MW00899342

MONTAUK TIME

~~by~~

PETER D. BOVÉ

Published by Taxicab Press, Montauk, NY
TaxiCabPress@gmail.com

Printed in the United States of America.

Editor: The Ghost of Ernest Hemingway

Cover Design: Sebastian Croitoriu

ISBN 13: 9781656622846

Montauk Time

Montauk Time

I

The seaplane makes a swooping left bank towards the Montauk Airport on East Lake Drive.

"George Washington built that lighthouse," says Kelly, a ruggedly handsome man with an unusually trusting face, as he peers out of the seaplane window at the Montauk Point Lighthouse situated atop the bluffs at the very tip of the stunning shoreline of Eastern Long Island. A shoreline on this day, studded with fishermen surf casting and surfers catching waves.

"I cannot tell a lie..." smiles Rollie, a one-time Navy Seal that Clint Eastwood would think twice about messing with.

Sally, 'Sal' as the boys call her, an extraordinarily beautiful woman in her mid-thirties who, if Renoir painted a supermodel... rolls her eyes, her sarcastic demeanor on full display.

"Too bad we can't land at the Yacht Club Marina like Lindbergh used to," Kelly remarks to the pilot.

The pilot turns to Kelly with a surprised look. "You a pilot?" he asks. Not many people know about that," he smiles happy to have a passenger who knows aviation. "This place was wide open back then. Lindbergh was one of only a handful of pilots flying in those days," he exclaims a big smile on his face.

"A heck of a time to be alive!" says Kelly losing himself in thought for a moment. He looks at his Patek Phillipe Moon Phase Chronograph wristwatch. "Dave and The Kid should be here by now," he says. "Why don't you give them a call Sal..."

Sal pulls a cell phone out of her Givenchy bag, hits speed dial and places the phone to her ear. “We’re about to land. You boys in Montauk yet?” she asks. She listens a moment, then turns to Kelly, “Heavy traffic through the Hamptons,” she tells him. Into the phone she adds, “We’ll see you at the Yacht Club.” Sal ends the call and places the phone back into her purse.

“I told them the train was faster than the Jitney on Fridays,” Kelly insists. He turns to Rollie and asks, “You remember that taxi driver we had last year?”

Rollie thinks for a moment, “The writer... Sparky!” Rollie smiles.

“You still have his number?” Kelly asks.

“I think so,” Rollie finds the number and calls. “Sparky, it’s Rollie from last summer. You driving?” he asks. “Excellent. We’re about to land, can you pick us up at the airport?” He looks up at Kelly and nods an affirmative. He listens a moment. “Three of us. Great, see you then.” He pockets his phone and looks at Kelly. “He’ll meet us on the tarmac in ten.”

“There’s the Yacht Club,” says Kelly pointing through the seaplane window at the Montauk Yacht Club.

Sal and Rollie peer out of the window.

“Nice swimming pool,” Sal smiles.

“In the Roaring Twenties, right where that swimming pool is now, was a high-end speakeasy with a casino next door,” Kelly says with a wry smile.

“A casino, hunh?” Sal muses.

"The Deep Sea Club," Kelly says looking over at Sal and Rollie. He gazes down at the site, "Can you imagine the action that place must have seen?" adds Kelly, giddy at the thought.

Sal smiles, "We could do some damage in a place like that!"

"A fool and his money are soon parted," Rollie grins.

They share a knowing laugh. The pilot cannot help but to be intrigued.

"Arthur Benson of Bensonhurst fame was the first to come out here and see Montauk as a resort destination. That didn't pan out, but in 1925, a guy named Carl Fischer ventured here and found a small fishing village named Montauk with about a hundred fishermen living in a squatters' village, owned by the railroad. There were no roads, no electricity and no plumbing. Just pastures, farms and a handful of wealthy families, mostly automobile manufacturers who Carl was friends with, and had built summer homes in the dunes east of Ditch Plains sometime back in the 1890s. All, except for The Seven Sisters, designed by Stanford White. One of which, as you know, Dick Cavett wants fourteen million dollars for," he says, peering at Sal and Rollie with raised eyebrows.

Sal shakes her head no and Rollie scowls, letting Kelly know they think Cavett is asking way too much.

"Carl ended up building the Montauk Yacht Club with The Deep Sea Club speakeasy and casino next door, The Montauk Manor, The Montauk Inn on Second House Road that's now Solé East," Kelly goes on. "Even a hotel of cabanas on the beach called the Surf Club that once had an Olympic-sized swimming pool."

"Sounds like he built the whole town!" Rollie adds.

"I like the pool," Sal comments.

"We'll be landing in a few minutes folks," informs the pilot.

They make a smooth landing at Montauk Airport. Sparky, the writer slash taxi driver, a tallish good-looking man in his mid-fifties dressed in khaki cargo shorts, a tee shirt and flip-flops, is standing on the tarmac alongside his minivan taxi waiting for them. When the plane stops, he drives over to pick up Kelly, Sal and Rollie.

"Great to see you guys again," Sparky says with a warm smile.

He steps out of the taxi, helps load the luggage and they pile into the taxi.

Sparky puts it in gear, turns to Kelly and asks, "Where to?"

"Montauk Yacht Club," answers Kelly.

"Couple of high rollers," comments Sparky with a raised eyebrow as they drive off. "How long you guys in town for?" he asks.

"Not sure yet. We're just taking a breather and maybe shopping for an estate," answers Kelly. "It's a little pricey but Dick Cavett's Stanford White house is on the market," he adds.

Sparky looks at Kelly through the rearview mirror, "That's right, you're a history buff," he says.

"I'll need a ride to the realtor's office in the morning," Kelly lets him know.

"Not a problem," says Sparky happily as they roll out of the airport on to East Lake Drive.

Starting at Gin Beach and Outer Beach State Park, East Lake Drive is a winding country road speckled with a few marinas, a family style restaurant, called Rick's Crabby Cowboy, that sometimes doubles as a Hipster Pop-Up Club in the summer, The Montauk Bungalows, across from the Airport, The Lake Club and an eclectic assortment of homes. Some are little more than shacks, while others are essentially mansions. The road hugs Lake Montauk ending at the Montauk Highway. The Lake Club is an old-school members only club with a few rooms, a marina and elegant dining hall. Sparky heads west on the highway and cuts up Old West Lake Drive, past the Crow's Nest Hotel and Restaurant, onward to West Lake Drive towards the Montauk Yacht Club. He makes the turn leading onto Star Island.

"See that guard house?" Kelly asks everyone, pointing at an old, stone guard house complete with a stone wall at the entrance to Star Island. "Back in the day, not everyone was welcomed to Star Island. There's a rich history to this place," Kelly states with affection, gazing out of the window. "You can feel it," he adds.

"I don't feel it," Sal says, digging into Kelly's non-stop obsession with history.

"Smart ass," Kelly quips "There was some serious money here about a hundred years ago."

"Oh? Do tell..." Sal says suddenly intrigued.

"Before Carl Fisher created Montauk, he was a wild racecar driver, inventor, industrialist and land developer who transformed the mangrove swamps of Miami into a winter playground for the rich and famous. The well-heeled..." Kelly tells them. "Trying to replicate his success in Miami, Crazy Carl, as he was sometimes called, envisioned turning Montauk into the Miami Beach of the North, in the form of a Tudor styled, gentleman's hunting and fishing paradise, and that he did! Although, mostly it was a roaring-twenties hotspot, frequented by movie stars, like Errol Flynn, John Barrymore and Marion Davies, even famous writers like Hemingway and F. Scott Fitzgerald roared it up out here. Distinguished big-money members included Vincent Astor, J.P. Morgan, Nelson Doubleday, Edsel Ford, Eli Whitney, Thomas Eastman and the Vanderbilts." He turns and gives Rollie and Sal a knowing look, "Our kind of people!" He grins.

"Oh, yeah..." Sal agrees with a knowing grin.

Sparky looks at each of them, intrigued, "You guys are definitely among the most fascinating fares I get in this town," he tells them with a shake of the head.

The three of them look at each other. A raise of the eyebrow from Kelly.

Any new books?" Rollie asks Sparky.

"Not sure what's next," he answers with a shrug of the shoulders. "Maybe I'll write about you guys," he suggests.

"Careful with that one, hotshot. Could be more trouble than it's worth," quips Sal.

Sparky gazes at her through the rearview mirror. Her wry smile is there to greet him.

"Interesting..." is all he can say.

Sparky stops at the reception area and pops the trunk. A bellhop helps with the luggage. Rollie rolls off a couple of fifties and stuffs them in Sparky's hand. He smiles and stashes them in his shirt.

"You guys have my number if you need me. See ya in the morning," he says before jumping in the taxi and driving off.

II

Enjoying a lavish breakfast on the deck of the Montauk Yacht Club, Kelly, Sal and Rollie are joined by Dave, a mechanical engineer with a physics degree, and The Kid, Kelly's protégé. A bright, good-looking young man in his mid-twenties from Brooklyn, who idealizes Kelly. Dave wears his hair longish and a bit wild. If you glanced at him quickly, Albert Einstein would come to mind. Kelly rifles through the morning paper.

He laughs out loud. "Listen to this!" he exclaims. They all look at Kelly. "A medieval chess piece missing for almost two hundred years could fetch a million pounds at auction after a family discovered that the object, which had been kept in a drawer for decades, is one of the long lost Lewis Chessmen." He glances up; all four are practically drooling wise. "The Lewis Chessmen," continues Kelly, "...a famous hoard of ninety-three objects, were discovered in 1831 on the Isle of Lewis in the Outer Hebrides. But the whereabouts of five pieces from the collection have remained a mystery. The family," he peeks from behind the newspaper, "that's us." They all can't help but to smile. "...has now been told the chess piece their grandfather bought for just five pounds in 1964 is one of the missing treasures," Kelly continues, "The antiques dealer, from Edinburgh, had no idea of the significance of the 8.8 cm piece, made from walrus ivory, which he passed down to his family." Kelly's broad smile. "Old Granddad..." he remarks in the Scottish accent he used for the con they had just pulled.

The crew cracks up laughing. Kelly looks up at The Kid. "You were great on this one, Kid. You're gonna be all right," he assures him.

The Kid smiles large, then downs the rest of his fresh-squeezed orange juice. “Man, that’s good OJ,” he comments.

They all look at him strangely. He looks back defensively and adds, “We always had frozen when I was growing up,”

Rollie raises his glass, “To the good life,” he toasts.

“To the good life,” the others chime in.

Kelly returns to the newspaper article. “They have looked after it for more than fifty years without realizing its importance, before bringing it to Sotheby's auction house in London. The Lewis Chessmen are among the biggest draws at the British Museum and the National Museum of Scotland in Edinburgh. A family spokesman said in a statement,” in his Scottish accent, Kelly reads, “’My grandfather was an antiques dealer based in Edinburgh, and in 1964, he purchased an ivory chessman from another Edinburgh dealer.’” He smiles at the crew.

Rollie smiles, “In the words of the great Menzies McKillop,” he adds in his own Scottish accent, “An old liar told me here; to think ahead and save my money. I should have spent it on ribbons. I should have learned the tune my dead grandfather played when the daft wife heard him resounding in the deep pine woods in early November.”

Kelly smiles at Rollie, then returns to the newspaper. "It was catalogued in his purchase ledger that he had bought an 'Antique Walrus Tusk Warrior Chessman.'” He looks up at Dave admiringly. “Amazing job on the Walrus tusk.”

“Why thank you, my good sir,” Dave muses also in his feigned Scottish brogue. They share a laugh.

Kelly buries his head back into the paper, “They are seen as an important symbol of European civilization and have also seeped into popular culture, inspiring everything from the children's show 'Noggin the Nog' to part of the plot in 'Harry Potter and The Philosopher's Stone.' Sotheby's expert Alexander Kader, who examined the piece for the family, said that his jaw dropped when he realized what they had in their possession." Kelly looks up at everyone. "It did, didn't it?" He smiles.

The crew cracks up laughing.

"I thought he was going to faint on the spot!" Sal says to uproarious laughter.

"He may not have fainted, but I'm quite certain the gentleman pissed his pants!" adds The Kid in his Scottish brogue, hoping to get a laugh, which he does. A smile of satisfaction comes to his face, having made the crew laugh even harder.

When things finally calm down, Kelly turns to Sal. "You should give Alex a call and see how he wants to proceed with the auction."

"Most assuredly, darling brother," Sal states in her own Scottish accent.

A big smile from Kelly. He sips the last of his coffee. "I better get over to the realtor," he says pulling out his cell phone.

He hits speed dial and places the cell to his ear. "Hey, Sparky... I need a ride to town. Can you pick me up at the Yacht Club?" He listens a moment. "Great, see you in five," He stands up, looks around, straightens his collar, "Time to buy us an estate," he says.

Sal lifts her Bloody Mary. "To old Grandpa," she says, continuing her Scottish accent.

The crew follows suit, lifting whatever drinks they have. "To Grandad," they toast in assorted Scottish accents.

Kelly smiles and struts off past the front desk. Sparky pulls up in his mini-van. "Hey Kelly," he says with a smile.

Kelly steps into the cab. "How ya doin', Sparky?" Kelly asks. "You serious about writing about us?" he continues, watching Sparky closely.

The always inquisitive Sparky looks at him through the rearview mirror. "That depends..." he answers with a wry expression.

"On what?" Kelly inquires.

"First off, where to?" Sparky asks.

"Compass Realty, good sire," Kelly smiles in his Scottish brogue.

Sparky drives off towards the town of Montauk. "You could be an actor with a Scottish accent that convincing!

Kelly studies Sparky through the rearview mirror. "What makes you think I'm not an actor?"

"I suppose to some degree we're all are actors on the great stage of life," Sparky says with a shrug of the shoulders.

Kelly smiles. "Naturally, you couldn't use our real names," Kelly adds, returning to the writing.

"Naturally..." Sparky says, grabbing sight of Kelly in the rearview mirror. "You look more like you could be a... James." He smiles at Kelly and adds, "Shaken, not stirred."

Kelly smiles. "I like it," he says. "James..." He muses, "It's a nice fit."

Sparky smiles, adding, “Regal, even.”

Sparky pulls up to Compass Realty, on Carl Fischer Circle in the center of town.

“Thanks, pal,” Kelly says as he hands Sparky a twenty.

Kelly steps out of the cab and takes in his surroundings. He notices the Carl Fischer Circle sign and smiles. “I love this town,” he says to himself as he walks over to the realty office and steps inside.

“Giovanna?” he asks a slender woman in her fifties seated at her desk.

“Mr. Kelly?” she responds with an engaging expression.

She stands and reaches out her hand.

“Please, call me John,” he smiles and takes her hand.

She gazes into his deep-blue, alluring eyes.

“Certainly, sir.” She stammers a moment, “I mean, John.” She giggles a bit, instantly attracted to him.

She looks down at her hand still in his, sighs a moment, then regains her composure, “Please, sit down,” she says, releasing his hand.

Kelly sits down across from her desk on an old, stuffed, red-leather chair and gets comfortable. Giovanna sits in her desk chair, organizing a few files as she speaks. “If I understand you correctly, you’re interested in the Dick Cavett estate,” she says with a professional manner as she attempts to disguise her attraction to him. An attraction the adept Kelly is more than willing to exploit.

"That's one idea," he says. "Only, at fourteen million, it feels somewhat overpriced to me," he states. Leaning forward, he adds, "Even for a Stanford White..." He gazes into her eyes and smiles. "The house to buy is Carl Fischer's old estate but I understand it just sold for nine and half million and is no longer available. Perhaps you can show me what other comparable properties might be available, and we can go from there," he adds with his charming smile.

She smiles back, running a hand through her hair, "I have some wonderful listings right now." She looks up at him. "Montauk is a great investment opportunity and is only slated to increase in value." She suggests gazing into Kelly's eyes dreamily. "If I was alive a hundred years ago, I would have bought the whole town!" She giggles, "It'd be worth many millions today," she adds.

"A billion maybe..." suggests Kelly with an enticing expression.

"Can you imagine?" remarks Giovanna, a coquettish smile on her face.

Her face takes on a dreamy quality as she imagines herself and her new, irresistible client bathing in the magnificent swimming pool of an impressive estate, stopping to sip Martinis and to make passionate love.

"Ahem..." she exclaims crossing her legs and trying to focus. "Let me see..." she says grabbing her book of listings. "We'll be more comfortable on the sofa."

She stands up holding the large three-ring-binder listings book and moves to the sofa and places the large book on the coffee table. "Can I get you anything?" she asks in her accommodating manner. "Coffee? Or a Pellegrino with lime perhaps? She smiles.

"That's very kind of you. Maybe later," he suggests, playing into her fantasies.

"You never know, John..." is her transparently coy response.

She takes a seat on the sofa placing the listings book on her lap and presents a few properties to Kelly. "This is an amazing estate with ocean views not far from the Cavett estate in Ditch Plains." She says moving closer to Kelly, balancing the large three-ring binder on her lap.

Kelly looks at the images. "That is nice." he says. "But let's continue," he suggests.

She flips through a few others. "Oh, I know! You're going to love this one." She flips quickly through a few pages and finds the property she's referring to.

"Go back a few pages..." Kelly says excitedly. "You had something there."

He looks up into her eyes and reaches out for the book. "Do you mind?" he asks, taking the large binder. Giovanna's breath quickens, her eyes following his masculine hands as he flips through the pages himself. "This one!" he states with a huge smile. "This is it!"

Giovanna looks at the page with a frown, "Oh, I'm sorry, this particular listing should have been removed." She holds the page and looks into his eyes, "It hasn't closed yet but this estate is in contract," she informs him.

Kelly appears sadly disappointed. "May I ask who bought it?" he inquires looking into her eyes.

Her reaction is less than forthcoming. Giovanna smiles. "I can't reveal client information," she stammers with a smile.

"Maybe I can make an offer that will convince them to let it go," Kelly continues.

"I can tell you that he's a major gem dealer from Russia. In fact, he's arranged for the Chase bank here in town to hold valuable gems in their vault for safe-keeping when he's in town," she boasts in an attempt to add mystique and an air of wealth to her listings.

"You don't say?" Kelly's mind works quickly, "I know a few gem dealers."

He looks into Giovanna's eyes and places his hand on her arm. "It wouldn't be Demyan Yusupova, would it?"

Her eyes light up. "Why John, you really know your stuff!" she exclaims.

"I know who Demyan Yusupova is..." he says feigning a humility that doesn't come naturally to him. "Russian rare gem dealer Demyan Yusupova is a descendant of Russian noblewoman, Princess Zinaida Yusupova, heiress of Russia's largest private fortune in her day." He looks into Giovanna's eyes.

Giovanna is excited, "Really... Russian royalty... I didn't know..." she says making a few notes in her notebook.

"Around the turn of the century..." Kelly continues, "...the Princess' only brother, Prince Boris Nicholaievich Yusupova died a child. Poor guy." he adds. "As head of one of the most important noble families in Russia, she also inherited the vast fortune," he says dreamily. "She grew up owning the largest collection of historical jewels in Russia, second only to that of the vaults of the Russian Imperial Family," Kelly tells her, enjoying his vast knowledge of historical fact, especially where jewels, antiquities and valuable art are concerned.

He glances at Giovanna who is noticeably impressed and smiles. “I love history…” he says with an innocent smile.

“So, I see…” Giovanna responds, dazzled by Kelly’s vast knowledge.

“The princess had a magnificent collection of stunning jewels,” he tells Giovanna. She smiles at Kelly with all the allure she can muster.

“The princess had twenty tiaras alone,” Kelly tells her.

“Can you imagine?” Giovanna exclaims. “The princess must have had quite the social calendar,” she comments running her fingers through her hair a second time while gazing into Kelly’s eyes invitingly.

“The list goes on…,” he states looking back at her. “There were hundreds of brooches, dozens of valuable bracelets, assorted objét d'art and literally hundreds of thousands of loose gems,” he says, not able to stop himself from imagining it for a moment.

Giovanna’s eyes light up. “John! You could be a professor,” she says moving closer to him. She looks directly into his eyes, “Very impressive,” she states, practically throwing herself at him.

“As I mentioned, I love history…” He smiles. “Some of the gems were world famous like the La Pelegrina pearl,” he says thinking for a moment. “My favorite has to be The Polar Star Diamond.” Kelly sighs at the thought of it.
“It’s a more than forty carat beast diamond.” He looks at her with a raise of the eyebrows. “We could do some damage with a gem of that caliber!” he adds.

Giovanna sighs. “We sure could…” she swoons as her imagination carries her back to that happy place with Kelly, only this time in glamorous attire in Kelly’s arms dancing under the moonlight on the veranda of an ancient castle.

"The La Regente Pearl is the fifth largest pearl in the world," he says looking into her eyes.

"That must've been some oyster," giggles Giovanna, her hand finding Kelly's knee for a moment.

They laugh. "And the 17th century Ram's Head Diamond," he says softly with a dreamy expression. He looks at Giovanna with a smile. "One of my favorites..." he adds with his enticing smile. "It's a nearly eighteen carat diamond," he says.

"Can you imagine?" comments Giovanna.

"Often," he assures her. "Then there's the 17th century Sultan of Morocco Diamond. An absolute behemoth at thirty-six carats, making it the fourth largest Blue diamond in the world!" he says, getting caught up in the majesty of it. "Another favorite is the pair of 17th century Diamond Earrings of Marie Antoinette, constructed from two thirty-five carat diamonds," he smiles.

Giovanna looks at Kelly with amazement. "I have to say John... this is just astonishing! I mean... you are a walking talking encyclopedia!" she states, as impressed as she is turned on.

"I do love my history," smiles Kelly. "The list is as impressive as it is immense. The Blue Venus Statuette Sapphire, a four-inch-tall sapphire statuette of the goddess Venus," he adds, with animated hand gestures. "The 15th century Ruby Buddha, a statue made from a more than seventy carat stone," he states leaning in close to her with affection.

Giovanna swoons over Kelly. "Oh John..." she looks at him with lustful eyes. They gaze at one another for a long moment. "What a life the princess must have led," Giovanna says finally.

Kelly smiles, then continues. "I can imagine," he says entranced. "But all good things must end," he adds with a frown. "She narrowly escaped the Russian Revolution and was forced to leave nearly all of her financial assets in Russia," he says sadly. "Luckily for her, she was one shrewd lady." He looks into Giovanna's eyes, "Royals..." he says flashing a charmingly comical smile. "She managed to hide her entire jewel collection in a secret vault in the Moika Palace in hopes that she would reclaim them upon their return to Russia. Only, communists don't mess around and, all those amazing treasures were found and sold by the Bolsheviks in 1925." He shakes his head in dismay, visibly upset. "Communism is the biggest political scam of them all!" he exclaims.

"Oh John..." Giovanna says sympathetically, running her fingers across his cheek, her passion overcoming her.

Kelly smiles, knowing he has her wrapped around his finger.

"Princess Zinaida did manage to smuggle out some of the major jewels but was eventually forced to sell them in order to fund her family's exorbitant lifestyle," he says sadly.

Giovanna looks at the remarkable Kelly. "You truly do love history, don't you?" she says.

"It's sort of a hobby," he answers, trying to sound innocent.

Looking down timidly, she says, "It's against our policy to reveal the identity of our clients, but since you guessed it right off the bat," She looks up into Kelly's eyes with a coy expression, "And then some!" she smiles, "He just fell in love with the house."

"Understandable," says Kelly. "That's a shame... I would love to have seen it," he says smiling. "On a lower level, yet much like Romanov and Bulgari, Demyan has successfully used his ancestry to fuel his stature in the world diamond market," he smiles.

Giovanna smiles back. "I see," she says, fascinated.

"I like a few of the estates you showed me," Kelly assures her. "Let me sleep on it, then come back and revisit them," he says.

"That would be wonderful!" Giovanna answers enthusiastically.

She throws him an enticingly sultry look, "Maybe there'll be another history lesson in it for me," she says, flirting with him.

Kelly smiles at her, "You never know, Giovanna, you never know..." He stands and takes her hand. "It was a real pleasure spending time with you," he leans over and kisses her hand, looking into her eyes.

She blushes with a sigh.

They walk to the door, Kelly turns and adds, "I'll call soon to set up another appointment."

"I look forward to it, "she answers.

Kelly walks off. She can't take her eyes off of him. When he's out of sight, she plops down at her desk and catches her breath. She lifts the phone receiver and dials a number.

“Hi…” she says.

Giovanna leans back in her desk chair and speaking into the phone exclaims, “I just had a meeting with the dreamiest man I have ever met.” She listens a moment. “He’s looking for an estate,” She sips from a coffee cup, “He is totally hot, and he knows history like you wouldn’t believe,” she says then holds the receiver to her ear and listens a moment. “Oh no… this guy’s way beyond him.” She closes her eyes and smiles as she recalls her infatuation, “Think Sean Connery as James Bond with the mind of a charming history professor,” she says dreamily.

III

"I have an idea," Kelly announces to the crew watching a beautiful sunset while enjoying local Steamers and Lobster on the deck of the Topside restaurant at Gosman's Dock.

"Here we go!" says The Kid enthusiastically.

Sal glances over at him and smiles.

"The foolish enthusiasm of youth..." Rollie says, sucking down a clam.

Dave cracks open a lobster claw.

Sal looks over at Kelly. "What are you thinking?" she asks.

"I had a very interesting meeting with an extremely talkative realtor this morning," Kelly tells them.

"Oh?" remarks Dave.

"Demyan Yusupova is in town," Kelly tells them, scanning the crew for reactions.

"Diamond Demyan?" asks Rollie.

"The one and only," Kelly answers leaning in. "He purchased the house we had our eyes on," he adds.

"Prick," says The Kid.

Sal rolls her eyes. Rollie liberates a giant lobster tail from its shell noisily with his fingers, soaks it in a bowl of melted butter and somehow manages to cram nearly half of it into his smiling face.

Chewing he states, "Man, I miss the sea when I'm away."

Sal watches this gruff display with her usual disdain. "It must be an absolute joy for you when we're not on a job and you can eat like the unmitigated slob that you are," she insists, sipping her cocktail.

The Kid laughs. Dave smiles as he sucks down a steamer.

"There's more," says Kelly excitedly.

"How much more?" asks Dave.

"Demyan, as you should all remember, is your typical Russian and very distrusting. He likes to keep his most valuable gems close to the vest." Kelly informs them, sipping his Prosecco.

"And?" asks The Kid excitedly.

"And... apparently, he's cut a deal with the Montauk branch of Chase Bank to hold his most valuable gems in their vault when he's in town," Kelly answers with a huge mischievous smile.

"This is supposed to be a vacation," presses Sal.

"Yeah! and I've never been on vacation before," The Kid adds.

"We just came off a hell of a run, Kelly. We could use a little downtime," remarks Dave, looking squarely at Kelly while sipping his Porter.

"Isn't client information supposed to be confidential with realtors?" Rollie inquires.

"Yeah!" exclaims The Kid. "How'd you pull that off?"

Kelly smiles at him, "Stick around, kid, and you'll learn all kinds of neat stuff."

The Kid swoons at the thought.

"Not to mention Monte Carlo," adds Rollie, looking around the table at his cohorts one by one.

"Monte Carlo's a tricky one. It's gonna take a lot of planning, Kel," insists Dave.

"Exactly!" Kelly answers. He sits up straight and looks at the crew challengingly. "Where is Monte Carlo?" he asks.

Sal rolls her eyes. "What's your point?" she asks, less than amused.

"Where's Montauk?" Kelly continues.

They look at one another a moment,

"They're both by the sea!" exclaims The Kid.

"See? The Kid gets it," Kelly says knowingly.

The Kid beams a great big smile as he looks the others over one by one, gloating.

"Save it, Kid," Sal tells him.

"You do realize there's only one road in and out of this town," states Dave as he sits back, sipping his porter.

"Which means it will be completely unexpected," Kelly assures them.

"Yeah, because with only one escape route, you'd have to be an absolute knucklehead to attempt a bank robbery in Montauk," Rollie argues.

Kelly peers at Rollie with a fretful expression. He thinks for a moment. "Y'know, John Quincy Adams insisted that,"

Before Kelly can finish, Rollie points his index finger up and exclaims, "Shit! ...Patience and perseverance have a magical effect before which difficulties disappear and obstacles vanish." He looks at Kelly and frowns. "Can't believe I missed that..."

Kelly looks at his pal. "Neither can I. You are the king of famous quotes, after all," says Kelly as he pats Rollie on the back.

"You two aren't going to have a quote-off, now are you?" asks Sal, sipping her cocktail.

"Maybe..." says Rollie always up to the challenge.

"Please, spare me." quips Sal.

"Difficulties mastered are opportunities won," Rollie laughs, quoting Winston Churchill.

"We'll need one hell of a plan," Dave insists.

"Another reason why it's perfect." Kelly says as he inspects reactions from the crew. "Of course, we'll have to figure a way to get all of us and the goods off the island before the FBI shows up," he continues.

Kelly stares his crew down one by one challengingly. "Consider it a rehearsal for Monte Carlo," he says, accompanied by his big smile.

"I'll need to get inside the bank," Dave says.

"Ok... you win," Sal retorts. "Dave and I will open up an account at Chase," she concedes.

Kelly's big smile. "C'mon Sal..." he starts, giving Sal his coaxing expression about to say something.

"Save it, hot pants. I said I'm in," she retorts. "But hold on," she says as a thought pops into her head. "What exactly do you mean by, 'When he's in town'?"

Kelly looks at her with a mixture of dismay and satisfaction that she caught it. The Kid, Dave, and Rollie stare at her, not sure what she's getting at.

"Kelly said Demyan keeps his gems in the vault when he's in town," she explains.

"Right..." Dave says, "How do we plan something that even by a modest consideration of broad strokes will certainly be a complex operation, and do so only when Demyan's in town to assure the gems will actually be in the vault when we rob it?" Dave asks, posing what Kelly already knows is a legitimate concern.

"Sal," he gestures with his arm outstretched towards Sal. "The beautiful Sally will entice Demyan to remain in Montauk long enough for us to rob the bank," he says with a bravado he hopes is contagious.

"You know I don't particularly have a fond disposition for Russians." Sal says, lighting a cigarette.

"Then you will derive an extra level of enjoyment and satisfaction when he's decided to stick around only by virtue of you showering him with flowery attentions," Kelly says, measuring Sal's temperature.

"I'll derive a special joy when I see my purse filled with his exotic jewels," she says, winking at Kelly.

"Now, all we need is a foolproof plan!" says The Kid with a youthful and fervent smile.

"We'll get a safety deposit box, too," Dave says looking up at the crew. "I want to get a look at the security."

"Naturally, you do," Kelly responds with a proud smile. "That's why you're the best crew in the world."

"True friendship is a plant of slow growth, and must undergo and withstand the shocks of adversity, before it is entitled to the appellation," states Rollie.

"George Washington…" says Kelly.

"Touché," says Rollie lifting his glass in a toast.

"In 1799, George Washington's distillery produced nearly 11,000 gallons, and was one of the largest whiskey distilleries in America at the time," Kelly adds raising his glass.

Rollie looks at Kelly with a satisfied smile, "Only you would know that."

"Better call Sparky to get us back to the Yacht Club," Kelly says looking at his wristwatch.

Rollie hits a recent number and holds the phone to his ear. "Hey, Sparky, it's Rollie and the gang. …Can you pick us up from that arch at Gosman's?" he asks. "Great, see you in five," he says and ends the call.

Sparky pulls up to Gosman's arch. Before long the crew appears.

"Hey, Sparky," says Rollie with a welcoming smile. "Montauk Yacht Club, please."

“Hey, guys,” Sparky says with a big grin as the automatic doors of his minivan taxi open. “Every time I see you guys, I get the sense that something fascinating is about to happen,” he says. He peers into the rearview mirror, “That something is afoot…” he adds with a wry smile.

“Writers…” says Rollie with a roll of the eyes.

“Always reading into things…” Kelly says looking at Sparky through the rear-view mirror. “Sparky and I have discussed his writing about us in his next book,” he says, addressing the crew.

“That would be cool!” exclaims The Kid.

“There’s nothing to write about,” insists Sal.

“I don’t want you using my real name,” insists Dave.

“Of course, all the names will be changed to protect the innocent,” Sparky assures them.

The crew cracks up laughing.

“Now that’s funny,” smiles Sal.

“See!” exclaims Sparky.

He pulls up to the main entrance of the Yacht Club.

“Can we make a reservation for nine a.m.?” Kelly asks.

“Sure… see you then,” Sparky answers.

The next morning just before nine o’clock Sparky pulls up to the Yacht Club. He takes the crew in one by one as they slowly fill the taxi.

“Where to, guys?” he asks.

“Chase Bank,” Kelly tells him.

“What’s my name gonna be?” The Kid asks, curious.

“Not sure yet. You’re a tough one,” he says.

“Is there a place close to the bank to have breakfast?” The Kid asks.

“Mr. John’s Pancake House is a few doors down, and Anthony’s right across the street. But for you guys, I’d say… Bird on the Roof, just around the corner,” he tells them.

Sparky pulls up to the Chase Bank and stops the taxi. He looks into the rear-view mirror at Dave and shakes his head, fascinated. “I would call your character Albert,” Sparky tells Dave.

“Albert?” remarks Dave.

“I look at you and Albert Einstein comes to mind,” he says giving Dave the once over.

“We’ll meet you around the corner at Bird on the Roof,” Kelly tells Sal and Dave.

“Good, I’m starving,” The Kid exclaims.

Sal rolls her eyes as she and Dave exit the taxi. Sparky pulls away. Sal and Dave stand there a moment and take in their surroundings.

“Is that the Police Station?” Dave comments with a question, knowing the answer.

“It would be right next door to the bank…” says Sal with a raise of the eyebrow.

They stroll up to the entrance, two different people, as they take on the persona of a married couple. Dave opens the door for Sal, and they enter Chase Bank.

“Darling, you know banks give me the creeps,” Sal announces in a precious voice loud enough to be heard.

“You’ll be fine, dear,” Dave tells her with a smile.

They approach the counter. “Good morning. We’d like to open an account,” Dave says.

“Certainly. I’ll get one of our account managers to help you with that,” the clerk tells them.

She picks up the phone and dials an extension. “Marge? There’s a lovely couple here who would like to open a new account.” She listens a moment as she eyes Sal and Dave, before replying, “Sure.”

Dave looks at Sal and winks. The clerk hangs up the phone and Marge walks over from one of the cubicles. “Good morning. I understand you’d like to open up a new account?” she asks in full banker-accommodation mode.

“And, a safety deposit box,” Dave adds.

“Wonderful. Right this way,” says Marge, leading them to her cubicle.

They follow her and sit down.

“You must feel an extra sense of security having the police station right next door,” Dave tells her with a knowing smile.

Marge looks at him with a sense of wonder. “You know, were it not for your voice, I would swear you were Albert Einstein.”

“I’m not nearly as brilliant as he was,” insists Dave. “But thank you for such a fine compliment all the same,” he adds with a broad smile.

Sal grins and pats Dave’s knee. “Don’t sell yourself short, darling.”

Marge shuffles a few papers around on her desk, “So... what type of account are you interested in opening?” she asks.

“Oh, you know... savings, checking...” says Sal as she looks at Dave lovingly.

“And a safety deposit box...” adds Dave, smiling at the account manager.

Marge organizes various papers for the loving couple to fill out and sign. What size deposit will you be starting with? Marge asks.

“What’s your security like?” asks Dave looking around the bank.

“Darling, what a silly question,” comments Sal. “He loves technology,” she adds speaking directly to Marge.

“I mean, being a small, quaint town and all... Sometimes these things can be overlooked,” he says.

Marge looks at Dave with an odd expression. “No one’s ever asked me that question before,” she comments.

Dave smiles, then adds, “Nowadays, it’s smart to have intelligent security cameras with video analytics...” he says with a smile. "...Motion sensing, facial recognition, and behavioral recognition can be used effectively to identify suspicious or abnormal activity in and around the bank," he adds with a broad smile.

"You'll have to forgive my husband, he sometimes forgets he's retired from the hi-tech security industry," Sal says. She looks at Dave lovingly, "You're an artist now, darling." She kisses him on the cheek.

Marge smiles. "Now, I see." She says looking directly into Dave's eyes. "Interesting profession, Mr. Quill. Fascinating..." she says almost giddy, apparently thrilled to be dealing with such a high-caliber client from the world of banking.

"Well..." Dave says, feigning humility. "Let's take a look at that safety deposit box, shall we," he says excitedly.

"Sure thing," states Marge, wrapping up the remainder of the paperwork. "Just sign these and we can continue to the vault," she says accommodatingly.

She rolls her chair back and stands. Sal and Dave follow her to the safety deposit boxes on the opposite end of the bank.

"The proper bank video surveillance setup can help deter robberies, or in a worst-case scenario, provide important images and evidence to law enforcement," Dave says in a very officious tone.

The account manager stops and turns to him, "I see you're passionate about your profession, Mr. Quill," she states.

"Call me Dave, please," he answers. "Recorded bank security camera images can be used to identify and track down suspects as well," he continues.

The account manager turns to Sal and says, "You are so lucky to have such a knowledgeable husband!" she says enthusiastically.

"You have no idea," answers Sal.

They enter the safety deposit box vault.

"Very impressive." says Dave approvingly.

The bank teller smiles. "What size should we get, dear?" Dave asks Sal.

"A big one, dear, a big one..." she says smiling at Dave lovingly.

A short while later the two lovebirds exit the bank arm in arm.

"Show off," says Sal.

"Whatever do you mean, darling?" Dave mutters.

"Nothing like showing your hand," she adds in her annoyed tone.

"I was just having a little innocent fun, dear," he laughs.

The two continue across the street to Bird on the Roof where Kelly, Rollie and The Kid are having breakfast. They join them. Kelly looks at Dave questioningly.

"Piece a cake," Dave states.

"Sure, if the manager doesn't put two and two together..." insists Sal with a roll of the eyes.

All three examine Sal and Dave.

“What happened?” asks Rollie.

The Kid takes a big bite into his bagel. “Yeah?” he adds.

“Dave showing off again?” asks Kelly.

“Just to the point of absurdity,” says Sal.

“Oh please!” exclaims Dave.

“Can I get you anything?” asks the attractive young waitress who has just arrived.

“Yes, you may,” answers Dave, handwritten menu in hand. “I’ll have the Decadent Nutella Strawberry French Toast with a large side of bacon,” he finishes, looking up at the waitress with a huge, hungry grin.

“Sounds yummy,” says The Kid flirting with the waitress.

“Just coffee for me, thanks,” adds Sal.

Kelly looks over at Sal with concern. “You should eat something, Sal,” he says.

“Why?” she responds in her oftentimes cynical tone.

“Breakfast is the most important meal of the day, Sal,” Rollie insists.

“I prefer my breakfast in bed,” she says as the waitress stands by waiting for the order.

“Better get me a three-minute egg, sweetheart, or the boys won’t ever leave me alone,” she says.

“One three-minute egg coming up,” she says jotting on her order pad.

“What is a three-minute egg exactly?” asks The Kid.

“It’s a fancy name for a soft-boiled egg,” says Rollie after he sips his tomato juice.

“So, what’s it like in there?” asks Kelly.

“A traditional digital security alarm system with Sonitrol audio verification... Your basic intrusion security alarm, enterprise access control system with video surveillance cams and video monitoring. Video alarm verification staff protection and panic buttons. Biometric authentication credentialing including vault access.” He looks over at Kelly with a shrug. “Nothing special,” Dave insists.

“The question is, can we get in, disable the alarms and do everything we have to do before the three-hour reset,” he adds.

“What three-hour reset,” asks The Kid, forever wanting to learn anything and everything he can from his experienced mentors.

“The alarm has an end-all safety element that will reset the alarm in three hours, even if the bank manager or an alarm company tech disarms it,” Dave tells them. “It’s a redundancy mechanism designed to thwart,” he looks up at everyone, “well... us, basically,” he says with a wise-ass smile.

They are all laughing when the waitress arrives with Dave’s breakfast.

“Thanks,” he says and waits for her to leave before he continues.

“Nothing we can’t handle,” Rollie says with a confident grin.

“The best part is that although they use the state-of-the-art Stanley Protection Net, we’re ninety minutes from the nearest monitoring system,” he adds taking a forkful of his decadent Nutella strawberry French toast. He bites into a bacon strip. “That’s good bacon,” he says, chomping on what appears to be his most-beloved food stuff.

“You do realize that bacon is probably the worst thing you can eat,” Rollie comments.

“Killjoy,” Dave responds as he places a huge strip of bacon into his mouth.

The waitress arrives with Sal’s three-minute egg.

“Are you sure I can’t get you something else?” asks the waitress.

“A Bloody Mary would be nice,” says Sal with a raise of the eyebrow.

“Ooooh... sounds good to me,” smiles the waitress knowingly.

The Kid throws her a sweet smile, “Where would you go for a great Bloody Mary?” he asks with his most charming smile.

“The Dock, hands down,” she says without hesitation.

“The Dock?” asks The Kid.

“Yeah, it’s a restaurant up at the commercial docks. Near Gosman’s,” she adds.

Leaning in, The Kid suggests, “Maybe you could show me some time.”

Kelly watches his protégé proudly.

"Sounds nice," she says moving closer to The Kid.

"What's your name?" The Kid asks.

Sal rolls her eyes, but we're not sure if she's world weary or slightly impressed. She glances over at Kelly with a knowing smirk. Kelly shrugs a smile.

"Rachel," she says, beaming.

"Rachel," repeats The Kid, looking deeply into her eyes. "A nice Biblical name," he says.

"Yes..." she says shyly.

Rollie watches the exchange with amusement. Even Dave pays mind for a moment while enjoying his decadent breakfast.

"It was my grandmother's name," she adds.

Kelly is impressed by the exchange.

"Why don't you give me your number and we'll put something together," he says boldly.

"I'd like that," she answers.

Kelly smiles his approval as he watches the waitress give The Kid her number.

"Waitress!" a patron at a nearby table shouts.

"Oops, gotta go." She smiles at The Kid sweetly, then attends the nearby table.

"The Biblical name comment was a nice touch, Kid," says Sal with a rare compliment.

Even Kelly is surprised by Sal's reaction.

"I thought so," says The Kid. He saves Rachel's number in his cell.

Kelly looks at the crew one by one, "Remember when we were here last year during the Fourth of July?" he asks with a mischievous grin.

"I wasn't with you guys yet," says The Kid, spotting Rachel and sending a sweet smile her way.

"Yeah, it was total mayhem," says Rollie.

"That's it!" exclaims Dave.

"Sure... the cops will be so busy with crowd control, it'll be like stealing candy from a baby," says Sal, finishing her three-minute egg.

"I have an idea," Kelly exclaims. "It came to me in a flash when we dropped you guys off at the bank. I've been brewing it up in my head since we sat down for breakfast," he adds.

"With the police station right next door, it better be one strong brew," says Dave.

"What stuck in my head was that turret on the roof," Kelly explains.

"What about it?" asks Sal.

Kelly looks at Dave. "This one falls on you, pal," he says.

"What's a turret?" The Kid asks.

Rachel, the waitress, comes over. “Anything else for you guys?” she asks, not able to take her eyes off of The Kid.

He looks at her with a huge grin. “I got everything I need,” he says, patting the cell phone in his shirt pocket.

She sighs. “You know, I don’t even know your name,” she says to The Kid.

“It’s Louie,” he answers.

“Louie,” she repeats with a hint of a swoon. “Like Louis Armstrong!” she states excitedly.

“Yeah, I guess so…” The Kid stands and stretches.

Kelly stands up and throws a couple of hundred-dollar bills on the table. “That cover it?”

Her eyes light up. “I’ll say.”

The crew exit Bird on The Roof and walk towards the Chase Bank. They get to the corner and stop.

Kelly points to the roof of the bank. “That’s a turret, Kid,” he says.

The Kid looks at the early American architectural feature on the roof of the Chase Bank.

“And?” he asks.

Kelly turns to Dave, “You think we can install a guided missile with a cavity large enough to hold the valued contents of that bank, including Diamond Demyan’s gems, on the Fourth of July?” he asks.

Dave looks at Kelly incredulously. “You know I can,” he says.

“That’s the spirit,” Kelly says with his huge grin.

“Not sure exactly how. Yet…” adds Dave as he stares up at the turret.

“Where there’s a will, there’s a way,” says The Kid.

Rollie pats The Kid on the back. “An oldie but a goodie, Kid,” he says.

“You want to break into the bank, install a missile, stuff it with Demyan’s diamonds and then blast it out to sea on the Fourth of July?” Sal asks, knowing the answer. “That’s actually brilliant!” she exclaims.

Rollie frowns a moment. “I don’t think fireworks, even Grucci fireworks, are enough of a distraction with the Cop Shop right next door,” he says.

“He’s got a point, Kel,” adds Dave. “That police station was the first thing I noticed about this location.”

They all stare at the bank a moment.

“What if we have a remote control get-a-way car the cops can chase?” The Kid exclaims almost without thinking.

“Kid! You’re a genius!” exclaims Kelly.

“Ha! Love it,” laughs Rollie.

“Not bad, Kid,” adds Sal with a wink.

“And we’ll blow out half the teller window with a smoke bomb to hide the fact that a six-foot missile is leaving the building,” Dave insists.

“And leaving a rocket trail,” adds Sal.

“They’ll never see it!” exclaims The Kid.

“The Kid’s right,” Kelly assures them.

Sal looks at the crew one by one. “Of course! The cops will be completely focused on the get-a-way car screeching away,” she adds.

“That’s right. They’ll figure that if the car’s speeding away, the loot is leaving with it,” Dave says.

“Precisely… at that point what’s happening at the bank will be moot,” Kelly concludes.

“Plus, if we time it just as the fireworks show is taking place, at least at first, they’ll have to consider that it’s fireworks gone awry,” Rollie adds.

“Since you’re the only one here who grew up racing cars in video games, you’re the natural choice for the driver,” Kelly tells The Kid.

“Now we’re talkin’…” The Kid smiles.

“This can work,” Rollie admits, imagining the scene in his head. “This can work…” he repeats.

They stand on the corner looking at the bank, then at each other.

“This *will* work!” insists Kelly with a huge grin.

“Damn, we’re good!” exclaims The Kid.

“We haven’t done anything yet, Kid,” Dave tells him with the voice of experience.

“Yeah, don’t get ahead of yourself, hot pants,” Sal quips.

“We’ve got three weeks to pull this off,” Kelly says.

He looks at the crew in earnest then looks up at the turret on the roof of the bank. “We have a lot of planning to do,” he says.

They stand there a moment, maybe dumbfounded just a little bit. Tourists walk by eating fudge or ice scream from the nearby Fudge Factory. But the crew is in another world.

“What’s that monstrosity?” asks Sal, pointing at the tall building at the north end of the Plaza.

“They call it the Tower,” Kelly tells her.

“What about it?” asks The Kid.

“It doesn’t exactly fit the rest of the town,” remarks Sal.

“Fischer envisioned a downtown filled with them, but never got around to it,” the knowledgeable Kelly tells them.

“You know, that would be the perfect starting point for a tunnel,” says Dave, thinking about the logistics of the massive undertaking they are considering.

“Wow…” comments The Kid looking at the Tower. “What tunnel?” he asks.

Dave looks at the young novice thief with a wry expression. “How else do you propose we get inside the bank in order to modify the turret, install a smart bomb, then fill it with all the goodies, in what I guess will be about a three-hour window, with the police station next door?” he quips knowingly.

The Kid assesses the situation, "Sounds like an immense amount of work to me," he says.

"If it were easy, anybody could do it," retorts Rollie.

The five of them stand there staring at the Tower. Rollie is imagining the massive undertaking of digging the tunnel, as is The Kid. Sal knows she'll have no part in the digging. Kelly is imagining the magnificent gems in Demyan's collection, and how close he is to finally getting his hands on them. Dave is making mathematical calculations in his head. Interestingly, not one of them is fearing the risks involved, only the problems to be solved in pulling off such a magnificent and unlikely robbery. Of all the thoughts they may be sharing, one is prevalent among all the others; if they pull this off, they're going to be legends in the worldwide community of thieves and grifters.

Kelly seems lost in another world. He just stands there staring at the Tower. He looks at the time. "Hey, Rollie, wanna get Sparky down here?" he asks.

He looks at the crew rubbing his jaw as Rollie hits speed dial. "We've got a bit of planning to do if we're going to pull this off," Kelly insists.

"Sparky! Hey, man, it's Rollie. Can you pick us up?" he asks. "The Chase Bank," he tells him. "Great, see you in three." Rollie smiles at Kelly.

The crew joins a group of boisterous young Irishmen in their twenties carrying beach towels, smelling of beer and suntan lotion, crossing the street towards the Chase Bank.

Sparky rolls up and the crew steps in. "Where to, guys?" he asks with his Sparky taxi smile.

"Yacht Club, pal," answers Kelly.

They drive past the Tower.

“Hey, Sparky, what’s with the Tower these days?” Kelly asks.

Sparky looks at Kelly through the rear view and smiles. “Being a history buff, I’m sure you already know that back in the day it was the business center of Montauk, but nowadays it’s condos and timeshares,” he answers, peering at Kelly.

“Man, I bet there’s some great views of the ocean from the top floor,” comments The Kid excitedly.

He looks at everyone hoping for a shared enthusiasm. When no one responds he adds, “I mean, sitting there right in the middle of town a few blocks from the ocean and all…”

Kelly’s eyes light up. “That’s it!”

“What’s it?” asks Sal.

Without hesitation, Kelly says, “We’re getting a condo in The Tower!”

Sal leans into Kelly, “I thought we were buying an estate,” he says.

“Yeah…” adds The Kid.

Sparky is intrigued. He knows there is more to these guys than buying an estate in town and he’s dying to know what it is.

He straightens himself out in the driver’s seat and says, “You guys should know that… this taxi is like a confessional…” He pauses a moment, then continues “…or like a shrink’s office… or, or like a lawyer’s…” He peeks through the rear view. "Whatever is said here is strictly between us," he says, trying to win their confidence.

Kelly smiles at Sal. She smiles back and tilts her head with a slight shrug of the shoulder. Kelly looks at Dave who gives Kelly a similar reaction.

Kelly looks up at Sparky. "How much would you charge us to be our driver exclusively for the next three weeks?"

The Kid looks at Kelly trying to follow his train of thought. Sparky plays it cool and says, "This taxi may not look like much, but it is strangely lucrative during the tourist season," he says, noticing Kelly's grin in the rear-view mirror.

"You tell 'em, Sparks," says Sal with an amused laugh.

"How lucrative are we talking?" asks Dave, entering the conversation just for the fun of it.

Sparky turns onto Star Island. Before he can answer the question, Kelly says, "We'll give you ten grand cash to be our driver, ambassador and guide through the Fourth of July."

Sparky pulls the car into the Yacht Club stopping at the main entrance. "And you can write about us. But only if you change our names," he adds.

Sparky puts the taxi in park and turns to face Kelly. "Ambassador? Guide?" he asks.

Sal looks at Kelly with a tilt of the head and raise of the eyebrows. Kelly smiles at Sparky with a wink and a nod, "You're a man about town, Sparky... Plus, I can tell you are someone who understands finesse," he says.

Sparky smiles and nods.

"As I'm sure you understand," Kelly pauses and scans the crew. "There are certain things in life that require a..." he turns to Sparky, "...an elegant approach," he states, arousing Sparky's already vivid imagination.

Sparky turns to Kelly, "Twenty-five hundred as a retainer, another twenty-five on June 21, the first day of summer..." he says, spanning the crew, "And the remainder at the end of the job." He looks directly into Kelly's eyes, doing his best to appear concise and official.

"He's fast on his feet," Sal comments with a grin at Kelly. "Eh, Sparks?" she adds, smiling at Sparky through the rear-view.

Sparky chuckles. "I knew it was only a matter of time before you asked."

"A real pro," comments Dave.

Rollie smiles at Sparky and with his index finger pointed up he states, "When you have confidence, you can have a lot of fun. And when you have fun, you can do amazing things," he says to Sparky.

"Joe Namath!" Sparky says in amazement. "Gotta love Broadway Joe..." he adds.

The crew is impressed.

Sal rolls her eyes. "Oh no, not another one..."

Rollie nods his head in approval and says, "Impressive."

"Confidence is not, 'They will like me. Confidence instead is, I'll be fine if they don't'," Sparky tells Rollie.

"Yup, another one..." says The Kid. "Where do you get this stuff?" he adds.

"Christina Grimmie," Rollie tells them.

"Yeah..." Sparky says, nodding his head and smiling at Rollie.

Kelly loves it. "He's one of us I tell you," Dave insists.

Kelly observes Sparky with a gleam in his eye, "Maybe..." he says. "Maybe..."

"I love great quotes," says Sparky. "I collect them," he says patting his MacBook which is in his knapsack between the two front seats.

Kelly looks at his watch. "Your first order of business is to find out how we rent a condominium in the Tower," he says, gazing at Sparky who stares him down with an expression that includes a raise of the eyebrow that says, "Show me the money." Kelly reaches in his pocket and hands him a fifty. "Come back in an hour and I'll have your retainer," Kelly smiles.

"So, it's a deal..." Sparky asks.

The crew exits the taxi. Kelly leans into the passenger side window and reaches his hand out. Sparky and he shake. "It's gonna be fun," Kelly says.

"I believe you," answers Sparky.

"What's for lunch? I'm starved," Sparky can hear The Kid retort as the crew walks away. He watches them with a wry smile. He knows something special is afoot. He doesn't know what it is yet. But there is a certainty in his heart and mind that this will be no ordinary gig. He takes out his MacBook from his satchel he keeps between the two front seats, opens a file and begins to type: *To suggest that they are an interesting bunch is an understatement. The commission is welcomed, not only for the financial reward, they're very generous, but it is more than apparent that something out of the ordinary is about to occur. I can't wait to find out what it is. Kelly's a real charmer and Sal, the only female in the group, is beyond beautiful and they're all of high intelligence. Each in their own way. Each possessing very different and distinct personalities. As though five worlds are colliding in a mutual, physical space of electrical plasma. A volatile brew just waiting for the right enzyme to ignite nothing less than a brilliant cacophony into a glorious explosion of light.* An expression of satisfaction covers his face as he closes the MacBook. He stows it in his backpack, starts the engine and drives off, his face still smiling from the expectation of what he just knows is going to be an extraordinary adventure.

IV

The crew assembles in Kelly's suite.

"I can't believe he knew that Joe Namath quote," Rollie comments as Kelly walks to the wall safe.

He opens it and counts off twenty-five one-hundred-dollar bills for Sparky's retainer from one of the stacks. Dave is seated, quietly scribbling notes in his notebook.

"After the roof, the foundation floor, if handled properly to avoid wall vibration, is the least sensitive part of a bank," he states.

The Kid lounging in a nearby chair asks, "Yeah, but how do we cut through the concrete floor of a bank without wall vibration setting off motion detectors?"

Dave looks up at The Kid. "Stick around, hot shot, and you'll learn something," he says.

"Please don't tell me you're thinking about cutting through with a thermal lance." Rollie complains. "I hate those things."

Sal pours herself a cocktail at the suite's bar, sits down and crosses her legs. She takes a long sip and asks Kelly, "How far do you think we can take Sparky?"

Kelly closes the safe. Walking towards the bar, he says, "I think he's game for anything." He pours himself a straight Irish whiskey.

Dave lifts his head from his notepad a moment, "Can he be trusted is the real question."

"We could give him a few tests," suggests Sal sipping her drink.

"Yeah!" The Kid perks up. "Like you did with me."

Sal laughs. The Kid takes a nonchalant posture and adds, "I mean, I knew what you guys were doing..."

"You did not!" insists Rollie.

The Kid waves him off.

Kelly looks over at Dave. "What about the work you were conducting with Ascarite?" he asks before taking a sip of his whiskey.

Dave looks up at Kelly a bit dismayed. "Never got it where it needs to be," he answers. "It's got potential though..."

"What's Ascarite?" asks The Kid, curious and eager to learn as always.

Dave peeks up from his notes, smiles and says, "Pour me a whiskey and I'll tell you."

The Kid laughs. "You're some kind of con man, professor."

He jumps up, struts to the bar and turns to Dave, "Neat, right?" he asks.

"Yeah."

The Kid pours a Maker's Mark, no ice, and walks it over to Dave.

"Ascarite is a highly corrosive material that theoretically dissolves concrete. But it only works in movies," Dave says, accepting the cocktail. "Thanks Kid," He takes a sip and continues. "It has potential... Just never got around to finishing my work with it," Dave looks at Kelly and Sal who have been following the exchange carefully. "My laboratory was invaded by Walrus Tusks before I could complete any serious work."

Kelly grins. "True... But look at the results!" he replies, his arms outstretched directing their attention to the fine accommodations of the Montauk Yacht Club.

"Touché," says Dave with a broad smile.

Kelly stands and addresses the crew. "I realize it has come as something of a surprise, but we..." in his Scottish brogue adds, "...my dear family, have a new and rather unexpected project afoot."

"Project Montauk!" exclaims The Kid.

Sal rolls her eyes.

"Interesting... You have good instincts, Kid," Dave tells him.

The entire crew turns to Dave unsure where he's going. He looks around the room. "None of you know about Project Montauk a.k.a. The Montauk Project?" he asks.

Kelly rubs his chin in thought. "You may have me stumped on this one," he concedes.

"It's sort of a legendary myth about Montauk surrounding the Radar Tower out at the point," he informs the crew.

“Countless articles in various journals have been written about it. Both *Stranger Things*, originally titled *Project Montauk* and *Unsolved Mysteries* have produced episodes about it,” he lets them know.

“Fascinating...” says Rollie.

Dave sips his whisky and looks around at the crew. They’re hooked. “Also connected to The Philadelphia Experiment...” he adds.

“The Philadelphia Experiment?” asks The Kid, a perplexed expression on his face. “What’s the Philadelphia Experiment?”

Dave sits up straight. “Potentially just another conspiracy theory. No one really knows for certain. The story goes that in the early days of World War II, October 28, 1943 to be exact, the Navy, it is thought, conducted an experiment using Einsteinian theory and Tesla engineering in an attempt to render a Naval Destroyer stealth to radar.”

“Wow,” Rollie comments, leaning in. “Invisible to radar in World War II?” he says excitedly.

“Must you really?” asks Sal directing the question to Dave.

Dave raises his eyebrows. “It may very well have been among the greatest tragedies of World War II, Sal. Many men purportedly lost their lives.” he says with a degree of emotion rarely seen in Dave.

He raises his glass looking upwards, as though to the deceased, and takes a swig of whisky. The crew listens intently.

“Naturally, the story is denied by the Navy, and there’s no evidence that any of it ever took place,” he says. “I suspect we’ll never know for sure, but ostensibly, the Navy parked a Destroyer at a harbor in Norfolk, Virginia. The ship used for the experiment was the USS Eldridge. The ship originated from Philadelphia, hence the name, Philadelphia Experiment. When the Navy conducted the experiment, not only did the ship become stealth to radar," he looks around the room with serious expression, "it disappeared entirely," he says dramatically.

The crew isn't buying into Dave's story. Being con artists and grifters, they are skeptical about most any story that strains credibility, conspiracy theories perhaps the top of the list.

"What do you mean disappeared?" asks Kelly.

"Legend has it that the destroyer somehow slipped through the space-time continuum and traveled past the dimensional vortex we know as 'now'," he says, his enjoyment of the story accompanied by a spooky grin.

"That's hard to believe," states The Kid.

"It certainly is," Dave concedes. "Yet, that hasn't stopped it from inspiring some serious scrutiny over the years," he adds, getting up to pour himself another whisky.

He pours the drink, turns to the crew and then leaning on the bar says, "Conspiracy theories are like that..." He examines the group, then continues, "The secret of that mysterious experiment and its terrible aftermath was kept for twelve years, until one day a guy by the name of Morris Jessup, author of a little-known book about UFOs, was summoned to the US Office of Naval Research. They got a hold of his UFO book and were intrigued with the strange handwritten annotations," he says, doing his best to imitate Boris Karloff's smile. "The weird thing about the unusual scribblings is that the notes were from three different characters, each in a different color of ink, yet all in the same odd handwriting,"

“I think I dated him once,” Sal quips, sipping her drink with a smirk, getting a laugh.

“The Navy was a bit on edge because the notes contained details of the Philadelphia Experiment thought to be Top Secret,” Dave continues. “Naturally the ONR,” he pauses and adds, “Office of Naval Research, wanted to know who had written the strange notes and how Jessup acquired them.”

Sounds par for the course,” Rollie tells them.

“Says the Navy Seal…” Dave comments, winking at Rollie. “During questioning, Jessup told them that he recognized the unique handwriting. That it matched the handwriting of a series of letters he’d received from a man who called himself Carlos Allende.” He pauses a moment and sips his drink. “Allende claimed he witnessed the Philadelphia Experiment from a nearby merchant marine ship. He says that during the experiment the USS Eldridge literally disappeared from the harbor in Norfolk, Virginia. When it reappeared a few minutes later, a number of the sailors’ bodies were integrated into the steel structure of the ship,” he states emotionally, sipping his drink.

“Jessup told the Navy that he figured Allende for a nut job. Especially when Allende told him how Albert Einstein spent several weeks mentoring him on subjects including invisibility and faster-than-light travel,” Dave says with a roll of the eyes. “Copies of the book, complete with the strange hand-written notes, were made public and the rest is history,” Dave says as he returns to the sofa.

“Yeah, but what does any of that have to do with the Montauk Project? How does Montauk play into all this?” The Kid asks, anxious for a punchline.

Dave looks up at him, emotionally distraught. “Forty years later in October of 1983 the Eldridge was spotted,” he looks at everyone deadpan, “...by several witnesses, off the coast of Montauk a few miles past the radar tower.” He takes a swig of whisky. “Anyway,” he says, “None of it may have ever happened.” He finishes his drink and places the empty glass on the table. “But if it did... then it had to travel through time to get there,” he says looking around at the crew one by one.

Dave smiles, looks over at Kelly and in his Scottish brogue says, “I return the floor to you, dear cousin.”

“That’s insane,” exclaims The Kid.

“Wild...” adds Rollie.

“See?” Sal says, looking into Kelly’s eyes.

Dave perks up and addresses Sal, “See what?”

Kelly takes over. “Sal has a theory that all con artists have an innate need to believe in fairytales... Essentially, to be conned themselves...” he tells his crew.

“Not true,” Rollie insists defensively.

“Wow, that’s depressing,” says The Kid.

“Look... we expend a huge effort creating realities that don’t exist, if we’re not diligent, we can sometimes lose track of what’s real and what’s not,” she says as she looks around at the crew with a rare sincere expression.

“Don’t sweat it, Kid.” Dave tries to ease the blow.

“If a part of us, often a large part of us, didn’t sincerely believe the lies we invent,” Kelly says looking around at the veterans in the group, "...the mark wouldn't buy into them."

"It's an essential part of the dynamic," Sal says, getting up to freshen her cocktail.

"The Kid looks around at his mentors. "I see what you mean," he says in realization. "Still..." he adds with a questionable look on his face, "Guess we need to be careful." The Kid straightens up in his chair.

"Always!" exclaims Rollie.

Dave looks over at The Kid. "It's important to keep things in perspective Kid," he says.

"That all makes sense but..." he looks down a moment, "Do you ever end up feeling guilty for the things you do?" The Kid asks.

Sal sits up straight, about to say something, but then looks over at Kelly. Dave leans forward running his fingers through his hair. Rollie cracks his knuckles.

"Is that what's happening to you?" Kelly asks walking over and patting The Kid on the back.

"I don't know," The Kid says, measuring it in his head.

"Missing your mommy, Kid?" Sal quips.

The Kid looks over at Sal with a mixture of disdain and maybe a touch of embarrassment. "Fuck you, Sal," he says without emotion to match the words.

"Consider the Chessman job we just pulled..." Kelly says. "How happy was Alexander Kader?"

"The Sotheby's guy?" The Kid.

“We made his day,” exclaims Dave.

“The Scottish Museum at Edinburgh and the British Museum are thrilled,” Rollie insists.

“To the tune of a million pounds...” smiles Dave.

“Kid, they'll make that money back in no time,” Sal informs him.

“That's true,” adds Kelly. “I mean you heard me read it in the paper. The Lewis Chessmen are the biggest draw at the museum,” Kelly reminds him.

They all look at The Kid. Each face showing signs of the wear and tear involved in dealing with their own inner demons. They've all gotten too close at one time or another. Too close to a mark or an object or their own conscience. The Kid's inquiries are triggering deeply buried ghosts they must all exorcise on various occasions in order to continue with their chosen profession as con artists, grifters and thieves.

Kelly sits on the arm of The Kid's chair. He looks at him in earnest. “No one has to know,” he says.

The Kid looks up at Kelly, his face an emblem of the huge question mark in his heart that already knows the answer.

“About what?” The Kid asks, unsure exactly which caper or what exactly Kelly is referring to.

He stares into Kelly's eyes. He's looking for something he can hold on to. He can feel the cold vacuous abyss beyond the precipice threatening his emotional well-being. He is not so inexperienced as to not already understand that he cannot let it creep in.

"Just that," Sal says breaking the tension. She leans forward, lights a cigarette and looks The Kid in the eyes. "Any of it," she says smiling, "No one ever has to know." She puffs her smoke.

"You keep it inside yourself as a... a kind of token. A source," Rollie says, attempting to explain what he knows is a complex concept.

"They don't want to know," adds Dave with a fatherly assurance.

"A source of what?" asks The Kid.

"A source of strength in the knowledge and precision that is our craft," Kelly says as he stands.

"Confidence," adds Sal.

"This is a confidence game, don't forget," Rollie summarizes.

Dave cups his hands. "It's a somewhat strange psychological phenomenon of life, Kid," He stands up and grabs The Kid's eyes. "No one is cheated who for one reason or another doesn't need to be cheated," he says.

The Kid considers this. They all look at Dave.

"You'll see it for yourself one day," Sal says, stomping her cigarette out in the ashtray. "One day it'll just add up," she finishes.

"It's the balance of equanimity," says Kelly. "What we do fills in the blanks..."

"Blanks?" The Kid inquires.

“The emptiness of otherwise uninspired lives,” Kelly tells him.

They sit there a moment in silence. Dave leans forward, picks up his notebook and scribbles something.

Kelly looks around at the forlorn crew and announces. “Now... back to the problem at hand,” he says. “Thoughts on the tunnel?” he asks Rollie.

“Shin has a micro TBM reversed engineered from Elon Musk’s device, he calls the Torpedo, that can handle our tunneling, no problem,” Rollie states confidently.

“TBM?” asks The Kid.

“Tunnel boring machine,” informs Dave.

“At least we’re not going El Chapo,” smiles The Kid, getting a big laugh.

A huge weight is lifted from the crew and the mood shifts. Kelly’s theory about the source of strength gained in the knowledge and precision of one’s craft takes center stage as the crew occupies themselves with solving the problems with detailed plans. The old adage; ‘Busy boy, happy boy,’ on full display.

“Shin’s better be faster than Musk’s, or we’ll be digging till next Independence Day,” Dave insists.

“Yeah, they call Musk’s TBM the snail behind his back,” Rollie says. “Shin figured it out. Even compacts as it digs so minimal removal will be required,” says Rollie happily.

“Removal could become a nightmare. I’ll take some readings, but I’ll guess earthen composition here just upwards of twenty-five percent,” Dave tells the crew.

“So, essentially, we’ll be digging through sand,” Rollie adds.

“With the occasional boulder deposited by the last ice age,” says Dave.

Rollie looks at The Kid with a big smile. “That’ll make our job a lot easier,” he tells him.

“Our job?” The Kid frowns, not wanting to be a part of the digging crew.

“Gotta pay your dues, Kid,” Sal tells him.

“We all do,” Kelly adds.

“I’m gonna need a set of blueprints for both the bank and the Tower.” Dave looks up from his notes.

“That’s yours, Kid,” says Kelly. “You can play an engineering student from RIT here for the summer hoping to get some research done.”

Kelly looks at his watch and sits down in one of the comfortable overstuffed chairs. The crew sit there silent a moment. Kelly looks at his watch again. “Better call Sparky,” he says to Rollie.

Kelly addresses Dave. “The Tower is definitely the closest feasible location to tunnel from,” he says.

“Agreed,” answers Dave, scribbling notes.

“Which makes it the only place to tunnel from,” warns Rollie.

Dave looks up with a smile. “Unless, of course, you prefer to tunnel from the police station.”

“It is much closer...” Sal quips.

“We’re going to need to create a serious maintenance issue at the Tower to get access below ground,” Dave informs them.

“I know,” says Kelly.

“Time to call your realtor girlfriend,” says Sal with a wise-ass smile.

The crew chuckles.

“You may have to take one for the team, boss,” says The Kid.

Kelly grins, happy to have The Kid back in the fold.

“Hey Sparky,” says Rollie speaking into the cell phone. “I have a stack of hundred-dollar bills with your name on it,” he says winking at the crew. “Yeah, call us when you’re here.” He ends the call, looks around the room with a shake of the head, “Sparky...” he smiles.

“Once we have access with a condominium in the building, we can scout the service area below and generate a plan.” “Whatever it is, it has to buy us three days for the tunnel,” Rollie informs them.

“And grant us access to the tunnel on the Fourth of July,” adds Dave. He looks at Kelly, “Even with condo access, we’ll need to find a way to hide the tunnel without killing our access to it on D-Day,” he says.

“Right...” Kelly says thinking.

“What about this smart-bomb-styled-missile doodad?” asks The Kid.

Rollie smiles. “There are salient advantages to having been a Navy Seal, Kid,” Rollie tells him.

“It’s practically CIA,” Sal adds, puffing on a smoke.

“It’s gonna have to be a custom job,” Dave tells Rollie.

“I know…” Rollie answers confidently. “Get me the specs, and I’ll get you the missile,” he says.

Kelly’s big smile. He pulls out his cell and hits speed dial, “Giovanna!” he says. He listens a moment, “Can I drop by in a few?” he asks in a sultry voice. “Great, see you then.” He stands up and addresses the crew, “I’ll see about that condo in the Tower.”

“Why don’t you just google Montauk Tower timeshares?” asks The Kid, pulling out his cell phone.

“Hold it right there, Kid,” Dave says sternly.

The Kid is miffed. “What’s your problem?” he asks defensively.

“Never google anything related to a job,” warns Kelly.

The Kid’s face remains a question mark.

“Google tracks everything,” warns Sal. “People are much easier to control,” she says looking at Kelly. “Why leave a bunny trail?” she states, eyebrows raised looking at The Kid.

“Right…” The Kid concedes in realization. “In that case, what’s for dinner?” he asks.

“What about that round restaurant with all the windows on the corner?” Suggests Sal. “It’s got a great view of the Tower and Chase Bank,” she adds.

Rollie's phone rings. He answers. "Sparky," he says. "Hey, what's the name of that round glass restaurant in town? ...Tacombi," Rollie repeats. He looks up at the crew, "Gourmet Mexican," he says.

Kelly shrugs indifferently, letting the crew know it's fine with him,

"We'll be out in a minute," Rollie says speaking into the phone.

"I think it's best if I have some alone time with Sparky," suggests Kelly, holding up Sparky's $2,500 retainer. He starts for the door and turns. "I'll send him back after he drops me at the realtor and then meet you at the Mexican joint in an hour or so."

"An hour?" asks The Kid. "I'm famished!" he insists.

"Kids..." Sal rouses.

"Give it a rest, Sal," The Kid says, cracking wise.

Kelly opens the door, turns to The Kid and says, "Order without me. I'll join you once I've secured the time-share."

"Charmer..." says Dave with a coy smile.

Sal walks to the bar and finds a candy bar and some cashews, "These should hold you until dinner," she smiles and hands the goodies to The Kid.

"Thanks, Sal," he says in a very sincere tone.

He wastes no time ripping open the candy bar and taking a huge energetic bite.

Kelly exits the Yacht Club. Sparky is there waiting. "Hey, Sparky," he says as he steps into the front passenger seat of the mini-van.

Here ya go, pal." Kelly hands Sparky his $2,500 retainer.

"The Tower doesn't offer time-shares, but you can rent or buy a condo," Sparky says counting the cash before stuffing it in his pocket.

"Renting works," says Kelly, spying Sparky with a wry knowing grin.

"Where to, sir?" Sparky asks, mimicking a driver of old.

"I need to see that pesky realtor again," he says smiling.

"Pesky hunh?" Sparky muses.

Kelly smiles at Sparky. "That's playing it down somewhat," Kelly says with a wink. "How'd you get a name like Sparky?" Kelly asks as they drive away.

"My surname is Sparcanella, Michael Sparcanella," he says. "I grew up near a Trotter Track... Roosevelt Raceway up island... There was a nearby bar a lot of the trainers, jockeys and groomers hung out in called Tom's Corner," he says, turning the corner onto Montauk Highway towards town. "I was a bit of a pool shark apparently," he says with a coy smile. "One night, after I'd learned to hustle pool, I was on fire winning loads of money at the table when a well-known trainer, John Chapman, warned one of his jockeys who had just entered the bar and put a quarter on the pool table, saying "Watch out, he's sparky tonight,"' Sparky smiles as he pulls up in front of the realtor's office. "The rest is history," he says with a shrug.

"Interesting," Kelly comments fascinated by this small piece of Sparky's history.

“I guess it is, isn’t it?” remarks Sparky with a sly smile.

“You ever been arrested?” Kelly asks.

Sparky looks over at Kelly with a tilt of the head, a smirk on his face. “Maybe... once or twice,” he answers.

Kelly gazes through the taxi window at the realtor’s office a moment as Giovanna stands at the window waiting for him to arrive. He looks back at Sparky and lets him know, “We’ll pick this conversation up soon.”

“I’ll look forward to it,” Sparky says with a smile. “I have a distinct feeling there’s more than meets the eye concerning you guys,” he adds daringly.

Kelly looks at him with a raise of the eyebrow.

“I have good instincts about these things...” Sparky offers as an explanation.

“I see,” says Kelly with his signature grin. “Would you head back up to the Yacht Club and pick up the guys?” I’ll meet everyone at Tacombi around the corner when I’m though here.”

“You got it, Kelly,” Sparky remarks with a smile.

“Thanks, Sparks.” Kelly says as he exits the taxi.

“Kelly!” Sparky yells after Kelly, who turns to face him. “I’ll let them know you could be late...” says Sparky, raising his eyebrows a few times, with a wise-ass grin.

Kelly’s laughing as he enters Giovanna’s office.

“Giovanna,” he gushes, arms stretched wide, smiling his charm.

Giovanna nearly swoons. “John,” she stammers. “How nice to see you again,” she states excitedly.

They stand there gazing into each other’s eyes. Kelly lays it on thick and Giovanna loves every second of it. Again, her mind instantly generates fantasies of romance with Kelly, only this time they’ve moved from poolside to more secretive environs. She’s trembling and Kelly lets her, gazing deeply into her eyes.

“I’ve decided that while I look for the perfect home, I’d like to rent a condo in the historic Montauk Tower,” he says smiling.

Giovanna continues staring into his eyes. “Yes…” she says finally. “That’s doable,” she tells him doing her best to appear professional. “Please sit down,” she says walking to her desk and motioning for Kelly to take the stuffed leather chair.

She sits at her desk, opens her computer and hits a few buttons. “The prices vary greatly depending on the floor and size of the unit,” she says smiling. “And availability…” she adds in her real estate broker’s tone.

Kelly sits silently watching her, a smile on his face. He chooses a unit and Giovanna sets it up. A short while later he walks to the door, “Thank you for all your help,” he says kindly. “You are fantastic.”

“Oh, John,” she blushes.

“Be back soon for the keys?” he smiles.

“I’ll have it all set up in a day or two,” she assures him.

They shake hands. Kelly exits her office. Giovanna stands at the door watching him walk away. She lets go of a big sigh. Her phone rings. She lets it ring while she watches Kelly's stride as he walks away. Kelly turns the corner towards Tacombi. He stops a moment and stares at the Chase Bank, then at the Tower. He judges the distance between them as a little over a thousand yards. He knows that he must see past the obstacles inherent in such a complex job, instead focusing on the success of the project, however outlandish. Kelly is a person who would rather be the passenger on a jetliner who must take the helm and land in an emergency rather than ride an amusement park roller-coaster. He isn't very adept at relinquishing control, and even when things careen way off course and become dangerous, he has a knack for always finding a way out. There is always a way to make it work. He stands in the middle of the sidewalk running every detail through his mind, belittling any obstacles that may arise, instilling positive associations to what most people would consider a gargantuan effort as well as an insane endeavor. A smile comes to his face. He smiles at two attractive bikini-clad women passing by on the sidewalk. One of the women turns back to him with a smile. Feeling confident, he continues towards Tacombi Restaurant where the crew are seated at one of the picnic-style exterior tables. Sparky is parked nearby.

“Buen dia,” he says taking the available spot at the table.

“So, what gives, Romeo?” Sal quips.

He acknowledges Sparky with a nod. “Apparently our Sparky was a bit of a pool shark in his youth.” Referring to him sitting in his taxi working on his MacBook. “And he has a record,” Kelly adds, turning back to the crew with a huge smile.

“Cool,” remarks The Kid.

“What for?” asks Dave sipping his Margherita.

"We didn't get that far," Kelly says, looking up at the waitress who has just arrived, menu in hand.

Kelly glances at the menu quickly and looks up at her, "I'll have the Crispy Local Tile Fish, and a Modelo Especiale."

"Crispy Tile and a Modelo," she repeats scribbling the order. She glances at The Kid with a sultry expression then struts off waitress style towards the kitchen.

"The tile fish is a good choice," assures Rollie referring to the plate in front of him.

Kelly looks at The Kid approvingly. "You're gonna be a real lady-killer one day, Kid," he says.

"That reminds me," The Kid exclaims, grabbing his cell phone. He clicks it a few times and puts the phone to his ear. "Rachel?" he asks smiling. "Hi, it's Louie. He gets up and walks to a nearby bench to speak in privacy.

Sal shakes her head. "Romeo II," she quips winking at Kelly.

"Tell us about Sparky, the pool shark," she says looking over at Sparky seated in his taxi typing away on his computer.

The waitress returns with Kelly's Modelo. "Your meal will be ready in just a few minutes," she assures him, taking notice that The Kid is not at the table.

"Apparently our Sparky grew up near a harness race track up island where he hustled pool at a nearby drinking establishment," Kelly says, sipping his beer and gazing over at Sparky, still focused on his MacBook.

"Interesting," says Dave. "All we really need is his discretion," he adds.

"His knowledge of the local fisherman may be of use also, don't forget," Rollie adds.

"That's right," says Kelly. He looks over at Dave, "Unless you want that missile filled with Demyan's diamonds floating out in the Atlantic unattended," adds Kelly as the waitress returns with his crispy local tile fish. "Thanks, this looks great," Kelly tells her.

"I promise it's amazing," she says.

"The promises of this world are, for the most part, vain phantoms, and to confide in one's self, and become something of worth and value is the best and safest course," quotes Rollie.

"Wow!" the waitress says, her eyes lighting up. "You're quoting Michelangelo!"

"Why, yes I am," Rollie smiles, charming the waitress with a sex appeal all his own.

"I'm an art major," the waitress tells Rollie.

"That's strange... I see you more as the work of art itself," he insists.

Sal rolls her eyes at Kelly who just smiles a shrug.

She giggles then spots The Kid sitting on the bench laughing loudly into his iPhone.

"Great!" The Kid exclaims. "See you then." he stands up and pockets the phone.

He turns towards the table and locks eyes with the waitress for a moment. "Hi," he says, using his charming smile as he approaches the table.

She struts off busily. When The Kid is close enough, Sal looks over her sunglasses.

“What do you have, a waitress fetish?” she asks The Kid.

They share a laugh as The Kid takes a seat.

“Hey, I mean... we’ve only been to restaurants since we got here,” he says defensively.

“Doesn’t matter anyway, looks like you’ve got serious competition with Mr. Michelangelo over here,” pointing her thumb at Rollie.

“Why? What happened?” asks The Kid instantly curious.

Kelly digs into his tile fish then turns the focus back to the job at hand, “I estimate a little over a football field of tunnel, Rollie,” he says, sipping his Modelo.

Rollie looks at The Tower across the Plaza over to the Chase Bank and says, “Sounds about right.”

“Tell me about Michelangelo,” insists The Kid.

“Unless you have a plan to acquire one, forget Michelangelo,” Kelly says. He turns to The Kid with a serious expression, “We have a job to do.”

“Fair enough,” says The Kid.

“All’s fair in love and war, Kid.” Rollie smiles.

“We have elevator, heating and cooling or plumbing that can gain access to the basement for a work crew,” Dave tells them.

"And I just rented us an available condo in the Tower," adds Kelly.

"When do we have access?" asks Sal.

"I sign and pick up the keys day after tomorrow," smiles Kelly. "Any update on the missile?" Kelly asks Rollie.

"Spoke to Shin early this morning. Because of the delicacy of keeping the rocket no more than one hundred feet above sea level, out of defense department sat-radar range, he'll need a full two weeks. Once he has the specs," Rollie adds looking at Dave.

"I'll have to estimate the specs," Dave adds. "Plus, I'll likely have to restructure the turret with a new support system, so it remains intact yet is hollow enough for the missile to fit inside," Dave says looking at Kelly.

"Yeah, till we blast it out over the Atlantic Ocean," says The Kid excitedly.

"Until then, please try to contain yourself," Sal tells him as she sips her drink, "This isn't the Indi 500 Kid," she adds.

"Not yet," smiles The Kid pretending to be racing, hands on an imaginary steering wheel. "When those cops are chasing the remote control get-a-way car, it'll be me they can't catch!" he says, adding motor-revving sounds and sharp-turn screeches.

Kelly smiles at The Kid's antics. "Interesting analogy, Sal," Kelly says turning to her.

"What is?" she asks.

"Carl Fischer... who built the Yacht Club, the Deep Sea Club, the Montauk Manor... and the Tower," Kelly continues pointing his thumb at the Tower.

“And the casino,” Sal interrupts.

“And the casino,” Kelly admits. “…began as a racecar driver,” Kelly tells them, looking at The Kid who perks up.

“The guy who built Montauk was a racecar driver?” The Kid asks.

“That he was,” Kelly tells him. “Carl lived life in the fast lane. The Deep Sea Club was the most glamorous speakeasy on Long Island. The club became a haven not only for the rich and famous of the day, like the Vanderbilts and Astor’s… John Barrymore and Errol Flynn… Carl was even friends with Al Capone,” he says, chuckling as he imagines the scene. “Writers like F. Scott Fitzgerald and Ernest Hemingway… The speakeasy and casino were, ‘the’ in spots. Even New York mayor Jimmy Walker would show up. Until a raid by the Feds in the early 1930’s shut it down” he tells them.

“The Mayor was secretly ushered out of the back exit wearing a kitchen apron,” Kelly enjoys sharing the spiciest bits of history, “A close-call escape… Old Carl lived life in the fast lane on and off the racetrack.” He gazes at The Kid. “Before he came here, he was a serious and famous racecar driver from Indiana who built the Indianapolis Motor Speedway,” Kelly continues.

“Legendary,” says The Kid. “What kind of car are we getting?" he asks looking at Rollie and Dave.

“A Crown Vic,” Rollie tells him.

“A Crown Victoria!?!” gasps The Kid. “A taxi?” He cannot believe it.

“Not just any Crown Vic,” Rollie assures him. “Until a decade ago cop cars were all Crown Vics… they have souped-up engines, drive trains, suspension, steerage... the whole nine," Rollie smiles.

"And they're ideal for installing the remote-control drive system I have in mind," says Dave. He looks up at the crew with a mischievous grin. "Plus, there is a certain irony using an old cop car to rob a bank," he adds.

Kelly and Sal agree. Rollie pats The Kid on the back, "I promise you, Kid, by the time my boys in Jersey are through with her, she'll be a racecar worthy of the Indi 500."

The Kid's happy to hear it. "I can deal with that," he says with a newfound smile.

The waitress meanders over. "Can I get you guys anything else?" she asks with a smile ...especially for Rollie.

The Kid can't help but to notice the lavish attention she is flowering on Rollie.

"She's Venus in blue jeans, Mona Lisa with a ponytail, ...she's a walkin', talkin' work of art. She's the girl who stole my heart..." Rollie sings arms outstretched. "Jimmy Clanton had to have written that song for you," he insists.

Kelly watches the exchange closely. He wants to see how The Kid reacts to a bit of adversity. As does Sal. Both are amused by the dynamics occurring between The Kid, Rollie and the pretty waitress.

"Only that song is older than you are," says The Kid, looking up at the waitress, vying for her attention.

She looks at The Kid sitting there pushing his handsome grin and says, "Poetry is like that." She turns her attention to Rollie and adds, "Like great art..." she smiles alluringly at Rollie, "…it's timeless." She says gazing into Rollie's eyes.

"Most philosophers don't come in such ravishing form as you," Rollie tells her.

"Ravishing, hunh?" she smiles flirtatiously.

"Absolutely ravishing… Perhaps we might discuss the ramifications of such an unlikely phenomenon over a bottle of wine some evening," Rollie charms.

She blushes a bit, "I would love that!" she says. She scribbles her number on a piece of paper and hands it to Rollie. "I'm Candy. Call me…" she says with a sexy smile. "We can discuss Michelangelo in depth," she adds, holding the piece of paper for Rollie to take from her hand, which he does.

The Kid is scratching his head.

Kelly intercedes asking "Sal? Guys…?" He looks around the table to be sure no one wants anything further from the waitress. Rollie and the waitress continue to gaze at one another deep in romantic thought.

"I'm good," answers Dave.

"It was all delicious," Rollie smiles.

"Scrumptious," quips Sal.

Kelly smiles as Rollie and the waitress gaze at one another. "Just the check then," he says.

The waitress doesn't respond, as though in a dream.

"Miss?" Kelly asks loudly looking up at her.

She snaps out of it, looks over at Kelly and says, “Oh... right...” she says. “I’ll be right back with the check.”

Sal looks over at Rollie, then The Kid, “You may have met your match, Kid.”

“Hardly,” The Kid responds looking over at Rollie with a wise-ass expression. The Kid checks Sal’s reaction, “I mean... not all women go gaga over Michelangelo.” He looks at the pretty waitress through the curved glass walls of the restaurant as she prepares the bill, “Freak,” he adds.

“Don’t be too sure about that, Kid,” assures Sal. “A little Michelangelo goes a long way,” she says, challenging The Kid’s meager defense.

“You should read more books, Kid,” Kelly tells him.

Dave looks at Rollie, “I need a large blackboard,” he says.

“Got that, Kid?’ Rollie asks.

“What? me?” The Kid protests. “Why am I elected to get a blackboard?”

“Because I’m getting the TBM, the guided missile and get-a-way car you get to have your Mario Andretti moment with,” says Rollie.

Kelly smiles at Rollie with a wink. Sal nods her head.

“It’s not all glamour and fresh orange juice, Kid,” Sal lets him know.

Dave watches The Kid’s reaction as he peers at his mentors one by one, a loving smirk on his face. “Fair enough,” he says, “Fair enough...”

"I hope you enjoyed everything," states the waitress as she places the check on the table.

"Everything was great, honey," says Sal.

"Absolutely delicious," adds Rollie smiling at her. He reaches into his vest pocket, pulls out her number and holds it up for her to see. "I'm looking forward to our seaside symposium."

"Me too," she gushes.

Kelly stuffs a few hundred-dollar bills in the check folder and stands up. "Everything was great, thanks again," he says.

She takes the check holder stuffed with cash as the crew saunters over to the taxi sitting in the shade nearby with Sparky typing away.

"Hey, gang," he says and opens the automatic doors for them. As they enter the mini-van he stows his MacBook and starts the engine.

"Any idea where to get a blackboard, Sparky?" asks The Kid.

Sparky smirks. "This is Montauk. We have fish, booze, surf, hotels and romance..." he cracks. "Anything beyond that is a drive out of town... or Amazon Prime," he says knowingly.

"Hey, Dave, how large a blackboard you need?" The Kid asks.

"A six-foot board will do..." he says with a nod of approval. "Don't forget the chalk... and erasers," he adds.

"Got that, Sparks?" asks The Kid, getting comfortable in his seat.

They all look at him, not sure whether to be angry or impressed. He looks at the crew from the rear of the taxi, his arms outstretched, a grin on his face, "It's about delegating," he says.

Kelly loves it.

"You're gonna be okay, Kid," Sal remarks.

Sparky's loving every minute of it. "I'll see what I can do."

Kelly can see in Sparky's expression and body language that he's sponging every word for his book. "You get all that, Sparks?"

"I have a photographic memory," he says, recognizing Kelly's double entendre. "Where we goin' anyway?" he asks.

"Back to the Yacht Club, pal," Kelly lets him know.

They take off around the Plaza and up Flamingo Avenue towards Star Island. Halfway up the hill a deer galivants across the road directly in front of the taxi. With a masterful maneuver, Sparky brakes and swerves to avoid hitting it.

"Damn deer," he grimaces.

"Nice move, Sparky!" says The Kid with a huge smile.

"They are the dumbest animals on God's green earth," Sparky insists.

"You have a lot of them out here?" Dave asks.

“They’re a menace!” Sparky insists, obviously frustrated by the beasts who have little concept of the automobile and who often just strut out into moving traffic without a care in the world.

“Night driving out here is like a video game! Don’t hit the deer for extra points…” he adds.

“I imagine hitting one could cause quite a lot of damage,” Rollie adds.

Sparky looks at Rollie. “We’re going to have to address this,” he says. “I wrote the County Legislature about it,” Sparky tells everyone. “They’ve been talking about culling the deer out here for twenty years. From Southampton to Montauk, people smash into them constantly. Even caused a few deaths,” he says mournfully.

“What’s keeping them from culling the deer?” Dave asks as they drive along towards the Yacht Club.

“That’s what I asked in my letter. It’s all politics!” Sparky answers, knowing the deal. “Unless they can win votes, rare is the politician who ever does anything simply because it’s the right thing to do,” he says in frustration.

“I hear that,” Navy Seal veteran Rollie says with a brotherly nod of his head.

“And! To make matters worse,” Sparky says with a noticeable degree of agitation, “This *is* the Hamptons after all… Idiot PETA members, most in leather shoes, not one a vegetarian, get all huffy about culling the deer,” he says shaking his head in incredulity.

“Until a deer smashes into their Land Rover,” Sal says with a wink to Sparky he catches through the rear-view mirror.

“If they were to cull half the deer population, process the meat and give it to food banks, kids who otherwise wouldn’t have meat in their diet could benefit from the venison,” he finishes matter of fact.

“That’s a clever idea, Sparky,” Kelly says looking over at Sparky.

“Only that could upset the PETA crowd,” adds Dave.

“If they want to see real mistreatment of animals, they should visit a slaughter house,” Rollie suggests knowingly.

“Never happen,” Sparky says pulling up to the Montauk Yacht Club.

He stops the car and the crew piles out.

“Feel free to grab a few hours, Sparky,” Kelly tells him. “But please keep your phone hot,” he adds.

“Yeah... Never know when one of the boys might get the sudden urge to meet a new waitress,” Sal adds, rolling her eyes.

She slaps The Kid on the butt, “Right, Kid?”

The Kid laughs. “You got that right, grandma.” He guffaws.

“Punk,” Sal quips with a snarl.

“Watch it, Kid,” Kelly warns him. “She bites!”

Sparky catches the exchange and laughs out loud. He is loving the crew more every day.

V

The following morning Kelly's crew is gathered in his suite. Dave is working out drilling equations on his laptop and Rollie's on the phone securing additional labor for the tunnel dig while The Kid polishes up on architecture. Kelly stands up and addresses the crew.

"All right, everybody, let's examine the broad strokes," he says spanning the room making eye contact with everyone. "Dave will get control of the phones at the Tower management office, reroute the maintenance call to us so we can create a work order and place our crew, secured by Rollie, onsite with the TBM." He looks at Rollie. "How we doing with labor?" he asks.

Rollie raises his eyes from his notebook, "The Frenchman's out so that leaves Moose's guys up in the Bronx," he answers, scribbling in his notepad.

"That's odd ...the French love the beach!" Sal quips.

"The Lithuanian?" Dave reacts excitedly. "That man has got a screw loose," he insists.

"Maybe a few screws loose," admits Rollie with a smirk. "But he's got the toughest guys I've ever worked with," Rollie adds, defending his old pal The Moose.

"I like the sound of that," adds The Kid.

"Old ass-lick himself..." Sal reminds them with her sarcastic tone. "There is something seriously wrong with that guy," she insists as she lights a cigarette.

"You're not exactly Mary Poppins, Sal," remarks The Kid. He winks at Kelly.

“The Kid’s got a point,” Kelly agrees.

“Hey!” Sal yells at Kelly defensively. “These are the waters we swim in, gang,” she says smiling at The Kid.

“Why not Shin?” Dave asks Rollie.

“He’s showing signs of stress on the quick turnaround for the custom rocket,” Rollie lets them know. “I don’t want to push him over the edge.”

“Fair enough,” Kelly agrees. “Okay, back to broad strokes.” He steers the crew back into the ABCs of the job.

He begins pacing the room as he lays it out.

“We use the condo at the Tower as command central and install our maintenance crew in the basement to repair whatever clever system failure Dave cooks up. We have to convince management there’s no short-term solution, …that it’s a complex problem. One that’ll require three to five days.” He tells Dave. Kelly turns to Rollie. “That should give you more than enough time to reach the bank with the TBM…”

Rollie nods an affirmative.

“Then, on the fourth, we go in and install the missile.” Kelly tells them.

“Which, considering basic construction technique, will involve restructuring the turret in order to hollow it out as well as devising an explosive hatch device that’ll blow the cap off, all done remotely from whatever boat we engage for our rocket retrieval and get-a-way,” Dave interjects.

“Which we know you will create a genius solution for…” Kelly assures the crew looking at Dave.

“Even with the preset stored images of the flight path, if that missile doesn’t have a clean exit, the presets on the guidance system could alter substantially. And seeing as the technology is designed for a far longer journey than four or five miles, less than a hundred feet above sea level, if it can’t correct the path in time, we may never see it again,” Dave adds as a warning.

“Hey, doc, maybe next time we go out to dinner, we’ll have a science major as our waitress, and you can score!” The Kid says.

Dave looks at The Kid amused. “Yeah, maybe, Kid…”

“Once our ‘The Great Escape’ styled tunnel is in place, including the dolly system, on Independence Day, we go in, install the rocket, fill it with the loot and blast it out over the ocean, just as the fireworks begin, where a commercial fishing boat we have secured with all of us aboard, will retrieve it and get us out of town,” Kelly summates. He looks around the room, “And I mean all the loot,” he says.

They look up at him, not sure why he wants to spend precious time inside the bank, robbing anything beyond Demyan’s exotic gems.

“Why waste our time with a measly few hundred grand cash, if that, and safety deposit box mementos, when Demyan’s diamonds are the only thing worth stealing?” asks The Kid with a bit of his know-it-all demeanor.

Kelly looks at his protégé. “Because it will help confuse the FBI if we take the cash and safety deposit box contents as well as Demyan’s exotic gem collection,” he informs him.

“Of course!” exclaims The Kid.

“Right.” agrees Dave.

"If we take it all they won't immediately suspect that we knew about Demyan's diamonds," Rollie adds.

"And seeing as your realtor fantasy lover wasn't supposed to divulge privy client info the way she did, it's unlikely she'll spill the beans," adds Sal.

"Okay... and this is the fun part," Kelly says smiling at The Kid. "I have learned, speaking with the illustrious Sparky, that back in the 1920s, a road that now circles the Montauk Downs golf course, called Fairview Avenue was a dirt racetrack," he smiles. "Originally we discussed Mario Andretti leading the cops west, down the stretch, towards Amagansett," he says referring to The Kid with lavish gesture. But, I think, in the spirit of history, ...and of racing, Carl Fischer's first profession back in Indianapolis, we bring them back to the racetrack," he finishes.

Everyone loves the idea.

"Nice touch" Rollie exclaims.

"You'll have 'em running in circles, Kid," Sal says smiling.

"Cool!" exclaims The Kid. "I'll get Sparky to drive me around it a few times to get the feel of it," he says closing his eyes, placing his hands on an imaginary steering wheel and mimicking a race car driver on a racetrack.

"By my calculations, we're gonna need twenty minutes, Kid," Dave says. He looks up at The Kid challengingly, "Think you can provide that?

"They don't have a chance against The Kid," he exclaims really getting into the air racecar driver bit he seems to enjoy.

"I've decided to add a heavy-duty steel Bull Bar to your racecar, Kid. That way, if a deer runs out in front of you it'll bounce out of your way like a hockey puck instead of potentially getting mangled in the steering wheel and the cops finding a crash test dummy behind the wheel instead of a bank robber, before we want them to" Rollie says animating the process.

"Cool," says The Kid. "The last thing I need is Bambi crashing through the windshield and messing up my run." He thinks a moment and then adds, "What about a James Bond style 50 Cal under the front bumper? I'll blow them all away," he smiles mimicking blowing deer out of the way with the 50-caliber machine gun.

"Leave it to the video game generation," Sal smirks. "You're such a gamer, Kid."

"Yeah, that's why I'm driving the get-away car and you're not," The Kid states with a smart-ass grin.

"You know, the race-track is actually the superior choice," Dave says looking up at Kelly with a wry expression. "Not to discount the lovely poetic aspect that inspired the idea, maestro," he says to Kelly, "...but there are actually two advantages to that route as opposed to running them down the Stretch. One, if we use the Stretch, East Hampton Police from Amagansett get involved and there's nowhere to go, whereas using the race-track keeps the focus local to Montauk, and with the cops full out dealing with the massive crowds here for the fireworks, The Kid will actually have less interference," he says knowingly. "Secondly, the cops will refrain from any drastic measures so as to not cause any serious damage to the valuable real estate up there," he says.

"Nice work, Dave," Kelly says.

“Plus, it’ll be more fun!” exclaims The Kid, air-racecar driving again, complete with full-on racing sound-effects.

“Plus, it’ll be more fun...” agrees Dave with a smile, enjoying The Kid’s enthusiasm and race-car driver antics. Dave realizes that The Kid is already in training, getting into character for his part in the heist. Dave appreciates and admires the simple intelligence in that.

Kelly stands up and addresses the crew, getting them back on track. “Fisherman around the world have a long history of smuggling. Montauk is no different. During prohibition it was booze,” he says.

“I’ll drink to that,” says Sal getting up and walking to the bar, pouring herself a champagne.

“The beach at the end of East Lake Drive is named Gin Beach for a reason...” he says egging on the mischievous nature of his crew. “Not a hundred percent sure, but I will venture to guess why...” he smiles with a fun suggestive tilt of the head. He looks around at the crew. “We’ll have to find a way to secure a commercial fishing boat captain and his vessel we can use as command central to track the missile, broadcast The Kid’s remote control get-a-way car signal and, naturally, to retrieve the missile we’ll have launched into the ocean due east...” he looks at Dave, “What? ...three miles or so?” he asks.

“Something like that,” answers Dave typing something into his laptop. “We’ll track the rocket with GPS until we can grab a visual,” says Dave.

“Then, when we have successfully retrieved the contents of the rocket, our commercial fishing boat captain will motor us up to Nova Scotia, where Sparky, having grabbed a flight from Montauk, and secured accommodations at the Fox Harbor Resort, will meet us at the commercial docks up there,” Kelly says with his mischievous grin.

He stands there a moment observing his crew seeking reactions, each deep in thought considering their role in the caper. After a long moment as the reality of what they are about to pursue sinks in, The Kid breaks the ice.

"This is going to be fun!" he exclaims.

The entire crew turns toward The Kid and stare at him, then in unison, crack up laughing.

"Some kind of vacation," quips Sal. She looks at her diamond-studded gold Cartier wristwatch. "Guess I better work on my tan," she says getting up from the sofa and leaving the suite.

"When is that chalkboard arriving, Kid?" Dave asks, getting back to business. "Time to get down to the nitty gritty.

"I'll track it now," The Kid says.

He taps his iPhone a few times, reads the screen, looks up at Dave smiling and says, "It'll be here Thursday."

"You remembered the chalk, right?" checks Dave.

"Even got you an extra eraser," The Kid announces proudly.

Dave folds up his laptop, stands up and asks, "Anyone up for a swim?"

The Kid looks at his watch, smiles and tells him, "Nah… I want to check out the racetrack on my way to meet Rachel," he says with a wink.

"That reminds me," says Rollie shrugging at The Kid with raised eyebrows.

He pulls out the piece of paper with the phone number of the pretty waitress art major, Candy, from Tacombi and dials.

“Hi… is this my favorite work of art?” he asks, smiling at The Kid with an all’s-fair-in-love-and-war expression.

“Sal’s heading down to work on her tan,” Kelly says to Dave.

“Oh, right,” says Dave. “I think I’ll join her.” He gathers his things and leaves the suite.

Rollie and The Kid get up to leave.

The Kid turns to Rollie, “What time are you meeting your waitress?” he asks.

“Our esteemed rendezvous is at eight o’clock… a local sunset paradise appropriately named The Montauket,” Rollie tells him.

Kelly looks at his watch. “Let me know when the taxi arrives.” He looks at the guys and adds, “Time to spend some quality time with Sparky.”

Rollie gathers the last of his notes and says. “Will do, chief.”

The Kid and Rollie leave the room. Kelly stands there alone for a moment and then walks to the bar slowly and pours himself a whisky, neat, no ice. He walks out to the terrace and takes a seat. He sips his drink and gazes out over the Yacht Club Marina admiring the yachts. He imagines Vanderbilt’s yacht tied up to the dock and the glamorous guests deboarding to enjoy the casino. He can hear the laughter amidst the wonderful music that was part of the roaring twenties… the clinking of glasses… the horse and buggies pulling up to the Deep Sea Club dropping off the rich and famous from their private train cars in the early days of the Long Island Railroad. He has long felt he was born in the wrong era and imagines himself as Charles Lindbergh landing his seaplane on Lake Montauk and how glamorous the Deep Sea Club must have been. He begins to work through the problems of the job ahead of him. A part of him in disbelief that he has actually conceived of such a radical, daring plan. Will it go well? What are the potential pitfalls? Will the crew hold up? Will The Kid? And what about Demyan? He runs the variables through in his head. Like baking a soufflé, every element must be precise and handled with care or the whole thing will collapse. He sips his whisky and remembers his very first con as a teenager in Chicago, how badly he felt about the older woman he took advantage of and how far he'd come. He thinks about the first time he met Sal. He sips his whisky and says her name softly with a wry grin. "Sally…" How quickly she made him and called him on it. But also complimented his mastery of style and how hard she had to work to figure him out. Shortly afterwards they were partners. He notices a two-mast ketch in the distance reefing the sails as it enters the inlet to Lake Montauk. He watches the fifty-footer motor towards the Yacht Club, admiring the captain proudly at the helm. Kelly, too, once again is at the helm now. He feels love and a great satisfaction for the crew he has assembled very carefully over the years… How great they have worked together in the past. Still the butterflies in his gut are fluttering just a bit. Better now than during the heist, he tells himself. Still, they rage inside of him, trying to work their way into his head. But then he considers the value of Demyan's exotic gems. He knows the potential is huge. Likely twenty million dollars… possibly more. Even on the black market. He runs through a short list of fences he will contact after the smoke clears. *The smoke clears…* he thinks to himself. He wonders how long they should stay in Nova Scotia after the heist. Is a quick get-a-way really best? Or should they stick around Montauk a while instead, act the innocents and enjoy the ride? It is enjoyable to witness the aftermath. Scotland provided that. "Good ole grandad..." he says softly in his Scottish brogue raising his glass. He smiles and sips the whisky. He looks at his watch, downs the rest of his drink, enters the room and takes a shower.

Stepping out of the shower, his phone rings. It's Rollie. "Sparky'll be here in ten minutes if you want to take the ride to town and cover the old racetrack with The Kid," he lets Kelly know.

Kelly smiles and glances at the time. "Yeah, I'll meet you out front," he says.

He hangs up the phone, picks out a button down, gets dressed, grabs a wad of hundreds, exits the room and walks past the restaurant towards the front desk. Rollie and The Kid are already there having an animated discussion. When he's within earshot, it becomes apparent to Kelly that their competition for the ladies has taken on a new dimension.

"You don't even know her name?" The Kid asks with incredulity.

"A rose by any other name..." Rollie states in his best Shakespeare.

Kelly is duly amused as he approaches the guys just as Sparky pulls up in his mini-van taxi. The automatic doors open.

"You should ride shotgun, Kid," Kelly tells him.

"Yeah," he answers as he gets in the passenger seat next to Sparky.

"Hey, Sparky," says The Kid.

"Hey fellas" Sparky smiles, happy to see the guys. "Where to?" he asks.

"We're going into town, but we'd like a tour of the old racetrack on the way," Kelly tells him.

"Fairview Avenue!" Sparky states. He looks at Kelly in the rearview. "You guys really love your history," he comments. "Mostly, only locals care about that."

"Not anymore," The Kid tells him. "Fairview Avenue Racetrack..." The Kid says, enthusiastically air racecar driving.

"The Kid here has dreams of being a racecar driver," Rollie adds, pointing at The Kid with his thumb, a smirk on his face attempting to provide cover for their true purpose of wanting to ride the old racetrack.

"Yeah," exclaims The Kid, escalating his air racecar driver antics.

"When he grows up," Rollie adds.

"At least I know the name of the girl I have a date with tonight," he says, leaning into the back seat.

Kelly gets a kick out of the exchange, as does Sparky. Kelly catches Sparky's eyes in the rear view and winks. Sparky smiles and turns onto S. Fairview Avenue off of West Lake Drive, towards the Montauk Downs golf course.

"The golf course was built by Carl Fischer. It was a ranch before that," Sparky tells them.

"I didn't know that," Kelly says fascinated.

They arrive at Fairview Avenue, "OK, this is where Fairview begins," Sparky tells them. "I'll guess they drove counter clockwise," he says as he pulls over, pointing north on Fairview Avenue. "I'm not sure why racetracks run counter clockwise."

"Not all tracks are counter clockwise," Kelly tells him.

Loving history as much as Kelly, but not nearly as knowledgeable, Sparky's ears perk up.

"Some exceptions include the Australian version of NASCAR they call AUSCAR," Kelly tells him "Horse racing is often run clockwise outside the US such as in England, at St Leger," Kelly tells them.

Sparky smiles at Kelly, "Man, I love that you know this stuff," he says.

"The decision to run horses counterclockwise in the US began in the days of the American War for Independence. The same reason we drive on the right side of the road here," Kelly says with a smile.

"With Independence Day approaching, this is great stuff to think about," says Sparky feeling patriotic.

"It was 1780, when the first circular US race track was established by William Whitley near his home in Lincoln County, Kentucky. A staunch supporter of independence from Britain, Whitley insisted that horses race counterclockwise, as opposed to clockwise which was the custom in England at the time," Kelly says with a wink and a smile for Sparky.

"You really know your history! Luckily, I have a photographic memory," he says smiling at Kelly through the rear-view mirror.

Rollie elbows Kelly in the back seat with an only slightly comical concerned expression.

"I'll be able to recall all this for the new book," Sparky says, looking over the crew he doesn't yet realize is actually a 'crew.'

"No idea where the starting line was, but I'll take us around and maybe it'll become obvious where the race started from, back in the day," Sparky says as he puts the taxi in gear and heads up Fairview Avenue.

Soon they're driving the twists and turns, peaks and valleys of Fairview Avenue which truly feels like a racetrack. An exciting and challenging racetrack...

"Wow!" exclaims The Kid. "This is awesome!"

A few deer run across the street directly in the path of the taxi. Sparky brakes just in time to avoid hitting one of them.

"Deer are the dumbest animals!" he insists. "You'd think after a hundred generations coexisting with the automobile, they might have figured it out," he adds. "Six hundred and forty-six collisions with deer this year so far," he complains. "It's insanity."

He takes it around the entire racetrack then makes the ninety degree turn onto S. Fairview, through some hairy turns then continue on a straightaway past the golf course entrance, back to where they began and pulls the taxi to a stop.

"So, that's the racetrack, hunh?" The Kid exclaims with a smile.

"Whatd'ya think, Kid?" Rollie asks.

"I like it!" he says with a broad grin turning to Rollie and Kelly in the second row of seats.

He turns towards the road ahead of them and asks, “Mind if we take it around a few more times?

“Sure, Kid,” says Kelly.

“Show us the way, Sparks.” Kelly says.

“If you say so, boss,” Sparky says with a smile that almost winks.

He steps on the gas and asks, “You guys aren’t planning to organize a race here, are you?”

The Kid gurgles up in laughter, looks over at Sparky and states, “In a way...”

After a few more runs around the track nearing the time the boys have agreed to meet their prospective dates, Sparky drops Rollie at The Montauket then The Kid at The Point Bar and Grill. Kelly moves to the front passenger seat.

“How about you take me on a sunset tour of the harbor?” Kelly suggests.

“Sure thing,” says Sparky. He turns up Edgemere Street towards Gosman’s Dock.

“You guys are truly fascinating,” he tells Kelly with a wry glance. “Mysterious...” he says with a mischievous grin.

Kelly is measuring how far to take it when he looks at Sparky, feigning innocence and asks, “Really? What exactly is it that you find fascinating about my friends and I?”

"That's just it," Sparky says as they pass the Surf Lodge. "Five more different personalities as a group of friends I have yet to meet," he says with a raise of the eyebrow.

Kelly glances over at Sparky and tilts his head. "You're a writer all right."

Kelly adjusts himself in his seat to get a better view of Sparky's mannerisms.

"I appreciate your keen sense of observation," he says. "It truly is well honed. Must have taken you years to develop,"

They arrive at the harbor area. Sparky pulls into the Gosman's Restaurant parking lot near the inlet, where hordes of tourists have amassed to enjoy a magnificent sunset.

"People come here nearly every night just to see the sunset from this spot," he says.

They peer out of the windshield at the many tourists taking selfies and the like.

"I suppose it began in earnest when I was hustling pool," Sparky says. "Sizing up my opponents was part of the game." Glancing at Kelly, a part of Sparky suspects he's not telling him anything he doesn't already know. "The key is knowing how a person will react before they do," Sparky continues.

Kelly's loving it. "I know exactly what you mean," he says, pleased by the realization that he had Sparky pegged all along.

"I had a feeling you would," Sparky says, feeling Kelly out. "In fact, I suspect you know about a lot more than history." Sparky looks over at Kelly hoping he'll reveal something juicy.

They stare at one another wondering exactly how much of what the other is theorizing about himself is accurate. A long moment passes.

“Have you ever worked as a fisherman?” Kelly asks.

Sparky chuckles a bit, enjoying the way Kelly changed the subject. “That’s really hard work, you know.” He says.

“I’d love to go out on a real fishing boat one day,” Kelly says. He turns to Sparky, “Just to see what it’s like,” he says.

“My favorite tips have always been fish,” Sparky admits. “Did you know that there’s shrimp in these waters?”

“Really?” asks Kelly. “One thinks of shrimp and far warmer waters come to mind,” he says.

“Yeah, they call ‘em Ruby Reds around here. No one is licensed to fish them, but netters get them by the pound when they’re going for Whiting or Squid,” Sparky tells him. “Big tasty suckers, too,” he says illustrating the average size of the Ruby Red with his thumb and forefinger. “I get them from the local fisherman every now and then. Since they can’t legally sell them, they give them away to friends and family. I’ve become one of those people,” he tells Kelly with a smile.

“Netters, hunh?” Kelly says, wondering about which type of fishing boat might be best for the job. “What are the other types of commercial fishing boats in Montauk?” Kelly asks.

“The same as all fishing towns, I suppose,” says Sparky. “Netters, draggers, trappers and longliners...”

“Longliners... They go out the farthest, don’t they?” asks Kelly.

“Yeah... Sometimes they have to hunt the fish down,” Sparky says matter of fact. “Longliners go after swordfish, tuna, even mako.” Sparky has learned quite a lot about fishing during his summers in Montauk.

“Where do commercial fisherman socialize in this town?” Kelly asks.

Sparky looks at him curiously, maybe a bit suspiciously.

“I’d love to hear some first-hand accounts about the adventures of commercial fishing,” Kelly adds knowing he may have broken his own rule by asking too direct a question. “I’m sure there are some amazing stories to tell,” he adds.

He looks over at Sparky to check the temperature. “Fishing in foul weather... sharks... sea monsters,” he says laughing.

“Mermaids...” Sparky adds to the list with a smile. “A lot of the fisherman in town hang out at Liars Saloon, Salivars or The Dock.”

“Liars Saloon, hunh?” Kelly smiles. “How apropos.” He smiles wryly and looks at his watch. “I promised Sal and Dave I’d meet them for dinner.” He looks over at Sparky with a sly grin. “Seeing as the studs are preoccupied with their dates, why don’t we slip by The Dock and Liars Saloon, just so I get a peek at them before we head back to the Yacht Club?” Kelly suggests.

“The Dock is just behind us by the commercial dock.” Sparky puts the taxi in gear and pulls around to The Dock Restaurant and parks.

“No locals,” Kelly says reading the amusing sign in the window.

"Stepping into the Dock is like stepping into the 1950s," Sparky says. "It'll be relatively quiet since it's a weekday."

"I have a few minutes, think I'll go have a look," Kelly tells him, stepping out of the taxi.

He enters The Dock Restaurant and scans the room. A classic long, dark-toned wooden bar fills the wall opposite the entrance with a few patrons who seem to know each other having lively conversation and a few tables are filled with diners. Kelly returns to the taxi.

"It's a true classic," he says to Sparky.

"The best Bloody Mary in town, too," Sparky tells him with a smile.

He puts it in gear and drives off. "Liars is just around the corner," he says.

They drive around the corner and pull in past the $1 Draft Beer sign on the street level then down the long bumpy dirt parking lot of Liars Saloon. "This is more of a rough and ready fisherman's bar," Sparky says. He turns to Kelly with a wry expression, "Yet, at three in the morning, everyone seems to end up here," he smirks.

"Interesting..." Kelly says.

"Maybe I can convince Sal and Dave into having a nightcap here later on," says Kelly looking at his watch.

"Back to the Yacht Club?" Sparky asks him.

"Yeah, we're dining at a restaurant called the Crow's Nest this evening, so we'll need you to take us there in a bit," Kelly says.

Sparky starts off towards the Yacht Club.

"Great choice... The Nest is a popular spot these days," Sparky lets him know.

"How's the book coming along?" Kelly asks.

Kelly is convinced there is potential for bringing Sparky deeper into the fold. Possibly making him part of the crew. But he knows he has to tread lightly and feel him out a while longer before confiding in him about anything serious. Sparky looks over at Kelly still unsure exactly what to make of him.

"Still formulating a story," he says. "Have some good character profiles based on you guys." He looks into Kelly's eyes. "Still waiting for something to happen that I can write about," he says, pulling into the Yacht Club.

"Interesting," Kelly comments. "What do you hope will happen?" he asks.

"Not sure," Sparky answers deep in thought. "There's something very mysterious about you guys," Sparky insists. "Not sure what it is, but there's something more to this picture..." He looks over at Kelly and rubs his chin. "I just can't put my finger on it yet," he continues.

"Or perhaps you have deductions drawn from keen observation, only you're not prepared to disclose them yet," Kelly suggests.

"Perhaps..." Sparky says with a wry smile. "Perhaps I have deduced certain potentialities that you're not yet ready to disclose," he states, sparring with Kelly.

"Sparky, I think you and I will become great friends one day," he says looking over at Sparky with a trusting smile.

He glances at his watch and says, “I better go fetch Sal and Dave.”

Sparky stops in the front. “I’ll be nearby when you’re ready,” Sparky assures him. “What time is your reservation?”

“Dinner at eight,” Kelly tells him.

“Great. I’ll just stick around.”

“Thanks, pal.” Kelly steps out of the cab.

VI

A short while later, Kelly, Dave and Sal step out of the Yacht Club, where Sparky is waiting in his taxi. The three con-artist thieves, step into the taxi.

“Hi, guys,” Sparky greets them. “Crow’s Nest, next stop,” he announces as he pulls away.

“Any recommendations, Sparks?” Sal asks in her naturally sultry manner.

“If you like spicy, you have to try the Moroccan East Coast Halibut,” he says without hesitation.

He looks in the rear-view mirror to check her reaction.

“Starting with the Beausoleil Oysters, naturally,” he adds.

Sal catches Kelly’s eye with an amused expression.

“What wine would you suggest with those oysters?” Kelly asks.

He looks over at Kelly with a knowing expression, “I would have the Shinn Estate Haven Sauvignon Blanc-Semillon,” he says with a wine enthusiast level of authority.

“I’m thinking lobster,” Dave says, licking his chops. “Haven’t had a good fresh lobster since the last time we were out here. Maybe an old school Surf n’ Turf,” he adds.

“Very manly of you, professor,” Sal quips.

“I suspect Dave masks his machismo under his professorial-like demeanor,” Sparky says, winking at Sal in the rear-view.

"Sparky... very astute observation," Sal says with a laugh. "I may have to start reading your books."

"There's a lot more to Sparky than may at first meet the eye," Kelly assures them.

"It seems so," Dave says, sizing Sparky up. "I didn't peg you as such a refined gourmand," he adds.

"I was raised in a European household," Sparky tells them. "The kitchen was the center of the home..."

"Fascinating," Dave says as they pull into the Crow's Nest parking lot.

"Perhaps Sparky would like to join us for diner," Kelly suggests to Dave and Sal, looking over at Sparky with a wink of the eye.

"Yeah, Sparks, why not?" Sal asks.

"Personally, I'd like to hear more about your pool-hustling days," Dave chimes in.

"That's very nice of you guys," Sparky says affectionately.

"C'mon... park this tub and meet us inside," Kelly says with a huge grin.

"If you insist," Sparky says with a lilt in his voice.

"I'll have an order of Beausoleil Oysters waiting for you," Kelly assures him.

"Now we're talkin," smiles Sparky. Three exit the taxi and Sparky drives off to find an available spot in the crowded parking lot.

He parks the taxi then sits there a moment wondering what the motive might be to invite him to dinner. He yanks out his MacBook and types; *Certainly, they are an engaging bunch. They're lucid in all kinds of ways... Bright beyond reckoning and highly entertaining... I can't help but consider that something more is at play..* Not wanting to keep them waiting, he stows the computer as his thoughts continue. He sits there a long moment thinking about the possible reasons they might have for inviting him to dinner. A few minutes pass and, he figures he better join them. He shakes his head in wonderous anticipation, exits the taxi, walks to the entrance and enters The Crow's Nest.

"Are you Sparky?" the lovely maître de asks.

"As a matter a fact, I am," Sparky answers with a big grin.

"Your friends told me you'd be along in a moment." she stops and looks Sparky up and down. "They described you to a 'T'!" she says. "Right this way," she adds with her congenial smile, leading Sparky into the dining area. They arrive at the table and, as promised, Beausoleil Oysters are at his place.

"Sparky," Kelly says with his signature grin, waving his arm and offering the chair at the table. "Your oysters await."

Sparky smiles and takes his seat.

"May I get you something to drink, sir?" the waitress asks Sparky.

"I don't think a Prosecco will hurt too badly," he says looking up at the attractive, rather tall, blond Swedish waitress, "Sparkling Pointe, if you have it," he adds.

"That's my favorite Prosecco!" she exclaims enthusiastically in a Swedish accent.

“In that case,” he looks around the table making eye contact with Sal, Dave and then Kelly, “In the spirit of Rollie and The Kid...” he says gazing up into the waitress’ eyes, “Perhaps you and I might enjoy a bottle together one evening,” he says, pouring on the charm.

“I’d like that very much,” she says with a comely smile.

She scribbles on her pad and looks into Sparky’s eyes, “I’ll be right back,” she assures him before turning around and skipping off for his Sparkling Pointe Prosecco.

“Pretty smooth, Sparks,” Sal quips, sipping her champagne.

“Indeed” adds Dave. “Which reminds me, how exactly did you become a pool shark at the tender age of...” Dave looks over to Kelly who is grinning ear to ear, loving the whole thing. “...What was it?” he asks turning back to Sparky, “Thirteen years old?”

Sparky sucks down an oyster just as his Prosecco arrives.

“Here you are, sir,” the waitress says placing his drink on the table in front of him.

“Sparky,” he says looking into her enticing, blue eyes.

“Sparky,” she repeats with a smile.

“And you are?” asks Sparky.

“I am Ewa,” she answers inspecting Sparky with an affectionate curiosity.

“Ewa,” he repeats, raising the glass in her honor. “To your intoxicating beauty.” He lifts the glass and sips the wine.

"We've all ordered, so if you know what you'd like, you should probably order it now," Kelly suggests.

"I'll have the Ewa..." he spurts out by accident. "I mean the Sea Bass," Sparky says among laughter.

"A Freudian slip?" the waitress asks with her charming smile.

"Waitress!" a voice calls out from a nearby table.

"I have to go," she says longingly, and darts off.

Sparky lifts another oyster, "Whatd'ya know about that..." he says amused at his own faux pas, looking over at Ewa who peeks back at him.

"Where were we?" he asks, already knowing the answer. "Oh yeah... I guess I was about thirteen when it started, but I didn't hustle pool in earnest till I was fifteen or so," he says as he sucks down another oyster. "These are local oysters, you know," He lifts his glass and takes another sip of the prosecco.

Sal delicately plucks an oyster with a cocktail fork and dips it in red wine vinegar, having taken Sparky's advice to order them.

"They are absolutely wonderful," she says.

"I suspected a bit of the playboy hiding beneath that unassuming demeanor," Kelly says, lifting his glass to Sparky.

"It's a rare foray that I venture into romance these days," Sparky lets him know.

"Spoken like a true poet," says Dave sipping his bull shot.

"Rare, perhaps, but seasoned nonetheless," Sal observes.

"Let's get back to your pool-sharking days," Kelly says. "I'm curious to hear more."

"Yes, where exactly did all this occur?" Dave inquires.

"How did it begin?" Sal asks sipping her champagne.

"Yes… beginnings are often very telling," Kelly agrees.

Sparky can't help but to smile at the attention.

"I suppose it began innocently enough," Sparky says looking at them one by one.

"As things often do," Kelly smiles.

"Touché," Sal says raising her glass. "Do tell…" she adds.

"As a youth I devoured books," he says, downing another oyster. "I rarely missed a library book sale… One day returning home from one, *The Hustler* by Walter Tevis was in the pile of books I'd purchased. I opened it, started reading it and couldn't put it down," Sparky tells them while he sucks down another of his oysters Beausoleil. "I had just made a new pal whose family had a regulation size pool table in their basement." He gazes around the table, shrugs his shoulders innocently and adds, "I was a natural."

"How natural?" Sal asks with a challenging smirk.

"Tell us about the first time you hustled someone," Kelly asks.

Sparky thinks back for a moment. A smile comes to his face.

“It was Tom’s Corner,” he says. “I was fifteen years old. True, I was six feet tall and already shaving, it wasn’t difficult to drink in a bar when underage in the early 1970s. A short beer was twenty-five cents, and the etiquette, at the time, was the bartender bought your every fourth beer…” He takes a sip of his Prosecco and continues. “Naturally, you bought him his drink of choice which for Whitey the bartender was Dewer’s Scotch Whisky,” he says fondly. “Roosevelt Raceway, a Harness Racing track or ‘Trotter track’ as we called them, was nearby so the place was frequented by owners, trainers, jockeys and the like,” he says, recalling days gone by.

“Trotters…” Kelly says fondly. “What has evolved into Modern Harness Racing began way back in ancient times. Assyrian kings around 1500 BC kept elaborate stables and professional trainers for their horses. Used for chariots in battles of war, in peacetime were used for the sport of hunting.” Kelly expounds his vast knowledge of history. “However, Harness Racing, as we know it today, began in Scotland,” he adds in his best Scottish brogue.

“Really?” Sparky asks.

“Horse and buggy drivers, cabbies…” he says smiling at Sparky, “began racing in the park for bets during the quiet hours and it caught on. Soon there were bookies and gamblers showing up at various parks in the wee hours just to bet on their favorite horse and buggy.” He says in his Scottish brogue.

“That is a very impressive accent,” Sparky says. You could pass yourself off as a Scotsman in Scotland with an accent like that!” he exclaims.

“Ha!” Sal can’t help but to laugh out loud. “Oh Sparky… you’re rich,” she says.

They share a laugh.

"I love you guys," Sparky tells them shaking his head with a laugh before finishing his last oyster. "Very mysterious..."

Ewa wheels a tray over with four entrees on it. She places Sal's in front of her. "One Moroccan Style East Coast Halibut," she says. Then Dave, "One Chef special Surf and Turf," she says placing Dave's elaborate meal in front of him. "One Local Sea Bass for you, sir," placing Kelly's plate down, "And also a Local Sea Bass for ...Sparky," she says affectionately, placing Sparky's meal down.

She arranges Sparky's dinner plate so that it is just right, then lingers a moment gazing into his eyes.

"Another Prosecco, ...Sparky?" she asks.

He looks up at her, "That would be nice, ...Ewa," he answers.

"I just love saying your name! Sparky..." she repeats with a giggle.

"Anyone care for another drink?" she asks the table.

"Yes, only allow me to confer with my wine connoisseur," Sal remarks turning to Sparky. "Monsieur Sparky?" she smiles.

Sparky looks at her with a wry expression that lets Sal know he's wise to their lavishing him with undue attentions. "With that dish," he looks up at the lovely Ewa and says, "I maintain the Shinn Estate Haven Sauvignon Blanc-Semillon."

Ewa smiles at him. "I couldn't agree more," she says, scribbling the order on her pad.

Dave smiles, looks at waitress Ewa and says, "As is apropos for my elaborate Surf and Turf, I'll have your finest local Rosé."

"Great idea!" Ewa exclaims and smiles at Dave. "I would have to say the Rafael Rosé," she tells him. "They grow a superior Vinifera grape."

"Hmmmm...? I think you've met your match, Sparky," Sal quips.

"It would seem so," Kelly adds, winking at Sparky.

"That sounds perfect," Dave tells her. A bottle, please," he adds.

Ewa scribbles the order down.

"Now, for the two local Sea Bass..." she looks at Sparky challengingly. "Everything from Chablis to Riesling is often paired, but for you two..." she looks at Sparky with a twinkle in her eye, "I suspect something more sophisticated, "I will defer to you entirely," she says to Sparky's smile.

"Surprise us," Sparky suggests.

Her eyes pop wide. "Okay," she giggles with a sweet smile.

She thinks for a moment, scribbles something on her pad and places her hand gently on Sparky's shoulder. "You are going to love this," she says before strutting off.

Sparky watches her skip away in her lively manner. He turns back to the crew who are all staring at him. The four of them trade long glances for a moment assessing the situation. They can only imagine what's going through Sparky's mind at this point. Kelly grins at him almost challengingly. Sparky looks at each of them directly in the eye, ending with Kelly and a raise of the eyebrow.

"So, why exactly are you guys blowing smoke up my ass?" he asks in earnest.

Sal lets out a loud laugh.

Dave laughs and refers to Sparky with his head, "A sure sign of higher intellect," he says to Kelly.

"He may be a keeper," Sal says also to Kelly.

"What do you *think* is going on here, Sparky?" Kelly asks.

Ewa returns with the wine. Sal and Dave are served first. She unwraps a bottle kept hidden by a linen napkin to reveal a Sauvignon Blanc from the Wölffer Estate Vineyards. She lifts it, shows it to Sparky, pours glasses for him and Kelly and then places it on the table between them.

"Ah yes..." Sparky says turning to Kelly. "From one of the oldest vineyards of Long Island; Perfection," he says, glancing up at Ewa.

"You are too kind, ...Sparky." She giggles. She spins on her heels and, once again, bounces joyfully through the restaurant toward the kitchen.

"Maybe I should change my name to Sparky," Dave says as he pours his Rosé.

"It seems to work..." Sal comments.

"Where were we?" Kelly reminds them.

Sparky sits back in his chair and examines them closely for a long moment. They sit quietly enjoying watching Sparky measure them up.

“If I were to dispel all logical explanation and let my imagination guide me, I would say you guys are engaged in something highly unusual,” he says with only a touch of comedic irony.

He pours a glass of wine, raises it to his mouth and takes a few sips. He places the glass down on the table, looks around the restaurant a moment, then, locking eyes with Kelly, says, “Something that requires a certain degree of stealthy investment.” He shifts his gaze to Dave, “Creativity...” He turns to Sal, “And perhaps something that may even blur the lines of ethical endeavor,” he adds, lifting his glass and taking another long sip of wine.

He turns to Kelly, “This truly is a great wine.”

Ewa returns, “Let me know if you need anything,” she says, smiling at Sparky.

“A meal fit for a king,” Dave comments before digging into his elaborate surf and turf.

Dave meticulously takes a prime piece of lobster with his fork, dips it into a ramekin of melted butter, digs the fork with the lobster on it into the steak, cuts off a large bite-sized piece and raises it to his face admiring it for a moment before fitting it into his mouth. “Superb!” he says once he’s chewed enough of it to speak.

Sal digs into her Moroccan-styled Halibut, “Oh, Sparky,” she says. “You are a genius!” She lifts her wine and toasts him before enjoying a decent pull.

“To Sparky,” Kelly toasts, raising his glass.

“To Sparky,” Sal and Dave chime in.

“I’ll drink to that,” says Sparky. With a wry smile, he raises his glass of Sauvignon Blanc. “So where exactly do I fit in?” he asks, already convinced that there is an element of intrigue afoot.

He takes a long healthy pull of his wine, places the glass down carefully and digs into his fresh local sea bass.

“Right now,” Dave says, looking over at Kelly, “if I may,” turning back to Sparky, “I’d like to hear more juicy details from your pool-hustling days,” Dave says, sipping his wine.

“Yeah, Sparks,” Sal says smiling at him. “Tell us about your biggest score,” she says.

“Wait,” Kelly says to Sal. “In the spirit of beginnings, I would love to hear the game that started you on the road to becoming the young hustler extraordinaire,” he says with his huge grin, taking a large forkful of sea bass and chomping on it. He pauses, looks over at Sal and asks, “Sal?”

She looks up at Kelly. “You’re right,” she admits, organizing a piece of Moroccan halibut on her fork. “I want to hear about the very first wager,” she adds.

Sparky looks around the table and with a big smile says, “I was fifteen... After I ran the table for three of four games, a tall gruff-looking man wearing a cowboy hat that I’d seen around but never spoke to before, places a quarter on the table, looks at me with a sly grin and in a southern drawl asks, ‘What’s the game, son?’”

“I told him it was eight ball.”

Sparky mimics the man’s Southern drawl, “Fifty bucks says I win.”

He takes a long pull of wine and enjoys another forkful of sea bass. The crew listen intently. "I knew I didn't have anything near fifty dollars on me at the time, but I agreed nonetheless," he says.

Kelly, Sal and Dave are instantly impressed.

"You may not have known it at the time, but you were also a con man," Dave tells him.

"Sparky..." says Sal with a coy smile.

Sparky laughs. "I suppose you're right," he says looking over at Dave.

"You did misrepresent yourself by agreeing..." Kelly says.

"True..." Sparky admits.

"You were lucky he didn't put his money down," Sal adds.

"That's right, and for all I knew, he didn't have fifty dollars either," Sparky says looking around the table, enjoying telling the story.

"Who won the break?" asks Sal.

"I did," Sparky tells her. "I sank the one ball and the three leaving the five ripe for the picking," Sparky says, enjoying more of his meal.

"And then?" Kelly asks.

"I sank the five... only I left myself in lousy position, missing the seven on a tricky bank shot the length of the table," he tells them.

The crew is soaking it in. Sparky looks them over, then continues the story.

"The cowboy ran four balls, then scratched," he says smiling. "Luckily..." he adds. "...because he was good," Sparky says as he finishes his glass of wine.

"And then?" Dave asks.

"Then, I sank the six and seven in succession, leaving myself in great position to sink the eight ball, which I did easily. I took his fifty and felt like Minnesota Fats," Sparky says cracking his knuckles with a fun smile.

"Merciless!" Dave comments.

"Did he have the money?" Kelly asks.

"Not only that, we played the next round double or nothing." Sparky smiles.

"And you beat him," Sal says knowing the answer.

They all look at Sparky, each with their own inner association of camaraderie.

"Amazing," Kelly says, admiring Sparky's gutsy move. "Fifteen..." Kelly raises his eyebrows in an I-told-you-so moment to Dave and Sal.

Sparky rests easy for a moment as he and the crew enjoy their meal when Ewa reappears.

"Will anyone be having coffee and dessert this evening?" she asks.

"Yes," Dave is the first to answer. "Sal?" he asks.

“I’ll have the Chocolate Budino and a macchiato, darling” she says.

“Sounds lovely,” Dave says, looking up at Ewa. “Make it two.” He adds holding up two fingers.

“Sparky?” Kelly asks.

“I’m feeling exotic,” he says. “A Fig Kaitafi and a double espresso for me.” Sparky says gazing up at her sweet smile.

“This is too much!” she exclaims. “That’s exactly what I would have!” she says, her hand finding its way gently on Sparky’s shoulder again.

“How convenient...” Sal says in her best dig. “When you two lovebirds finally make it to dinner, you’ll only have to order once,” she says with a smart-ass grin.

Sparky rolls with it and looking into Ewa’s eyes, says, “That will allow us more time to speak of poetry and the stars,”

Ewa sighs at the thought of it.

“Ahem...” Kelly clears his throat. “If I may interrupt for a moment, I will have the olive Oil Cake and a cappuccino, please,” he says.

Ewa manages to scribble the orders on her pad and floats off.

“I wonder if she’s a pool shark, also,” quips Sal.

“Don’t laugh,” says Kelly “There is a famous female billiards player from Sweden named Ewa Laurance, who holds several championship titles. Word has it, she’s one hell of a pool shark as well!” he adds.

“Ewa…” Sparky says dreamily.

“Yes?” Ewa asks as she arrives with the coffee and dessert.

Sparky opens his eyes, sees Ewa and says one word, “Magic! …I say your name and you appear.” He looks into Ewa’s eyes. “I could get used to that,” he adds with a smile.

Ewa giggles, then finishes serving the coffee and dessert. She stands there a moment, gazing at Sparky.

“You can bring the check whenever you have a moment,” Kelly tells her.

“Okay,” she says, still smiling at Sparky.

“Waitress!” a voice calls out.

“Enjoy your dessert.” she says and runs off.

“What is it with the Swedes and older men?” Sal asks digging into her Chocolate Budino.

“I’m not sure,” Sparky says. “However, I’m finding it very agreeable at the moment.”

“Swedish researchers believe it’s a biological phenomenon,” Dave says, ever professorial in his response. “A woman faces a big investment when choosing a partner; she’s going to go through nine months of pregnancy and will need nutritious food and shelter in order to reproduce, as well as the resources for it. An older man with his finances in order and a high social status is a safe choice.”

Ewa returns with the check and places it in front of Kelly. She turns to leave but Kelly stops her. He opens the check presenter, reaches into his pocket, pulls out a wad of cash, places four hundred-dollar bills in the presenter, folds it and hands it to Ewa. “Everything was excellent,” he says.

“Especially the service,” Sparky adds, smiling at Ewa who smiles back at him sweetly.

She bounces away. They finish their coffee and dessert. Sparky scans the table, looking at them one by one.

“This truly is a real treat. Thank you for inviting me along. It has been my honor dining with you this evening. Although…” he says with a raise of the eyebrow, “I’m still curious as to why you guys are blowing smoke up my ass,” he says with an agreeable smirk.

Kelly makes eye contact with Sal and Dave. Kelly lifts the cappuccino to his mouth, gazes over at Sparky with his charming grin and says, “If you can indulge us, my friend, we will reserve our right to remain mysterious for just a little while longer,” he says.

Sparky finishes his espresso, looks over at Kelly and says, “I suppose a little mystery is good.” He glances at his watch. “I’ll say my goodbye to the lovely Ewa, pull the car around and meet you out front,” he tells them.

He stands up, looks at them one by one, shakes his head and smiles. “Just for the record,” he says smiling, “I love you guys.”

He turns and walks towards the exit stopping to have a word with Ewa. Kelly and the crew watch as Sparky and Ewa exchange telephone numbers.

“Look at the smiles on those two,” Dave comments.

"Luckily for me, there seems to be no shortage of romancing in this town," Sal says referring to the mission at hand and her likely part in it.

"That reminds me," Dave says, "The blackboard should be arriving tomorrow." He looks at Kelly, "Time to get down to brass tacks."

Kelly doesn't respond. He's thinking about Sparky and how they should proceed. After all, in essence, Sparky is their wheel man. Should they need to improvise in an adverse situation, it would be best if he were in the loop and not just a livery driver. It seems to Kelly that Sparky would be game. He certainly seems intelligent and perhaps just nefarious enough to understand the need and crucial importance of secrecy. But it is a lot to entrust to someone who has not been tested in an actual emergency. There's no way of knowing just how he might react in any given situation. And from his years of experience, Kelly knows that in situations such as this, unexpected situations arise often.

"We might want to concoct a scenario that will test Sparky's ability to think on his feet," he says to Sal and Dave.

"That qualifies as brass tacks..." Dave says getting up from the table.

"We'll have to find something out of town," Sal adds.

"Agreed," Kelly says as he gets up from the table.

"Let's sleep on it," he says. "Something will come to me."

Dave pulls Sal's chair for her and the of them walk towards the exit, stopping to say goodbye to Ewa. They step out of the Crow's Nest and Sparky is out there in the taxi, engine running. They approach the taxi.

“Sparks!” Sal says as they enter the taxi. “I suspected you possessed dimensions not seen by the naked eye,” she says as she gets comfortable in her seat. “But I had little idea to what degree.” She smiles at him through the rear-view.

“Touché,” says Dave as he and Kelly hop in.

“Yacht Club?” Sparky asks.

“Yeah, we better call it a night,” Kelly says as they drive off. “Naturally, our two Romeos are still out and about, so I suppose you'll be hearing from them at some point,” Kelly adds.

“There's no shortage of romance in this town,” Sparky says, reminiscing Ewa.

“We now officially have a third Romeo in our esteemed little group,” Sal says, taking a friendly poke at Sparky.

“I can't help it if the ladies find me irresistible, Sal.” Sparky laughs.

“Touché, hot pants, touché,” Sal says with a giggle.

VII

The next morning, Dave exits the shower to find a message from the front desk slipped under his door. He walks to the hotel phone and dials. “Front desk?” he asks. I see a package arrived for me today,” he says, pausing to listen to the response. “Great, if you can have it delivered to John Kelly’s suite in an hour that would be perfect. Thanks,” he says before hanging up.

He grabs his cell phone and texts Kelly that the blackboard will be delivered to his suite in an hour. Dave’s getting dressed when his phone makes a telegraph sound alerting him that he has received a text. It’s from Kelly. One word, “Breakfast?”

He texts back, “Meet you in five.”

The crew assembles for breakfast on the patio of the Yacht Club restaurant.

“What a night!” The Kid says.

“Oh? ...get her to kiss you?” Sal asks.

Rollie and Dave join them. Sal looks up at Rollie with a smart-ass expression. “The Kid was just about to disclose his Don Quixotesque exploits of last night,” she says.

“Maybe she let him kiss her,” Rollie says with a smirk.

“More like Don Juan, honey,” The Kid lets Sal know.

“Like I said...” she quips.

“Play nice, kids,” says Dave as the waitress comes over.

Kelly arrives and before the waitress can utter a word, he grabs her eyes and pointing at The Kid says, "The Kid'll have your large, fresh-squeezed orange juice."

"Thanks, chief," says The Kid. "They don't believe I made out with Rachel," he tells Kelly.

"I'll have the eggs benedict with a cappuccino," Dave tells her.

"Make that two," Kelly tells the waitress.

"Just half a grapefruit and a coffee for me, doll," Sal says.

"Steak, bloody, and eggs over easy," says The Kid.

"Make that two," adds Rollie. "Only medium rare for me and I'll have your tallest glass of tomato juice with a giant wedge of lemon, please," he adds.

The waitress scribbles it all down and smiles at the crew. "You guys are quick," she says before dashing off.

"You have no idea," smiles Rollie. "Or at least some of us are..." he says, polishing his nails on his shirt trying to get a rise out of The Kid.

"I've given this considerable thought and have decided to bring Sparky in," Kelly says, looking over the crew.

"Sparky?" The Kid asks.

"If he'll agree," Kelly adds.

"In what capacity," asks Rollie.

"He can have my tunnel-digging duties," says The Kid with a huge smile.

"Fat chance, hot pants," Sal says, winking at Kelly.

"*Did* you make out with her?" Kelly asks The Kid.

"What do you think," The Kid says with an I-can't-believe-you-just-asked-me-such-a dumb-question look on his face.

"While you two were out romancing, we took Sparky out to dinner," Dave says looking back and forth from The Kid to Rollie.

"Really?" The Kid asks.

"And what did we learn about our illustrious author?" asks Rollie.

"Not only was Sparky a class A pool shark in his teens," Sal says, "he is a natural-born con man," she adds.

"Even if he doesn't realize it," Dave adds.

"That's all well and good, but we just met him," says The Kid, doubting the wisdom of bringing Sparky into the fold. "Why should we bring him in?"

Kelly looks at everyone with a serious expression. "As always, Kid, I'm glad you asked," Kelly responds. "Two reasons, Sparky has a line on the commercial fishing boats in town, so we will likely need his assistance in securing a boat, and, to be sure, this is the more significant of the two, it is unwise to have a wheelman who doesn't know the score." He looks around at everyone. "It's too risky," he says.

"How do we know he can be trusted?" asks Rollie.

"We have to test him," insists The Kid without hesitation.

"Sal?" Kelly asks.

“Sparky can be a real asset,” she assures the rest of the crew.

When the waitress arrives with their coffee and juice, Rollie looks up at her. “Would you please bring me a larger wedge of fresh-cut lemon?” he asks, squeezing the lemon into his tomato juice and shaking an amazing amount of black pepper into the glass.

“Right away, sir,” the waitress answers.

She stands there a moment watching Rollie continue to shake an obscene amount of black pepper into his tomato juice. Kelly sips his cappuccino.

The Kid downs his fresh squeezed OJ, looks at Rollie and asks, “So?”

Rollie laughs. “Yield nothing to love that is denied to discretion,” says Rollie, quoting Minna Antrim.

“That reminds me,” says Sal speaking to Rollie and The Kid. “You guys have some serious competition on the waitress romancing front with Sparky on the scene,” she says.

Kelly and Dave laugh.

“We’re talking a six-foot Swedish blond to die for,” Dave lets them know.

“Sparky...” The Kid says nodding his head and smiling. “On the prowl...”

The waitress arrives with Rollie’s lemon and the breakfast orders. She serves them up and the crew digs in.

“That’s just it,” Kelly says. “Sparky’s romance happened so naturally...”

“Yeah Kid, there was no ‘prowling’ as you would have it,” Sal says with a raise of the eyebrows.

“Sparky seems very capable,” Dave says before delivering a forkful of eggs benedict to his mouth. He washes it down with coffee and adds, “However unassuming he may appear, there are definitive signs of advanced intuitive intelligence. A real edge.”

“He’s very likable,” Sal adds.

“He wants something to write about...” Rollie says, cutting into his medium rare steak and eggs.

Kelly listens intently to the crew deliberate the pros and cons of making Sparky a part of the crew.

“So, let’s give him something to write about,” Kelly says, smiling at everyone.

After breakfast, the crew gathers in Kelly’s suite. Once Rollie and The Kid set up the chalkboard, Dave immediately begins sketching various scenarios involved in pulling off the unlikely venture. Dave stops for a moment looking at the blackboard.

He turns to Rollie and asks, “How’s Shin doing with the missile?”

“I have Moose’s crew picking it up and bringing it out day after tomorrow. That gives us thirteen days till blast-off,” he says smiling.

“Sparky,” Kelly says into his cell phone. “How ya doin’, pal?” He listens a moment. “Can you grab me at the Yacht Club in ten?” He looks at Sal as he listens, “Great, see you then," he says, hitting end. "It's time to have the talk with Sparky," he says to everyone.

"Come with me, Sal?" he asks. "I think it'll soften the blow if you were part of the exchange," he adds.

"Yeah," she says. "You think he can find out where Demyan is staying?" she asks.

"I was counting on Giovanna for that," Kelly says. "I'll go see her after we meet with Sparky," he tells her.

"So, no Sparky test?" Rollie asks.

"Yeah?" The Kid chimes in.

"I don't think there's time. His reaction will be test enough. Plus, I have a good feeling about him," Kelly says looking at Dave, who pays close attention. "You'll have to trust my instincts on this one," he adds looking around at everyone.

"I'm with Kel," Sal says lighting a cigarette and looking around the room at everyone.

"He's ripe for the picking," Dave adds, looking up at Rollie and The Kid.

Kelly looks at his watch, "C'mon, Sal," he says standing up, "Sparky'll be here any minute."

"Even though Jann Mardenborough became the great racecar driver he is by playing Gran Tourismo on PlayStation, I'm going to rent a car and drive around the old racetrack every evening till we pull this off," The Kid says. "I want to know every bump and turn in that road before it's time," he says.

"You sure you're just not attempting to get out of tunnel-digging duties, Kid?" Rollie asks with raised eyebrow.

“Hey, you have your expertise… I have mine,” he smiles, kicking back on the comfortable arm chair. “Digging tunnels isn’t one of mine,” he adds.

“Remember, counter clockwise, Kid,” Kelly reminds him.

“Right…” The Kid says.

“I have a better idea,” says Dave leaping up with a smile. They all look at Dave. “We videotape the old racetrack in HD, now, and modify Gran Tourismo using that track as the new course. The Kid can learn that track driving like he will the night of the heist,” Dave tells everyone.

“That’s a brilliant solution, Dave,” says Kelly.

“You can do that?” The Kid asks.

“Absolutely… It’ll be far more valuable to practice on the same apparatus you’ll actually be using for the real thing,” Dave tells him. “By the time race night comes along you’ll know every inch of that road in HIDEF,” he adds.

“Great work, Dave. See ya later, guys,” Kelly says with a smile.

Kelly and Sal leave the room and walk through the hotel corridors past the marina towards the front desk.

“Nearly a century ago, some pretty amazing people took this walk,” Kelly says a nostalgic gleam in his eye.

“I wonder if Mary Astor ever hung out here back in the day,” muses Sal.

She and Kelly stop and look at one another.

“You know we’ll be legends if we pull this off,” he says with a grin.

“If, cowboy?” she asks taking Kelly’s forearm in her hand. “Any serious doubts I should know about?” she asks.

“You know, I take nothing for granted,” he reminds her.

“Smart man...” she says as Sparky pulls up.

“Hey, Sparks,” Sal says as he steps into the taxi.

“Hungry?” Kelly asks Sparky as he gets into the passenger seat.

“I could eat,” Sparky tells him.

“What about George’s Lighthouse Café up at the Lighthouse?” Kelly asks Sal.

“Sounds perfect.” Sal winks at him.

Sparky looks at the two of them and smiles. “George’s it is,” he says stepping on the gas. “They have a wonderful calamari,” Sparky tells them.

“Have you spoken to Ewa?” Sal wants to know.

“Maybe...” Sparky says with a wink into the rear-view mirror as he drives off.

“The boys looked a bit worried when I mentioned that there may be some serious competition in the crew,” Kelly says introducing the concept of a ‘crew’ through word association.

“Yeah... Romeo I and Romeo II wanted to hear all about your exploits at the Crow’s Nest last night,” Sal quips.

"They could learn a thing or two about style from the likes of you, pal," smiles Kelly.

"You were pretty smooth," Sal says. "You're assuming the moniker of Romeo III," she says smiling at Sparky. "That was a rare display of cool-school womanizing," she adds.

Sparky lets go of a laugh, checking Sal out in the rear-view mirror as he drives along the picturesque highway to the Lighthouse.

"I didn't plan it that way, you know. It just, ...sort of happened," Sparky tells them.

"Precisely!" says Kelly looking over at Sparky. "You're a natural," he adds.

They enter the Montauk Point State Park. Kelly gazes up at the Lighthouse as they drive by.

"Looks different from the ground," he says.

Sparky pulls up to the restaurant and stops the taxi. "I'll park this beast and meet you inside," he says.

"Fair enough," says Kelly.

He and Sal exit the taxi and stand there a moment while Sparky pulls into the parking lot.

"Whatd'ya think?" Sal asks watching Sparky drive away.

"I planted a few seeds," he says. "We'll see..."

"Not too subtle either," Sal says, lighting a cigarette.

"I was being intentionally transparent," Kelly says.

"You succeeded," Sal says with a giggle.

"C'mon, let's grab a table with a view of the great ocean sea, ...as Columbus called it," Kelly says while gazing out at the magnificent view of the Atlantic Ocean.

They stroll towards the entrance of George's Lighthouse Café.

"I can't help but to imagine there's a part of Sparky that already knows what's about to happen," Kelly says as he opens the door.

Sal steps in, looks Kelly in the eyes and says, "I think you're right. I think he's been waiting for this his whole life." Sal reflects on what they had learned about Sparky the night before at dinner.

"Almost as though his pool hustling days were the warm-up act and he's been waiting for Act II ever since," Kelly further theorizes.

They enter George's and the Maître D greets them. They ask for a table with a view of the ocean. The Maître D leads them to a table near the large windows overlooking the ocean beyond the terrace.

"This work for you folks?" he asks.

"This is great, thanks," Kelly says, pulling a chair for Sal.

"Our friend's parking the car. He'll be here in a minute," Kelly says.

Sparky parks the taxi and begins walking towards the restaurant. He's thinking about why Kelly and Sal have asked him to lunch. Things are getting awful friendly, but he can't help but consider that there might be a driving force behind it. Something beyond a gregarious act of kindness or friendly socializing. He decides he's just being unduly suspicious and shakes it off. He enters George's Café and finds his way to Kelly and Sal's table.

"Hey, guys." Sparky takes a seat.

"You mentioned calamari, so we ordered some for the table," Sal tells him.

A waitress arrives with the calamari and Sparky digs right in.

"Calamari is best right out of the pan," he says, squeezing some fresh lemon onto the calamari and munching on a large bite. "You'd be hard pressed to find fresher squid than here in Montauk. Netters go for squid the whole year long," Sparky says, enjoying his calamari. "They won't start hitting quotas till spring, so it's always fresh," he adds.

"How far out do they go?" Kelly asks.

"Just a few miles offshore but that could be anywhere from Massachusetts to Virginia," Sparky says.

"You know a lot of commercial fishermen?" Kelly asks popping a piece of calamari into his mouth. "That is good," he says. "It practically melts in your mouth."

"That's how you know it's fresh," Sparky tells him. "Squid only becomes rubbery when it isn't fresh," he adds.

They order mussels in white wine sauce, clam chowder and lobster rolls. Sparky looks up at Kelly and Sal sucking mussels off the shell. "So, what are you guys up to anyway?" he asks in a no-nonsense manner.

Kelly looks at Sal with his huge grin. "He's no slouch, Sal," he says slyly, bolstering Sparky's suspicions.

“Sharp as a tack,” Sal looks at Sparky, furthering the effort.

“I’ve come to realize that, as the inquisitive observer that you are, being a writer... That, you’re more than curious as to what exactly such an unlikely group of people are doing in Montauk together,” Kelly says as she pops another mussel into his mouth.

“Not to mention our odd requests...” Sal adds sipping her wine.

“My favorites are the blackboard and the racetrack tour,” Sparky says with a coy grin. “To name only a few...”

Kelly and Sal smile at one another. Kelly gestures to Sparky. “Seeing as you’ve decided to write a book about us, I thought perhaps now is the time to...” Kelly looks at Sal a moment, then adds, “...fill in the blanks.”

“I would love that,” Sparky says as the waitress arrives with three bowls of Clam Chowder.

“Who gets the Boston Clam?” The waitress asks.

“That would be me,” Sal answers. “Manhattan is a bit too earthy for me,” she adds.

“Sal is sometimes very delicate,” Sparky says as he looks at Sal.

“Your lobster rolls will be out shortly,” the waitress tells them.

“Thank you,” Kelly says as she struts off. He takes a spoonful of chowder. “Oh, that’s good,” he says.

He smiles at Sparky, wipes his mouth with the napkin and says, “Learning about your pool-hustling days left quite an impression on us.”

“Truly fascinating…” Sal adds.

“It reveals a part of you we would not have suspected exists,” Kelly tells him.

“A part of you that is yearning to return even,” Sal suggests, sipping her wine and then giving Sparky a coy, knowing expression.

“Curious that you should say that,” Sparky says reminiscing. “There have been moments… late at night… when I find myself playing out scenarios in my mind of what may have happened had I continued along that path,” he says.

“I know just how you feel,” Sal says, giving Sparky a sympathetic smile. “It’s as though you’ve left a part of yourself behind along the way.”

“Interestingly put, Sal.” Sparky says connecting with Sal’s insight.

“A part of yourself that has never stopped calling you from far away,” she adds.

“Yeah…” Sparky agrees. “And every now and then, you swear you can almost hear him… Way out in the distance… Catch a glimpse of him as a shadow from the corner of your eye,” Sparky says introspectively.

The three of them sit there a moment in silence considering what was said. How having left parts of oneself scattered about and abandoned for one reason or another throughout life. How they become ghosts that can pop up and haunt you as regret, loss or temptation.

“It’s more of a curiosity than a full-blown regret,” Sparky explains, “Yet, still a pestering force that has to be reckoned with from time to time,” he adds.

Kelly and Sal know all about that. Kelly’s torn between considering if Sparky is indeed ripe for the picking, battling his own demons of the same nature that he himself has contended with his entire life, or just reminiscing. Sal is thinking the same. Sparky is wondering if this is one of those times. They sit there in silence considering the gravity of the situation at hand, as though the three of them are standing over a precipice, not knowing what awaits them if they were to leap. Several moments pass in silence. The spell is broken when the waitress appears with their lobster rolls.

She serves them. “Let me know if there’s anything else I can get you.”

“Sal?” Kelly asks looking over at Sal.

“Another wine, please,” she says.

“I’m good,” Sparky says as he lifts his lobster roll off of the plate and takes a healthy bite.

“Just the wine then,” says Kelly before he too digs into his Lobster Roll.

Kelly looks out at the ocean a moment.

“What if I told you we might have a way for you to resurrect that lost part of yourself?” Kelly asks Sparky in earnest. He looks directly into his eyes. “To all that is Sparky…” he adds.

Sparky takes a large bite of his lobster roll. While chewing, he slowly and deliberately looks back and forth from Sal to

Kelly. They would likely give a small fortune to know what he's thinking. He wipes his mouth, places the napkin on his lap and leans back in his chair.

"That would depend," he says.

Kelly looks over at Sal whose face is little more than a question mark. Sparky truly is no slouch, as Kelly had commented earlier. He knows they want something very specific from him and that it must be pretty dynamic because they're tender-footing their way very cautiously. Sparky smiles at them finally, almost laughing, letting them know he's on to them.

"So, what exactly do you have in mind?" he asks.

Kelly smiles at Sal.

"Sharp as a tack," she repeats.

"You're right about us being up to something beyond buying an estate," Kelly admits.

Sal takes a bite and watches the exchange between Kelly and Sparky like a kid eating popcorn at the movies.

"What we are attempting is nothing short of legendary," Kelly tells him. "Originally we came to Montauk, innocently enough, to vacation and shop for an estate," he says.

Sal can't help but to giggle. Kelly turns his head. Sipping her wine, she looks up at him. A satirical smile, "Innocently may be a bit of a stretch," she comments.

Sparky is more than amused watching the two of them spar. Whatever is happening, he likes them and is very curious to learn exactly what is going on, however cool he must pretend to be in order to not show his pre-ordained enthusiasm.

"Legendary, hunh?" Sparky asks. He looks back and forth between Sal and Kelly. "In what arena?" he asks.

Kelly leans in and speaking in a low voice, says, "We've learned that a gem dealer has cut a deal with the Chase Bank to hold his most valuable gems while he is in Montauk and..."

Before Kelly can complete the sentence, "You're going to rob the Chase Bank?" Sparky asks incredulously.

The three of them stare at one another a moment. Kelly and Sal are impressed at Sparky's quick and spot-on assessment of their endeavor.

"You do realize there's only one road out of town," Sparky says with raised eyebrows.

"We do," says Sal taking a lady-sized bite of her lobster roll.

Sparky leans towards Kelly, "That would indeed be legendary..." he says.

The three of them sit quietly as it sinks in. For Kelly and Sal, that they just disclosed nefarious plans to their taxi driver. and for Sparky, that they just disclosed nefarious plans to their taxi driver; him. A few moments pass.

"How much are the gems worth?" Sparky asks breaking the silence.

"Not sure..." Kelly answers sipping his wine. He looks at Sal a moment, "But we imagine somewhere between five and twenty million," Kelly tells him.

"How exactly do you propose to successfully rob the Chase Bank in Montauk with one road out of town and the Coast

Guard Station on Star Island?" Sparky asks, always seeking details.

"The blackboard..." answers Sal.

The waitress returns with Sal's wine.

"Thanks, doll," says Sal taking the fresh glass of wine.

"You're welcome," says the waitress, unsure what to make of Sal's vernacular, "doll." She walks away shaking her head, perplexed.

"The blackboard..." Sparky repeats adding a few things up in his head. "I suspect it will have to be a very complex plan," he adds.

"It's genius!" Kelly says excitedly thinking through some of the details of the elaborate plan in his head.

"So... you in?" asks Sal sipping her wine, looking into Sparky's eyes.

"That depends," he answers.

"We're back to that, hunh?" Sal says smiling.

The three of them laugh out loud, as the thrill of the exchange overtakes them for a moment.

"Essentially, where you're concerned, very little has changed," Kelly tells him.

"You're still our hired livery driver, only now you know why," he adds.

Sparky stares at Kelly unsure what to make of what he just said.

“So why tell me at all?” he asks.

“You have us convinced that you would act quick on your feet, ...that you’re both bright and trustworthy,” Kelly tells him. “Were anything to go awry and an adjustment needed to be made on the fly, a wheelman in the mix, in my experience, could very likely become a key factor,” he adds.

Sparky attempts to put such a scenario together in his head.

“Plus, we like you, Sparks,” Sal says. “It’d be fun to have you on the inside,” she adds.

Sparky looks back and forth from Kelly to Sal.

“Thanks, Sal,” he says.

“I like you guys, too,” he adds. He looks Kelly in the eye. “Your instinct to trust me is sound,” Sparky says. “To begin with, I believe that honor, even honor among thieves, may be the last commodity left in this world. Plus... I’m no fan of banks...” he says leaning in. “Banks have been robbing us blind since the money changers in the Temple,” he says. “Those gems are insured. I won’t lose any sleep because the bank has to cover the value of them if they went missing,” he adds with a mischievous shrug of the shoulders.

Sal smiles and raises her glass, “Welcome aboard, Romeo,” she says to Sparky’s broad smile.

“What’s with the old racetrack?” Sparky asks. “How does that figure into all of this?”

“I’ll tell you what, come back with us to the Yacht Club and we’ll tell you all about it, Kelly says getting the attention of the waitress, who saunters over. “Can we have the check, please?”

The waitress glances at Sal a moment, then back to Kelly. “Sure, doll,” she says with a wink.

As the waitress leaves to fetch the check Sparky turns to Sal with a broad grin, “You leave a lasting impression,” he says pointing his thumb at the waitress.

“Touché, baby,” she says raising her glass and downing the rest of her wine.

VIII

A short while later Kelly and Sal with Sparky in tow enter his suite where the crew is hard at work. Dave labors over the formula for the tunnel dig on the blackboard, Rollie's on the phone speaking with the Moose, and in a set of headphones totally oblivious to his surroundings, The Kid is playing Gran Turismo with the Thrustmaster Ferrari 458 Spider Wheel and Pedals Set on a PlayStation. Dave and Rollie stop what they're doing and stare at Sparky. They all just stand there a moment staring at one another.

Finally, Dave walks over to Sparky with his hand outstretched, "Welcome to the crew, rookie," he says with a knowing smile.

Sparky loves every moment of it.

"The blackboard…" he says, shaking Dave's hand.

Rollie ends the call, walks over to Sparky and in a no-nonsense attitude, says, "I'll have no problem breaking your neck if you break your word," he says matter-of-factly.

"And I wouldn't hold it against you," Sparky says, reaching out for a handshake.

Rollie gives him a giant hug. "Welcome aboard, wheelman," he says smiling.

"I insisted on headphones," Dave says referring to The Kid.

Dave turns to Sparky, "The first thing I'll need from you is to drive me and The Kid from the Chase Bank to the racetrack at night, so I can videotape the route." He looks at The Kid. "Gran Tourismo was good enough for developing a racecar driver like Jann Mardenborough, and it's good enough for me. Only, we'll need to customize our version so The Kid will be versed on the actual route, so that it's second nature by blast off," says Dave, forever thinking the technical aspects of the job through.

"Good call, Dave," says Kelly.

"You can add a video of the racetrack to Gran Tourismo?" Sparky is impressed at the thought of it.

"Sure," Dave says smiling. "It's a 'video game,' isn't it?"

"Impressive..." Sparky says, nodding his head. "Albert Einstein, all right..." Sparky says sort of to himself.

Kelly refers to The Kid who remains deep into the video game, unaware of Sparky being there. "Somebody want to bring him into this dimension?" he asks.

Rollie laughs, walks over and standing behind The Kid, leans down and removes the headphones. "It's medication time," Rollie says into The Kid's ear.

It jolts The Kid into the world of the living. He sees Sparky and leaps up.

"What the..." he yelps.

He calms down and smiles at Sparky, "They brought you in, hunh?" Hey," he says in a friendly tone. "From one wheelman to another... welcome aboard." He walks over to Sparky and offers a handshake.

"I still don't know where Demyan's staying," Sal says.

"Demyan?" Sparky asks.

"He's the gem dealer I mentioned," Kelly tells him.

"Nobody gets killed in this, right?" Sparky asks.

"We're not hitmen thugs," says Kelly, surprised at the question.

"Any moron can kill someone and take their belongings," Dave tells him.

"We are more like extraction professionals," Sal assures him.

"I see," Sparky says, "So why do we need to know where Demyan is?" he asks.

"Fair question," Kelly says.

"Sal, the beautiful Sally, will make sure that Demyan remains in town for the Fourth of July Fireworks display," he informs him.

"He rarely strays far from his precious gem collection," Rollie tells him.

"His deal with Chase Bank is that they hold his gems when he's in town," Kelly adds. "Demyan is Russian and Russians are extremely distrusting... Demyan likes to keep his gems close to the vest." Kelly says, confiding in Sparky.

"I see..." Sparky says looking around at everyone, still not a hundred percent sure about his expanded role in the crew.

"Sal, by virtue of her irresistible allure, will coax Demyan to remain in town for the fireworks," Kelly adds.

"Fireworks?" Sparky inquires.

"The night we plan to pull off our caper," Kelly tells him.

"And in order to do that, I need to know where he's staying," Sal adds, tapping her watch.

"That's easy," Sparky says.

The crew is all ears. They stand there staring at Sparky, curious what he has in mind.

"He's kinda famous, right?" he says. "Or at least of some renown... a big deal for the town... Famous Russian gem dealer moves to Montauk..." he says sounding like a headline.

"Seeing that he purchased an estate from that loose-lipped realtor, I'd say probably yes," Sal states winking at Kelly.

Kelly shrugs his shoulders and smiles. He turns to Sparky, "What do you have in mind?" he asks.

"I could pose as a reporter for the society pages of a local rag and ask around," Sparky tells them.

"Brilliant!" Kelly says with his famous grin.

"Sharp as a tack," Sal agrees.

"He's one of us, I tell ya," adds Dave.

"I can't believe you guys didn't think of that..." Sparky says, smartassing them. "Being con artists and all..." he adds.

"I love this guy!" says The Kid.

"Give me a couple minutes," Sparky says.

He pulls out his cellphone and finds a quiet corner of the room. After a few moments he returns to the group.

"As I would have predicted, Gurney's Resort on the old highway," Sparky tells them. "The priciest spot in town..."

"You're up, Sal," Kelly says.

Sparky looks at Sal. "I have an idea," he tells her.

"Talk to me, Romeo," she says.

"Would you know this Demyan if you saw him?" Sparky poses the question to everyone.

"Sure..." Kelly answers.

"Rent a cabana on the beach at Gurney's..." he says. "That'll give you access to the whole place and you'll be sure to run into him," he deducts. "Russians, especially wealthy Russians, are ostentatious so he should be easy to spot," he adds.

"Writers are natural-born con men," says Dave, rubbing his jaw. "Through observation, they, the good ones... have a detailed understanding of human motivation," he says.

"Well said," Sparky smiles, happy to be understood and appreciated.

"Time to get us a cabana at Gurney's" Kelly says.

"Scarpetta is the restaurant at Gurney's," Sparky tells them. "And it's one of the best restaurants in town," he adds.

"Great, I'm famished," says The Kid.

"You're always famished," Sal says.

"Okay, Kid, make us a reservation at Scarpetta for five, no, six." He looks over at Sparky. "For this evening," Kelly tells him.

"Dinner for six coming up," he says.

"Better make it a late reservation," Rollie tells him. "Russians like to dine late," he adds.

"Dinner at ten," The Kid, says phone in hand.

"Meanwhile…" Dave says, "We have a rather complex theft to orchestrate… so if it's all right with you guys, let's get down to brass tacks," he says pointing to the blackboard.

"I'm all ears, professor," says Kelly as he takes a comfortable seat on the sofa.

"Grab a seat, Sparks," Sal says, also sitting down facing the blackboard.

Sparky smiles and takes a seat.

Dave turns to Rollie, "What's the update on the torpedo and the crew," he asks.

Rollie steps in front of the blackboard and addresses everyone.

"The maintenance crew will grab the TBM from Shinn up in the Bronx and be here tomorrow night," he says.

Kelly looks at his watch, "I pick up the keys for the Tower condo from Giovanna tomorrow, so we'll have access to the building long before they arrive," Kelly tells them.

"What's a TBM?" Sparky asks.

"Tunnel boring machine," Dave tells him.

Kelly stands up, "This is the itinerary for this evening," he says, pacing the floor and looking around the room. "Sparky takes Dave and The Kid for a video-taping drive from Chase Bank around the race track, then we all get dolled up for dinner at Scarpetta, where the irresistible Sal connects with Demyan."

He stops a moment. Something is bothering him. A thought comes to mind, "Ah!" he exclaims. "Can any of the Romeos grab a date for this evening?" he asks.

The Kid and Rollie look at each other unsure why Kelly's asking.

"It'll be more natural if Sal isn't the only woman at our table…" he tells them.

"Not a problem," says The Kid, "Rachel is dying to see me again," he brags.

"I'll wager Romeo III can convince Ewa to join us," Sal says, winking at Sparky.

"Well, I suppose…" Sparky says.

"Are you kidding?" Sal says pushing it. "She was practically drooling," she adds.

"Oh, please," The Kid remarks.

"I'll give Candy a call," Rollie says.

"Great," Kelly says. "And Kid, don't forget to change the reservation once we have a new number," he tells him.

The Kid shakes his head affirmatively, the phone to his ear. "Hi, baby," he says into the phone. "Busy tonight?" He listens a moment. "Hahaha, me too!" he says, giving the group a thumbs up and listening into the phone. "You know it! Pick you up at 9:30," he says, smiling ear to ear. "One down," he says big-shoting it for the group. "What are you slow pokes waiting for?' he adds. "I have dinner reservations to make," he says tapping his watch with a smart-ass grin.

Sparky dials a number and places the phone to his ear. "Ewa?" he asks looking around at the crew, "It's Sparky," he says. He walks away and smiles big as he listens. "I've been thinking about you, too," he says, finding a quiet corner of the suite to finish his exchange. He ends the call and walks back to the group. "Ewa will meet us there a bit after ten," he says.

"Swedes…" Dave says knowingly. "The women are very independent," he says.

Rollie reappears, "Candy will be joining us," he says smiling.

"Guess we're the only ones flying solo, chief," Dave says to Kelly.

"Which simply opens the door for endless possibilities," Kelly says looking over at Dave with his mischievous grin.

"That makes nine of us for dinner," The Kid says picking up his phone and hitting a recently dialed number. "Yes, hello… This is the Sparky party," he says winking at Sparky who perks up suddenly. "Yes, there will be nine of us dining this evening instead of six," he says. He listens a moment, "Great…see you then."

Sal smiles at Sparky. "This party is sparky all right, so it's fitting…" she says.

"Touché, Sal, touché…" Sparky says with a broad smile.

"I'm going to rest up before dinner, and you guys," referring to Dave, Sparky and The Kid, "have a movie to make..."

Dave looks at his watch, "Let's meet out front at seven-thirty," he says to Sparky and The Kid.

"You got it, pal," says Sparky heading for the door.

At seven-thirty Sparky, dressed nicer than usual, pulls the taxi into the Yacht Club to find Dave and The Kid with a few small duffel bags. Sparky opens the automatic doors and they step inside.

"I'll need somewhere out of the way near town to mount the HD Cam onto the hood mount." Dave says.

"Not a problem," Sparky says.

They drive into town.

"Will the program give me contour sensation?" The Kid asks.

"The visual will be enough for your mind to react without the Disneyland vacuum manipulated seat apparatus," Dave assures him.

Sparky turns into a gravel parking lot near the soccer field at Fort Pond.
"Only in Montauk would they name a lake, Fort Pond," Sparky comments.

Dave looks through the windshield at Fort Pond, "That is rather large to be considered a pond," he says.

"Yeah, but with the entire Atlantic Ocean down the street, I suppose it's all relative," Sparky says, pulling the taxi behind a large hedge at the rear of the parking lot.

Dave's already into the duffel bag. He pulls out a camera mount attaches it to what resembles truck tie-down straps with ratchet-tightening levers. He quickly mounts the small HD cam onto the hood of the taxi and adjusts the positioning to best resemble the view from the driver's seat. He tests the remote-control device a few times, sticks it in his vest pocket, then looks at Sparky and The Kid. "Let's do it," he says.

They jump into the taxi and drive to the Chase Bank. Sparky pulls up to the bank.

"Stop there," Dave says, pointing to a spot near the bank. "I've given the starting point only rudimentary thought. Let's get out and walk around, ...see if we can find the ideal starting point," he says.

The three of them get out and stand on the circle side of the bank.

"What's the deal with this small parking lot?" Dave asks Sparky referring to a smaller lot adjacent to the main parking lot.

"Not sure, but I've seen cars parked here for days without being bothered," Sparky tells them.

"We need it to appear for the cops as though the getaway car has just left the rear of the bank," Dave says.

"Why the rear?" Sparky asks, "The entrances are in the front and the side," he says pointing.

"I plan on an using an explosive device to blow out the teller window and half the wall around it," Dave says.

"Wow..." says Sparky imagining the destruction.

“We need to distract attention from the missile blasting off the roof as much as possible,” says Dave matter of fact, “Plus, this is the side facing the police station…” he adds.

“I see…” Sparky says looking around.

“I say we park it right there,” The Kid says pointing to a spot on the street near the rear of the bank. “Will I have reverse controls?” he asks Dave.

“You’ll have every driving feature being in an actual car would provide,” Dave says.

“Genius!” The Kid says.

“Then why not right there,” Sparky says pointing to a parking spot.

“That could work,” Dave says. He looks at The Kid. “When we’re through the tunnel and everything is set, I can give you your first of two cues,” Dave says walking towards the spot.

“Then you’ll back up slowly and pull up next to the building. I’ll give you three seconds before I blow out the back of the bank, then you screech off towards the race track,” he says.

“Okay, let’s get in the taxi and work it through, …see how it feels before I videotape the run,” Dave suggests.

They get back in the taxi, The Kid riding shotgun, then drive the entire course from the bank to once around the track.

“That feels good,” The Kid says.

“Yeah, I think that’ll work,” Dave says.

"I purposefully stayed off Montauk Highway," Sparky says looking at Dave in the rear-view, "I've been here for the Fourth of July fireworks, and it is a mess," Sparky tells them. "After the fireworks are over, it's bumper to bumper for well over three hours with everyone trying to get out of town," he tells them. "You'll likely have to illegally pass a few cars just to make the first turn," he says.

He looks at The Kid with a serious expression, "Just be aware that people walk on the streets in this town as though cars don't exist," he says. "It's really strange but sort of a custom here," he adds. "Plus, most of them will be smashed."

"Yeah, try not to kill anyone, Kid," Dave tells him.

"All right you guys," he says, "Knock it off, will ya," yells The Kid. "I counted four turns before I reach the racetrack," The Kid says.

"That's right," says Dave.

"Yup, once you're out of the bank parking lot..." Sparky tells him.

"Right," says The Kid.

"Okay, let's run one through from the start," Dave says. He looks at Sparky in the rear-view and adds, "Include backing out of the parking spot."

Sparky gets the taxi into position. "I'll give you an action cue like filmmakers use once I'm rolling," Dave tells Sparky.

"Ready when you are," Sparky says.

"Rolling..." Dave announces, "Aaaand... Action!" he says.

Sparky backs out of the spot and drives the entire run. When they return to the starting point on South Fairview Avenue, Dave stops recording and asks Sparky to pull over so he can check the playback. He plays it in fast forward...

"It's all here," he says smiling.

"Good work, guys," Dave says.

"Let's eat!" says The Kid.

"Yeah, let's eat," says Dave.

They drive to the Yacht Club. Dave packs up the equipment. Sparky checks the time.

"Our reservation is in twenty-five minutes," he says. "Better get the others together, it's a ten-minute drive out to Gurneys," he adds.

"Meet you back here with the crew in fifteen, "Dave tells him.

"I'll be here," Sparky tells him.

"You look great, by the way," Dave adds before he struts off.

A short time later the entire crew with Rachel and Candy in tow pull up to Gurney's Resort. Everyone exits the taxi. Sparky tells the valet, someone he's acquainted with from years of driving taxi, that he's joining them for dinner and to park the car.

"Ooh, la, la," The valet comments.

"Just park the car, hot shot," Sparky says with a wink stuffing a ten spot in his hand.

A short time later, the crew is assembled around a large table, sipping cocktails and looking at the menu. There is an empty seat next to Sparky. Sal looks around the restaurant,

“No sign of him yet,” she notes.

Rollie turns to Candy. “Would you like to take a tour of Gurney’s with me? I’ve never been here before,” he says.

“I haven’t either,” she says. “I’ve heard so much about it, it’ll be fun!” she adds.

Rollie winks at Sal, stands up, looks around the restaurant and starts heading towards the bar with Candy. He turns, and looks at Kelly, “Order me the charred octopus, will ya?” he asks.

Kelly nods an affirmative. Rollie takes Candy by the hand.

“Would you like an appetizer?” Rollie asks. “These guys can order for us and it’ll be here when we get back,” he adds.

“The yellowtail looked awesome!” Candy says with a smiling lick of the lips.

“I’ll be happy to procure the awesome looking yellowtail for the lady,” Kelly says in his charming way.

Rollie and Candy walk off. Candy doesn’t know it, but this is recon, looking for Demyan.

“What time is Ewa arriving?” Kelly asks Sparky.

“What am I, Kreskin?” Sparky asks with a smirk.

Kelly, Sal and Dave laugh.

“Who’s Kreskin?” asks The Kid.

“Don’t ask me,” says Rachel.

“The Amazing Kreskin, was a self-professed psychic who ended up with his own television show in the 1970s,” Kelly tells them.

“Yeah, but he was just a con man,” Dave adds looking up at the younger members of the group who’ve never heard of him.

“A damn good one,” says Sal with a smirk. “His TV show lasted five years…”

“I’ll look him up on YouTube,” Rachel says. “I want to work in entertainment,” she says. “I have a communications degree…” She looks into The Kid’s eyes and adds, “It’s important to know as much as possible about the industry.”

The Kid gazes at her adoringly. “With a face like yours, all you’ll have to do is smile for the camera, baby,” The Kid assures her.

Rachel gives him a sweet kiss. Sal rolls her eyes.

“Hi, Sparky,” says Ewa’s charming voice. Sparky looks up to find Ewa standing there.

“Ewa,” he says.

“Hope I didn’t keep you waiting,” she says in her sweet demeanor.

The Kid’s jaw has nearly dropped to the floor as Ewa truly is a stunning woman.

"Not at all," Sparky says as he stands up and pulls the chair out for her. "We haven't even ordered prima piatti," he adds.

Sparky stands there ready to adjust the chair beneath her when she sits, but she just stands there.

"Aren't you going to kiss me?" she asks in her Teutonic yet somehow alluring tone.

Sparky smiles and gives her a gentlemanly kiss.

Ewa wraps her arms around his shoulders and kisses him back with a bit more passion. When she's through, she looks out over the table. "Good evening, everyone," she says before taking her seat.

Sparky glances at Kelly with an innocent shrug, then a wink of the eye.

"Hi, Ewa," Sal says. "Nice to see you again."

The waitress appears and takes their orders for drinks and appetizers. A short while later Rollie and Candy return arm in arm chatting lively. They stop a few feet from the table.

"Art reveals mystery to the eye, which only the heart can see," Candy says.

"That's brilliant," Rollie says impressed. "Who said that?" he asks.

"I did," says Candy smiling. "In my dissertation..." She folds her arms around Rollie and they share a kiss.

"You truly are a work of art," he says.

They make it to the table finally and sit down. The waitress arrives with appetizers and cocktails. Sal lifts her prosecco in a toast.

"To the artist hidden inside all of us," she says.

Kelly and Dave look at one another knowingly.

"You know they have a firepit area here which is very special," Rollie says looking directly at Sal.

"Really?" Sal asks. "I love firepits," I'll have to venture over there and take a look," she adds.

"I highly recommend it," Rollie says.

Candy looks at Sal, oblivious to the doublespeak. "Yeah, it truly is wonderful, the crackling of the fire... the ocean waves crashing on the shore..." She looks up at Rollie and kisses him.

"Candy... Ewa... Rollie... I ordered a few bottles of prosecco for the table," Kelly says waving his arm over the table in a welcoming gesture," Please help yourselves."

"In that case," Candy says, pouring glasses for Rollie and herself, "Buon appetito!"

Sparky pours a glass of prosecco for Ewa.

"To your loveliness," he says toasting her.

"And to yours," she says with a coy smile as she lifts the glass and takes a sip.

The waitress arrives.

"No rush, but when you guys are ready to order entrées, just let me know.

"Ooh," Candy says, "Want to go family style on the halibut and the seared scallops?" she asks Rollie.

"Sounds perfect," Rollie says.

"Know what you're having, baby?" The Kid asks Rachel.

"I'd love the watercress salad and the Branzino," she says, looking at The Kid with sweet-doe eyes.

"Duo of veal for me," Dave tells the waitress.

"Ewa? Sparky asks.

"I would like the black cod," she says.

"A black cod for my friend," Sparky tells the waitress. "And halibut for me," he adds.

"Sal?" Kelly asks.

"I'll have the wild black bass," she says, looking up at the waitress.

"And for you, sir?" the waitress asks Kelly.

"Has to be the halibut," he tells her. "But first could you bring watercress salad for the table," he adds as he raises his glass to Candy.

The waitress jots it all down and takes her leave.

"I think I'll have a peek at that fire pit before my entrée arrives," Sal says, filling her glass with prosecco.

"I think you'll really love it," says Candy. "That's the first thing Rollie said when we got there," she continues, "Sal is going to love this..."

"It's true," Rollie says with a wink.

Sal gets up, grabs her drink and saunters across the restaurant floor.

"Your friend is very beautiful," Ewa tells Sparky.

"Said the pot to the kettle..." Sparky remarks, gazing deeply into Ewa's eyes.

"Touché, my friend," Dave says raising his glass to Sparky, "Touché..."

Sal makes her way through the restaurant and out to Gurney's Oceanfront Deck. She quickly spots Demyan's rather boisterous group at one of the fire pits downing shots of Stoltsynia Vodka. She saunters over and looks down at one person in particular, Demyan Yusapova. Sal, in a most sultry alluring manner, smiles directly at Demyan.

"Anno, Anno," she says.

"Vell... Hello!" he says with a lascivious smile, "To vat do I owe the honor of such a sweet flower sayink hello to me?" he asks with the boisterous tone of an ostentatious Russian who has been drinking vodka for hours.

"You are all having so much fun! How could I possibly resist?" Sal tells him.

"Then please, you must join us for some wodka," he says, inviting her to sit down.

"Vladimir, ...wodka for the lady!" he orders a man who is apparently a subordinate.

Vladimir sheepishly pulls one of several bottles of Stoltsynia Vodka out of a tub of ice and pours a tall, narrow glass for Sal.

“Please, sit down,” Demyan asks invitingly.

“I would love to,” she says with an amorous lilt in her voice.

She sits closely next to him and accepts the glass of vodka from Vladimir. She lifts the glass high.

“Nostrovia,” she says before drinking the entire glass down.

Demyan is duly impressed.

“Vell! ...an American who drinks like a Russian,” he says, pleased at her ability.

“I’ve left friends at a table,” she tells him sadly.

“Friends? Or a man?” he asks, not wasting any time.

“No man,” she assures him stroking his cheek sweetly.

She stands up and hands Vladimir the glass.

“If you’re still here when we’ve finished our meal, I would very much love to come back for another vodka,” she says, staring into his hungry eyes.

“Demyan,” he says holding out his hand.

“Sally,” she tells him, placing her hand in his for him to kiss, which he does.

“I’ll see you soon...” she tells him invitingly. “Demyan,” she adds in her most sultry delivery.

"For you, I vould vait..." he assures her.

"Until then," she says.

"Until then," he repeats and stands to see her off.

Sal turns and leaves, turning back to glance at him and yes, he is devouring her with his eyes. She giggles, blows him a kiss and steps onto the large ocean view deck, making her way to the table just as the waitress is completing her service.

"Perfect timing," Rachel says.

"How was it?" Kelly asks.

"There's vodka," she says.

"Nostrovia!" remarks Kelly.

"Let's eat!" announces Dave.

"Yeah, I'm starved!" says The Kid.

"There's a headline," Sal says looking at Rachel. "I hope you have plenty of snacks at your place," Sal says, winking at Rachel.

"I'll make sure to have some on hand," she says gazing lovingly at The Kid. "I wouldn't want you to lose your strength, Louis darling," she adds, running her hand across his cheek.

"Waitress..." Dave calls out with his finger raised. He looks over at Sparky, "What Long Island red would you suggest with the veal?" he asks as the waitress arrives.

"If they have a bottle, the 2014 Paumanok Cabernet from the North Fork," he says looking up at the waitress.

"I think we have some of those," the waitress says jotting it down.

"Great, I'll have a bottle," Dave tells her.

"Buon appetite, everyone," says Kelly with a huge smile, raising his glass.

"Buon appetito," everyone toasts raising a glass.

Candy stabs a seared sea scallop with her fork, "Every time I eat a scallop, I can't help but to think of Botticelli's Venus di Milo," she says, munching on her scallop, then giggling almost uncontrollably. She grabs a hold of herself. "I'm sorry," she says. "And now…" she says looking into Rollie's eyes, "I can't think of Venus di Milo without thinking of you singing 'Venus in Blue Jeans' to me," she says throwing her arms around Rollie and kissing him passionately.

"Romeo II takes the lead by a head," Sal says sort of to herself.

Dave and Kelly get a chuckle from Sal's commentary.

They all dig in to their dishes and enjoy the meal with much banter and imbibing of fine Long Island wines.

"We should all take a walk down to the beach after dinner," Kelly suggests.

"Let's," says Sal.

"That sounds wonderful," Candy says looking up into Rollie's eyes, before feeding him a scallop with her fingers.

After dessert the crew heads down to the water. Demyan and company are still at the fire pits drinking vodka.

“Ah!” he shouts, spotting Sal. “My leetle flower,” he exclaims. “Kav you come to enjoy another drink with your new friend Demyan?” he asks in his buoyant manner.

“I wouldn’t miss it for the world,” she says, taking a seat next to him.

She turns to Kelly and the gang, “I’ll meet you guys back at the hotel.”

“Vladimir, a wodka for the lady!”

Kelly can hear as he strolls down to the ocean to meet the others. He shakes his head and smiles, “Sally,” he says to himself.

IX

The next morning the crew is assembled in Kelly's suite.

"I can pick up keys for the Tower condo in an hour," Kelly tells everyone. "What time is Moose's crew due to arrive?" he asks Rollie.

"They're meeting Shin in the Bronx at six, to pick up the TBM, so figure sometime around ten o'clock or so," he says.

"I'll have a work order in place well before then," Dave assures them.

"Great," says Kelly, glancing at Sparky.

"Man! You guys work like a well-oiled machine," Sparky comments.

Kelly turns to Sal, "How's Demyan?" he asks.

"He can't live without me," she smirks, puffing on a cigarette.

"I'll have the Gran Tourismo, Montauk edition, ready tonight, Kid. "It's nearly finished rendering," Dave tells him.

"Awesome..." The Kid says. "How about some lunch?" The Kid asks everyone.

"It's take-out for me." says Dave, "I need to grab a chopper back to the city and pick up some equipment," he adds.

"Let's try that Gig Shack joint," Rollie says.

"Sounds good, I can walk to the realtor's office from there," Kelly says.

"Giovanna will be thrilled," Sal quips.

Kelly smiles with a shrug of the shoulders.

"I fear I may have over stimulated her fertile imagination a bit," he says with raised eyebrows.

"I'll need a ride to the airport, Sparky," Dave tells him. "See you guys tonight," he says, looking over the crew.

"Hey, Sparky, meet us out front when you get back from the airport?" Kelly asks.

"Shouldn't be more than half an hour, or so..." Sparky lets him know.

Sparky walks through the Yacht Club towards the parking lot, somewhat amazed at what he is witnessing. He drives the taxi around to find Dave waiting, drops him at the airport and heads back to the Yacht Club. He pulls up to the front entrance and as he waits for the crew to arrive, opens his MacBook. He accesses the file he's made entries into since first meeting the crew and writes everything that he can recall from dinner at Scarpetta and what had just happened in Kelly's suite. His face is electric. He laughs out loud a few times as he types away. The Kid is the first to appear. He steps into the taxi and sees Sparky on the MacBook.

"You really writing a book about us?" The Kid asks.

Sparky looks over at The Kid with a wry expression. "Yeah," he says saving the file before folding the computer.

"What's my name gonna be?" The Kid asks.

"I haven't decided yet," he tells him carefully, placing the computer in his backpack between the seats, "The Kid is a strong favorite," Sparky tells him with a certain degree of trepidation.

He observes The Kid's reaction. "It's not your real name... and it's what everyone calls you, so, it's unique and it fits," Sparky tells him.

"I guess..." The Kid says, thinking for a moment.

The Kid doesn't look thrilled. Sparky quickly runs through other names in his head he might use for The Kid.

"Yeah, why not?" The Kid says with a sudden enthusiasm Sparky didn't expect.

The Kid looks over at Sparky, "If it was good enough for Billy The Kid, I'll take it!"

Kelly and the others appear, jump in the taxi and they take off for the Gig Shack in town.

"The Gig Shack is a premier local hangout," Sparky tells them as they drive down West Lake Drrive, "Never know who you might run into. A lot of surfers... locals... tourists, of course, even owners of other restaurants will show up just to get away from their own places for an hour.... And for a good meal," he adds.

"So, there's good chow?" asks The Kid.

"Top-notch!" Sparky tells him. "Sort of a Global Surf Cuisine that does its best to stay true to its Montauk roots," he adds.

He pulls up to the Gig Shack and opens the automatic doors. The crew ambles out. Candy is walking by on her way to work, sees Rollie, jumps up excitedly and wraps her arms around him.

"What a cool run-in!" she exclaims.

The rest of the crew grab a table, leaving them to smooch on the sidewalk. The maître d' sets menus down and sends a waitress over. They order some wine, as Rollie and Candy stand on the sidewalk in front of the Gig Shack hugging and kissing.

"I dreamt of you all night, and now I'm late for work," she says. "See you later?" she asks.

"I can't tonight, Venus baby. Unfortunately, I have some business I must tend to," he tells her. "But soon, ok?"

"You know it," she says with one final kiss.

Rollie makes his way to the table the gang has gathered around.

"You're a true inspiration," Sal says with a coy smile.

"You're going to need all the inspiration you can get," Rollie says giving Sal a knowing look. "…If my memory serves me correctly regarding the way you feel about Russian men," he adds.

She lifts her glass to Rollie, "It does serve you correctly, Romeo…" she says sipping her cocktail. "C'est la gare," she says smiling with a shrug of the shoulders.

"What's la gare?" asks The Kid.

"It's war, Kid," Rollie tells him.
"C'est la gare means, Such is war," Kelly tells him.

"Interesting…" comments The Kid.

"The French have a saying for everything," Kelly tells him. "It's as though the entire language exists solely to express poetic encapsulations of the unfathomable," he adds.

The Kid listens, as always, to his mentor, soaking it up like a sponge. "Vive la France," he says mimicking a Frenchman.

The waitress arrives with the wine, "You guys know what you're having?" she asks.

"Let's start with the mussels and grilled French baguette for the table," Kelly says looking up to whom he suddenly feels is a very attractive woman. "Hello," he says, suddenly flirtatious.

"It's contagious," Sal quips, referring to Kelly's exchange with the attractive waitress.

She pours herself a glass of chilled Rosé. Kelly ignores her as he continues to gaze into the eyes of the attractive waitress with his signature grin. She responds in kind until Rollie, menu in hand, attempts to break the spell.

"I'll have the seared local sea scallops," he says.

The waitress doesn't respond.

"Kelly," Kelly says, his hand outstretched.

"Mihaela," the pretty waitress says with a strong accent, taking his hand and holding onto it.

"Romanian?" Kelly asks.

"Yes!" the waitress exclaims. "How did you know?" she asks.

"Lucky guess," Kelly says.

"Oh sure..." she says, giggling.

"Ummm... Miss?" Rollie asks loudly.

"A fella could starve in this place," Sal says in her smart-ass tone.

"I think my friends want to order," Kelly says, letting go of her hand

"Oh, yes!" the waitress responds finally as if from a dream. "Sorry..." she says, looking at Rollie and still glowing from her exchange with Kelly.

"I'll have the seared local sea scallops," he repeats.

She scribbles it down. "And for you, miss?" she asks Sal.

"Just keep the wine coming, doll," she says.

"I want the spicy tuna tartare taquitos," says The Kid.

"OK," she says scribbling, then grabbing Kelly's gaze again.

"The sea scallops sound lovely," Kelly tells her.

"Yes..." she says scribbling on her order pad. "Wonderful..." she adds with a deep sigh before strutting off.

Sal sips her wine, then looks over at Kelly with a you're-busted expression. "Thanks, toots, but I think I've got Demyan under control," she says.

Rollie knows what she's talking about, but The Kid is miffed.

"I don't get the connection," he says looking at Sal with his now-signature inquisitive face.

She looks at The Kid. "Kelly's attempting subliminal suggestion technique," she says, sipping her Montauk Rosé. "To make my job with Demyan easier," she says. "Flow more naturally…" she adds.

The Kid fails to grasp the complexity of what Sal's describing to him.

"You see, Kid, romance is contagious largely due to the biological drives that influence all of us through the subconscious," Kelly says trying to explain the science of suggestion through desire to him.

"Sal must romance Demyan," Rollie tells him, "and be convincing at it," he adds turning to Sal.

"Being surrounded by romantic, even sexually charged exchanges will ignite specific neurons in the brain to that bias, even when we are unaware of it," Kelly tells him.

The Kid thinks it through for a moment, then smiles.

"Fascinating… You guys truly are amazing!" he says.

Kelly looks at Sal, "Although, Sal… in this case, there is a genuine attraction," he says to her almost sternly.

"You were laying it on pretty thick, Romeo," Sal says with a smirk.

She and Kelly stare at one another in a near duel of wits. Sal pours a Rosé and lifts the glass.

"What do you think Sparky's doing right now?" she asks.

"I'll guess he's parked in the shade somewhere, writing about us," Kelly says, looking around the immediate vicinity to see if Sparky is parked nearby.

"Sparky's naming me 'The Kid' in his book," The Kid announces.

The three of them look at him amused.

"Hey, if it was good enough for Billy The Kid, it's good enough for me," he tells them, happy with his name de plume.

Mihaela, the waitress, arrives with the mussels, scallops and seared tuna taquitos.

"Everything looks wonderful," Kelly says, gazing into Mihaela's eyes.

"Truly..." She stares at Kelly with a sensuous smile.

She floats off as Rollie and The Kid dig in.

"You should at least have some mussels, Sal," Kelly suggests, sucking one down himself. "Ah... the essence of the entire sea exists right here in this tiny shell," he exclaims.

Sal smiles. "You cad." she says. "Okay, I'll have a few," she adds.

Kelly looks at his watch. "Time to meet Giovanna and get keys to the Tower," Kelly tells them.

He sucks down a few more Mussels. "Be back before you know it," he says standing up to take the walk a few blocks away to the realtor's office.

"Not if Giovanna has her way," Sal quips.

Kelly returns a short time later with the keys in hand.

"Let the games begin," he says, jangling the keys while taking his seat.

"Hey, Rollie, let's ask Sparky to pick us up at the Tower in, say, twenty minutes," Kelly says.

"What's for dessert?" The Kid asks.

"Sparky says we should try the homemade ice cream at John's Drive-in," Rollie says, hitting speed dial.

He puts the phone to his ear, "Hey Sparky, can you pick us up at the Tower in twenty minutes?" he asks. "...OK, see you then," he says, ending the call.

Mihaela appears, "Anything else for you?" she asks.

"Just the check, please," Kelly says sadly, working a 'sorry to have to go' angle. "But perhaps we'll meet again," he adds.

"I'm here four days a week," Mihaela tells him.

Kelly smiles at her longingly.

"I'll get your check," she says.

The Kid stands up and stretches. "So, where's this ice cream joint?" he asks.

"Hold your horses, Kid." Rollie tells him.

Mihaela returns with the bill and hands it to Kelly who rolls off two hundred-dollar bills and stuffs them in the check holder.

“And on the fifth day?” Kelly asks her.

She looks down at her feet a moment, then up into his eyes, “On the fifth day, I am free.”

“You must join us for dinner one evening,” Kelly suggests.

“I would like that very much,” Mihaela says.

She scribbles her number on the order pad, tears it off and stuffs it in Kelly’s vest pocket. “I look forward to hearing from you, Kelly,” she says with a giggle.

Kelly takes her hand and kisses it gently looking up into her eyes. “Until then,” he says.

The crew strolls across The Circle and find their way into the Tower. When they get to the elevator, Kelly presses the up button.

“We’re on the fifth floor,” he tells them. “Carl Fischer had his penthouse on six back in the day, but nothing on six was available,” Kelly tells them.

They take the elevator up and Kelly leads them to the unit.

He unlocks the door, turns towards the crew before swinging the door open, “You’re gonna love the view,” He says.

He opens the door and there it is. The Atlantic Ocean coastline can be seen for miles. It is truly stunning. The crew, minus Dave, who remained at the Yacht Club customizing Gran Tourismo for The Kid, take in the majestic view.

Kelly looks at his watch, “Dave should be finished soon,” he says. “We’ll go get him, then return here for some recon and to meet Moose's guys. Time to get this show on the road," he says.

"I have an eight o'clock with Demyan," Sal says.

They look at one another a bit awestruck at the many prospects facing them.

"Sparky should be here by now," Rollie says.

"Let's hit it," says The Kid. "I'm excited to start driving the old racetrack," he exclaims with a big smile on his face. "After a quick stop for ice cream, of course..."

They grab the elevator down and exit the historic Montauk Tower. Sparky is waiting outside the entrance.

X

They pile into the Taxi.

“Where’s this ice cream joint you mentioned.” The Kid asks Sparky.

“Right around the corner,” Sparky tells him.

“Someone should call Dave and ask him what flavor he wants,” Sal suggests.

“Pistachio…” Rollie tells them.

Sparky drives the few blocks to John’s Drive-in, and they jump out to get loads of ice cream. They return to the Yacht Club to find Dave hard at work in the suite testing Gran Tourismo, Montauk edition. The Kid nearly wets his pants when he sees it.

“This is so cool!” he exclaims.

“Not a glitch to speak of,” Dave says. He looks up at The Kid. “Fun, too,” he says.

“We brought you some Pistachio,” Sal tells him holding out a pint of ice cream.

“Thanks, Sal,” says Dave.

He gives The Kid the driver’s seat and grabs the pint of homemade ice cream.

“Hey… Kid…” Dave calls out.

No response as The Kid is already deeply engrossed in the game. Dave walks over and pulls one of the headphones off.

“Did you email the building plans for The Tower?” he asks into his ear.

The Kid turns around, “I emailed them this morning,” he says with a smile.

The Kid wastes no time getting back into Gran Tourismo.

“I’m going to work on my tan,” Sal tells everyone, walking towards the door.

“Good luck tonight, Sal,” Kelly tells her with an encouraging smile.

“You too, doll,” she says before exiting the room.

“Okay, we have six hours to create a maintenance issue and get a work order in place. Rollie, you need to find the best access to the basement,” Kelly says, looking at his watch. “Maintenance for The Tower,” he says handing Dave a piece of paper with the contact info for the outfit that maintains the Tower.

“Let me grab a shower and I’ll meet you guys outside,” Dave says, stuffing the notes in his pocket while enjoying a rather large spoonful of Pistachio ice cream.

“Sparky’s standing by. I’ll load the equipment into his taxi. So, whenever you’re ready...” Rollie tells him.

A short time later Kelly, Dave and Rollie are in the taxi heading to The Tower. Sparky at the wheel...

“Where can we make copies of this key,” Kelly asks Sparky holding up the key to the Tower Condo for Sparky to see.

“Becker’s Hardware. It’s a block away from the Tower. We’ll stop on the way,” he tells them.

Kelly turns to Dave, “So what emergency have you decided on?” he asks.

“Plumbing,” Dave says. “Specifically, sewage drainage...” he adds.

“Good idea,” says Kelly nodding his head imagining the potential mess such a situation could cause. Then imagining the management company rep imagining the same mess.

“I even made a stink bomb, just in case we need a convincer,” he Dave having fun with a spooky grin.

“Brilliant,” says Sparky. “You guys think of everything,” he says.

“Even you, Sparks, even you...” Kelly tells Sparky, looking at him through the rear-view mirror with a wink.

They pull into the parking lot behind Becker’s hardware and Sparky pulls into one of the three narrow parking spaces at the rear entrance.

“Be right back, Kelly tells them stepping out of the taxi.

A short time later Kelly appears with half a dozen condo keys. He jumps into the taxi and Sparky drives up the block to The Tower.

“Sal might need you at some point this evening, but stick around for a while,” Kelly tells Sparky as they pull in.

“No problem,” Sparky says smiling.

"I'm sure you have some notes to make for your book," Kelly says, smiling as he exits the taxi.

Sparky just grins.

"I printed these out before we left," Dave says referring to building plans of the Tower. "The external service entrance is tucked away around the side of the building," he says as they enter the Tower. "There's secondary access by a staircase that should be just around that bend," he says referring to a little hallway behind the elevator banks.

"No one's around. Let's take a look," says Kelly.

They wander over and find the door. It's locked. Rollie pulls out his Multiple Elite lockpick set.

"Wait!" says Kelly. He holds out his hand, "It's been a while... don't want to get rusty," he says.

Rollie hands him the lockpick set and within moments, Kelly unlocks the door.

"Just like the old days," Rollie says.

"Thanks pal, that meant a lot to me." With the smile of a twelve-year-old, Kelly hands Rollie his lockpick set.

"If you guys are done reminiscing," Dave says, passing them and heading down the stairs with his head mounted coal miner's flashlight.

"Wow, these foundation walls must be three feet thick," Rollie says.

"Which is why it has to be plumbing," Dave tells him. "The only things in and out of here are the water main and sewage pipes," Dave says knowingly, walking along the foundation wall looking for an opening.

“Here it is,” Kelly says, banging on a large cast-iron twelve-inch pipe.

Dave pulls out his compass, “Perfect,” he says. “This Tower is North by Northeast of the bank and this pipe is South by Southwest,” he states happily with a smile. “That means the service entrance should be right over there,” he says referring to the right of the sewage pipe.

He walks twenty feet or so and shines his light on two large steel doors.

“Let’s see exactly where this exits to,” he asks Rollie.

Rollie whips out his lockpick set and unlocks the door. It reveals a wide stairway heading up. He follows it and unlocks the next set of doors. Daylight pours in. He walks out and smiles.

“Couldn’t have ordered a better way in,” Rollie tells them. “We can back the van in from over there, and load the TBM in right here,” he says, rubbing his jaw, envisioning the load in. “No reason we can’t start work tonight.”

“You better get on that work order,” Kelly tells Dave.

“No problem, I already have a connection ready to intercept their phone lines,” Dave says. He looks up at Kelly with a proud mischievous smile. “Ingoing and outgoing calls,” he adds. “Now all we have to do is clog the pipe,” he smiles.

“I’ll get the gear,” Rollie says, moving towards the exit.

“Yeah, but take the lobby,” Kelly says. “We don’t technically have access to the service entrance yet.”

“Right,” Rollie says as he heads to the set of steps they first walked down.

Kelly and Dave watch him a moment. Kelly turns to Dave.

“This is gonna work,” he says excitedly.

“Did you ever have any doubt?” Dave asks.

“Yes.” Kelly admits.

They stand there a moment in silence.

“In for a penny, in for a pound,” Dave says.

Kelly gives Dave an odd look.

“Rollie’s not here to lend an apropos quotation, so I thought I’d fill in,” Dave says laughing.

They crack up laughing. A needed release of pent-up nerves as they embark on what most thieves wouldn’t even joke about doing. The best in the world consider it to be nothing less than monumental. Rollie appears with the duffel of tools to find Kelly and Dave in uproarious laughter. He begins to laugh as though it were contagious. The three of them laugh nearly to tears.

“Okay…” Dave says, catching his breath and looking at his watch. “We have a schedule to keep,” he says in a serious tone.

This ignites another bout of laughter. The three of them are laughing so hard they can barely breathe.

“Dave’s right,” Kelly says. “We have a hahahahaha,” he dissolves into belly-aching laughter.

Finally, the three of them calm down and get to work.

"This is my own Freon-generated, pipe-freeze device," Dave says proudly. "I'll have this pipe frozen solid in a matter of minutes," he adds. "When the toilets start backing up, the Suffolk County Water Authority will be getting a call," he says with a devious smile. "Water Authority," He says holding an imaginary phone to his ear and answering a call in a perfectly unenthusiastic government employee demeanor.

"You're a genius!" says Rollie.

"An artist!" Kelly insists.

"They'll call their local plumber first, that's the tricky part." Dave tells them. "We have to hide the freezer device, and a warming strip closer to this wall or a plumber will discover that it's frozen," Dave explains to them. "We'll dig in about four feet around the sewage pipe where I'll rig my Freon generated freeze element, with the edge warmer closer to the wall, then hide them both from view," Dave says illustrating what he means.

Rollie starts breaking away some of the earth surrounding the pipe with a pick ax, then a shovel.

"Where do you get a Freon-generated, pipe-freeze device?" Kelly asks.

"I invented it," Dave says. "Brainstormed it on the flight into the city, and put it together in my shop this afternoon," he tells them blowing on his fingernails then polishing them on his chest with a devious smile of satisfaction.

"You deserve the Nobel for science," Kelly says, smiling at his old pal.

"How long do you predict before we get the call from management?" Rollie asks, digging away.

"It depends, but as an occupant you can call and complain immediately," Dave says to Kelly.

"How long should it take?" Kelly asks looking at his watch.

"You'll know when you try to flush and it backs up on you," Dave tells him. "Maybe fifteen, twenty minutes after the freezing element is in place,"

Rollie stops digging a moment. He looks at his watch, "The crew will be here with the TBM in six hours," he says, smiling. "Maybe more with the add-on of the Water Authority stop in Yaphank to pick up some uniforms and a service vehicle," he says.

"Perfect... That should give us a lot of leeway," he adds.

"I'll hack into Water Authority computers and add this emergency service to their log," Dave tells them.

"Naturally, being a government agency, it could be weeks before they figure anything out," Kelly says smiling.

"If ever," Rollie says placing the shovel down. "Freeze away, doc," he says smiling at Dave.

Dave walks over and inspects the pipe, "That's plenty of room," he says. "Once the elements are in place, we'll pack the dirt back in and clean up any mess," he tells Rollie. "Can't have any fresh dirt around for the plumber to find," he adds.

"As a resident of a fifth-floor condominium, I feel the need to flush some toilets," Kelly says with a big smile. "See you guys later," he says taking the stairway up to the lobby.

Back at the Yacht Club, Sal is at the pool working on her tan, getting ready for her date with Demyan. The Kid is familiarizing himself with the old race-track on Gran Tourismo Montauk Edition. Sparky, on call, is sitting in the taxi typing away on his MacBook which he has balanced on the steering wheel. "*Despite being criminals, they're a lovable group*," he writes. "*While dining at Scarpetta...*" he goes on. He sits there a moment recalling recent episodes with the crew and what is about to unfold. A smile comes to his face. He shakes his head in amazement and continues writing.

XI

Within hours, Montauk Plumbing and Heating is on the scene at The Tower. Before long, they alert the management company that the problem appears to be the main sewer line and that they will have to call the Water Authority. Kelly, Dave and Rollie are relaxing in the condo with some takeout when Rollie's phone rings.

"Yeah," he answers. "Sounds good," he says nodding at Kelly and Dave. "Makes sense," he says into the phone. "We'll be ready to rock and roll by the time you guys get here," he says. He listens a moment, "Okay, see you then," he says.

"They've scouted the Water Authority yard in Yaphank and as soon as it's dark, they'll grab some uniforms and the truck," he tells Kelly and Dave.

"Great," Kelly says enjoying one of the elaborate hamburgers from the Montauk Circle Restaurant across the street from The Tower. Dave's cell phone rings. He looks at the number and nods his head at Kelly.

"Water Authority," he answers. He listens a moment. "Yeah," he says, sounding bored and world weary. "Montauk Plumbing and Heating?" Sure, I know dose guys, ...I trust 'em," he says convincingly. "We'll have a crew out there as soon as we can," he says. He listens a moment, "Tonight..." he says feigning the short patience of a blue-collar government employee. "That's the best I can do, honey,' he says finally. "We're all the way out in Yaphank for crying out loud," he says looking over at Rollie, "Maybe two hours, maybe three..." he says. Rollie gives him an affirmative. "Yeah, we have the keys," Dave says. "Okay, meanwhile make sure no one flushes or showers till we can get in there, see what the problem is and correct it," he says finally. "Last week we had an apartment complex in Huntington clogged for hours cause some kid flushed her stuffed tiger down the drain... damn kids!" he adds smiling. "Right," he says into the phone. "I'll call you the minute we know what's going on," he says. "All right, doll..." he says listening. "Sure, give it to me," he says. "And try to relax," he adds. "You did all you could do..." he tells her with an air of encouragement. "Okay, talk to you later," he says, ending the call.

"Nicely done," says Kelly smiling at Dave.

"A real blue-collar pro," Rollie says. "I feel like I just got off the phone with Con Ed," he says and laughs.

Rollie and Kelly watch Dave punch a cell number into his phone.

"Her cell number," he says.

Kelly and Rollie look at each other, obviously impressed.

"You know I have a photographic memory," Dave reminds them.

A few hours later everything begins fall into place. Moose's Lithuanian's arrive with the TBM and a Suffolk County Water Authority truck. They load in and Rollie supervises assembly of the TBM. Dave gives them the parameters of depth and direction and the boys start drilling. First, they cut through a large enough section of the steel reinforced concrete foundation facing South Southeast for the TBM to fit, and then into the sandy soil that is the East End of Long Island. Dave warns them that they will likely encounter a few boulders along the way left behind from the last ice age.

"Ice age?" one of Moose's crew asks in his thick Lithuanian accent. "What are you, Bill Nye, the Science Guy?" he asks.

“Just dig, smart-ass,” Dave tells him.

Demyan arrives at the Montauk Yacht Club in a dark blue Ferrari. Sal acts impressed as she steps into the car.

“Nice ride, Demy,” she comments with her sultry coy smile.

“Demy… I like that,” he says before screeching off. “Like pet name,” he says, showing off his driving skills.

Sal can’t help but to think how envious The Kid would be. “Not so fast, hot pants,” Sal says. “Let’s enjoy the night air,” she tells him.

“Ah… you like my taste in car,” Demyan says, glancing over at Sal, seeking approval.

“Very much,” she says, cool as a cucumber. “It’s a real man’s car,” she says, spatting his thigh and smiling at him.

Demyan is distracted enough that he nearly hits a deer in the middle of the road.

“Dumb animals!” he yells, screeching to a stop.

Pulled over on the side of West Lake Drive, he turns to Sal, and as cool as he can manage, asks, “So, my leetle Salishka, vhere shall we have dinner zis evening?”

“I don’t know, lover, why don’t you choose?” she says playing into his machismo.

“Maybe zee Surf Lodge,” he says. “It is the hot spot of Montauk and vee should try it,” he says.

“Sounds divine,” Sal says. “I was told at dinner the other night that one of the owners, Jayma, is the goddess of Montauk,” she tells him.

“No! You are zee goddess of Montauk,” Demyan insists with a ‘Pepe le Pew’ smile.

“Tomorrow my yacht will arrive, and my chef vill make for us real Russian food,” he says matter of course.

“Nostrovia,” Sal says, smiling. “I love the water.”

“Goot!” he says, feeling victorious as he screeches off.

Back at The Tower, the crew has the TBM in place and are about to start digging. Dave is in the parking lot sitting in the passenger seat of the Water Authority service vehicle. He dials a number on his cell.

“Yeah, how ya doin…’” he says. “Dis is da Water Authority ova here,” he says. He listens a moment. “Yeah, we got a serious problem on our hands,” he says sounding dire. “The sewer main is completely blocked, but we can’t tell exactly how far in the clogged section is so we’ll have to dig till we find it, before we can make da repair,” he states. He listens a moment, “Uh hunh…” he says. “Dat’s right,” he says smiling. “There’s no way to tell till we get in there,” he tells her. “I don’t know,” he insists. “Could take a few hours, could be days… There’s really no way to tell,” he warns her. He listens a moment. “Miss, no reason to cry,” he says. “Crying won’t help a thing,” he says. “All’s we can do is hope and pray for da best,” he says in the best blue-collar sympathetic voice he has. “Yeah, I know…” he says. “I’ll call the minute we got something definitive den. Yeah, okay. Goodbye,” he says.

He ends the call then laughs to himself. He sits there and laughs aloud. Kelly walks up to find Dave seated in the van all alone, laughing to himself.

“Management call?” he asks, already knowing the answer.

Dave looks over to him, “You missed a classic,” Dave tells him.

“How much time do we have?” Kelly asks him.

“Could take a few hours, could be days... Dere’s really no way to tell,” he repeats in character.

Kelly gets a good laugh out of it. “You’re a genius,” he says. “How are the boys doing?” he asks.

“Let’s go see,” Dave says.

They enter the service entrance walk down the steps till they reach Rollie and the Lithuanians behind a classic workman-styled enclosure made of hanging tarps. Dave and Kelly enter the ‘Workman Only’ area and find Rollie.

“How we doin?” Dave asks.

“Better than expected,” Rollie tells him. “Shin’s modifications are exceeding original specs,” he says with a broad smile.

“When do you estimate we’ll reach the bank? Dave asks.

“Drilling round the clock, two days tops,” he says over the sound of Lithuanians drilling.

“That gives us a two-day cushion,” Kelly says.

“And I just may need it for the turret modifications which I’ll be guesstimating,” Dave says, clasping his hands.

Kelly looks around the immediate area, “What do those guys eat?” he asks.

“They said they wanted pizza,” Rollie tells him.

“Okay, I’ll go get the pizza. Be back in a few,” he says.

“I’ll head back to the service vehicle in case anybody shows up,” says Dave. “Like my shirt?” he asks Kelly, referring to the Suffolk County Water Authority shirt he’s wearing.

“It’s you, Mel,” says Kelly.

Dave grabs the name patch that says Mel on the shirt.

“That’s Supervisor Mel to you, bud,” Dave says smiling.

“He’s a good boss,” Rollie says to Kelly with a smile.

“Make those Everything Pizzas,” Rollie tells him. “And some Cokes with that pie,” he adds.

“You got it. Roll… be back before you know it,” he says. Kelly grabs his phone as he exits and calls Sparky. “Sparky!” he says. “What’s the best pizza in town,” Kelly asks.

“Ah… there’s a lot of debate about that in Montauk. Some insist it’s Sausage’s others, La Prima Vera… But, for me it’s Pizza Village,” he says.

“Okay, meet me at the Tower, will ya? Time to feed the crew,” he tells him.

“On my way,” Sparky says. He closes up his MacBook, puts the taxi in gear and hits the gas.

Before long Sparky appears at the rear entrance of The Tower.

“How’s it goin’ down there?” Sparky asks.

"Great!" Kelly tells him. "We're ahead of schedule," he adds.

They drive to Pizza Village.

"Do you know of a commercial fisherman, who, shall we say, has an adventurous streak?" Kelly asks Sparky with a wry expression.

"How adventurous? Sparky asks as he pulls up to Pizza Village.

"Adventurous enough to let us use his boat as command central and to track a missile filled with stolen bank loot a few miles out to sea, then get us to shore safely," Kelly says matter of fact.

Sparky looks at him, not sure who he could possibly approach for such a task. "There has to be at least one captain out there who'd jump at the chance, but no one's coming to mind," he says.

"Think about it a minute, I'll order the pizza," Kelly says, looking at his watch.

He steps out of the taxi and into Pizza Village. Sparky watches him through the large windows of the pizza shop, admiring the way he interacts with people, how he seems to make everyone he encounters feel special and rare.

"The art of the con..." Sparky says to himself softly.

Kelly returns to the taxi and steps into the front passenger seat. Kelly tells him, "It'll take fifteen minutes... Let's grab a cooler, ice and some cokes."

Sparky puts it in gear and drives p the street to the IGA.

“Any ideas on a nefarious captain?” he asks turning to Sparky.

“I have a few ideas, but,” he says looking into Kelly’s eyes, “I’ll need to test the waters... See who might best fit such a unique voyage,” he says to Kelly’s smile.

Kelly shops for the cokes, cooler and ice. Sparky helps him put it all in the luggage bay of the taxi.

“Do you have any problem being the one to approach them?” Kelly asks, stepping back into the taxi.

“I would prefer it that way,” Sparky tells him. “How much time do we have?” he asks.

He drives back to Pizza Village.

“July Fourth is ‘D’ Day,” Kelly says. “Today’s the twenty-eighth, so we have five days. The tunnel will be ready by July 1st... I’d like to have someone in place in two or three days,” Kelly tells him.

“What can I offer as compensation?” he says looking at Kelly knowingly. “Whoever it is, they’ll likely want an advance to secure the vessel and the crew,” he adds.

Sparky picks his brain trying to think who, how and why a commercial fishing captain would take on such an outlandish crime.

“We don’t want a total cowboy, yet it has to be someone daring...” Sparky says, thinking aloud almost to himself.

“Exactly,” Kelly says smiling.

“You’re a natural, Sparks! We’re lucky to have you on board,” he adds.

Sparky thinks about that for a moment. There have been substantial changes to the situation, and however generous it is, they haven't discussed an adjustment to his original deal of $10,000 to match his increased participation in the project.

"How lucky?" Sparky asks with a sly smile.

Kelly is grinning ear to ear.

"I'm glad you asked," answers Kelly still grinning. "Naturally, now that the dynamic has... evolved, our agreement will also," Kelly tells him. "Once we've secured a commercial fishing boat captain and his boat... After the robbery and retrieval at sea," he says still thinking, "When the dust settles... you meet us wherever we end up," he says. "How does $250,000 sound?"

They sit there a moment silent. Kelly checks the time, then peers into the pizza shop. He sees two large everything pizzas coming out of the oven. He turns to Sparky with a smile.

"My pies are ready," he says pointing at Village Pizza with his chin.

He steps out of the taxi. Sparky measures the risk he is taking verses the potential earnings. Essentially, he has the perfect cover. He's hired to drive tourists around during their stay. If they break the law and are caught, he can't legally be held responsible. It's actually a pretty clean deal. He's deep into his inner deliberation as Kelly exits Pizza Village. Sparky opens the passenger side automatic doors,

Kelly places the pizzas on the back seat, and they take off for The Tower.

"Securing a commercial fishing boat captain will be tricky. I have to be extremely covert, finding a way to choose the right man for the job without revealing too many details of what the job is until he's agreed to do it," Sparky says, pulling into traffic on Montauk Highway. "In the event, he isn't game," he adds.

He turns left past the Chase Bank towards the Tower and pulls into the parking lot where Dave is seated in the emergency vehicle.

"If he isn't game…" Kelly repeats.

Sparky stops the car, puts it in park and turns to Kelly.

"Then we have a problem," they both say in perfect synchronicity.

The two just sit there smiling at one another in amazement. Dave struts over.

"You guys just waiting for the pizza to get to the right level of cool?" he asks in his blue-collar Suffolk County Water Authority supervisor persona, "or are we gonna feed the crew?"

The three of them crack up laughing. Sparky holds out his hand to Kelly.

"It's a deal," he says.

He and Kelly shake on it.

"Of course," Sparky adds, "I am a taxi driver…" he looks at Kelly with raised eyebrow, "And you ALWAYS tip the driver," he says with a smile to challenge Kelly's.

Kelly loves it, "I'm sure there'll be a substantial gratuity," he says.

They get out of the taxi to find Dave grabbing a slice and a coke.

"Got a napkin?" Dave asks. "Never mind, I'll use my sleeve," Dave tells them. "More fitting of Mel." He wipes his mouth with his sleeve.

They can't help but to crack up laughing.

Sparky and Kelly are still laughing as they grab the pies and the cooler of iced colas. They arrive at the work site past the hanging tarpaulin to find Rollie and the Lithuanians taking a break.

"Perfect timing," Rollie says.

He grabs one of the pizza boxes and sets it on a folding table.

"Ah! Pizza!" one of the Lithuanians exclaim.

He tears open a box, grabs a slice and rips off half the slice with his teeth. As he chews the gargantuan bite, he wipes his mouth with his sleeve. Sparky and Kelly look at one another and break into hysterical laughter.

The Lithuanian looks at them and says, "OK, so I vas hungry!" he says. "Vee are working kere!" he says excitedly.

Kelly grabs a bottle of coke and offers it to him,

"Vat! No beer?" he asks incredulously. "A working man must kave beer!" he exclaims loudly as the other Lithuanian shoves him aside to get to the pizza, "Move it, Matis," he says.

Rollie looks at Kelly with a shrug of the shoulders.

"They drink beer all day," he says. "Seem to be immune to it."

"Cold beer comin' up," Kelly tells the Lithuanians.

"Goot!" he says, grabbing another slice.

"Make it Jovaru Alus," the Lithuanian says, taking another gargantuan bite.

"Jovaru Alus it is. Let's go, partner," Kelly says to Sparky. "Be right back," he tells Rollie.

Kelly turns a moment, "You need anything?" he asks Rollie.

"I'm good, thanks."

They get outside to find Dave seated in the emergency vehicle on the phone doing his best Mel impression. He ends the call and looks over at Kelly.

"Everything good?" Kelly asks.

"Yeah... just stringing her along," Dave says.

"Great work, Mel," Kelly tells him.

"Hey, check on The Kid, will ya?" Dave asks. "Make sure he's okay with the Gran Tourismo. Didn't have the chance to check it as thoroughly as I would have liked to," he adds. "We don't need The Kid clamming up and trying to hot-dog it," he tells Kelly as a forewarning.

"Good point, Mel," he smiles.

Sparky's waiting in the taxi when Kelly gets there.

"Montauk Beer and Soda's right around the corner," he tells Kelly. "Dottie runs the place and is a real sweetheart," he adds.

"Does she know any fisherman?" Kelly asks.

"What are you, a mind reader?" Sparky says looking at Kelly.

Sparky hits the gas and they drive a few blocks away to Montauk Beer and Soda.

"She knows everyone in town," Sparky says as they pull up. He turns to Kelly, "But, she's no idiot... She'll read into this real quick and this *is* a small town after all," he says. "Liars is our best bet. And the Dock," he adds entering Montauk Beer and Soda.

"Hey, Dottie," Sparky says with a smile.

"Hi, sweetheart," she says smiling.

"You have any Jovaru Alus?" he asks.

"What is that, Lithuanian?" she asks.

"Not sure, someone asked me to get a case or two," he tells her with a shrug,

"Let me check, honey," Dottie tells him.

"Two six-packs left," she says.

"I'll take 'em both," Sparky tells her. "Any way you can order a few cases?" Sparky asks. "These guys are staying a while," he says.

"Probably sharkin..." Dottie says. "Lithuanians love shark meat," she says. "No sweat, honey, truck's comin' tomorrow... "Hey Lou!" She says loudly to the back of the store. "Add a few cases of that Lithuanian beer for tomorrow's delivery."

'You got it, Dot," he says.

Sparky pays for the beer. "Thanks Dottie, see ya tomorrow," he says.

"OK, doll," she says. He grabs the beer and heads to the taxi where Kelly's on the phone talking to The Kid.

"All right, Kid. Keep up the good work, pal," he says and ends the call.

They drive off towards The Tower. When they get down to the worksite with the beer, Kelly lets Rollie know he and Sparky are going out to secure a commercial fishing boat. They jump in the taxi and head up to the Harbor to find a captain.

Meanwhile at the Surf Lodge, Sal and Demyan enjoy shots of Stolichnaya as local rocker Nancy Atlas performs.

"You drink like Russian!" Demyan tells her, downing a shot, pleased with her ability to drink.

"I'm impressed you can keep up with me, Demy." She laughs.

"Smarty pants, hunh?" he says laughing then leaning over trying to grab a kiss.

"Not so fast, hot-pants. We've only just met," she tells him teasingly.

"Okay... Okay... I love goot challenge," he says pouring another round.

"So do I, Demy," she says shooting down the Stolichnaya. "So do I..."

XII

Sparky and Kelly arrive at the Dock Restaurant. Sparky pulls in close to the commercial docks at the end of the short street.

“Somewhere out there is our vessel,” Kelly says.

“Just gotta find the right one,” Sparky says.

They gaze out over the commercial boats for a moment.

“Let’s take a walk down to the end,” Sparky suggests.

“Yeah, good idea” Kelly agrees.

They walk out onto the old massive timbers of the wooden dock, stopping occasionally while Sparky explains what he knows about the different types of rigging on each boat.

“I don’t think we want a netter,” Sparky says referring to a commercial fishing boat rigged with a large spool of green and white fishnets. “I think a longliner would be best,” he explains, referring to a sixty-foot boat rigged for longline fishing. “They mainly go for swordfish around here, and tuna sometimes,” he tells Kelly as they head back towards the Dock Restaurant.

“How’s the food here?” Kelly asks.

“Surprisingly good,” Sparky tells him. “We should eat at the bar,” he adds.

“Good idea,” Kelly says.

He smiles at Sparky, impressed at his being fast on his feet and always thinking.

"At first glance, it looks like a period bar that might serve a decent hamburger." He turns to Kelly and adds, "They only offer like five entrées, but they make the best clam chowder in town and the soft shell crabs are not to be missed," he tells Kelly.

They enter the lively Dock Restaurant and grab a seat at the bar.

"What'll you have?" a somewhat gruff yet attractive, tattooed female bartender asks.

Kelly glances at Sparky.

"Guinness for me," Sparky tells her.

"Make that two," Kelly tells her.

She pours the beer and serves them up.

"Can we see a menu?" Kelly asks.

"Sure," she says pulling a few damp menus from under the bar.

They sip the Guinness for a while in the din of the noisy bar.

"I wonder how Sal's doing," Kelly says, sipping his stout.

"From what I've been able to discern of Sal, I'll guess she has the Russian wrapped around her little finger," Sparky says taking a healthy swig of his Guinness.

Kelly smiles. "You're probably right. Sal and I have been together the longest," Kelly tells him, glancing at the menu.

Sparky smiles. "How'd you guys meet?" he asks.

"That's a long story for another day," Kelly assures him.

"You know what you're having?" Sparky asks, looking over at Kelly.

"The chowder and crabs you suggested feel good," he says.

Sparky gets the bartender's attention.

"Yeah, we'll have two Montauk chowders and two soft shell crabs," Sparky tells her.

"You got it," She says grabbing the menus.

Two men at the end of the bar are talking about fishing.

"Listen," Sparky says pointing at them with his chin.

"I had a tuna at the end of the snood must a been three hundred pounds," the old timer says sipping his Budweiser. "I was about to yank it in when a great white reared up and snapped it right off the hook," he says. "Nearly took my hand along with it," he says, shaking his head. "Sportsman don't know what it's like out there," he says. "Always writing those damned articles about how bad longlining is for the fish population.

"Idiots!" his friend says. "The bycatch from us longliners is a fraction of netters and draggers," he says sipping his Budweiser. "But you never see complaints for those guys, always the longliners," he says frustrated. "As though the DEC isn't enough of a problem," he says. "Hell, yes! It seems we got more regulations than fish nowadays," he says.

"And Seggos is all talk," his friend says angrily.

Sparky and Kelly listen intently.

“Miss…” Sparky says to the bartender.

“Yeah?” she asks. “I’d like to buy a round for our hardworking fishermen,” he says gallantly referring to the two men seated a few stools down at the bar. The men hear the exchange, look over at Sparky. Kelly raises his Guinness.

“Gents…” he says with a smile.

The bartender grabs two bottles of Bud and serves them up. The men raise their bottles.

“Thanks, fellas,” one of them says.

“Couldn’t help overhearing what you were saying about fishing regulations,” Kelly says.

“Yeah, we longliners get it six ways from Sunday, and in some ways the draggers got it even worse than us,” fisherman number two says.

“New York only gets seven and a half percent of the state quota for fluke, while North Carolina and Virginia each get more than twenty percent,” fisherman number one says, gulping his Budweiser.

The Bartender serves up the clam chowder.

“I’m guessing you guys are suing them?” Sparky says shaking black pepper into his chowder.

“Yeah, Bonnie Brady, of the Long Island Commercial Fishing Association’s overseeing that,” fisherman two tells them. “They leave us little choice but to sue,” he says. “Damned quotas were set decades ago! Based on incomplete data of the coast-wide catch,” he adds.

"It just doesn't apply anymore," fisherman one insists.

"Decades?" Kelly says, sounding astonished.

"I went to the meeting last year and told Seggos,", he sips his beer, then looks up at Sparky and Kelly and adds, "He's the state commissioner of the DEC. We grilled that son-of-a-bitch for two hours, I told him that the reason there's no young people in the room is because our quota isn't big enough. There's nothing to give new people incentive to become fisherman anymore."

Kelly reaches out his hand. "Kelly," he says.

"Hank," fisherman number one says, shaking Kelly's hand.

"I'm guessing it's tough enough making a living as a commercial fisherman without having government bureaucrats up your ass," Sparky says.

"You got that right, chief," Hank heartily agrees.

"I'd love to get out there sometime," Kelly says. "See what's it like, first hand," he adds. "Sparky here's a writer, and part of his book involves a commercial fisherman," Kelly tells them.

"Oh, yeah?" Hank asks.

"Wouldn't you like to get out there?" Kelly asks turning to Sparky.

"Man! Wouldn't I!" Sparky says enthusiastically. "Probably more work than I can handle," he adds, smiling at the fisherman.

"Hey, you guys want a shot?" Kelly asks. "What do you fellas drink?" he asks.

"Most people would assume rum, being fisherman and all, but I think Jameson's," Sparky says looking at the two fisherman.

"Or tequila," Kelly adds.

"Whatdy'a think, Buddy?" Hank asks, turning to his friend.

"I could drink a tequila," Buddy says.

"I'm Buddy." He reaches out to shake Kelly's hand.

"Hey, Buddy," Kelly says.

"I'm Kelly and this is Sparky," he tells him.

"Hey, Sparky," Buddy greets Sparky.

"Buddy," Sparky says, raising his glass.

"What about you, Hank?" Sparky asks.

"Tequila works for me," he says with a broad smile.

"Miss?" Sparky asks the bartender.

"Tequila?" she asks knowingly.

"Casamigo, if you have it," Sparky says.

"Four Casamigos comin' up," she says.

"Unless you're game?" Sparky asks her.

She looks at him and smiles.

"Five Casamigos!" she exclaims, pouring a fifth shot for herself. She raises her Tequila. "Gents," she says before shooting it down. "Damn, that's smooth," she says.

"You're a writer?" Hank asks Sparky, sipping his Tequila.

"Yeah, I'm writing a book," Sparky tells him.

"And it's about fishing?" Hank asks, shooting the rest of his Tequila down.

"Not entirely," Sparky says, sipping his Tequila.

Kelly listens closely. As does Buddy. Even the bartender is intrigued.

"If it's not about fishing, where does the fisherman come in?" Hank asks.

"Another round for everyone, please," Kelly tells the bartender.

"Sure thing, doll," she says, giving the handsome and charming Kelly a sweet smile.

"It has fisherman in it... The part with the fisherman is," Sparky looks at Kelly a moment. "Sort of an ode to the prohibition days of old when some fisherman also ran booze from Rum Row," he tells Hank.

The Bartender serves up the drinks.

"Ah..." Hank comments with a broad smile, "You're talkin' my Grandad now," he says with a noticeable degree of affection.

"You don't say?" Kelly asks, happy to hear they're speaking with a descendent of a rumrunner.

"I was just a teenager, startin' to work on the boats longlining. He told me some stories all right," Hank says, reminiscing.

Hank looks up at Sparky and Kelly, “You two really want to get out?” he asks.

“I would consider it an honor,” Kelly tells him.

“I’m game,” Sparky agrees.

“All right then, I’m the ‘Sally Ann’ at the end of the dock back here,” Hank says pointing over his shoulder at the commercial dock at the end of the street Kelly and Sparky took a tour of before entering the restaurant.

The Bartender serves up the soft-shell crabs.

“These look great, thanks,” Kelly tells her.

“We sail at dawn,” Hank says, finishing his beer and standing up.

“Be there or be square,” Buddy tells them, also getting up to leave.

“We’ll be there,” Kelly assures them.

“Enjoy your meal, fellas.” Hank says with his hand on Kelly’s shoulder. “And thanks for the cheer,” Hank says referring to the bar with his chin.

“Anytime,” Kelly tells him.

“See ya, Lou,” he says to the bartender.

“See ya round, Hank,” she says. “Good luck tomorrow,” she adds. “You guys, too,” she says to Sparky and Kelly.

Sparky and Kelly are ecstatic as they dig into their delicious soft-shell crab. They finish the meal, leave a good tip and take their leave. Back in the taxi they look at one another.

"Hank just may be the ideal captain for our mission," Kelly says.

"Yeah..." Sparky says thinking about it. "He might see it as an opportunity to live up to the legend of his grandfather," he says.

Kelly looks at his watch, it's ten o'clock. "Dawn," he says.

"I'll pick you up at 4:30," Sparky says. "You have a pair of deck shoes?" he asks Kelly.

"I'll improvise something," Kelly says smiling. "We'll check in on Rollie and the Lithuanians, then straight to bed," he says, raising his eyebrows at Sparky.

"What a life," Sparky says, pulling away.

They stop at The Tower to find Dave asleep in the Suffolk County Water Authority emergency vehicle. Kelly looks at him asleep in the passenger seat, then over at Sparky and says, "A true government employee."

Rollie and the Lithuanians are moving along at a good pace so Sparky drives Kelly to the Yacht Club and pulls up to the front entrance. He turns to Kelly who appears deep in thought. "I can't believe you guys are really doing this," he says.

He looks over at Sparky with a quizzical look.

"Don't think about it too hard," he says, his hand on Sparky's shoulder, "It'll scare you, half to death..." he adds.

Sparky looks straight ahead running his hands through his full head of hair.

"After all, only a crazy person would rob the Chase Bank in Montauk with one road out of town," Kelly says smiling.

"And the Coast Guard down the street," Sparky adds pointing to the end of Star Island.

Kelly steps out of the taxi, "See you at dawn," he says.

Sparky watches him walk into the hotel with a wry expression and a shake of the head, most of him in disbelief that he has become a part of this audacious scheme. He sits there a moment and thinks back to his pool-hustling days. He realizes now that, at the time, he was too young to have the degree of perspective that would allow him to understand what was really happening. In the years since it has become clear to him that it was his age that allowed him to be challenged so readily and for such high stakes. He recalls the time he made nearly five thousand dollars and how frightened he was walking home that night. He thinks about the time he was beaten up by three sore losers who accused him of being a much older man. A hustler playing a boy to trip up his marks. He's lost in thought, being torn a bit from the emotional impact of the memories, when he hears a familiar voice.

"Hi, Sparky," Sal says standing at the driver's side window, having just been dropped off from her dinner date with Demyan. "Where were you just then?" she asks.

He looks at her, still feeling a bit emotional from his recollections. Recollections of a part of his life he'd presumed long gone.

"Second thoughts?" she asks in a rare sensitive moment.

"Kelly and I are going fishing tomorrow," he says.

She smiles, “Oh? Do tell.”

“We met a longliner at The Dock and he invited us to go out with him,” Sparky says with a big smile on his face. “At dawn...” he adds with a somebody’s-gotta-do-it shrug of the shoulders. “His grandfather was a rumrunner during prohibition,” he continues.

“Sounds a likely candidate,” Sal says, intrigued.

“I’ll be here at 4:30 in the a.m. to pick Kelly up,” he says.

“Fishing at dawn...” she says, glad it’s not her. “You better get some sleep, Sparks,” she says with a sweet smile. “I’m happy you’re a part of the crew for this one,” she says, holding his arm for a moment.

“Me too,” he says smiling at her. “Me too...”

He puts the taxi in gear and pulls away. Sal watches for a moment as he drives off.

“Sparky...” she says to herself with a wry smile.

XIII

With less than a week till D-Day, the plan is developing nicely. The Lithuanians are making great headway digging the tunnel, Sparky and Kelly might just have found the perfect commercial fishing boat captain, The Kid will be able to drive the old racetrack blindfolded by blast off and Sal has Demyan wrapped around her little finger. Sparky rolls up to the Montauk Yacht Club to find Kelly there waiting. Kelly looks at his watch, smiles at Sparky and steps into the taxi.

“I thought for sure I’d have to wake you up,” Sparky says.

“Let’s go fishing,” Kelly says.

“I got us some coffee,” says Sparky, handing Kelly a takeout Brazilian coffee from 711.

They drive over to the commercial fishing dock, step out of the taxi and stroll up the old timbers of the dock doing their best not to look like the two landlubber greenhorns that they are. Hank’s already aboard the forty-six-foot Thames-built wooden-freezer trawler rigged for longlining named Sally Ann. He sees them and shakes his head, smiling ear to ear, surprised that they actually made it.

“Morning, fellas,” he says, laughing a little. “Have to admit, I’m a little surprised to see you two,”

“Permission to come aboard?” Sparky asks.

“Come on up, fellas,” Hank says, impressed that they knew to ask.

The two neophytes climb aboard the large vessel, neither quite sure what to expect.

"Welcome aboard the Sally Ann," Hank says like a true captain. "I can't tell you how many guys just like you two, who I've invited out because they expressed an interest, that never showed up," Hank says while organizing some floats and tie lines around the deck.

Two crewmen arrive carrying large heavy bags of groceries and climb aboard.

"Hey, Hank," one of the men says.

"Morning, Steve," Hank says. "This is, um, what are your names again?" he asks.

"Kelly," Kelly says grabbing one of the large grocery bags from Steve.

"Thanks, man," Steve says.

Hank is impressed and seems pleased by Kelly grabbing one of the heavy bags. So is Sparky.

"If you're gonna carry that, follow me down below," Steve says, stepping below deck into the cabin.

Sparky follows suit and grabs a bag from the other crew member.

"Sparky," he says.

"Evan," the crewman says with a Jamaican accent. "Come on, man," he says. "We load this down below," he tells Sparky.

A few minutes later they return to the deck to find two other longliners aboard.

Hank starts the large diesel engine. Smoke billows from the large exhaust pipes that run up the sides of the helm. Hank and the crew check various parts of the boat.

“Check the livewell,” Hank tells Steve.

“You got it, Skipper,” Steve shouts.

He moves briskly over to a control panel, flips a switch then goes below. Hank checks the stays to make sure they’re nice and tight.

“Livewell’s up and running,” Steve reports, returning topside.

Hank looks around one last time. The crew stands by in anticipation.

“Okay fellas… let’s shove off,” Hank tells them.

Some of the crew head to the gunwales, untie bowlines and yank in the bumpers as Hank puts her in gear and pulls out of the dock. They move through the harbor and putter through the inlet. The dawn light is starting to show colors as Hank opens up the throttle and heads out to sea. Kelly and Sparky join Hank at the helm for the ride out to the shelf. When they arrive, the crew bait hooks set at the end of the snoods attached to the mainline by swivels, then drop them in the water. As Hank mans the ship, he explains how they’ll mark the end of the line with a buoy then go back and reel in the mainline to see if they’ve hooked any fish.

“I could fill my holds back when. Did so a few times,” Hank tells them. “But not anymore,” he says sadly. “Federal regulations set by the NOAA has set some pretty stringent limits these days,” he says. “Makes it tough to make a good living anymore.”

Kelly looks over at Sparky and winks. “There have to be ways to make up for that lost income,” he says to Hank. Hank gives him a curious look. “I mean, having such an impressive vessel as this,” he checks Sparky’s reaction, “There must be the occasional opportunity,” he says.

“Yeah, like your grandfather did during prohibition,” Sparky adds.

Hank smiles. “Those were the days,” he tells them.

“Sure were!” Kelly says with enthusiasm. “Prohibition created a booming industry of rum-running and bootlegging. This place with its close proximity to New York City, access to water. Being isolated, Montauk was a significant hub for rum-running,” Kelly says, espousing his vast knowledge of history.

“You a professor or just a history buff?” Hank asks.

“Kelly loves his history,” Sparky tells him. “As long as I’ve known Kelly, he can go off in detail about all kinds of historical events,” he adds.

“My old grandpa told me how they used the fog to lose the Coast Guard. The rain, too,” Hank says smiling. “He was a dragger by day and rum-runner by night,” Hank says and laughs at the memory. “He told me he’d go out fishing all day, go home, have dinner with the family, then after dark get out his Chris Craft thirty-foot twin and ride out to the twelve-mile mark just outside US Territorial Waters, where cutters from Europe, Nova Scotia, even Jamaica would wait for the likes of Grandpa to show up in their speed boats,” Hank tells them.

“That puts a new spin on the romance of the sea,” Sparky says smiling.

"Oh yeah... Grandpa told me that during prohibition, nearly every night, they would sneak out of Fort Pond Bay in their speed boats and head straight for the Rum Line, as he called it... They'd bring boat-loads of booze back to the shores of Gin Beach, Shagwong and Oyster Pond," Hank says, getting deeper and deeper into the heroic romance of the rum-running days of his renegade grandfather. "Local fisherman could outmaneuver the Coast Guard most of the time, too," he says with a coy smile. "Knowing these waters, the way they did, those Coast Guard boys never had a chance," he says happy to talk about the rum-running days of his grandfather.

"Knowledge is power," Sparky says smiling at Hank.

"That's right," Hank says turning to Sparky with an agreeable yet curious expression. "And once the booze made it to shore, most all of it was loaded into secret compartments custom built into the false bottoms of trucks and cars, then transported up island and New York City for distribution," he tells them.

Kelly smiles, "That was a major boom for port towns all over America back then," he says, smiling at Hank.

"It was hard work," Hank says. Some nights he even had Grandma and my dad out there loading up the trucks!"

"Only, before too long, gangsters like Dutch Schultz and Al Capone turned pirate, hijacking competing rum-runners," Kelly adds with a saddened face.

"That's right," Hank says. "My grandpa told me a story or two about Dutch and Capone," he says thinking back. "Said they fought Dutch's boys off on Whiskey Road in Yaphank one night," he says. "Ran 'em into a tree, shooting out their front tire in a chase." He laughed.

"Yaphank, hunh?" Kelly says looking at his watch wondering how Dave, Rollie and the Lithuanians are making out.

"That's when he got out," Hank tells them. "It just got too damn dangerous," he says. "Al Capone mostly worked the North Fork," he says. "But he was down here often enough to be a problem. Bad enough fighting weather and the Coast Guard, but when the likes of Dutch Schultz and Al Capone are shooting at you, it just stopped being worth the trouble, old Grandpa told me," Hank says, reminiscing.

"More than anything else, all the Volstead Act achieved was creating the American gangster," Sparky says.

"Yup," Hank says, agreeing with Sparky.

Steve shows up at the helm, "We're set, Skip," he tells Hank, looking at Kelly and Sparky curious, bordering on suspiciously. Maybe a little jealous.

"Okay, Steve, turning around." Hank steers the boat around for a go.

Steve heads back to the deck.

"Rum-runners figured out how to take advantage of a bad situation," Kelly says trying to imagine what it was like.

"Yeah, a lot of fisherman got in on the action back then," Hank says. "Till Dutch and Capone showed up," he adds. "By then it was either work for one of them or get out," he says with a serious expression as he maneuvers the boat.

"What about now?" Kelly asks.

He can sense Hank working a slew of considerations in his head. Hank's no greenhorn. He's been around the block a few times...

"I had a feeling there was something more than fishing on your mind when you guys actually showed up this morning," Hank tells them as he makes the run at just the right speed, as though it's second nature to him.

"If an opportunity came up that involved breaking the law, but had great rewards," Kelly says as nonchalantly as he can, peeking over at Sparky, "Would you consider taking the risk?"

Hank looks at Kelly, then at Sparky. He steps out of the cabin and calls to his lead man, "Okay, Steve, goin' in," he calls out. "Let's see if we caught any fish." Hank turns the boat around so the crew can check the hooks they've been setting since reaching the shelf.

He motors back to the buoy where they started. The boys gaff the mainline and start checking the snoods. Like a well-trained relay team, they pull in the empty hooks, pull them off the swivels and set them back in their proper place for the next run.

"Fish!" Steve calls out.

Hank idles the throttle. The team sets a gaff into a huge swordfish and yanks it on deck.

"Whoooo! She's a big girl," Jamaican Evan screams, wrestling the swordfish onto the deck where it can be gutted and put in the freezer hold till they get back to shore.

Five more are brought in the same way. Sparky and Kelly watch closely, fascinated by the process.

"Set the line!" Hank yells to the crew once they have all the fish in the hold. He glances at Kelly then Sparky, "We'll take one or two more runs then head back," he tells them.

"Just wanted to give you fellas a taste of what it's like out here."

"Dropping," Steve yells out.

Hank revs the throttle just a bit so they can set the hooks in the water at twenty-foot intervals. He gazes out over the vast ocean.

"What do you have in mind?" Hank asks Kelly, turning towards him with a curious smile.

Kelly and Sparky look at one another.

Kelly smiles, "I can't provide you with too many details. Until I know that there's a genuine interest," he says.

"It's basically a retrieval," Sparky tells Hank.

"Retrieval, hunh?" Hank asks, looking at Sparky.

"Yeah... one night with a small crew of five tracking a six-foot rocket full of loot, till it parachutes down into the water, then retrieve it" Kelly tells him.

"It'll be a lot closer to shore," Sparky tells him.

"Just a few miles out," Kelly adds.

Hank listens as he maneuvers the boat into position for another run. "What kind of money are you fellas talking about?" Hank asks, looking from Kelly to Sparky, then back at Kelly.

Kelly smiles, "Ten grand in advance. You keep that even if we lose the rocket," he says while looking Hank in the eyes. "If we're successful, when all is said and done... $250,000," Kelly says, smiling. "Clean cash in small bills."

“Rocket, hunh? How big is this rocket? What exactly is involved?” Hank asks, looking Kelly dead in the eyes.

“Rocket… missile… About five or six feet long,” Kelly tells Hank with a smile and a shrug playing it down. “We track the rocket, grab it when it hits the water, empty the contents, just a medium-sized duffel bag worth,” he tells him illustrating size with his hands. “We let the rocket sink, you get us out with the loot, and you’re done.” He says patting Hank on the back.

“Sounds simple enough,” Hank says. He turns to Kelly with his elbow up on the wheel, “But if you’re offering a quarter million, it’s gotta be worth half,” Hank says, smiling at Kelly with an I’ve-been-around-the-block expression.

Sparky nods his head smiling. Kelly looks at Sparky, then at Hank.

“What did I tell you?” Kelly asks Sparky.

Hank and Sparky just stand there watching Kelly get excited.

“Montauk holds a rich history of seaman defying the odds, …and the law!” he says with his broad smile. He offers his hand to Hank for a handshake. “I knew you were the right man for the job,” Kelly says. “If you’ll have it?” he adds with as much humility as he can muster.

“You got yourself a deal, Kelly, my boy,” Hank says shaking his hand.

Hank turns to Sparky and reaches out his hand. He and Sparky shake on it.

“This is gonna be legendary,” Sparky says looking Kelly in the eyes with a wink and a smile.

"Ya hear that, Grandpa?" Hank says loudly, gazing out to sea. Then laughing like a kid on Christmas morning. "Tell me something, Kelly," Hank says. "When exactly do you plan to accomplish this elaborate caper of yours?" he asks.

"Independence Day," Kelly tells him placing a huge trust in Hank.

Sparky seems a bit surprised Kelly revealed the actual date.

"I see." Hank says. "The entire town'll be preoccupied with Grucci's fireworks... Especially the cops," he adds. "Meanwhile you guys will be..." he gazes at Sparky then Kelly. He doesn't want to get ahead of himself. "I'll need to know what it is you're stealing eventually," he says.

He steps out to Steve and the crew, "You boys about ready?" he shouts.

"Baiting the last few now, Skipper," Steve yells back.

"Let's see if we can haul in the limit," Hank tells Sparky and Kelly.

They do catch the limit and get back in after sunset. Hank invites Kelly and Sparky to have a beer at The Dock Restaurant while Steve puts the fish to market, and the crew prepares the boat for the next day. Hank, Sparky and Kelly grab stools at the bar and order a few beers.

"So far you guys are good luck," Hank tells them gulping his iced-cold Budweiser.

Kelly and Sparky smile at each other.

"What makes you say that?" Kelly asks.

"I know you noticed the groceries, 'cause you were gracious enough to help carry them down to the galley... I was prepared to get you guys back tonight, no matter what the case, but it usually takes a bit longer than 12 hours to hit my quota these days," he tells them.

"Happy to be of service, Hank," Sparky says raising his beer with a smile.

"He usually attracts women, but fish are good, too," Kelly tells Hank referring to Sparky. "You should see the Swedish gal he picked up the other night at the Crow's Nest," Kelly tells him.

"Swedish, hunh?" Hank says sipping his beer.

Kelly looks at his watch.

"We have to run, but," Kelly tells Hank. He looks around to be sure no one is listening, "We should get together to run through details sometime over the next few days," he says speaking to Hank in hushed tones.

"You say you're going out in the morning," Sparky says. When will you get back?" Sparky asks, looking past Kelly at Hank.

"Oh, just a few days," Hank says.

"Today's the twenty-ninth... Let's say evening of the first?" he says turning to Hank.

"Sounds good," Hank tells him.

"Sparky's our wheel man and can pick you up here," he says. "Sometime around nine work for you?" Kelly asks.

Hank smiles, "That'll be fine," he says.

Hank sips his beer and thinks a moment.

"I want to thank you guys," Hank says. He turns to them a warm smile on his face, "You fellas have woken up a part of me I thought was gone forever," he says. "Old Grandpa would be proud," he says, lifting his beer up in a toast. "To you, Gramps," he says looking upward, draining the beer in the glass.

Kelly and Sparky take their leave and drive down to The Tower to see how the crew is getting on with the dig. When they get there, Dave is speaking with two young police officers who have pulled up in their cruiser.

"Just drop me off like any other passenger," Kelly tells Sparky. "I'm a tenant and you're a taxi driver, after all. Important to keep up appearances," he says with a wink.

Kelly steps out of the car walks towards the entrance, then approaches Dave and the police officers. Sparky pulls away like he might have dropped off any passenger.

"Hey... Mel, right?" Kelly says reinforcing that they've met. "Evening, officers," Kelly says in a nonchalant cordial manner. "Can we flush yet?" he asks Mel.

"Nah..." Dave tells him. "This one's a real mystery," he says. "With a little luck the place will be back to normal tomorrow," he assures Kelly. "But don't quote me on that," he says hands up in a blue-collar frustration. "We had a deal like this in Port Jeff last fall," he says, matter of fact. "The Sherlock Holmes of plumbing would've been stumped by that one," Mel says laughing.

"Thanks again for all your hard work Mel," Kelly says. "Night, officers," he says to the cops as he ascends the steps to The Tower and enters.

He takes the elevator up and spies down through the fifth floor rear window. The cops get in the cruiser and drive away. Kelly jumps back into the elevator and rides it down. He walks outside keeping his cover as the nice tenant.

"What was that all about?" Kelly asks Dave.

"Hey, it's a small town," Dave, as Mel, tells him, arms stretched out.

"How are the boys doing?" Kelly asks.

"They're doing fine. I walked out and found those two rookies sniffing around," Dave tells him.

"Looks like we got us a boat," Kelly tells him.

"Yeah?" Dave asks.

"Sparky and I went fishing all day. The captain's grandfather was a rum-runner," Kelly says with a smile.

"Ah… he's got the gene," says Dave, fascinated.

"Yes, and I think we succeeded in reminding him of that," Kelly says. "I'm going to check on Sal and The Kid," Kelly adds as he pulls out his phone, hits a recent number and brings the phone to his ear. "Coast is clear…" he tells Sparky. "I need to get back to the Yacht Club," he says.

"OK…See you in a few," Sparky answers.

Kelly ends the call and pockets the phone.

"How's he doing?" Dave asks.

"He's loving every minute of it," Kelly retorts with a huge grin.

"There's greatness in that man," Dave says as Sparky rolls up in the taxi.

XIV

It's July 3rd. The crew is gathered in Kelly's suite where they'll meet the latest addition to the crew, longline fishing boat captain Hank. With everyone in attendance, they'll run through the entire plan one last time before the big day.

"Sparky went to pick up Captain Hank, and should be here in a few minutes," Kelly tells the crew looking at his watch.

"Do we have to call him Captain Hank, or will Hank suffice?" Sal asks, eyebrows raised.

Kelly looks around the room at his crew. They've come a long way since Scotland. The respite they had planned in Montauk didn't quite go quite according to plan but Kelly is buzzing inside, as is the entire crew, filled with energy.

"That reminds me," Kelly says. He picks up the hotel phone, "Room service, please," he says. "Yes, can I have a six-pack of Budweiser brought to suite six? ...Great, thanks," he says, hanging up the phone.

"Hank, it is," Sal quips.

Kelly looks at her with a familiar smile for his oldest partner.

"Hank is a descendant of rum-runners," Kelly tells the crew with a smile. "You'll love him," he adds.

Moments later Sparky enters the suite with Hank in tow. Kelly walks over to them.

“Great to see you, Hank,” Kelly says with a giant hug. “Everyone, Hank,” he says, presenting Hank to the crew. “Hank, everyone,” he says with a smile.

“This is Dave, our scientific wizard who has set up the technical aspects of our little project,” he says.

Dave shakes Hank’s hand. “How ya doin, Cap?” he says with a smile.

“So, you’re the nut who’s making all this possible,” Hank says with a smile, shaking Dave’s hand.

“More than they’ll ever admit,” Dave says with a wink.

There’s a knock at the door followed by the words, “Room Service!”

“I’ll get it,” Rollie says moving towards the door. Rollie opens the door to reveal a room service attendant rolling a tray with a six-pack of cold Budweiser, beer glasses and a bucket of ice.

“Thanks,” Rollie says stuffing a bill in the attendant’s hand.

“You’re welcome, sir,” he says smiling.

“Beer, Hank?” Rollie asks stuffing some of the bottles in the bucket of ice.

“Sure,” Hank says.

“Glass or bottle?” Rollie asks.

“Seeing as there’s a lady here, I’ll have my beer in a glass, please,” Hank says, smiling at the stunning Sal who stands up and introduces herself.

“Sal,” she says with a warm smile, her hand out for a handshake.

Hank kisses her hand. “The pleasure’s mine,” he says.

Rollie pours the beer and walks it over to Hank, who is quite naturally enamored by Sal’s extreme beauty. “Rollie,” he says handing Hank the glass of beer.

“Nice to meet ya, Rollie.” Hank accepts the drink.

“I’m Louie,” The Kid says reaching out to shake Hank’s hand. “But everyone calls me The Kid,” he adds.

“The Kid, hunh?” Hank says, shaking his hand. “Good to meet you,” he says.

Hank takes a big swig of beer. “You’re right,” he says turning to Sparky, “These guys are all right.”

“A cold beer sounds good,” The Kid says moving over to the cart and pour himself one.

He lifts it and toasts Hank. “Cheers,” he says.

“Welcome aboard,” Sal says, lifting her prosecco.

Kelly pours himself a whiskey and turns to the crew, “We need to run through the goings-on for tomorrow, so get comfortable,” Kelly says with his signature grin, plopping down on a comfortable chair.

“Have a squat, Hank,” Sal tells Hank, pointing to the sofa.

“Don’t mind if I do,” Hank says.

Sal takes the seat next to him while the rest of the crew find places to sit down. Dave pours himself a whiskey and sits on the sofa next to Sal. Kelly leans forward in his chair.

"As I may have mentioned, Hank is descended from a family of rum-runners," Kelly says proudly.

"I salute your renegade spirit, my good man," Dave says, raising his glass.

Hank raises his bottle in a gesture to Dave.

"So, what exactly is it you have planned?" Hank asks, getting up to pour himself another beer. He sips the beer, "All I know so far..." he says looking around at everyone, "...is we're retrieving some kind of rocket you're launching out to sea," he says.

"That's right," says Rollie.

Hank laughs as he returns to his seat next to Sal.

"What's your part in all this?" Hank asks the beautiful Sal.

She sneaks a glance at Kelly, not exactly sure how far she should take it. Kelly nods his head extremely slowly, imperceptibly to most, signaling Sal it's okay to tell all.

"I'm playing the mark, making sure he stays in town for the 4th," she says, looking at Hank with her coy smile.

Sparky watches everything closely, fascinated by the dynamic of the exchange between Hank and the crew.

"Okay..." Hank says. "But how does the rocket fit into all this?" he asks finishing off his beer. "That's what has me most intrigued," he admits, getting up to pour himself another beer. "Seems kind of extravagant is all," he says as he returns to the sofa.

"It is indeed extravagant," Kelly admits.

"You think that's extravagant, no one's told you about the remote control get-a-way car I'll be leading the cops on a wild goose chase with yet," The Kid says, air-race-car-driving sound effects and all.

Hank gets a kick out of The Kid's antics.

"This just gets more interesting all the time," Hank says glancing at Sal, then Kelly. "Why don't you just lay it out for me?" he asks.

"I will," Kelly says.

"You a Marine?" Hank asks Rollie, looking him up and down.

"Good call," Sal tells him.

"Navy Seal," Rollie tells him. "Decommissioned…" he adds.

"I can always tell a military man," Hank says.

Kelly stands up, walks over to the bar, pours himself a whiskey and turns to Hank.

"It all started when I asked a realtor about an estate we were interested in purchasing," he tells him.

"Except the damn Russian put an offer on it first," The Kid tells him.

"That aside," Dave says. "Due to the proximity of Montauk," he leans past Sal to make eye contact with Hank, "…one road out of town and all," he says. "We decided to stuff the loot in a missile and send it out over the ocean using the fireworks as a distraction," Dave explains.

“Where we can retrieve it with none the wiser,” Kelly says finishing Dave’s description of the plan.

“I see,” Hank says. “Clever...” he adds, impressed.

“After we retrieve the rocket, you take us out past old Rum Row to a yet-undisclosed location,” Kelly says.

“International waters,” Hank says knowing the reference of Rum Row. “My Grandfather told me all about the Rum Line,” he tells the crew. “After a day of fishing, he’d take a speedboat out there to find schooners, clippers and barques all lined up in a row, filled with booze from Jamaica, Canada and as far away as Europe, waiting for the likes of old Grandpa to show up and buy it,” he says trying to imagine the scene. “He was quite the character...”

“I bet he was,” Sal says looking into Hanks eyes.

He looks over at Kelly “Then what?” he asks.

Then you drop us in Nova Scotia,” Kelly says.

“That isn’t too far, is it?” Sparky smiles at Hank.

“I’ve fished out there before,” Hank says. “Good swordfish off Nova Scotia,” he adds, sipping his beer.

“Which is our cover...” says Kelly smiling.

They talk for a while making detailed plans until the Budweiser’s gone, then part ways, agreeing to meet on the 4th of July. Sparky gets Hank home and they call it a night.

XV

It's July 4th. Everything the crew could do to prepare for such an outlandish caper has been done. They've checked out of the Yacht Club and moved everything onto the Sally Ann for the retrieval and trip to Nova Scotia.

Sal has successfully strung Demyan along. She even received a lovely Sapphire necklace. Demyan has arranged for he and Sal to view the fireworks from an extravagantly catered tent on the beach featuring Russian Caviar and bottles of Stolichnaya frozen in blocks of ice. The Kid is primed and pumped for his car-chase with the cops around the old 1920s Montauk racetrack. Sparky has renamed The Kid's character in his novel to Mario, in honor of Mario Andretti. Hank has set Sparky up with a two-way radio so they can contact him with updates.

Dave has successfully devised a fast and easy way to retro-fit Shin's rocket into the turret with explosive bolts and now that the tunnel is completed, the Lithuanians have returned to the Bronx. They were able to return the Suffolk County Water Authority emergency vehicle unnoticed. Of course, they can't give themselves too much credit for that one, as it is a government agency after all, and we all know how ridiculously inefficient and aloof a company run by a government bureaucracy can be. The Tower management agency is thrilled that the toilets work again and Giovanna the realtor has had nightly fantasies about swimming naked in the perfect swimming pool in the perfect mansion with Kelly since the whole thing began.

Rollie and Candy may have fallen in love. The same goes for The Kid and Rachel. Kelly has checked and rechecked everything three times and Hank is speaking to the spirit of his Grandfather on a regular basis. Dave is a bit concerned about it, but Kelly thinks it's a good sign. Still, deep down in his innermost self, Kelly is wondering if this project is just too insane an idea to actually pull off. But then he thinks about the legendary status pulling it off will bring him and his crew in the nefarious world of con artist thieves internationally and his fears magically melt away. Sparky has 100 pages of his novel written and is giddy with excitement about how all of this will turn out.

Montauk is buzzing with excitement. The police have their hands full dealing with the massive influx of people arriving in town for the July 4th Grucci fireworks. Kelly, Dave, Rollie and The Kid are in the Tower basement three hours and ten minutes before showtime. Shin's rocket is standing by to be placed onto the 'Great Escape' styled dolly that will glide the rocket through the long tunnel they dug from the Tower to the bank.

"Okay, let's go get that loot," Kelly says grabbing a hold of the line he'll use to reel the rocket to the bank.

He crawls into the tunnel and rolls towards the bank on the wheeled-dolly-system Dave designed. Rollie and The Kid fit a second dolly into place on the tracks then lift the heavy rocket into the dolly and secure it. Rollie pulls the line till it's taut, then gives it three tugs signaling to Kelly he can reel it in. The rocket disappears into the dark tunnel. The others follow suit. Rollie successfully digs a large enough opening alongside the water main at the bank for Dave to crawl through and disable the alarm systems. Rollie and The Kid enlarge the hole so the rest of them and the rocket can enter the bank. Dave cracks the vault and there they are: Demyan's diamonds and assorted exotic jewels in a velvet-lined Haliburton case. Kelly looks at them and smiles. "There's a of gems here," he says, happily surprised.

"Dave assesses the collection, "Somewhere around twenty million," he says smiling at Kelly.

The Kid helps Dave up to the turret with his tools. Kelly grabs Demyan's loot and passes it up to Rollie who passes it to The Kid who runs it up to Dave who gets it into the rocket. The four of them work quickly and efficiently to empty the vault and contents of every safety deposit box in the bank. The rocket is filled with the loot, sealed and armed.

The plan is for Dave to set the rocket off remotely along with a large explosion at the teller window just during the grand finale of the fireworks show when they are a few miles out to sea on the Sally Ann. After getting the crew to the boat, Sparky will stand by at the Montauk Airport waiting for word that they've got the rocket. At which point he will board a private plane to Nova Scotia and rendezvous with the Sally Ann the next day.

Sparky is seated in his taxi at The Tower parking lot waiting for everyone and get them to the Sally Ann. Kelly, Dave, Rollie and The Kid run up the steps to the lobby. They slow everything down to a normal pace, exit the building like tourists on vacation, walk to the waiting taxi and get in.

"How'd everything go?" Sparky asks, excited to see them.

"Like clockwork," The Kid says.

"Sal has likely given Demyan the slip by now and should be here any minute," Kelly says as he checks the time.

The plan is for her to make her way to the Tower on foot from the beach, since the entire town is gridlocked and Sparky picking her up at the beach in the taxi just couldn't have worked.

"There she is," says Sparky pointing at Sal crossing the street.

Sparky races over and she jumps in the taxi. Sparky wastes no time driving to the dock.

"I'm sure glad we picked such a safe small-town bank to open our account in, dear," Sal says to Dave.

The crew cracks up laughing as Sparky races up Flamingo Avenue to the Commercial dock. He pulls up and the crew exit the taxi.

Kelly looks over to Sparky with an excited smile. "See you tomorrow in Nova Scotia," he says.

"Nova Scotia," Sparky repeats with a knowing smile.

"See ya, Sparks," Sal says, kissing him on the cheek.

"See ya tomorrow," Dave says patting him on the shoulder.

"Yeah, pal," Rollie adds.

"Hey, I like Mario by the way," The Kid lets him know.

Sparky watches the crew move quickly up the dock to the Sally Ann. Hank is already aboard, alone this time, idling the diesel engine. Hank sees them walking up the dock.

"Well, Grandpa, it's time to do or die," he says sipping a beer.

The crew steps aboard the Sally Ann.

"Hello, Hank," Sal says in her sultry way holding out her hand.

"Hello there, Sal," Hank says taking her hand and helping her aboard.

“No time to waste,” Dave reminds everyone.

Hank returns to the helm. “Okay then… Shove off, fellas,” he yells. “Like I showed you,” he adds loudly.

Sal watches as Kelly, Dave, Rollie and The Kid untie the lines and pull in the bumpers like a seasoned crew. She walks over and joins Hank at the helm as they idle through the inlet. Once they’re through, Hank opens it up until they’re out a few miles past the point.

“It’s T minus twenty-two or fifty-two minutes, Dave says looking at his watch.

“What’s this twenty-two or fifty-two minutes stuff?” Rollie asks.

“The closest the town can get to a starting time is between 9 and 9:30 p.m.,” he says with a cynical raise of the eyebrows. “I can see the Grucci fireworks barge,” Dave says peering through the high quality antique spyglass he brought along to see when the fireworks begin so he can start the countdown.

The Kid is in the galley with his remote-control live-cam Gran Tourismo Dave rigged to drive the Crown Vic parked in the spot they picked near the bank and ready to take the cops on a wild-goose chase.

“The fireworks will last for only twenty-five minutes, so we have to be right on the mark,” Kelly says. He turns to Rollie. “How’s the car?” he asks.

“Filled up and ready to roll,” he says. “We’ve tested the auto controls six ways to Sunday,” Dave assures Kelly. “If it starts, we’re home free,” he adds with smart-ass grin.

The three of them crack up laughing. Nerves are running high and they should be. Sal walks over to them from the helm and lights a cigarette.

“Hank’s talking to an invisible grandfather,” she says.

“That’s ok,” Kelly says. “It’s a good sign,” he adds.

Dave is doubtful.

“Hank’s grandfather was a rum-runner out here during Prohibition, don’t forget,” Kelly reminds him.

“And that makes it ok?” Sal asks in her cynical way.

“My point exactly,” Dave says peering through the spyglass. “They just shot up the starter flare,” Dave says excitedly looking at Kelly, then Rollie and Sal.

Kelly checks his watch. “Twenty-five minutes,” he says.

“I’ll go check on The Kid,” Rollie says.

“Make sure he’s got a clear view of the bank,” Dave tells him. “He has to be screeching past that cop shop the second the explosion occurs.

“You got it,” Rollie says with a big smile stepping below deck.

“We haven’t had this much fun in a while,” Kelly says, looking at Dave and Sal.

The three of them peer off into the distance where they can see the glow of the fireworks and hear the delayed sound from a few miles away. Dave checks the mobile device he has rigged to blast off the rocket.

“Time to join Hank at the helm,” Dave says.

“Good idea, we may need to guide him once we start tracking the rocket,” Kelly says.

“I’m hooked into his GPS system,” Dave says with his mad scientist grin. “He’ll be fine till we get close enough to see it, then it’s all hands-on-deck to grab a visual,” Dave says as they join Hank at the helm.

“You guys realize that you’re all crazy, right?” Hank says with a smile as they enter the cabin.

“Moments away,” Dave says looking through the spyglass. “As soon as the rocket launches, I’ll patch it through to your GPS tracking system I rigged and you’ll be able to track it,” he tells Hank.

“You got it, Einstein,” Hank comments smiling.

He continues to navigate the Sally Ann towards Dave’s approximation point a few miles offshore. Hank turns to Kelly, suddenly remembering something. “What about Sparky? ...Couldn’t make the soiree?” he asks, keeping the boat on course.

“Someone had to stay ashore,” Kelly says. “Sparky’ll grab a flight out of Montauk to Nova Scotia, soon as we give him the word that we’ve retrieved the rocket.”

“Sparky...” Sal says with a fond smile. “What do you imagine our Sparky is thinking about right now?” she asks everyone.

“I don’t know, but whatever it is, it’s probably going into his book,” Kelly says with a warm smile for their new pal.

“Looks like a finale to me,” Dave says peering through the spyglass.

“I better go supervise Mario Andretti,” Kelly says dashing off to the galley to make sure all goes well with The Kid.

He arrives below deck to find The Kid at the Gran Tourismo steering wheel with Rollie standing behind him, ready to troubleshoot any problems.

“Start your engines,” Kelly says like a race track announcer. The Kid starts the motor and revs it up a few times. He looks up at Rollie standing behind him. “Feels good,” he says.

“Trust me... It’s a race car, Kid,” Rollie says.

Kelly peers at the screen. He points to the glowing window of the otherwise darkened structure of the bank on the screen. “That the drive-in window?” he asks.

“Yes sir!” The Kid says totally pumped up for his car chase. The Kid points to a rectangular section at the top of the screen, “That’s the rear-view,” he says.

The three of them stare at the screen. BOOM! The screen flashes white.

“That’s it!” says The Kid excitedly as he puts it in gear and screeches past the police station.

He heads towards the racetrack the way he’s rehearsed dozens of times now.

“Hahaha! Got one!” he exclaims.

Kelly and Rollie look at one another giddy, then at the screen. They can see the flashing lights of a police cruiser in the rear-view. The Kid spins onto South Fairview past the golf course then makes the first turn on the track, cops in pursuit.

Kelly pats Rollie on the back with a big smile, “You guys got this. I’m going up to help find us a rocket-ship full of loot!” He laughs as he ascends the companionway to topside.

He dashes into the helm.

“We’re tracking it now,” Dave says pointing to a little speck flying through the air of the boat’s LCD computerized GPS tracking screen.

“How’s The Kid?” Dave asks, watching the spec on the screen get closer and closer.

“When I left them, a cop car was hot on his tail passing the golf course,” Kelly says.

“You guys truly are something else,” Hank says, impressed by the amazing and unlikely feat the crew is pulling off.

“It’s a living,” Sal says flirting with Hank.

Kelly can’t help but notice the dynamic developing between Sal and Hank. He’s a bit surprised until he remembers reading how women have found commercial fisherman, much like lumberjacks and fireman, to have great sex appeal.

“Sorry I’m gonna miss The Kid’s epic car chase,” Kelly says.

“Oh, I didn’t tell anyone but I’m recording the whole thing on a computer chip I installed,” Dave says. He looks up at Kelly, “As a gift for The Kid,” he says, “Plus, so we can all watch it later,” he says.

Down below, The Kid is having a ball running the cops in circles around the racetrack. “C’mon...” he says, “Come and get me!” he exclaims. “If you can!” he screams out loud. “Sucker!” he says, laughing as a cop car crashes into the trunk of a large tree.

Sparky is parked at the airport with his MacBook up on the steering wheel, writing everything that has happened so far, shaking his head, stomping his feet and laughing out loud a few times. Out at sea things have turned a bit strange with a surprise weather event brewing.

“Look at that,” says Hank, referring to the screen as he maneuvers the boat towards what he predicts should be the intercept point.

He looks out at the ocean. “Wasn’t forecast, but looks like we got some weather ahead,” he says, sounding miffed.

He looks back at the screen which begins flickering and flashing wildly. “I’ve seen a few things out here,” he says. “Me and ole Sally Ann have ridden out some rough seas, haven’t we, gal?” he says, patting the instrument panel.

He looks out to sea again, “This is a strange one,” he insists.

“The rocket must be getting close,” Dave insists. “You guys get on deck, see if you can grab a visual,” he says.

Kelly and Sal run out to the bow and start scanning the sky towards the west, the direction the rocket would be coming from. The wind has increased and electrical flashes from lightning far above are increasing. In the helm, the instrument panel is going completely haywire. Rollie and The Kid run up to the galley, still laughing from the chase.

“Did you see that one cop fly through that fence?” The Kid shouts laughing.

They leap onto the deck to find a whirlwind of weather as waves begin crashing into the side of the boat. The sky, although it's a high ceiling with whatever's going on happening a few thousand feet above the ocean, is lighting up bigger and brighter than the Grucci fireworks.

"There it is," Kelly screams.

Dave comes running out to the deck as Rollie and The Kid run over.

"See it?" Kelly asks, pointing up into the sky.

"There she is!" Dave says, "About a hundred feet high," he adds.

The Sally Ann heaves to and fro as the sea becomes more violent by the second. The five of them stand there in awe as the rocket parachute opens and begins floating down. Kelly and Dave run into the helm to assist Hank with the intercept. Dave points out the position of the rocket to Hank who maneuvers the boat towards the descending rocket full of the stolen loot. Sal runs into the cabin.

"Time to call Sparky ship to shore," Kelly says.

"We can do that?" Sal asks.

"Right there on the radio," Hank says pointing to the ship's radio.

"What do I do?" Sal asks.

"Just lift the handset, press the button, and say 'Ship to Shore,'" he tells her.

Sal lifts the handset, "Ship to Shore," she says as Kelly joins them at the helm.

Sparky, seated in his taxi at the airport typing away, hears the scratchy voice on the portable radio Hank gave him and grabs it. He presses it and speaks into it.

“Sparky here,” he says.

Sal passes the handset to Kelly.

“Hey, Sparky, we’ve run into some foul weather, but we have the rocket in our sights,” Kelly tells.

“Yee Ha!” Sparky exclaims. “See you in Nova Scotia,” he says. No one answers.

“Hello? Hello?” Sparky repeats.

Nothing but static. Back on the ship the weather has become serious.

“Anybody got eyes on it?” Dave shouts to Rollie and The Kid on the foredeck.

“There it is,” yells The Kid.

Dave gets it in view and points it out to Hank who is having difficulty keeping the boat on course with the weather worsening. “See it?” shouts Dave pointing it out to Hank as he gets knocked around. “Right there!” he screams pointing to the rocket in the sky.

“Got it,” says Hank steering the boat toward the rocket he can barely see descending.

With multi-colored lightning flashes surrounding it and lighting it up, the rocket suddenly disappears into thin air.

“What the?” Dave gasps.

“It was right there!” says Hank.

Kelly looks at Dave. “What do you make of it?” he asks.

“I’m not sure… It’s as though it disappeared out of thin air!” Dave says miffed.

Sal runs to the helm. She’s holding on tightly as the Sally Ann gets knocked around like a cork in a washing machine. The sky is a spectrum of exploding colors beyond any lightning anyone has ever seen and dropping closer every second.

“Hold on tight, little lady,” Hank shouts. “I’ve never seen the likes of this before,” he shouts at Sal who is holding on tightly. Hank, being the experienced and brave seaman that he is, puts his arm around Sal and looks into her eyes. “If it weren’t for this damned storm, I’d really be enjoying having this moment with you,” he says with a smile, holding her tightly.

Sal may be frightened, but she’s also as cool as they come.

“Hank,” she says leaning in to give Hank a kiss.

They get tossed apart as the boat begins twirling around. The boys on deck hold on for dear life.

“What the hell is it, Dave?” Kelly asks screaming.

“It’s possible the Montauk Project is more than just a conspiracy theory,” Dave yells back. “Hold on tight, you guys,” Dave tells them. “I think things are about to get weird.”

The boat begins twirling around and around as the sky and sea appear to have merged. Electrical flashes come within reach of the Sally Ann. Finally, it’s as though they are flying through a violent electrical maze of some kind, Thunderous explosions made of electricity engulf them.

Hank and Sal are locked together at the helm getting tossed around. Then in a flash, it's dead quiet. The Sally Ann is floating in a netherworld of sorts seen only in nightmarish dreams. Then boom! The ship crashes into the sea surrounded by a dense fog, although it feels more as though the sea crashed into the boat, since they were floating not falling. The Sally Ann comes to rest finally as a scattering of crackling electrical charges fade away in the thickest fog any of them have ever seen.

Kelly, Dave, Rollie and The Kid run to the helm to find Hank helping Sal to her feet.

"What on earth was that?" Hank exclaims. "What was in that rocket anyway?" he asks.

"Nothing but jewels, cash and the personal effects from safety deposit boxes," Kelly assures him. "You guys all right?" he asks Sal and Hank. "You guys?" he asks turning to Dave, Rollie and The Kid.

"No injuries here," Rollie says.

The dense fog sits perfectly still as nary a breeze exists. They all stare at Hank.

"Did you guys notice how we crashed into the sea but didn't feel like we were falling just before it hit? Hank asks.

"Yes!" exclaims Dave.

"That's right," Kelly says thinking back to that moment.

"Yeah..." The Kid says.

"Doesn't make sense," Rollie chimes in.

"The Montauk Project..." Hank says surprising the crew, "I'd heard of it most of my life... but never believed it was real," he says.

"Till now..." Dave says.

"Till now..." Hank repeats, looking over at Dave with a befuddled expression. "Not even the wild stories old Grandpa use to tell me compare to this," he says.

"Ship seems all right," Hank says as he grabs the wheel.

They remain there speechless for a moment unsure of what just happened. Hank is fiddling with the instrument panel, but nothing is working. Dave checks the satellite GPS on his iPad. Nothing...

"Electrical storm must have short circuited everything," Dave tells them.

"Compass still works," Hank says checking the old school floating magnetic compass mounted to the dashboard.

"Our heading remains east by northeast," he says looking at it.

He looks up at the crew with a strangely surprised expression. They let that tidbit soak in a moment then walk out to the foredeck hoping for the fog to clear.

"How long can that rocket float?" Kelly asks Dave.

"It's airtight and will float indefinitely unless it's damaged," he says. "...or begins to leak from rot... but that would take years," he says peering off the bow hoping to see something.

"Highly unlikely we'll find anything till this fog clears," Hank tells them. "I've seen the gray lady this thick before," he says. "But not often," he adds, looking at Sal with a sweet smile. "I'm glad that you made it all right, Sal," he says.

"Gray lady?" The Kid asks. "What's the gray lady?"

"It's an old-time sailor's term for the fog," Hank tells them. "My Grandfather would tell me how they would lose the Coast Guard in the britches of the gray lady," he says with an eerie smile and a chuckle.

After a long while, the crew speechless, a slight breeze begins to pick up and the fog begins to clear a little bit. They peer off the deck into the water hoping to find the rocket, but the fog is still too thick to see anything. Hours go by and the crew is beginning to worry.

"I realize it can be unnerving for a gang of landlubbers adrift at sea, but the strange weather has settled down now, and the fog will clear up eventually," he says. "Just gotta wait it out," he says.

"Hank's right," Kelly says. "We all best try to relax."

Hank leans down and opens a cabinet door, "Maybe a rum?" He produces a large bottle of Jamaican rum.

"Now you're talkin." Smiles Sal. "We have any glasses under here?" Or do we just pass the bottle?" she asks leaning over to check if there are any glasses in the stash hold Hank pulled the bottle from.

Sal produces enough glasses to go around and Hank pours a healthy drink for everyone.

"Fair winds and following seas," he says raising his glass of rum.

They toast and enjoy their rum for a while before the faint sound of a ship's bell is heard in the distance. Hank's the first to hear it.

"You hear that?" he asks cupping his ear. "Quiet!" he yells.

Everyone strains to hear what Hank hears. A few moments pass.

"What was it?" Sal asks.

"I could have sworn I heard a ship's bell clang," Hank says not fully believing his own ears.

The crew look at one other with queer expressions, not sure what to think. Dave pours himself another rum. A gust of wind sweeps through the ship and the fog begins to clear a little.

"Set sail, fellas! The gray lady's liftin' her skirt," they hear faintly from a distance in what sounds like old Irish brogue.

"What was that?" The Kid asks.

Another gust of wind clears enough fog to reveal a full moon. In the moonlight, they can see the ship the voice came from; a three-masted clipper ship from the 1800s about a hundred yards off the port side of the Sally Ann.

"Would ya look at that?" Kelly says, peering out at the great ship of old.

"What kind of boat is that?" The Kid asks.

"It's a clipper," Kelly says somewhat astonished.

“For hundreds of years, ships like that carried people, animals and goods across the globe,” he says, peering out at the majestic ship.

They all rush to the portside bow to get a better view. Dave whips out his spyglass and peers through it.

“Look!” he says in near disbelief.

As the fog continues to clear, a few other large period vessels come into view. Schooners, barques, clippers and the like are out there in the moonlight lined up in a row.

“Unless my eyes deceive me, men are loading boxes from those ships onto small power boats,” Dave says peering through his spyglass in amazement.

“Give me that thing!” Hank exclaims grabbing the spyglass.

The clipper they had first spotted, with its sails up now, slowly begins to catch some wind and falls away from the pack heading east. Hank scans the area, then focuses on one boat in particular.

“Man-oh-man.” Hank is astonished at what he sees.

“This is weird,” Rollie exclaims.

“Tell me about it,” Sal says in a near state of shock peering over the bow.

“Where are we?” The Kid asks, gazing out to the strange scene on the moonlit sea.

“If I’m still breathing, those are rum-runners,” Hank says, dispelling logical doubts and believing his eyes.

“Let me take a look,” Kelly says reaching out his hand.

Hank hands him the spyglass in a near hypnotic state. Kelly places it up to his eye and scans the area. Dave, Rollie, The Kid, Sal and Hank stand there in awe hoping Kelly can tell them what exactly is going on. The unmistakable sound of a motor boat hitting the waves becomes louder and louder until two men in a speedboat packed with booze races by a few feet off the port side of the Sally Ann. The occupants waving, shouting and laughing.

“Ya better hurry!” “We may have got the last of it!” one of them yells as they speed away.

“Did you see that?” The Kid exclaims, having a difficult time trusting his own eyes.

“Yeah, but I’m not sure I believe it,” Rollie says, dazed from the strangeness of what they are witnessing.

“Where’s that rum?” Sal quips, walking towards the helm and pouring herself a stiff drink.

Hank rushes to the helm. “Where’s my damn binoculars,” he says sort of to himself.

Hank grabs his binoculars and runs to the bow to join the others. Kelly continues to scan the goings on through the spyglass.

“You’re not going to believe this,” he says turning to face everyone.

He looks at Dave in particular, “You’ll have to fill in the blanks on this one, pal, but I think...” he stares at them one by one, as Sal returns with the rum. “I believe the question is not where are we, it is when are we,” Kelly says, placing the spyglass back up to his eye. “Because... unless I am mistaken, this is Rum Row of the 1920s,” he tells them.

"You're crazy!" The Kid protests.

"That's it," Hank exclaims looking through his binoculars. "It's either that or we've all lost our minds," he says, laughing.

"I think you're right, amigo," Dave says peering through the spyglass.

"Let me see that thing," Sal says, handing Dave her rum and grabbing the spyglass.

She lifts it to her eye and looks through it, "They're loading boxes, all right," she says, handing Rollie the spyglass. "Here, see for yourself," she says.

Rollie gazes out at the line-up of large period sailing vessels.

"Wow..." is all he can utter.

"Let me see!" yells The Kid grabbing the spyglass.

"What the?" He says looking through it.

"There's only one explanation," Dave says finally.

He looks up at everyone with the most solemn expression, "We have somehow travelled through a window of space-time and arrived here," he says, staring out to sea at the bizarre scene. "Just like Kelly said," he adds.

The six of them stand there in a state of inexplicable awe staring out to sea as the large ships hoist sails and begin to move away heading east, south or north, but not one leaves international waters towards them. Kelly turns to the crew. He looks them over one by one, trying to judge their condition. He's long had the ability to roll with the punches, get himself out of scrapes, wiggle out of tight impossible spots. And he's been in many... He runs through some of them in his head. The many times when he thought all was lost, how he found a willingness to risk everything and take a leap of faith. A journey through unknown waters. It is the quality that most allows his crew to follow his lead into what can often be defined as the abyss. Once again, he finds himself standing over that precipice, unsure what to do, as do most of the others. A smile comes to his face.

"Will the engine start?" Kelly asks Hank, breaking the strained silence.

Hank looks up at Kelly and slowly comes out of his dazed state of mind.

"Only one way to find out," Hank tells him.

He makes his way to the helm.

"Wherever we are, we have a rocket to find," Kelly reminds his crew.

Dave looks up at him, "Yeah, only if we did cross through a dimension of time, the rocket went through before we did," he says, ever the scientist, "It may be somewhere else entirely," he says.

Rollie pulls himself up by the bootstraps, "We'll never find out standing around," he says.

He walks to the helm, "You got a spotlight?" he asks Hank.

Hank looks up at him as if stepping out of a dream.

"The stow just outside this cabin," he says pointing to the bow.

“If it’ll work,” he adds.

Rollie steps out to the bow and finds the light. He plugs it in and turns it on.

“It works!” he exclaims pointing it into the water.

The working light provides a level of normalcy for everyone.

Kelly joins Hank at the helm.

“Here goes,” Hank says turning the key.

The motor turns and soon the diesel engine is running. A huge smile comes to Hank’s face. He pats the dashboard fondly.

“That’s a girl,” he says, revving the motor.

The crew perks up upon hearing the engine roar. Dave and The Kid join Rollie in searching for the rocket. Hank puts it in gear and starts moving very slowly. He turns to Kelly. “We’ll make a spiral pattern widening the degrees incrementally,” he says turning the wheel as tight as it’ll go.

“Best give those guys another set of eyes,” he tells him. “Not much good you can do in here,” he says.

Kelly looks at Hank fondly. “True adventure, my friend,” he says, patting Hank on the back. He gazes out to the sea, “This is once-in-a-lifetime stuff,” he says.

Hank smiles, “Has anyone ever told you that you have a knack for understatement?” he asks as he idles around the pattern he’s set for the search. “If here truly is the 1920s, I can’t help wondering…” He looks at Kelly, not sure whether to say what’s on his mind. He gazes out to sea. His expression changes from dire to hopeful then bewilderment, “My Grandpa might have been out there tonight,” he says, looking at Kelly, unable to hold back the smile of a ten-year-old on Christmas morning. A tear comes to his eye. Kelly moves over to him and puts his arm around his shoulder gazing out at the mysterious moonlight flickering on the water of the great ocean sea.

“Maybe....” Kelly says. “Maybe...”

They stand there for a moment contemplating the intensity of what just happened. Hank turns to Kelly and looks into his eyes.

“You do realize that if this is indeed the 1920’s, there’ll be an extra charge for time travel,” he says. They both crack up laughing. They laugh so hard the crew stops what they’re doing and turn to the helm to see what’s going on.

“Absolutely,” Kelly tells him.

He walks out to the bow and joins the others still laughing.

“What’s all that about?” Sal wants to know.

“Hank just hit us up with a time travel fee,” he says to the crew with his signature grin.

“Hank...” Sal says fondly, then turning to look at him at the helm. “What a guy,” she adds, waving to him.

“We may not find it here,” Dave says.

“Why do you say that?” Kelly asks scanning the water with the others as Rollie continues to light up the immediate area with the powerful spotlight.

Dave looks up at Kelly, “That rocket slipped through before we did,” he says. “If it is here, wherever here is exactly, it may very likely have arrived here before we did and that opens the door to several possibilities," he tells Kelly while still thinking it through in his head. "One of those speedboats may have crashed into it," he adds with a disappointed expression.

"Or yanked it out of the water and cracked it open," Kelly theorizes.

He and Dave just stand there, considering the possibilities.

"Since we don't know for certain, we just keep searching," Kelly surmises finally.

They join the others at the bow searching for the rocket.

"Hey! What's that?" asks The Kid, as he points excitedly at something floating in the water.

Hank sticks his head out from the helm.

"What d'ya got?" he yells.

The Kid points to the right, "Go that way!" he yells.

Hank rolls his eyes. "That's starboard!" he yells back. "Landlubbers..." he complains to himself.

He steers the Sally Ann towards the object floating in the water. When they get close enough to identify it, they see it's a case of booze. Kelly grabs the gaff and hooks it.

"Careful, hotshot," Sal tells him. "That's vintage booze," she says.

"Actually, it isn't," Dave tells her.

"Oh, right..." she says.

Kelly guides the box of booze around to midship with the long gaff. Rollie reaches over the side and gets it aboard to discover it's a case of Henrick's Gin. Everyone gathers around. A giant gray whale swims slowly by a few feet away, and blows its spout, soaking the crew.

"Cheers to you, too," Rollie says to the whale as it sucks in a lung-full of air and dives below. Hank and the crew gather around to inspect the wooden case of gin.

"I have a theory about gin," Sal tells everyone.

They all turn to Sal, curious to hear her theory. She smiles at them and explains, "Wine... cognac... brandy... all go to the head... Whiskey... Whiskey goes to the body... Gin?" she says, looking each of them in the eye, "Gin goes everywhere..."
The crew is laughing at Sal's theory as Hank appears with glasses for everyone, "After what we've been through, I'd say we've earned a drink." He hands the first glass to Sal.

"My kind of guy," Sal says smiling at Hank.

Kelly opens the case, cracks open a bottle, and pours drinks all around.

"To the mysteries of the sea," he toasts lifting his glass.

"Here, here," Dave says in the Scottish accent he used for the Lewis Chessman caper.

The crew shares a good laugh, likely releasing pent-up nerves from their recent harrowing experience.

"What's that all about?" Hank asks.

"I'll tell you all about it sometime," Sal tells him with a wink, sipping her drink. "That's good," she says.

"I've never had straight gin before," The Kid remarks as he takes a healthy swig. "Wow, not bad," he says.

"Yeah, because it's top-shelf gin," Dave tells him. "You can survive cheap whiskey, cheap rum, even cheap tequila, rye and vodka, but gin…" he says with authority, "Gin *has* to be top shelf." He grins at the more experienced drinkers who all nod their heads in agreement.

"There is no booze in the world worse than cheap gin," Sal tells The Kid.

They continue to search for the rocket. After a few hours of dedicated effort, nothing is found, and the crew begin to tire.

"We all better get some rest," Kelly tells them. "The sun will be up in a few hours. We'll have a better chance of finding the rocket in the daylight anyway," he says.

"Good idea," says Hank. "Best just to let her drift awhile," he says, hands on his hips. "If that rocket is out here, we'll likely come upon it moving along in the drift. You all catch some shuteye" he says as he takes his last sip of gin. "That is good," he says, winking at Sal.

"What about you?" Rollie asks, "Don't you sleep?"

"Someone's got to keep watch, son," Hank tells him.

"I can take the first watch," Rollie tells him.

"Oh right… Navy Seal… Fair enough," Hank says with a smile. "Wake me in two hours," he tells him. Hank addresses the crew. "C'mon, bunks are below," he tells them, heading down the gangway below deck.

Sal, Dave and The Kid follow.

Kelly looks at Rollie, "You sure you're ok?" he asks.

Rollie smiles, "Stayed awake for three days once on a mission in the Persian Gulf," he says. "I've been trained for this kind of thing. Don't sweat it, boss," he says. "Get some shut-eye."

"Okay, see you in a couple hours." Kelly pats Rollie on the back.

Kelly walks to the gangway, turns a moment and says, "Pretty amazing, hunh?"

Rollie looks out over the ocean. "Pretty amazing..." he says.

Kelly joins the others below and grabs a bunk. Rollie grabs a comfortable position on deck and takes in the night sky as the boat gently rocks on the moonlit ocean. A thought occurs to Rollie. He jumps up and walks the perimeter of the Sally Ann just in case the rocket ended up in the boat and was missed in the commotion. He walks to the aft deck and back, but nothing there. The gray whale makes another appearance, but this time Rollie's ready for it. He ducks into the cabin just as the whale sprays another fountain of water onboard. Rollie rushes to the bow, Ha!" he yells.

"Thought you had me, didn't you?" he yells laughing.

XVI

A few hours later as the sun appears on the horizon, Hank steps on deck. He's happy to discover Rollie awake.

"I miss anything?" Hank asks him.

"That whale made another appearance, but I outsmarted him and leapt into the cabin just as he sprayed the boat again," Rollie says, smiling.

"It's another world out here, isn't it?" Hank says, patting Rollie on the shoulder.

"You better get some rest, son," he says.

"Good idea," Rollie agrees.

"You'll find a free bunk down there," Hank tells him.

Before long Kelly and Dave appear on deck. They continue the search for the rocket. By midday, the entire crew is back on deck looking for the rocket. Hank fixes them all some sandwiches. They continue to search for the rocket through the night. Dawn breaks and sunrise right behind it.

Kelly turns to Hank and the crew, "We can't stay out here forever," he says.

"We have plenty of water and some fishing poles," Hank says. "We could stay out here longer than you might think," he adds. "But there's no point to it he says," looking west. "It's time we go ashore... See what's what," he adds.

"The rocket could have washed up on the beach," Kelly suggests.

"Possibly," Hank agrees.

"Let's go see," says The Kid.

"With a little luck we're still in Montauk," Kelly says.

"What about rum row?" Dave asks.

"Rum lines existed from Maine to Florida during prohibition," Kelly tells him.

"Makes sense..." Dave says.

Hank makes his way to the helm. He starts the big diesel engine, lets it warm up a bit, then comes about, revs the motor and heads west towards what he believes will be the shoreline.

A short time later they spot land in the early morning light. Hank smiles. "It's Montauk all right," he says, pointing to a square-looking island. "That's Block Island," he tells them. He turns to starboard, "The inlet we came out of is only a few miles west," he says, glancing at Sal who is standing next to him.

"We're fortunate to have such a knowledgeable seaman as our captain," Sal says admiring Hank's seamanship.

Dave smiles. "Tellin' me," he says. "Without GPS, astral and coastal navigation is all we have," he says. "Hey, Hank, are you versed in celestial navigation?" he asks.

"I know enough to not always follow the setting sun if I want to head west," he says.

“Why not? Doesn’t the sun always set in the west?” Sal asks.

“Sure... but not always dead west,” Hank tells her. “There’s a forty-four-degree variance between the vernal and autumnal equinox.” He says knowingly. “Follow the sun west in the winter from the middle of the Atlantic and you could end up in Bermuda, little lady,” he says, smiling at her.

“And he calls me Einstein,” Dave quips.

Kelly pops his head into the cabin. “If the inlet’s there, we know it’s later than 1927,” Kelly tells them.

“That’s right,” says Hank. “Carl Fischer didn’t dynamite the lake into the bay till ‘26 or ‘27 sometime,” he says.

Seagulls show up and they know they’re close.

“That’s Culloden Point,” Hank tells them, pointing to a high bluff off the starboard side as he hugs the coastline.

“Would ya look at that?” Kelly says.

A beautiful wooden Stephens Cruiser yacht motors past them heading out to sea. A festive group aboard waves hello at the Sally Ann. The crew wave back.

“There it is,” Hank says.

They motor through the inlet and enter Lake Montauk.

“Wow...” Hank says. “Amazing...”

Kelly knows enough to see that it is a totally different place. “There’s the yacht club...” he says, pointing.

“We can put in over there,” Hank says, pointing to the far end of the dock.

Hank maneuvers the Sally Ann to the far end of the dockside of old. Rollie and The Kid tie on. They sit there on deck and watch a while.

“Even the air smells different,” Hank says.

“Look over there,” Kelly says, pointing to a building where horse-drawn coaches and period automobiles pull up picking up groups of well-dressed people of the day arriving at a large Tudor building at far end of the Yacht Club.

“That has to be the speakeasy,” says Dave.

“The Deep Sea Club...” Kelly says with an air of romance, as he peers out at the scene smiling.

To their credit, none of them have fainted from the shock of having travelled to the 1920s.

In many ways Kelly is living a longtime dream of his.

“Look how they’re dressed,” Sal comments as he watches the fine ladies step out of coaches and automobiles. “We need some clothes,” she says, tugging at the little black dress she wore on her date with Demyan.

“Now’s a heck of a time to think about shopping, Sal,” The Kid says, cracking wise.

“She’s right,” says Kelly.

“Sure is...” Dave adds. “We’ll stick out like sore thumbs without finely tailored period attire.”

Rollie reaches into his pocket and pulls out some cash, "My money is too new to buy anything here," he says, his face a giant question mark.

They stand there a moment, silent, just staring at each other, unsure what to do.

"You guys are thieves, aren't you?" Hank asks with a wry smile.

"I love this man," says Rollie.

"Hank's right," exclaims Kelly, already thinking of a way out.

"He most certainly is," says Sal smiling at Hank.

"Let's do what we do best," Kelly says with a shrug, his arms in the air.

He gazes out over the marina. "There are some very fine yachts here. Where's that scope?" he asks, checking around the deck.

Dave produces the vintage spyglass. Kelly peers through it at some of the elegant wooden yachts docked closer to the Deep Sea Club.

"It'll be dark soon," says Kelly.

"They loved cash in the 1920s," says Sal.

"That's right! We didn't have credit cards yet," Kelly says looking at the crew. "Cash was king."

"There's probably a safe on every one of those boats just filled with cash waiting to be liberated," Rollie says, rubbing his jaw while gazing out over the marina. He cracks his knuckles, “Back to basics,” he says, locking eyes with Kelly.

“You guys are too much fun.” Hank smiles.

It’s quiet for a moment as they struggle emotionally to come to terms with the different world in which they find themselves. They know that they’ll have to adjust their thinking in order to apply their various expertise to a new set of rules, both technically and culturally.

“Y’know, now that we’re back in Montauk, I can’t help but to think about Sparky,” Kelly says, looking at everyone.

“Yeah,” Sal agrees. “I’d hate it if he thought we took a powder,” she says.

“He was a good man,” says Dave.

“You say that like he’s dead or something,” Sal retorts, looking at Dave with raised eyebrows. “Sparky *is* a good man,” she says with a coy smile.

“Fair enough, Sal,” Dave says with a nod of the head. “Then again...” he says suddenly, thinking it through, “Now that we’re in the 1920s, it would not be at all inaccurate to say that Sparky ‘will’ be a good man,” he says.

Everyone stares at Dave. As much as it is sinking in that they have travelled through time, confronting the ramifications are mind boggling. They know that nothing will ever be the same. It’s as though they’ve leapt off that precipice that has haunted each of them for years, and this is where they’ve landed, ninety years in the distant, yet, not too distant, past. They stand there a moment trying to not let all manner of crazy emotions that are stirring overwhelm them. A long moment passes in absolute silence as their minds race through myriad circumstances brought about by travelling through time.

“You know something Sal… I’ll bet there are closets full of neat clothes on those yachts,” says The Kid breaking the spell.

Kelly looks at him and smiles.

“Time to make a plan,” Kelly tells them, smiling, feeling a great satisfaction that he had seen the potential and pulled The Kid off the streets when he did. “It’s moments like this,” he says, throwing his arm around The Kid, “it’s moments like this that make me love you.”

Kelly looks at his wristwatch, then realizes it may or may not be the correct time. He looks at Dave pointing at his watch hoping for some kind of answer from the scientist, but Dave just shrugs.

Kelly looks up at the sky, “It’ll be dark soon,” he says with a devious grin.

“Crews will likely remain aboard those yachts…” Rollie tells Kelly.

“Likely,” Kelly agrees, “but when the cat’s away…” he says, looking at Sal.

Kelly looks over at Hank. “You wouldn’t have a women’s bathing suit aboard that will fit Sal, by any chance, would you?” he asks.

Hank smiles. “I just might,” he says.

“Old Sally Ann has doubled as a pleasure craft on occasion,” he admits with a wry smile. “I’ll go poke around,” he says standing. “Sal?” he says holding out his hand.

Sal rolls her eyes, takes his hand and goes below with Hank.

Kelly, Dave, Rollie and The Kid remain on deck.

Kelly peers through the spyglass, “This is beyond fascinating,” he says. “All my life I’ve imagined scenes just like this,” he says, placing the spyglass to his side for a moment. “And here it is,” he says.

“This is gonna be fun,” The Kid says, smiling at his mentor.

Kelly peers through the spyglass observing the luxury yachts, most measuring over two hundred feet in length. “There’s a fine example of the Gilded Age,” he mutters. “Pay close attention, Kid. There’s a lot to learn here. The Gilded Age society in which we suddenly find ourselves frequently engaged in social comparison, valuable in determining human behavior in any age,” he tells him. “Take a look at these yachts” he says, handing the spyglass to The Kid. “Each is desperately attempting to outdo the other in order to increase their measure of self-worth, in order to enhance a feeling of superiority,” Kelly tells him.

“They’re doing a great job,” The Kid says peering through the spyglass. “That one must be two hundred and fifty feet long!” he gasps.

“Two hundred and seventy, to be exact,” Kelly tells him.

“How can you tell that by looking at it?” The Kid asks, doubting Kelly.

“That’s the North Star, Kid. Cornelius Vanderbilt’s classic built in 1853, a luxury yacht which set the standard by which all others were measured,” Kelly tells him.

“Either way, these are truly awesome boats,” The Kid says looking through the spyglass.

“Yachts, or ships, Kid,” Dave tells him. “Never boats,” he adds.

“We’re on a boat,” Kelly tells him. “A very special boat,” he adds, when he sees Sal in a rather skimpy bikini stepping on deck.

Dave, Rollie and The Kid turn to see what he’s talking about. Sal is indeed a stunning figure in a tight and skimpy bikini. She is a devastatingly gorgeous vixen to be reckoned with. As well as they know her, and as familiar as they are with her physical beauty, which often disappears for them, working in such close proximity, Sal in a bikini cannot be easily dismissed. The men’s jaws drop to the deck.

“Wow!” gasps The Kid. “Not bad for an older broad,” he says.

“Fuck you, Kid,” she quips.

Kelly walks over to her. “Woman in distress?” he asks her.

“I seem to have fallen in,” she says in a helpless flapper persona, “Would you have a towel I could borrow?” she says adding a Mid-Atlantic drawl Cary Grant would envy.

“Not a ship’s captain or crew for a hundred miles will be able to resist you for one moment, Sal.” Kelly smiles.

“Nary one chance in a million,” Dave adds. “And once we get into Alva Vanderbilt’s closet, no gentleman in this age will have a breath that you won’t possess,” he tells her.

“Spare me,” she says.

“Wait till we deck you out with some of her wardrobe,” Kelly says, picturing it in his mind. “Alva and the other ladies in her little blue blood society were in constant competition for the finest apparel, so you know there will be some fine garments for you to grace with your extreme beauty,” he goes on.

“Laying it on kind of thick, aren’t we?” she says defiantly, hands on her hips.

Kelly smiles. “What do you say, Hank?” he asks turning to Hank.

“Nary a chance,” Hank says, looking Sal up and down, imitating Dave.

They can’t help but to crack up laughing.

“Boys...” she quips, joining in the laughter.

“Okay,” says Kelly. “As soon as it’s dark enough we hit the North Star for the wardrobe and whatever’s in the safe,” he says. “Rollie, knowing Sal is our primary diversion, I defer to your experience in boat invasions for logistics,” he says with a gesture meaning for everyone to listen to Rollie.

“Yachts or ships, Kelly... Never boats,” The Kid says, raising his eyebrows at Kelly and then winking at Sal.

A few hours later, Sal slips into the water and swims quietly over to Vanderbilt’s yacht, the North Star. She swims out to deeper water yet remaining close enough to be seen and heard. She begins to flail her arms in the water helplessly screaming for dear life.

“Help!” she yelps. “I can’t swim!” she yells.

The captain of the North Star, hearing the voice of a woman in distress, rushes to the bow where Sal continues to yell for help, as she flounders in the water. The captain spots her and without hesitation, leaps into the water to save her. The entire staff and crew of the North Star gather along the starboard to watch their heroic captain save the damsel in distress, allowing Kelly, Rollie, Dave and The Kid to sneak aboard unseen at the stern. They move quickly through the huge yacht. Kelly and Rollie search for the safe, Dave and The Kid for the wardrobe. Sal is having fun pretending to drown as she stealthily swims father and farther away from the ship. Kelly and Rollie find the safe.

"Diebold," Rollie says on one knee looking up at Kelly.

"Go figure," remarks Kelly. "Here," he says, holding out a tall, thin highball glass for Rollie to use as a stethoscope. "I grabbed it on the way."

Rollie places it over the area above the combination dial where the tumblers are and begins to crack the safe. It takes them longer than expected but finally they're in.

"Phew," says Kelly, looking at the stacks of cash.

"Okay," Kelly says, "Just enough to set us up, but not so much as to be easily noticed," he says.

Rollie grabs stacks of bills. Kelly brings a stack to his face and breathes in.

"Smells the same," he says.

Rollie sniffs a stack. "Timeless," he says.

They close up the safe and rush off the yacht, being careful to stay quiet and low. Meanwhile, The Kid and Dave have filled an entire shipping trunk with clothing and are scurrying it across the dock to the Sally Ann while the entire North Star crew remains engaged in assisting the poor, stunningly beautiful woman who had tragically fallen into the water. And now a soaking wet Captain as well. The crew of the North Star manage to get them both onto the yacht safely. The staff dries Sal off with warm towels, then wraps her in a white, terry-cloth robe. Dave and The Kid get the large trunk to the Sally Ann where Hank is there to help load it onto the boat. They are laughing hysterically from the rush, just as Kelly and Rollie appear. Kelly grabs the spyglass, brings it to his eye and focuses on the deck of the North Star. He watches Sal, on deck with the Captain, being catered to by the staff. A short stout nurse standing nearby looks at her watch, then reaches up and pulls an old mercury glass tube thermometer from Sal's mouth, reads it and nods okay. Sal is given a hairbrush and brushes her hair as an attendant holds a large round handheld mirror for her. She finishes brushing her hair, gives the Captain a hug and a friendly kiss, thanking him profusely, then steps off the yacht. She walks the long way around, hiding out for a while, in order to not be seen climbing aboard the Sally Ann. The crew gathers below to inspect the contents of the trunk filled with garments, Dave and The Kid lifted from the North Star.

Dave looks around at the crew, laughing, "We didn't have time to try anything on," he says.

They pull out the garments and lay them out on the bunk beds. Kelly tries on a silk, three-piece pinstriped suit jacket. Dave pulls out an ivory tusk walking stick.

"It's the finely crafted accoutrement that can bring a gentleman's attire to the level of elegant," Dave says, handing it to him.

"Is that a Fedora?" Kelly asks.

"It most certainly is," Dave says, handing the fine hat to Kelly.

Kelly takes it and it's as though it were made to order.

"Nothing fits me in here," says Rollie, disappointed.

Hank watches totally amused by the crew's adept thieving skills. He finds how calm they remain throughout to be very impressive. Sal steps down the gangway wearing the terry cloth robe, her hair brushed back perfectly.

"I could get used to the Vanderbilt lifestyle," she says, flipping her hair back.

"I grabbed something special just for you, Sal," Dave says digging around in the trunk. "Here it is," he exclaims and hands her a fine, long, feminine cigarette holder.

"How posh," she says modeling it with an elegant flair.

"What is posh, anyway?" asks The Kid.

He looks around the room and adds somewhat defensively. "I mean I know it means, y'know... fancy schmancy, and all, but where's it from?" he asks.

"There's actually a huge debate among historians about that, Kid," Kelly tells him. "Most reasonable people understand that it is an acronym for Port Out Starboard Home," he says. "P.O.S.H... But diehards argue that it isn't an acronym at all," he informs The Kid. "On ocean voyages between Britain and India or Africa, the most desirable cabins... the ones that didn't get the afternoon heat, and most often had sight of the coast, were on the port side going out and on the starboard side coming home," Kelly tells him.

"Yes, dahling, my higher-priced luxury tickets were always stamped with the letters POSH," Sal tells him in her best Mid-Atlantic drawl.

"Yeah, but because no one has any proof, it remains a hot debate." Dave pops open a fine top hat and puts it on.

"Hey! Now that we're here, in that era, maybe we can find a ticket marked POSH and settle the whole thing!" says The Kid excitedly.

Kelly smiles at The Kid's enthusiasm, "Maybe, Kid... maybe..."

Dave tries on a jacket, but the sleeves are at least an inch too long.

"I'll look like a circus monkey in this," he says diving back into the stack of clothing they've emptied from the trunk.

Sal begins sorting out some of the silk dresses and gowns from the trunk. She pulls out a thin silk dress with spaghetti straps, a beaded headband and a boa. She poses, holding the dress against her body.

"Look at these!" Sal says excitedly, yanking out one dress after another. "Coco Chanel..." she remarks holding one against her body and posing.

She tosses it on the bed and continues rummaging through the trunk.

"This one is a Jeanne Lanvin," she exclaims. "Nice..."

She tries on several outfits until she finds one to her liking with pointy shoes and all. She fits a cigarette into her new cigarette holder and lights it. Kelly appears decked out in a silk pin-striped Zoot Suit.

"Why don't you fellas put some ensembles together while Sal and I conduct a short reconnaissance of the Deep Sea Club and Casino, Kelly tells them.

He grabs his Fedora and looks at Sal with a huge grin. “Shall we, deary?” he asks.

“We must… I’ve been told the casino is wonderful this time of year,” she remarks coyly in her best Hoy Poloi.

Dave, Rollie and Hank continue to try on suits. Kelly grabs a healthy stack of cash, slips it into his vest pocket and smiles.

“Let’s go win some money,” he says to Sal.

“Let’s,” she answers.

They climb up the gangway to the deck and slip around to the far side of the Sally Ann where they can step off unnoticed. They stroll along the promenade arm in arm towards the club. It appears that Kelly has never been happier in his life. It is as though all his dreams have come true. Alive in the roaring twenties!

“I’m home,” he says, standing still a moment and taking in the scene. “I’m home…”

Sal looks up at Kelly. His face is beaming.

“I know,” she says and gives Kelly a warm hug. “I know, baby…”

As they stroll closer to the speakeasy they can hear a swinging version of ‘Blue Skies’, a popular Jazz hit of the era, pouring out of the club. They walk to the entrance where a doorman greets them and welcomes them. Kelly slips a large bill into his hand as they walk by.

“Thank you, sir!” says the doorman watching as they enter the speakeasy.

Kelly bends his arm up to his shoulder and twinkles a few fingers as a you're-welcome to the doorman. The club is boisterous, filled with rich and famous party people roaring it up. They approach the bar, passing the jazz band with a glamorous vocalist singing "Shaking the Blues Away."

"Two martinis, please," Kelly orders.

"Dry," Sal adds.

They take in their surroundings in utter amazement as they sip their cocktails. Loud laughter erupts at a table near the rear of the club. Sal and Kelly look over.

She pokes Kelly, "Is that Errol Flynn?" she asks, her eyes lighting up.

"It most certainly is," Kelly answers, his smile so large it captures a tear rolling down his cheek.

"Errol Flynn..." Sal says dreamily.

She watches closely as the movie star cavorts with a distinguished group of the rich and famous.

Kelly looks at Sal with the face of a child, "I feel as though I have woken up in a wonderful dream," he tells her near tears.

She places her hand gently on his shoulder, "So I see..." she says, looking up at him with a sweet smile. "Now I'm going to live one of mine," she says.

She takes her drink and galivants over to the table where Errol Flynn is seated with other illustrious members of the Deep Sea Club that includes John Barrymore, Mae West, W.C. Fields and F. Scott Fitzgerald. Looking absolutely stunning, she walks directly to Errol Flynn, looks down at him seated at the table, strokes his cheek with more confidence than most any lady would have had at the time and coos.

“I know you prefer your girls on the younger side, deary,” she says, making eye contact with everyone seated at the table. “But I promise the sheer knowledge I hold in my pinky will undo any and all such silly little desires of screwing the farmer’s daughter,” she says staring into Errol Flynn’s surprised eyes with a sultry expression.

I wasn’t there, but I would wager Errol Flynn was trembling, if only just a little.

“Rather well put, by a dear woman of extraordinary measure,” exclaims F. Scott Fitzgerald, raising his glass to Sal and finishing off his gin and tonic.

“Ah, yes…” says W.C. Fields, looking at Errol Flynn. “A rather divine intrusion,” he remarks as he looks the gorgeous Sal up and down. “I can say that I’m almost glad I came here tonight,” he comments and raises his martini to Sal.

“Come over here, lovely… Have a sit down,” Mae West tells her, yanking a chair from a neighboring table and patting the seat. “Let’s talk a while,” she adds, sipping her signature cayenne pepper martini.

Errol Flynn looks at Sal. “It’s true, I like my whiskey old, and my women young,” he says. “However, you, my dear lady, are a goddess who transcends both age and preference.” He lifts a glass of whiskey to Sal before taking a long sip.

“Says the Tasmanian Devil in the flesh,” John Barrymore comments to uproarious laughter.

"Anyone can be a movie star with the dashing good looks of Adonis," W.C. Fields jokes, looking at Errol Flynn. "Try being one with the appearance of a lowly farm hand," he says as he finishes off his Martini with a Vaudevillian bow, to more boisterous laughter. "Waiter!" he says loudly. "Another dozen martinis, please." He turns to John Barrymore. "Why I don't like drinking out..." he says agitated, "At home I never have to wait for the drinks to be made..."

Sal is beyond thoroughly amused. She glances over at Kelly sitting at the bar sharing intimate conversation with none other than the beautiful Marion Davies, a dreamy look in his eyes. After a while Kelly and Sal decide it's time to stroll next door to the casino.

"When we first flew into Montauk and you said there was a casino here in the 1920s, I never imagined in a hundred years, I'd actually be inside of it," Sal says as they enter the casino floor.

"A hundred years," Kelly repeats. "Doesn't feel that long a period of time suddenly," he comments as he takes in the wonderful environs of the casino.

"I smell money," Sal says with a nefarious grin.

"So do I, toots," Kelly says with a huge grin. "So do I..." He gives Sal his arm as they stroll towards the roulette table.

"I'll bet Dave could do a number on that old wheel," Kelly says.

"A night raid to plant a fix?" Sal asks, looking into Kelly's eyes.

"Sounds lovely, doesn't it?" he says smiling. "They must close the doors at some point," he says. "Either way, we'll hire one of those horse-drawn carriages to take us to the

Montauk Manor and book some rooms," Kelly tells her. "The Sally Ann sticks out like a sore thumb," he adds thinking alud. "It's only a matter of time before someone wonders what it is and begins making inquiries," he says as a loud cheer from a group of folks at the roulette wheel fills the room. "We'll have to find a convenient place to stash it," he adds.

"We have to acquire clothes for the crew," Sal says.

"We should go shopping in town first thing tomorrow," Kelly adds.

They continue strolling through the casino and stop near the craps table.

"While you were cavorting with the likes of Errol Flynn, I learned that there is a first-class haberdashery in town," Kelly tells her. "But right now, I'll need a distraction at the craps table," he says, winking at Sal, his mind reeling a mile a minute.

"It's been a while," she says, looking at Kelly, maybe feeling he's about to bite off more than he can chew. "Think you still have it?" she asks, always game despite the odds.

"Like riding a bicycle," he says, finding a spot at the table and laying some cash on the velvet.

They have some fun betting and intermingling with the guests. It's pretty hectic and there is a lot of action happening all at once. Kelly even wins a few pass line bets. Sal has been ordering drink after drink, playing the drunken flapper, knocking into and insulting people at the table. Kelly skillfully pretends to continually attempt to reel her in, apologizing to the other gamblers at the table. A shooter is taking a longer-than-usual time to roll. Sal points to him with her drink which splashes everywhere.

"You gonna marry those dice, honey, or roll 'em?" she slurs before cracking up at her own joke.

The shooter craps out.

"Craps!" Sal yells, falling into the young gentleman standing beside her. "Figures..." she adds.

The man is practically holding her up and keeping her from falling to the floor. She turns around, her face inches from his.

"Hi, honey," she coos very suggestively. "What's your name, babe?" she inquires in her most sensuous demeanor, her hands all over him.

"Seven out. New shooter!" announces the croupier.

It's Kelly's turn to roll the dice.

"C'mon, you bones! A little bit of love," Kelly says, talking to the dice. "Give them one of your magic kisses for me, baby," he says holding out the dice for Sal to kiss.

"Can't you see I'm busy?" she asks, annoyed, hanging on to the young man. "Oh, what the hell?" she says. She kisses the dice, "Seven come eleven," she slurs before Kelly rolls the dice.

Although it's been some time, this isn't the first time Kelly and Sal have played the couple on a party. Kelly lucks out and rolls a seven.

Oohs, ahs and cheers for Kelly from the crowd.

"The gentleman rolls a natural. Come bets pay," the boxman announces, paying the pass bets.

The stickman pulls in the dice, then shoves them back to Kelly, who picks them up and kisses them. Gamblers place their bets on the table.

“Bets are on,” the boxman calls.

“Give these sweet babies another magic kiss, sugar,” he says, moving closer to Sal.

“Lemme have ‘em, she slurs,” before falling head first into Kelly very hard, knocking him down, also knocking over the woman standing next to him and several others to the ground screaming, cursing or laughing. Kelly makes a big fuss over it as the dealers rush over to assist in helping the ladies who were knocked down, get to their feet.

“Ya dumb oaf,” she yells at Kelly who, unknown to anyone, has the dice palmed in his hand.

“You were supposed to catch me,” she insists drunkenly. “Take me home, she insists.

In the milieu of women wiping cocktails off of their dresses and collecting themselves, Kelly looks up at the boxman with the sincerest apologetic expression anyone has ever seen.

“I best get this little lady to bed,” he says among insults and threats of some of the gamblers still brushing themselves off.

“I do believe that is the best solution, sir,” the boxman agrees, happy to be getting rid of them.

Kelly carries her out of the casino kicking and screaming. They hurry back to the Sally Ann laughing all the way. Hank and the crew are there waiting when they appear.

“What a party!” Sal says still in character, hiccupping.

They help Sal aboard. Kelly gets on deck, reaches into his pocket and produces a pair of dice.

He looks at Sal. “Just like riding a bicycle,” he says.

“Yeah, you still got it.” She smiles.

He hands them to Dave.

“Got enough tools around here to do something with these?” he asks.

“Load dice in an era when they were still getting away with bristling?” He smiles. “I can load these little ladies to roll up or down, with no one the wiser, while standing on my head balancing an egg yolk,” he boasts.

“I believe you could,” Hank says, smiling in amazement at his newfound friends.

“An egg yolk?” The Kid asks challengingly. “Why not the whole egg?” he wants to know.

Dave looks at him, his eyebrows raised, a little tilt of the head. “Have you ever attempted to balance an egg yolk while standing on your head?” Dave asks matter of factly.

“I’ve never even heard of someone trying to balance an egg yolk standing on their head,” he says.

“My point exactly,” Dave answers, index finger pointed upwards.

Hank smiles at the exchange as he looks around the marina... The sound of jazz of the 1920s still rolling faintly in the distance.

“That doesn’t make any sense,” The Kid insists.

“Now you’re getting it, Kid,” Dave tells him with a smile.

“We’ve gotten some odd looks while you two were gone,” Hank tells Kelly and Sal.

“We decided we should try to stash the Sally Ann,” Rollie says.

“Agreed,” Kelly says, pulling out a wad of cash from bets he’d won before the fiasco.

But Sal... Sal reaches into her silk stockings at her inner thigh and pulls out a billfold. She opens it, pulls a thick wad of cash from it and looks up at everyone with a smart-ass grin.

“The young man was loaded,” she says, handing the billfold to The Kid. “Here Kid, don’t ever say I never gave you anything.” She hiccups.

“How many of those cocktails did you actually drink?” Kelly asks.

“All of them,” she says, losing her balance while readjusting her garters and falling onto Hanks lap.

Hank holds her steady.

“Thanks, doll,” she says to Hank holding the wad of cash safely up in the air.

“Here, count it,” she says to Kelly.

“I could see you setting him up for the lift, but then when you made the knock-everyone-down move, the timing of which was perfect, by the way, I figured you gave up on it,” he says taking the wad from her and counting it.

“This has to be your smoothest lift of all time,” he says.

“You should’ve seen it,” Sal says looking around at everyone. “I flirted with Errol Flynn,” she says, laughing.

“*The* Errol Flynn?” asks Dave.

“*The* Errol Flynn,” she repeats.

Kelly sits down, clasps his hands and looks out over his crew one by one.

“What we have here, gentleman, Sal...” he adds turning to Sal, “is...” he pauses a moment searching for the right words.

They’ve all seen Kelly like this before. They each find a place to sit down. So much has happened so quickly, even Kelly, the smartest and most adept at quickly adapting to any situation among them, having always been able to get himself out of the tightest scrapes, is having a difficult time summarizing the how, what and where of their uncanny situation.

“What we have here... is a living museum,” he says finally looking at everyone with an earnest face that calls out for each of them to put their best thinking to what he is about to tell them.

“With our combined knowledge base...” he states looking around at everyone, “The cornucopia of our various expertise accumulated over many years, in a far more technologically advanced age, having studied the greatest cons of the greatest con artists from time immemorial,” he says, smiling at them fondly with love in his heart for each and every one of them, “Learning from the best of the best...” he continues.

The crew glances at one another in anticipation of what's coming next.

"We've lost the missile," he says suddenly, "An unfortunate event. Fair enough. But!" he says standing up with a face that asks them all to never lose hope, "What lays before us is an opportunity to make history," he insists, realizing the instant those words left his mouth, how strange and bizarre saying that actually is. He cracks up laughing.

"History!" he says, laughing loudly.

Dave begins to laugh, then Sal, Rollie and The Kid. Soon they are all whooping it up. Even Hank is laughing so hard, he must hold his sides.

"There is an immense amount of money here, so ripe for the picking... It's just plain silly!" he says. "We are in the roaring twenties!" he exclaims, his arms outstretched. "There are some amazing possibilities here for us to explore." He paces the foredeck.

"Of course!" Dave says. "Think about it!" he exclaims, his mind reeling. "We know more than everyone we will meet here combined," he says looking around at everyone excitedly.

"The things we could do," Kelly says, the tone of his voice coaxing the others.

They sit there, each deep in their own thoughts, considering everything that has happened since pulling off the Chase Bank heist and stepping aboard the Sally Ann. A long moment passes as the popular jazz of the 1920s wafts softly across the marina from The Deep Sea Club.

"One thing you've always taught me," says The Kid breaking the silence, looking at his mentor with a genuinely warm and sincere expression, "I remember you telling me these exact words," he says with his eyes closed. He looks up at Kelly, "Kid, you have to roll with the punches..." he says as he thinks back to some of the earliest exchanges he's had with Kelly. "From the very start you always maintained that I must make the best of a bad situation," he says, looking out into the harbor, "And... that if I can do that, I'll learn that maybe it's not the situation that's bad, but only my thinking," he says finally.

Kelly smiles broadly and winks at Sal.

Rollie nods his head, "Throw me into a pack of wolves, and I'll return leading the pack," he says looking around at everyone seated around the foredeck.

"Always look for the silver lining, Kid..." Sal says, lighting a cigarette in her new cigarette holder.

"They're right, Kid," Hank says as he's trying to recall something. He looks over at The Kid, "In silent sorrow they drop their salted tears, shall our soul be a feast of kelp and brine, the wasted tales of wishful time," he says, deeply affecting everyone.

Rollie looks at him, "Adler," he mutters. "Nice..."

"Life is a game of roulette, Kid," Dave says.

Kelly's eyes perk up as do Sal's.

The roulette wheel..." Sal exclaims.

"There is a roulette wheel in the casino that is dying to meet you," Kelly tells Dave.

"Oh?" Dave asks with a smile.

"Okay." Kelly stands up. "Has anyone else found an outfit you can wear?" he asks.

“I found a suit that works,” Dave tells him.

“I could pass,” says The Kid. He looks up at Kelly. “Not my style,” he adds with a shrug.

“You have to make it your style,” Sal tells him.

“Okay, Sal, Dave and I will hire a horse-drawn carriage to take us to the Montauk Manor, where we’ll book rooms for everyone,” Kelly tells them. “Kid,” he says smiling at his protégé, “You stick around and scout the casino. We need to know where the back entrances are, what time they close and for how long.” He points to Dave. “Dave needs absolute privacy for his rendezvous with our lovely roulette wheel.”

“A place like this often had a trip-wire alarm system,” Dave tells The Kid, “See what you can find out.”

“It’s likely that there will be guards to contend with,” says Rollie, cracking his knuckles.

Kelly smiles at Rollie. “Which you will attend to, I’m sure,” he says. “We’ll book the rooms, secure some period elements needed to rig the roulette wheel, then Dave and I will meet you back here,” he tells The Kid. “Marion tells me there’s a fine haberdashery in town. Tomorrow, we go shopping,” he says.

“Sounds good. Daddy needs new threads,” Rollie says rehearsing being a swell in the 1920s.

“On that subject, I’ll go get into my period duds,” Dave says, coifing his hair. “C’mon Kid,” Dave says patting The Kid on the back. I’ll help you with your tie,” he says, smiling at The Kid.

"Be back in a jif," The Kid tells Kelly and Sal with a smile that could have come from the roaring twenties.

"Now you're getting it, Kid," Sal says. "Jot down your sizes, Rollie dear, and tomorrow I'll have you styled up like a real swell."

"Anything but gray," Rollie tells her.

"No gray... Got it," she says.

"Hank and I will find a place to stash the Sally Ann." Rollie tells them.

"Perfect," Kelly says turning to Hank, "Probably best to stash the Sally Ann somewhere not too far from a road so we can access it when we need to by horse or automobile, yet somehow remain secretive," Kelly says. "The Montauk Highway that runs all the way to the Lighthouse, Deep Hollow Ranch and those Stanford White homes already exists," he says.

"The highway's a good call. I've already given this some thought," Hank tells him. "I believe the nearest place that will give us cover, as well as access to the highway is a cove down by what's now The Crow's Nest," he says, then shakes his head and smiles. "Now the Crow's Nest..." he repeats looking up at Kelly, Sal and Rollie. "Never thought I'd see a time when 'now' would become a relative term," he says, laughing.

"Touché," Dave says as he reappears from below looking the dashing intellectual of the 1920s.

The Kid steps up right behind him, looking dapper.

"Whatever you guys do," Hank says looking at Dave's getup, "I'll stick with the Sally Ann," he says.

They all look at one another, then at Hank.

“You wouldn’t leave us behind, would you, deary?” Sal asks in her flapper.

Hank laughs, “Where would I go?”

“Good point…” she says.

“Besides, I’ve grown pretty fond of you guys,” he says, looking around and smiling at everyone.

“We feel the same way about you, Hank,” Dave says.

Kelly sets The Kid up with a wad of cash.

The Kid flips through the cash, and then turns to Kelly and Dave. “I’ll catch you on the flip side,” he says with a wink while stuffing the cash in the billfold Sal gave him.

“As crazy as things have gotten, this is the most fun I’ve had in a very long time,” Hank says, looking at each of them.

“We’ll meet you guys behind what will someday be the Crow’s Nest, tomorrow at Sunset,” Kelly says.

“I’ll make my way out to the road,” Rollie tells him.

“We’ll be there,” Kelly says. He turns to Sal, “C’mon, toots, let’s secure our lavish accommodations at the Montauk Manor,” he says.

“Let’s,” She answers.

Kelly, Sal and Dave step off the far side of the Sally Ann and make their way to the speakeasy, where several horse-drawn carriages are standing by. They approach the carriage in the very front of the pack.

"Allow me," Dave says stepping ahead of them, "Hey, cupcake," he says, smiling at the driver. "We're done with the whoopee for the moment," he smiles raising his eyebrows exaggeratingly. "And what a party! Oh! It was simply divine," he says wiping his brow with his handkerchief. "Would you be kind enough to take my friends and I to the Montauk Manor?" he says with a huge smile.

The driver looks at Dave like he's seen it all before. "Certainly, sir. Step right in," he says pointing to the back with his thumb.

"Come, darlings, I've secured us a wagoner to the Montauk Manor," he shouts to Kelly and Sal who are dancing to the smooth jazz emanating from the Deep Sea Club.

"Is there a dance floor aboard?" Sal asks, playing the drunk flapper.

"No, it's just a little hop-a-long," Kelly says, helping Sal aboard.

The driver turns up the kerosene lanterns fixed on either side of the carriage and slaps the reins. The horse neighs and begins moving along in a slow trot.

"Look!" Sal says pointing at the driver, It's Ben Hur!" she exclaims as the driver pulls away.

"My apologies," Kelly tells the driver, looking at Sal. "You see her favorite driver is a fellow named Sparky and we can't seem to find him of late," says Kelly, looking at Dave and Sal.

"Sparky," Sal says with affection. "What a guy!" she says.

"I wonder if he ever made it to Nova Scotia," Dave ponders.

The three of them think back to their pal Sparky as the horse-drawn carriage clatters along the Star Island Causeway.

“Hey Dave, if we’re here now, riding along this causeway, will we still be here driving along it with Sparky a hundred years from now?” Sal asks trying to wrap her head around how this could really have happened and what it might mean.

“Good question Sal,” says Dave. “We find ourselves in a strange predicament having traveled through time...” he says. “Scientists and philosophers have pondered riddles like this for millennia,” he says. “They strain definition of reality.”

“But how can we speak of something in the past tense when it hasn’t happened yet?” she asks perplexing herself with linear-time dimension.

“If you remember it happening, it happened, Sal,” Kelly says matter of factly.

“Basically, yeah,” Dave says, nodding at Kelly.

“That’s just it,” Kelly says. “It did happen. We were there when it did. I remember it like it was yesterday,” he says.

“Yet relative to where we are now in the timeline of life on earth, it won’t occur for, as you say, a hundred years from now,” Dave tells them, trying not to get lost in the complexity of it all. “We left the timeline that we were in and now we’re in a new one,” Dave continues. “What’s about to happen to us hasn’t happened yet where we are now, but when we were back in 2019, it did,” he says. “Or did it?” he asks Sal and Kelly with that eerie face he likes to make at moments like this.

"Wait a minute," Kelly says. "What if we were able to return to 2019 and we did things here that change..." he says, stopping in mid-sentence suddenly, realizing something, "...the course of history? Does that mean that what has already happened will happen again only differently?"

"It can't!" the three of them exclaim in unison. They laugh together, uproariously tickled by the mysterious riddle of it all.

The driver raises his eyebrows, shaking his head. "Absinthe," he says to himself.

"Wait! That's it!" Kelly exclaims, "Dave," he says trembling from the thrilling thoughts he's having. "This can be the greatest con of all time!" he says grabbing Dave with his eyes which have turned from excited to electric. "And if anyone in the entire world, in the entire history of all mankind, can pull it off, it is you, my friend," he says.

"What on earth are you dreaming up now, handsome?" Sal sticks a cigarette in her cigarette holder and lights it.

"You are a genius!" Dave says looking at Kelly. He spins around in the carriage grabs Kelly's arms and faces him. "We'll go down in the books of all time," he says.

"You guys care to fill me in?" Sal asks.

Dave looks at her in a super excited state. He and Kelly are shivering with excitement.

"We got here, right?" Dave poses the statement as a question. "If..." Dave says, "and it is admittedly the biggest 'if' of my career, but if I was able to figure out how to get us back," he says.

“We can put something into effect now that will pay off like a slot machine when we get back and are able to capitalize on it,” Kelly finishes.

“Wow...” Sal says feeling faint from the depth of intensity the proposition proposes. “But how?” she asks.

“No idea,” says Dave, “Not yet...” he adds with his mischievous grin.

The three of them attempt to absorb the complex idea at hand.

“There’s something strange out there in the ocean,” Kelly says, staring at Sal.

“A break in the space-time continuum. A slip if you will, ...a window through a further dimension that somehow looped us into the same place, but at a different point in time,” says Dave. “It’s pure conjecture on my part, really, but then again, here we are. He looks at them, his hands spread wide.

They sit quiet a moment as the horse clatters the carriage slowly along Flamingo Avenue in the direction of the Montauk Manor, a gargantuan three-story manor with 140 units, a ballroom, restaurants and shops, situated high on a hill across from the Long Island Railroad. A Packard Super Eight Phaeton races by, blowing its horn at the slow-moving horse-drawn carriage.

“Driver, darling? Sal asks.

“Yes?” answers the horse drawn carriage driver.

“What is today’s date?” she asks.

“As of midnight,” he says rather curtly, “today is July 6, miss.”

The three of them look at one another, heads thrown back.

"That's right," says Dave.

"And driver... What year is it?" she asks.

The driver rolls his eyes.

"It is 1929, miss," he says.

"July 6, 1929," Sal says looking at Kelly and Dave.

"Ninety years to the day," Dave says.

They sit still a moment, their heads spinning, attempting to fathom the fact that the day is the same, the place is the same, but not the year. Kelly's eyes pop. "That means," he says excitedly, "theoretically, the rocket should be here," he says, nearly trembling.

"Or at least that it could be here... Or could have *been* here," says Dave. "Or that it's on its way here," he adds.

Kelly and Sal look at him unsure why he is suggesting so many options.

He looks at them with a genuinely sincere expression, "The rocket disappeared into thin air while we were still aboard the Sally Ann before whatever that storm was, began to affect us directly," he says, raising his eyebrows at them. "It left us behind for a few minutes..." he finishes.

The three of them sit there recalling the strange journey they took aboard the Sally Ann just two days before.

"The rocket, it appears, travelled through whatever slip in space-time that exists out there, before we did," he says.

“But that doesn’t guarantee it travelled the same route or at the same rate,” he says, patting Sal on her shoulder.

“But if it did?” Sal asks.

“If it did… and we locate it, that reinforces my developing theory that the loop is consistent,” Dave says. “That there is something unique to Montauk, that provides a passage through space-time, confined to its own locality. To Montauk…”

Kelly is putting it all together in his head and like he always does, is developing a plan.

“This is what we’ll do,” he says, getting their attention. “We will integrate ourselves into the world of The Montauk Yacht Club and The Deep Sea Casino,” he tells them. “Get to know people. See what we can learn… If the rocket did land here and was found, someone’ll know about it,” he says. “Let’s say we find it, Dave,” Kelly says sounding like a question. “Is it possible you can get us back?” he asks with a sincere tone of voice.

Sal is surprised to hear Kelly ask that question. She looks into his eyes with a tilt of her head, “You’re home, remember?” she asks.

Kelly looks into her eyes, his face filled with emotion. He turns away and peers out of the carriage window as it travels down the hill on Flamingo Avenue towards the Manor. He glances up at the star-filled sky above and smiles, “I am and I’m not,” he says.

XVII

Back in 2019, Sparky waits in Nova Scotia, unsure what happened to his new friends out at sea two nights before. The way the ship-to-shore transmission ended so abruptly and his flight to Nova Scotia having been delayed for six hours due to reports of an unexpected electrical storm at sea that night, has him worried that something has gone terribly wrong. All having gone well, the Sally Ann should have pulled into Nova Scotia sometime before dawn the next morning, on July fifth. It's now the sixth and Sparky's not sure what to do. He knows he can't alert the coast guard. Even if they are drifting out there he's convinced that between Dave, Hank, Kelly, Rollie and The Kid aboard, even Sal with her own brand of brilliance, they'll find a way to rig something up that will get them moving again. Besides, Hank may have already contacted someone to help them get safely to shore. Alerting the Coast Guard could very easily land them all in jail. Sparky calls a friend back in Montauk he trusts enough to check on the Sally Ann, but as of midnight there's still no sign of her at the commercial dock. He's decided to stick around Nova Scotia a few more days since meeting there is what they had agreed on. Whatever took place, he refuses to consider that they intentionally left him behind. He's seated at a dockside café typing away on his MacBook, writing everything that has taken place since he got the first call from Rollie. *I'm forced to speculate with wonder the mystery of where they might be right now*, he types.

The waitress approaches. "Anything else for you, sir?" she asks.

A thought occurs to him. "Is there a newspaper nearby?" he asks.

"I'm sure I can round one up for you," she says smiling.

"And another glass of Cabernet," he tells her.

A few moments later she appears with the wine and a copy of *The Chronicle Herald.*

"Thanks," he says smiling up at her.

A quick search through the newspaper finds an article about the stunning bank robbery in Montauk. A wry smile comes to his face. He rifles through the article reading some lines aloud to himself.

"...what officials say involved very clever planning. The robbery occurred on the Fourth of July, during the Independence Day fireworks celebration, as local law enforcement was inundated with controlling the hordes of spectators who arrive each year to the quaint seaside town..." he reads aloud.

"...The FBI are uncertain whether or not the thieves were aware that Mr. Yusapova's gems were being kept in the bank vault for safekeeping," he reads with a smile. "No suspects have been named in connection to the elaborate, highly unique bank robbery. Mr. Yusapova is being investigated for insurance fraud by both the FBI and CIA," he reads and laughs softly.

He folds the newspaper and gazes out to sea. "They're out there somewhere," he says to himself.

And that they are. Kelly, Sal and Dave are in the horse-drawn carriage they hired to take them to the Montauk Manor. The carriage moves slowly but steadily up the curving steep road past the horse stables and glass-enclosed indoor tennis courts around the last hilly bend to the Manor entrance. The driver whoas the horse to a stop and yanks the brake.

“Thank you, good sir,” Dave says loudly while opening the carriage door and stepping out.

“Would you mind sticking around a while and wait for us?” Kelly asks as she hands the driver a five-dollar bill. “We won’t be long,” he adds with a smile. “Only long enough to secure lodging and grab a tidy-up,” he says.

“That will be fine, sir,” says the driver, taking the bill with a nod of the head.

They saunter over to the majestic entrance of the Montauk Manor where a doorman welcomes them inside. Beautiful tapestries hang from the spacious lobby and opulent ballroom. Kelly and Sal secure a few apartments while Dave pokes around. Sal stays behind to have a hot bath as Kelly and Dave meet at the bar for a cocktail before grabbing the horse-drawn carriage for the slow ride back to the Casino to meet with The Kid. They exit the Manor and step into the carriage.

“The Kid’s come a long way,” Dave says as the carriage pulls away.

“Yeah, he’s really coming into his own,” Kelly says, thinking about how far The Kid has come during the three years he’s been with them.

Dave pulls out a handful of tools from his jacket, looks at them and smiles.

“Nice.” Kelly grabs a pair of pliers from the 1920s.

“Found the maintenance room,” Dave says while looking at the rudimentary tools. “My great uncle had tools like this when I was a little kid.” He admires the long narrow screwdriver he’s procured. “Cut my teeth on tools just like this.”

Kelly hands him the pliers. Dave plays with them for a moment, then puts them in his pocket.

Gazing out of the carriage window he asks, "What do you make of Hank wanting to stay with the Sally Ann?"

"I've been wondering about that..." Kelly says. "I think it has something to do with his grandfather. His involvement in our project has ignited a deep connection to his past. He may be fixated on reclaiming his heritage..." Kelly smiles. "Hank's grandfather, having been a rum-runner, I don't think there's one chance in a million he won't head out to Rum Row at some point," Kelly says.

"I think you're right," says Dave.

They ride along in silence for a while. The driver steers the carriage from West Lake Drive onto Star Island. The driver slows down to a stop as one of two armed guards stationed at the guard house walks over.

"Good evening, Keegan," the driver says to the guard, whom he seems to be very familiar with. "A coupla swells..." the driver tells him pointing over his shoulder with his thumb.

The guard peeks through the carriage window. Kelly and Dave smile at him and the guard waves them through. The carriage continues on to the Deep Sea Club.

"Interesting," Kelly says. He tells the driver that they arrived by yacht, and that this is their first time visiting. He asks if they check all the carriages entering Star Island. The driver lets them know that not only is it a very exclusive club, but that the local constabulary organize raids on occasion.

"Primarily when they're looking for a payout from Mr. Fischer," the driver adds. "When that happens, the guard must quickly telephone the raid into the club," he tells them.

The Driver pulls the carriage up to the Deep Sea Club where the party is still going strong, and whoas the horses.

"Driver! How late does this hotspot kick until?" Dave asks.

"Oh, they'll usually shut it down sometime after four a.m.," he tells them. "But after dinner hours the next day, she's right back at it," he says looking in the rear view.

"Seven days a week!" he adds.

"What d'ya know about that…" Dave comments.

Kelly and Dave step out of the carriage. Kelly places a couple of twenty-dollar bills in the driver's hand. The driver's eyes light up.

"Thank you, sir!" he says with the first smile he's made since they hired him. Kelly lets him know that after the club and casino close they might stick around to watch the sunrise after which they would like him to take them back to the Montauk Manor. The driver enthusiastically agrees to stick around exclusively for them. Forty dollars in 1929 is more than five hundred in 2019. Enough to buy a fleet of horse drawn carriages at the time.
"I'll be right here when you need me, sir," he says tipping his hat with a broad smile.

Kelly and Dave stroll over to the Deep Sea Club like a couple of swells. They enter the casino to find The Kid and see what he's learned about what alarm system the casino may be using. Attracted to a large boisterous crowd at the craps table they meander over to discover it's The Kid who's causing the huge commotion, winning bets on throw after throw, a gorgeous blond at his side.

"One more time, Mario!" a man at the table yells, slamming a stack of chips on the pass line.

Kelly watches and smiles. "Mario..." he says to himself, amused.

He's happy to see The Kid enjoying himself after the harrowing experience they'd all just gone through.

"Kiss 'em for me, baby?" The Kid asks the blond placing the dice close to her lips.

The crowd is going absolutely wild. Kelly and Dave stand back calmly enjoying the show. The Kid shakes the dice in his hand a few times amidst the calls for seven.

"Hit it, baby! Hit it!" a man calls as the dice roll the table into the backboard.

The crowd goes wild as the dice roll a seven. Bets are paid out. Dice are collected and once again pushed to The Kid who is slightly preoccupied smooching with the blond who seems to adore him. Dave leans up to Kelly and tells him that The Kid's having too much fun to break in, so he's going to check out the roulette wheel. Kelly looks at his watch, it's nearly three a.m.

"I'll join you," he says.

They saunter over to the roulette wheel and watch a while. Kelly and Dave both suspect the wheel is likely rigged to favor the low-paying numbers, increasing the house's odds of winning by not having to pay out high-paying inside bets. Even though the most popular bets are 'even-money' bets, because they cover close to half of the possible outcomes and pay even money, there are still plenty of daredevils who play the straight bet, wagers that pay out at thirty-five to one. The house hates having to pay out those bets, so various nefarious riggings were devised over the years to decrease the chances of high-odds bets ever winning.

Dave smiles at Kelly, “New table,” he says.

“Brand new,” Kelly answers.

“I’m thinking the batteries,” Dave says.

One of the ways casinos in the late 1920s rigged tables to favor even money bets was by hollowing out one of the legs and slipping in two large batteries. There are screws along the edge of the table that appear to be simply a part of the table’s design, which they are. But one of them, conveniently located on the croupier’s side was often a button made to appear as just another screw holding the table together that when pressed caused two wire thin metal pins to project out from the wheel beneath the surface catching the electrical charge from the batteries. This caused the wheel to stop in whatever section the pins were placed in, always on the even money bet areas. Paying out even odds wasn’t so bad. But if enough ‘straight’ bets hit, at thirty-five to one, it could break a small house. They decide to lay some straight bets in order to plant the seed with the croupier that they’re a couple of high rolling swells that like the high odds. They’ll come back tomorrow and repeat the exercise again so after they figure out how to sneak Dave in to work his magic and those same bets start paying off, the croupier will figure they’re just getting lucky. At least for a little while... Long enough for them to rake in some serious cash. Kelly and Dave find a spot at the table. Kelly places a stack of chips on thirty-five. The croupier eyes Kelly closely as he would anyone throwing big money on high-odds straight bets. What the croupier doesn’t realize is that Kelly and Dave are watching him even closer. The croupier spins the wheel and announces, “No more bets,” then throws the ball. As the ball circles the spinning wheel the croupier casually leans on the table. Everyone betting has their eyes on the ball spinning around the wheel, many calling out for their number, red or black. Everyone except Kelly and Dave that is. They are focused on the croupier's subtle but recognizable pressing of the secret button. Kelly and Dave smile at one another. They stick around, placing a few more straight bets to be sure the croupier will recognize them when they return, occasionally looking over at the commotion The Kid is causing at the craps table.

"Shall we?" Kelly asks Dave pointing at the craps table with his chin.

"Not having any luck here," Dave says raising his eyebrows at the croupier.

As they approach the craps table, it erupts in more uproarious cheers. Kelly stops walking suddenly and grabs Dave by the shoulder.

"You didn't fix those, did you?" he asks.

Dave gives Kelly a defensive look. "There is such a thing as luck, you know!" he says.

Kelly smiles as he watches The Kid gather his winnings into a large stack of chips, laughing, kissing the blond and tipping the croupier. Dave and Kelly manage to get close.

"Mario!" Kelly shouts, his arms outstretched.

He gives The Kid a giant hug. "It's been ages! Absolutely wonderful to see you again," he shouts winking at the blond. "David's here," he says, looking around.

"Hi, toots!" Dave says patting The Kid on the back. "I think I'll ride your wave a while," he says managing to squeeze close to the table and place a stack of chips down.

"New roll!" the croupier announces.

The frenzied betting starts all over again. After winning a few bets, Dave breaks away to cash in his chips and poke around a little to see what he can learn about the alarm system the casino is using. The Kid's lucky streak continues as he wins roll after roll. A short time later the house lights flash on and off a few times signaling patrons that the casino is closing for the night. It's five a.m. The Kid bids farewell to his new friend and cashes in his chips. The three of them exit the casino arm in arm boisterously recalling the high points of The Kid's winning streak. They locate their horse-drawn carriage, greet the driver and hop in.

"Can you take us to the inlet, please?" Kelly asks. "We'd like to watch the fishing boats going out," he adds.

"Certainly, sir," the driver answers with a big smile, happy to see Kelly again.

He pulls the carriage away and heads up to the inlet. The Kid is electrified counting his large wad of cash.

"Did you see that?" The Kid asks Kelly practically bouncing off the seat of the carriage.

"We saw enough," Kelly tells The Kid smiling.

"You were on fire, kid!" Dave says.

"Red hot!" The Kid says recalling his amazing run at the craps table.

"Kelly was convinced you were using the smart dice," Dave says laughing.

"Nah..." he says, looking over at Kelly. "But I did have a good luck charm," he says licking his lips.

“What was her name?” Kelly asks.

“Monica…” The Kid tells him dreamily.

“I hope you were kind enough to share some of your good fortune with Monica,” Kelly says.

“Of course!” The Kid exclaims. “I’m not a scoundrel.”

“She has a room with a few friends at the Montauk Inn,” he lets them know.

Kelly asks him what else he learned while they were gone. The Kid tells him that Al Capone runs security for Carl Fischer at the casino. And even though Capone is in a Philadelphia prison right now, no one expects him to be gone for long.

“Capone didn’t mess around,” Dave says looking at Kelly with a serious expression.

“No, he didn’t,” Kelly says.

“However, I believe the proper vernacular is that he doesn’t mess around,” Kelly says smiling at Dave. “But then, neither does Rollie,” he says.

The carriage pulls up to the inlet and stops. The Kid looks over at where Gosman’s restaurant was the last time they were here.

“Strange…” he says gazing out at the moonlit water of Lake Montauk. “We had lunch there just last week,” he says looking back at Kelly and Dave.

The three of them sit quietly a few moments gazing out at the water considering all that has happened as dawn begins to break over Block Island Sound. A few fishing boats appear lined up one after the other, idling through the inlet, heading out to sea. Dave comments how the rigging is not that dissimilar from the modern-day boats that were docked alongside the Sally Ann.

“One of those fishermen could be Hank’s grandfather,” says Kelly.

“Wow... Can you imagine if Hank gets to meet him?” The Kid says envisioning it. “I never knew my grandfather,” he says with a hint of sadness.

The sky becomes lighter by the second. Kelly looks at his watch, then asks the driver to take them to the Montauk Manor. The driver gets the carriage moving.

“Any thoughts on the roulette wheel?” Kelly asks Dave.

Dave tells Kelly that he’s been building a plan in his head since he first laid eyes on it.

“Seeing as there’s no way I can set new pins with pliers and a screwdriver, I thought if I were able to dismantle their pins, then rewire the wheel with just enough copper wire set in a stationary position that will continually protrude outward, they will receive a jolt from the battery terminals hidden under the surface favoring whatever position I set them in whenever the croupier closes the circuit by hitting his little secret button,” he explains smiling.

“Which as we witnessed last night, was every time we placed a straight bet,” Kelly says smiling at Dave.

“When we stop winning, we’ll know the wires have frayed too much to receive the jolt anymore and we fold up shop,” Dave says.

“How long will the wire set-up last?” Kelly asks him thinking the scam through.

“Hard to say exactly... It could last several weeks, depending on how many high rollers show up.” Dave tells him.

“How long will you need to rig the table?” Kelly asks.

“I’ll need about an hour,” Dave tells him.

“The toughest part will be getting in and out without setting off the trip wire alarm system, Capone’s men nailing us, and doing so, all between closing time and daybreak,” The Kid says chiming in.

“Very concisely stated, Kid,” Dave says thinking for a moment.

Dave looks at Kelly, “Well?”

The horse-drawn carriage clatters along Flamingo Avenue towards the Montauk Manor. Dave and The Kid stare at each other waiting for an answer with question marks for faces. A few minutes pass.

“We need a diversion,” Kelly says finally thinking aloud. “A raid!” he exclaims.

“Of course!” Dave says smiling. “The guard house is there primarily to alert the speakeasy when the cops decide to raid the place,” he adds.

“Wow!” The Kid exclaims. “Just like in those old gangster movies,” he says. Kelly and Dave smile at The Kid who suddenly realizes, “Great... where do we get guys to play the cops around here?” The Kid asks, frowning.

“Rum-running fisherman,” Kelly says thinking quickly with his don’t-I-always-have-a-solution expression

"That could work," Dave says.

They tell The Kid what the horse-drawn carriage driver had told them at the guard house: "Mainly when they want a payout from Mr. Fischer..."

They decide they'll have to find Hank's grandfather, then convince him to round up some fellow renegade rum-running fisherman they can disguise as cops to raid the Deep Sea Club with Kelly playing the new captain. Dave, Rollie and The Kid will borrow a few uniforms from the police station, then hijack a cop car and a paddy wagon. Kelly will explain to Carl Fischer that he's the new Police Captain and the rest will fall into place. With the casino emptied and Capone's goons out on the street cracking wise with the cops as the payoff is taking place in the speakeasy, Dave will have time to rig the Roulette Wheel in the casino. The three of them play out the raid in their heads as the horse-drawn carriage clatters down Flamingo Avenue.

"Wait a minute!" Kelly exclaims. "Using cops is too risky," he says.

"I think they'll miss the paddy wagon..." The Kid adds.

"Yeah... too many variables," Dave surmises. "It's just not practical," he adds. "The cop uniforms would have to fit the fisherman, who are all probably local and casino employees, also being locals, would likely know them not to be cops," he says thinking it through.

"Yeah... and where did all these new cops suddenly come from in a tiny town like Montauk?" The Kid adds.

They sit quietly thinking as neither the sun rising nor the clattering sounds of the carriage moving along Flamingo Avenue towards the Manor do little to distract them. The

Kid is sad and frowns. Dave is forlorn. The driver turns the carriage up the last hill towards the Manor.

“Unless we were FBI,” Kelly says looking over at his pals with a huge grin.

“G-men!” says The Kid.

“Brilliant,” Dave says. “We can fit them all in cheap government suits... I can fake some ID’s... We’ll need a camera,” he says looking at Kelly.

“And firearms,” says The Kid.

“Not even Capone’s men are going to shoot it out with the Feds,” Kelly assures them.

“Think Hank will go for it?” Dave asks in earnest.

“Is it even worth it?” asks The Kid, maybe losing a little heart, perhaps the strain getting to him.

“What do you suggest?” Kelly asks him. “Go straight in the 1920s?” he asks.

“This is what we do, Kid,” Dave adds. “Wherever we are...” he says.

“You mean whenever we are...” The Kid says with a big smile.

Kelly and Dave laugh it up.

“You’re okay, Kid,” Kelly says as the Driver whoas the horse to a stop.

They look up to see that they are at the entrance of The Montauk Manor.

“Welcome back, Kid,’ Dave says stepping out of the carriage.

Kelly turns to the driver. “Would you mind taking us to town for some shopping this afternoon?” he asks.

“It will be my pleasure, sir,” the well paid driver says with a smile.

“Say two o’clock?” he asks. “Guys?” Kelly asks addressing Dave and The Kid.

“Capital!” Dave says strutting off towards the entrance.

“Sounds like the cat’s meow,” says The Kid, laughing and catching up with Dave.

“Two o’clock it is then.” Kelly says to the driver, slipping a twenty-dollar bill into his hand.

“See you then, sir,” the driver says as he happily stuffs the bill in his pocket.

“What’s your name anyway?” Kelly asks.

“Chapman,” he says. “John Chapman, but most call me Chappy,” he says.

Kelly smiles. “See you later then, Chappy,” he says as Chappy gets the horse moving and pulls away.

Kelly peers out at the beautiful view of Fort Pond Bay at sunrise a moment and then strolls into the Montauk Manor with his hands in his pockets like a man without a care in the world.

XVIII

Later that morning Kelly, Sal, Dave and The Kid enjoy a lovely brunch at the Montauk Manor restaurant as a woman dressed in a silken gown strums a Harp nearby, filling the manor with lovely if somewhat ghostly melodies.

“How’s the orange juice, Kid?” Sal asks.

“Better than the Yacht Club!” he says, polishing off his third glass.

“Time for a rundown of what’s next,” Kelly says to his crew.

“Nuts and bolts,” Dave adds.

“Okay...” Kelly organizes his thoughts. “There are some high rollers here and we need to appear as affluent as they are in order to blend in and continue our search for our rocket,” he says while sipping his coffee. “The roulette wheel and the loaded dice should yield enough cash which will allow us to create the illusion of having greater wealth than we actually do,” he says.

“All contingent upon Hank’s willingness to hunt down his grandfather,” Dave says, looking up at everyone.

“Some nice duds won’t hurt...” The Kid adds.

“Now you’re getting it, Kid,” Sal tells him with a smile. “I hope we’re not asking too much of Hank on this.” She looks into Kelly’s eyes with a tenderness not often seen in Sal.

They finish brunch then stroll outside to find Chappy waiting nearby in his carriage.

"Good day to you, Chappy, sir." Dave tips his hat.

"Good to see you again, Chappy," Kelly says. "To the finest haberdashery in town, please."

"The pleasure is mine, sir," Chappy replies.

The four of them enter the carriage and take the ride to town. They head down Edgemere Street as a roadster races by.

"Oh, man!" The Kid exclaims. "I have got to get me one of those!" he says, leaning out of the buggy to watch it race away.

It's not long before they can see The Montauk Tower looming in the distance.

"Surreal…" Dave says, his jaw dropping just a bit.

"Truly stunning," Kelly comments.

"I forgot all about the Tower," Sal says.

"Man! You should 'a seen the chase'!" The Kid says, returning to his air-racecar driver mode for a moment.

The crew go shopping and buy clothes for everyone. They're not able to find a camera but there is a photographer in town who can make passport photos when the time comes. Dave finds enough billfold parts to make FBI IDs if and when they get enough fisherman to play the agents. He also purchases a few essential tools he'll need to rig the roulette wheel. Now it's time to visit Hank and convince him to take the trip to Rum Row and seek out his grandfather. The four of them are gathered on the sidewalk not far from Chappy and his carriage.

“How do you propose we explain to Chappy that we’re meeting a friend on the side of the road in the middle of nowhere?” Sal asks, placing some of the many packages she’s carrying on the sidewalk. “At sunset…” she adds.

“He doesn’t appear to be overly judgmental,” Dave comments.

“I’ve been paying him well,” Kelly says.

“Chappy… Sparky…” The Kid comments.

“Sparky, he’s not,” Sal quips.

“Sun sets in an hour,” Kelly says looking at his watch. “I say we throw caution to the wind,” he says looking over at Chappy seated in his carriage. “Let me talk to him alone for a moment,” he says. Kelly walks over to where Chappy is standing by in his carriage.

“Chappy!” Kelly says loudly with a warm welcoming wave and his signature grin. “I’m hoping I can have a word with you before the others join us,” he says, looking back to see the crew hanging back.

“Certainly, sir,” Chappy answers dutifully.

Kelly leans into the driver’s seat, “You see, Chappy, my good man, Hey!” Kelly says, suddenly changing the direction and tone of what he was about to say. “Do you have an interest in the literary arts, per chance?” he asks with a genuine expression anyone would believe.

Chappy gives Kelly an agreeable look of surprise. “Funny that you should ask that, sir.”

“First of all, please, call me Kelly,” Kelly tells him.

Chappy gets comfortable in his posture, “Okay… Kelly,” he says smiling. “As a matter of fact, I have dabbled in the literary arts,” he says, looking Kelly directly in the eyes. “In my youth, I once dreamed of pursuing the life of an author,” Chappy admits. “A celebrated author,” he adds.

“Fancy that!” Kelly says with a smile so large even the crew watching from half a block away notice.

Chappy gives Kelly an inquisitive look that borders on suspicion, “What, in God’s name, caused you to inquire such a very specific question of that nature?” Chappy asks, unsure whether to be flattered or apprehensive of Kelly’s interest in his literary exploits.

Kelly smiles and glances over at the crew a moment. “We recently had in our employ a driver, not unlike yourself, who indeed had a lively interest in the literary arts. He’d began writing a book about my friends and I and you, my dear fellow, remind us of him. I promised the others I would make a sincere inquiry,” he says looking over at the crew getting their attention, pointing at his wrist watch. “Mind meeting us up there?” Kelly asks, pointing up the street at the crew. “We seem to have made more purchases than we are able to carry,” he adds.

“Certainly, Mr. Kelly,” Chappy smiles.

Kelly struts briskly up the street to the crew. He stops and stands there a moment staring at Dave, Sal and The Kid with an astonished expression, “The irony is astounding,” he says smiling at them.

“Don’t tell me he’s a writer?” quips Sal, puffing on a cigarette through her glamorous cigarette holder.

“Aspiring,” Kelly says with a big smile.

Chappy pulls up and whoas the horse. He helps the crew load the packages into the luggage compartment, tying the rest onto the roof rack. They step inside the carriage.

“Back to the Manor then?” Chappy asks.

“Actually... we have a friend who’s anchored in Lake Montauk near the highway not far from those Stanford White estates,” Kelly tells him. “We promised to fetch him at sunset,” he adds speaking loudly from inside the carriage.

“A bit of an adventure, then...” Chappy says as he turns the carriage around and heads due east of Montauk.

Sal and Dave smile at each other.

“Chappy is an author,” Kelly announces to the crew loud enough for Chappy to hear.

“Now, I wouldn’t take it that far, sir” Chappy says. “It’s true that in my errant youth, I once imagined the possibility of the literary profession,” he says.

“Errant youth, hunh?” Dave comments with a droll smile.

“No reason to be modest with us, Chappy, dahling,” Sal assures him.

“You tell him, toots,” The Kid says, acting the young swell of the time.

“There’s no shame in supplementing one’s income as one labors on his magnum opus,” Dave insists.

Chappy considers Dave’s assessment as they travel eastward along Montauk Highway to the somewhat vague destination on the side of the road. We can safely assume that Chappy has seen his share of unusual goings-on while carting passengers to and from the Deep Sea Club, yet he senses something very unique about this particular group, although he can't quite put his finger on it. *They're an odd bunch,* he thinks to himself.

"What is it that you would write about, Chappy?" asks Sal, genuinely curious.

Chappy ponders Sal's question. He's thought about it quite a lot over the years yet has never taken the time to encapsulate it in words, to define it in theme or substance. Now he's being asked for the first time ever and he is not sure how to express it in such terms of what it is exactly he would write about. A long silence follows as they clatter along The Montauk Highway.

"Love, honor and daring," Chappy blurts out suddenly.

Kelly throws his head back raising his eyebrows. A huge grin comes to his face. Sal, Dave and The Kid have similar reactions.

Kelly is the first to respond, "You're a poet, Chappy! A true poet."

"Touché." exclaims Dave.

"The genuine article," says The Kid.

"Chappy..." Sal remarks warmly with a sweet smile.

"Who are your favorite authors?" Dave asks curious.

"Oh my..." Chappy exclaims. "Everything from Montesquieu, Shakespeare and Cervantes to Nathanial Hawthorne, James Joyce, Fyodor Dostoevsky and Mark Twain, whom I believe has birthed what is now considered modern literature with his wonderful novel, Huckleberry

Finn." he tells them, feeling comfortable in his skin, as they clatter along the Montauk Hwy looking for Rollie.

"Fascinating..." Kelly comments looking at the others.

"Truly..." admits Dave.

"Of course, there's also Jonathan Swift, Henry David Thoreau, Walt Whitman, Emily Dickenson, Louisa May Alcott and Jacob Riis. Even some rather obscure scribes such as Ingersoll Lockwood and Sir Francis Bacon. I have also read many of the great philosophers from Plato and Socrates to Dante Alighieri, Kafka, William James and Proust... I am not a fan of Plato!" he announces sternly. "I prefer Socrates, the first monotheist, who there is every indication was poisoned by the likes of Plato..." he contends slapping the reigns with a charged vigor. "I also enjoy some contemporary literati such as D.H. Lawrence, William Faulkner, F. Scott Fitzgerald, Ernest Hemingway and the like... Also, Virginia Wolff..." He finishes.

The crew look at one another with raised eyebrows, impressed.

"Very impressive," states Dave. "Have you read Einstein?" Dave inquires.

"I have perused his General Theory of Relativity..." he says looking into the rear view mirror trying to get a good look at Dave. "As a matter of fact, you sort of remind me of him..." adds Chappy.

"You must have quite to library, Chappy!" says Sal with a sweet smile.

"Amazing... hunh Einstein," remarks The Kid elbowing Dave with a laugh.

"Save it Kid..." says Dave.

A few miles east of town, sunset fading and the sky becoming darker by the second, they spot Rollie on the side of the road.

“There he is!” exclaims The Kid.

“He’s a working man, Chappy,” Kelly lets him know.

“I presume some of the packages we loaded aboard contain appropriate evening wear for the gentlemen...” Chappy comments as he whoas the horse to a stop.

“Right you are, Chappy,” says Kelly. “Will you meet us on the other side of the road? We’ll head back to the Manor so our friend can bathe,” Kelly says, jumping out of the carriage.

He runs across the Montauk Highway and gives Rollie a hug.

“How far is the boat?” Kelly asks as Chappy turns the carriage around.

“Not a three-minute walk,” Rollie tells him.

Kelly jogs over to the carriage and lets Chappy know he has to have a word with the captain and that they’ll be back in a jif. Kelly and Rollie head through the reeds towards the water.

“How’s Hank?” Kelly asks.

“He’s talking to his grandfather again,” Rollie says.

“With a little luck he’ll get to meet him in the flesh soon enough,” Kelly says.

They come upon the ship barely outlined against the dusk sky.

“Permission to come aboard, captain,” Kelly says.

They climb aboard and Kelly reveals their plan to seek out his grandfather, hire some renegade rum-runners and stage a raid on the casino in order to buy them time to rig the roulette wheel and acquire some operating capital.” Hank listens intently and then looks out to sea.

“Ya hear that, grandpa?” he says with a dreamy smile on his face.

“How’s your fuel?” Kelly asks.

“We left full, so we can still make it to Nova Scotia if we have to,” Hank tells him.

Kelly smiles, walks over to Hank and takes him by the shoulders. “We’ll be back in five or six hours,” Kelly tells him looking into his eyes then giving him a big hug.

“OK, fellas.” Hank replies.

“C’mon. We have a lovely gray flannel suit in your size waiting for you,” Kelly says to Rollie.

“Smart-ass,” Rollie says as they leap off the Sally Ann and head back to the carriage.

Kelly and Rollie step into the carriage. Dave, Sal and The Kid are happy to see him. Chappy heads towards The Montauk Manor.

“Nothing personal, Chappy, but where can a fella buy a hot rod around here?” The Kid asks showing Rollie the wad of cash he won the night before.

"The Kid killed it at the craps table last night," Dave tells him.

Rollie's impressed. "With straight dice," Kelly adds.

"As regards purchasing an automobile, the concierge at the Manor can make arrangements for you," Chappy tells The Kid.

They pull up to The Montauk Manor, where a bellhop assists them with the packages. Kelly asks Chappy to return in four hours or so. Chappy agrees to return after he dines. Rollie gets a bath and puts on his new set of duds, no gray… He meets the crew, minus The Kid, in the large festive restaurant on the main floor of the Manor. Rollie takes a seat and orders.

"Where's The Kid?" he asks.

"He's making inquiries regarding purchasing the fastest roadster available," Dave tells him.

The waiter serves the first course.

"There's something unnatural about dining without a glass of wine," Sal comments. "It's uncivilized," she adds.

"We should get Hank a nice hot meal," Rollie suggests.

"Good thinking," Kelly agrees.

The Kid returns and grabs his seat.

"What are we having?" he asks. "I'm famished."

"There are some things, apparently, that time cannot change," Sal comments about The Kid always being hungry.

They dine while reveling in the astounding events of the past few days.

“Dave thinks he can get us back,” Kelly tells Rollie and The Kid.

“If anyone can, it’s you, doc,” says Rollie.

“Hey!” The Kid exclaims. “There are automobile races here, right?” he asks looking at Kelly.

Kelly’s eyes light up, “You might have something there, Kid,” he says.

“No one knows that track better than I do!” The Kid exclaims going into his air-racecar driver mode.

“I can attest to that,” Rollie says, smiling at The Kid still air-racecar driving.

“Spare me, Kid, will ya? This isn’t a video game…” Sal rolls her eyes.

“No, it’s not, it’s much more exciting!” The Kid insists.

“I’ll venture to presume wagers were made,” Dave says.

“Exactly,” Kelly says.

“Kid, you just might have come upon a third source of revenue for us,” Kelly says thinking aloud, “And, a way to ingratiate ourselves deeper into the gambling set,” Kelly says, looking at his watch. “But right now, it’s Rum Row,” he says.

He looks at the crew one by one seated around the table, dressed in their finest 1920’s attire.

"We are living history..." he says making a grand gesture taking in the amazing dining room they find themselves in.

Kelly checks his watch. "Chappy should be back by now," he says turning to Sal. "You coming with us?" he asks.

"Wouldn't miss it for the world," she says as she lights a cigarette.

The waiter brings a meal covered by an elaborate room service dome on a tray for Hank.

"We have a carriage waiting outside," Kelly tells him, handing him a five-dollar bill.

The waiter gladly accepts the generous tip with a big smile, calls out to a nearby bellhop. "Oh, boy!" he shouts across the room. The young bellhop skips over. "These fine people will require this tray transferred to their carriage."

"Yes, sir." The young bellhop takes the tray.

The crew make their way to the waiting carriage. The bellhop carefully places the tray aboard. Kelly slaps a five-dollar bill into his hand.

"Thank you, sir!" he says, smiling ear to ear.

"You clean up rather nicely, sir," Chappy says looking at Rollie.

"You're not so bad yourself, Jeeves," Rollie answers cracking wise.

"The name is Chappy, smart-ass," Sal scolds him.

"He's a writer," Dave adds as they climb into the carriage.

"No shit?" Rollie smiles.

A short time later they are all aboard the Sally Ann. Chappy stands by in the carriage parked on the side of the road with a fresh notebook, a new fountain pen and a lit lantern. He opens the notebook and begins to write. *If something nefarious is not about to occur, then a simple case of benign insanity is at play,* he writes. He gazes upward to see a shooting star streak across the night sky. A smile comes to his face. He hears the roar of a nearby diesel engine and looks out towards the reeds.

Not far away, Hank is at the helm surrounded by the crew aboard the Sally Ann. Rollie and The Kid, down to their shirtsleeves, hoist the anchor. Hank puts her in gear, and they move slowly out from the cove of what will one day be the Crow's Nest's private beach. They continue slowly past the Montauk Yacht Club towards the inlet. Once through the inlet, Hank opens her up a little for the twelve-mile ride out to the International waters of Rum Row.

"It's a good thing you know these waters as well as you do, Hank," Dave says pouring himself a rum. "Anyone care for a drink?" he asks before putting the bottle away. "Most people would be lost without GPS," Dave adds, sipping his drink.

Sal steps alongside Hank, "Are you nervous about possibly meeting your grandfather?" she asks.

"I'm not sure what to feel," he says, gazing out to sea.

"What's his name?" Kelly asks, appearing in the cabin.

Hank smiles, "Danny... Danny Sullivan."

"Think you'll recognize him?" Kelly asks.

"Recognize him? What am I gonna say to him?" Hank exclaims. He looks at Kelly. "I'm your grandson from the future?" he says, shaking his head. "It's all so strange." He keeps the boat on heading using the compass. "Rum Row ought to be coming up here pretty soon," he says.

"It might be best if you don't tell him who you are," Dave interjects. "At least not at first..." he adds.

"We didn't think this through as thoroughly as we should have," Kelly says, looking at Dave, then at Hank. "I'm sorry about that, Hank," he says.

Hank shrugs his shoulders in a sympathetic gesture, "Everything's happened so fast. "Don't be too hard on yourself," he says with a smile. "Knowing my grandfather, I suspect he'd find it amusing to portray a G-man all right," Hank says, laughing. "And from the stories he told me while growing up, every rum-runner out here would jump at the chance to get back at Capone, any way possible," he adds.

"Understandable..." Kelly says. "Capone... Dutch Schultz... They were nothing more than pirates stealing booze from hard-working fisherman trying to make a few extra bucks bootlegging," he states passionately.

"That's how Grandpa saw it," he says as remembering the stories from his youth.

"Look!" The Kid shouts from the bow, spotting a Clipper in the moonlight up ahead.

As they get closer, a Schooner and another Clipper ship appear.

"Rum Row..." Kelly says sort of to himself, amazed that they are actually there to experience what he considers a rich part of American history. "I think we should hang back until some rumrunners show up," Kelly suggests.

“We have to be wary of the Coast Guard, as well,” Hank says, turning on the radar. “We should put the boys on watch,” he adds.

Kelly runs out to the bow to ask Rollie and The Kid to split up, one at the bow and one at the stern, to keep watch for the Coast Guard. Kelly returns to the helm. Hank turns to the three of them with a serious expression.

“Now, when I was back in my own time, if I had met my Grandfather here in the 1920s, wouldn’t he have remembered it?” Hank asks somewhat perplexed.

Dave looks at Sal then at Hank with a knowing and solemn expression, “Funny thing about time is that, ya see... it hasn’t happened yet. You haven’t met your grandfather... So, the answer is no. And even if you were to meet now, it wouldn’t change what has already happened between you in the past even though that past is now technically in the future, relative to the timeline we are presently in. See?” Dave says patting Hank on the shoulder.

“We can’t change what’s already happened...” Hank says, thinking aloud.

“Right,” Dave says.

“Now, if we do make it back to our time, you’ll remember... because it will have happened to you and you’ll still be alive,” Dave adds. “Then again,” Dave says thinking it through a bit further, “It will have happened to your grandfather, so he will have remembered it,” Dave says, taking a sip of rum and becoming dumbfounded suddenly.

“Better pour me one of those,” Hank says, straining to comprehend the implications traveling though the dimension of time can bring about.

Dave hands him a rum. They gently clink glasses and drink.

“I guess the real answer is, I’m not sure exactly.” Dave takes a healthy swig. “For every action, there is an equal but opposite reaction…” he says sort of to himself. “Wait! Getting back to our conversation of the other night, if we were to put something in motion here now, in this timeline…” he says, thinking it through.

“Such as?” Sal asks.

“Such as a major land purchase or large stock option,” Dave says thinking as he speaks.

“And we put it in a trust…” Kelly interjects finishing Dave’s thought. “When we get back…” Kelly says, dreaming of the greatest scam of all time.

“If we get back,” Sal adds.

“When we get back,” Kelly says, looking at Sal with determination.

“We can cash in on it then…” Sal says with a sly grin.

Dave contemplates the idea. “It’s the ultimate scam every con artist has dreamt of since the beginning of time, but has never been able to pull off!” Dave says excitedly.

“Sure…” Hank says. “Everyone’s imagined going back just one day before the big lotto or the Kentucky Derby knowing the winning numbers or the winning horse…” he says smiling.

The four of them stand there in awe, their minds reeling at the possibilities. Hank hears a speedboat approaching from far off in the distance.

"Ya hear that?" Hank asks turning to check the radar.

Kelly, Dave and Sal strain to hear it.

"Yes!" Kelly says.

"The rum-runners are back," says Sal.

Dave leans out to the bow to take a look.

"We have one approaching," shouts The Kid from the aft deck.

Rollie and The Kid lean over the port side trying to get a better look at the speedboat on the moonlit ocean.

"There it is!" The Kid yells from the stern.

Kelly jumps up and down waving his arms in an attempt to get their attention. He runs to the helm. "Can you get us closer?" he asks Hank.

Hank puts the Sally Ann in gear, revs the engine and steers towards Rum Row catching up to the speedboat as it slows down to approach one of the ships.

Kelly puts his arm around Hank's shoulder, "Ahoy, right?" he asks.

"Ordinarily, sure, that'd work... But if you want these fellas trust, we best buy some rum," Hank tells him with a smile.

Kelly reaches into his pocket and pulls out a wad. Hank looks over and sees the size of Kelly's stack of one hundred-dollar bills. "You won't need that much, unless ya want to buy the ship as well," he says, laughing.

Kelly gives Hank a serious look, "I'm going to ask for Danny Sullivan," he says. "You sure you're okay with this?" he asks.

Hank takes a deep breath and turns to Kelly, "I think so..." he says. "Yeah..."

"How close can you get?" Kelly asks looking ahead at the speedboat ride up alongside the clipper, "Can we get alongside like that?" he asks Hank.

"I'll see what I can do," Hank tells him as he expertly pilots the Sally Ann alongside the large ship.

Another speedboat approaches. Kelly runs to the bow and yells out to one of the men on the clipper.

"Rum, gin or whiskey?" he asks loudly.

He grabs Rollie and hands him a few hundred-dollar bills.

"See what you can get for this," he says. "I'm going to find Danny Sullivan," he says with a sudden, strange smile.

"What a world," Rollie says. "What a world..."

Kelly runs to the stern as close as he can get to one of the speedboats loading booze.

"Ahoy!" he shouts. "Have ya seen Danny Sullivan?" he shouts. "Looking for Danny Sullivan," he yells cupping his hands around his mouth adding a megaphone effect.

"Never heard of him," one of the men on the speedboat shouts.

"Sal!" Kelly exclaims to himself. He runs to the helm, "Sal! I need your expertise," He says, grabbing her by the hand

and dragging her out to the stern. “We need to find Danny,” Kelly tells her.

Catching on quickly, as usual, Sal strikes an alluring pose, “Hiya, fellas,” she coos. “Where’s my sweet Danny?” she asks suggestively.

One of the men gets sight of her, and shouts, “Danny’s married, but I’m available, sweetheart,” he says with a huge grin on his face, fixing his hair and tucking in his shirt.

“It’s a start,” Kelly says, elbowing Sal.

Rollie has tied onto the clipper and now he, The Kid and Dave are loading cases of booze onto the deck of the Sally Ann. Hank grabs his binoculars and meanders out to Kelly and Sal.

“I’d recognize him from early photographs I’ve seen,” Hank says peering through the binoculars at a third speedboat that has just arrived tying on to a nearby schooner.

Kelly looks at Sal, emotions are running high. Two more speedboats race onto the scene.

“That’s him!” Hank exclaims.

He begins to tremble looking through the binoculars.

“Unbelievable...” he mutters as he brings the binoculars down to his side and peers out at the boat.

Sal takes the binoculars gently from his hands. Hank begins to weep.

“He was much older when I knew him... Look at him out there, king of the rum-runners,” He says wiping the tears with his sleeve. “Guess we better get over there,” he says.

Kelly runs to the bow where Rollie, Dave and The Kid continue to load in boxes of illegal booze. “We see him, you guys done loading?” he asks excitedly.

“Just about,” Rollie tells him.

They grab the last few cases and a sailor on the clipper throws them the bowline. The strong Rollie shoves the Sally Ann off. Kelly runs to the helm with Hank and Sal.

“We’re clear,” Kelly tells Hank. He takes one look at Hank and stops. “You all right, partner?” he asks.

“I’ll be okay,” Hank says taking a deep breath. “Just hard to fathom seeing old Grandpa Danny as a young man.” He looks into Kelly’s eyes with an intensity that could only exist in a situation such as this.

“Coming about,” he shouts, shifting to captain mode.

He steers the Sally Ann towards the schooner where he spots Danny and pulls up alongside them.

“Danny!” Hank yells from the helm. “See if we can tie on,” Hank tells Kelly who runs to the stern, grabs the line and leans over the boat holding it in his hand.

“Can we tie on? Someone here needs a word with you!” Kelly shouts to Danny who’s loading cases of Irish whiskey onto his Chris Craft. “Danny!” Kelly shouts.

Danny loads the last case that will fit onboard, then looks up at Kelly.

“What is it?” he shouts.

“We need to speak with you!” Sal coos loud enough to be heard.

"Well, pretty lady, what's the likes a you doing out here on such a fancy fishing boat?" Danny asks.

"You wouldn't believe me if I told you... But please, come aboard, I promise, it's a surprise and half," She says smiling.

"No harm will come to you," says Hank, appearing suddenly alongside Kelly and Sal.

Danny takes his eyes off the gorgeous Sal and looks at Hank, suddenly dumbfounded. The two men stare at one another speechless. They don't know why exactly, but there's a connection. Rollie, Dave and The Kid watch the scene in astonished silence. Sal wipes a tear from her eye.

"Unbelievable," Kelly utters to himself.

After what seems an eternity, Kelly throws the line to Danny's mate aboard the Chris Craft. Hank steps forward and puts out his hand for Danny to grab onto. Danny takes Hank's hand and Hank pulls him aboard the Sally Ann. The two men stand there staring at one another.

"Have we met?" Danny asks.

"Hank Sullivan," Hank says putting his hand out.

The two men shake hands.

"Danny Sullivan," Danny says, sure that something is amiss without a clue as to what exactly it might be.

"I've come a very long way to see you," Hank says, breaking down suddenly, hugging Danny, in tears. "Grandpa..." he says softly.

"What did you call me?" Danny asks, breaking away.

Dave appears with a bottle of rum and some glasses. He places them down on a crate and pours a few stiff drinks. He lifts two glasses filled with rum and holds them out for Danny and Hank.

"Ladies first," Danny says referring to the beautiful Sal.

"You don't have to ask me twice," Sal quips, pouring herself a stiff one.

Kelly, Dave, Rollie and The Kid join them.

"To the future!" Kelly announces, raising his glass. No one can argue with that sentiment. All raise their glasses.

"To the future." They all toast before taking swigs of the rum.

"So, what exactly is all this about?" Danny asks beyond curious. "What kind of vessel is this?" he asks looking around the Sally Ann. "I see it's a fishing boat all right, but none the likes of which I've seen," he adds looking them over one by one.

Hank hasn't taken his eyes off of Grandpa Danny since he stepped aboard. Speedboats come and go, loading up from the row of clippers, schooners and barques that have lined up to sell their wares to the rumrunners, but aboard the Sally Ann, it is as though time has stopped.

"You the captain?" Danny asks Hank.

"This is my boat," answers Hank.

"Figured as much," Danny says. "Question is," he says rubbing his jaw taking in the crew, "What are you doin' out here at the rum line with a bunch a landlubbers?" he asks.

“No offense,” he says smiling at Kelly and Sal, then at the others.

“Is it that obvious?” Rollie asks.

“Fraid so...” Danny says with a smirk.

“You might want to take a seat,” Sal tells him.

“Yeah, we best sit down,” Kelly says. “What we have to tell you is a bit outside the everyday,” he assures him.

“In that case, pour me another rum,” Danny says, holding out his glass.

Sal obliges and pours Danny a stiff drink.

“Ya see,” Hank starts. “I’m... we’re... It all started when... Ah shit... Look,” he says. “Either you’re gonna believe it or not, but we were out doing a different kind of rum-running 90 years from now in 2019, got caught up in a strange electrical storm, and ended up here a little over four days ago,” he says.

Danny looks at him like he’s crazy. He stands up wary of what he’s being told, backing away, “This the looney bin at sea or what?” he asks taking a stance ready to defend himself or leap into the ocean, if need be.

“We seem to have passed through a space-time dimension of some kind and ended up here,” Dave tells him in as sincere a tone as he can.

“We all know it sounds crazy,” Kelly says. “We’ve been grappling with it for almost a week now,” he adds.

“Here, look at the helm,” Hank suggests walking to the helm. “This instrumentation is from a different time,” he says. He looks back at Danny, who hasn’t moved.

“No one is going to hurt you, Danny,” Sal assures him.

“We’ll stand back,” Rollie says.

“Good idea. Let’s all move to the bow. Give Danny some room,” Kelly says, walking to the bow.

The crew follow him as Danny slowly moves to the helm with Hank.

“What in God’s name is this stuff?” Danny exclaims looking at the now fuzzy GPS screen and other electrical gauges and radar, keeping one eye on the crew at the bow.

“See that?” Hank says pointing at the radar screen referring to each blip on the radar screen as it bleeps scanning the immediate vicinity. “There’s that clipper... The schooner... The barque...” Hank tells him pointing from the dots on the screen to each of the ships they represent. “Your Chris Craft is this speck right here,” Hank says, pointing to a blip on the screen.

He refers to another, “This speck halfway to shore just sitting there is likely Coast Guard,” Hank says, winking at Danny. Another blip appears moving towards them at a fast pace. “Watch this speck,” Hank says, pointing at it. “Probably a speed boat coming to buy some rum,” he says, peering out of the cabin to the stern. The blip is getting closer. He hears the speedboat. “Now watch,” Hank says pointing behind them. “There it is!” exclaims Hank. Danny turns from the blip on the radar screen to the speedboat a few times until it becomes apparent, the blip on the radar screen and the speedboat are indeed the same.

“That’s the damnedest thing I’ve ever seen!” he exclaims, looking at Hank suspiciously.

“That’s what I’ve been trying to tell you,” Hank says.

“Whatever else is going on around here...” Danny says, checking to make sure the crew is still at the bow, who stand there patiently waiting, “...that could be a handy gizmo to have in these waters,” he says smiling at Hank suddenly.

Hank pours them some rum.

“Us rum-runners know these waters better than those Coast Guard captains anyways, but it’d be a welcomed blessing to have an edge,” he says raising his glass and winking at Hank.

Hank lifts his glass and they share a drink. Danny peeks over at Kelly and the crew who continue to keep their distance.

“Okay, let’s say, just for arguments sake, that you somehow passed through time... How do you know who I am and what do you want?” he asks.

Hank looks at him in amazement, unsure what to say. He looks out at the crew gathered on the bow, then back at Danny.

“I’m your grandson in the future and when I was a boy you told me stories about your rum-running days. That’s how I knew where to find you,” Hank blurts out.

Danny’s eyes pop open wide.

“You slip something in my rum?” he asks, smelling the drink and backing away from Hank. “I’ve heard of things like this,” he says. “What’s in here? Absinthe?” he asks, looking closely at the glass of rum. “That stuff makes people crazy,” he says.

“Your son William is my father,” he says.

Danny gazes at him, suspiciously wary of the incredulous tale he’s being told. He’s a bit spooked and begins slowly backing away towards the stern.

“I know about the Grand Duchess,” Hank says finally.

Danny looks at him in shock. “Who told you about that?” he asks furiously. “No one knows about the Duchess!” he insists looking around and backing away towards the stern.

“Grandpa, wait!” Hank yells moving towards Danny. “You told me when I was twelve years old,” he says. “You were trying to teach me something about certain women, and you told me all about the Duchess and what happened,” Hank tells him in earnest.

Kelly and the crew listen to the fantastic tale, on edge, wondering if they’re about to lose Danny.

“The Duchess, hunh?” Sal smiles looking up at Kelly.

The crew knows there’s nothing they can do and hang back. Danny is poised to leap into the drink.

“I’ve heard about enough of this craziness,” he says ready to leap.

“You met grandma at Tiny Underwood’s,” Hank tells him.

Hank stares at Danny, who stares back, wrestling with what is a fantastical and extremely confusing exchange he cannot begin to fathom. He sits on the siderail exhausted.

“Danny! We got’s to go!” his shipmate, still aboard the Chris Craft tied on to the Schooner, yells at him.

Danny looks out at him and motions for him to hold on. “I’ve experienced some strange goings-on out here on this ocean,” he says, looking up into Hank’s eyes. “But nothin’ comes close to this,” he says, shaking his head. “Either you’re all nuts, or I am,” he says, looking at the crew still gathered at the bow, then at Hank.

“Or what we’re telling you, as crazy as it sounds, is the truth,” Sal says gently taking a few steps towards Danny.

“Look, I’ve got to get my whiskey ashore,” Danny says pointing over his shoulder at his Chris Craft as he steps towards them, “let’s say everything you’re telling me is the truth, God help us all. Now what?” he asks looking at Hank.

Hank is somewhat speechless. He looks over at Kelly, “May I?” Kelly says, looking at Danny with his trusting grin.

“Please,” Danny says.

“We ended up here in your time after a wild and strange electrical storm,” Kelly says walking towards Danny.

“It’s taken us a few days to even begin to come to terms with all of this,” he says looking around at his crew. “We have a proposition for you and about six of your friends,” he says reaching into his pocket. “I know you have to go now, but if we can meet somewhere onshore in an hour or so, we can tell you all about it,” Kelly tells him. “See if it’s the kind of easy money you guys would like to capitalize on,” he says smiling at Danny. “Here’s a deposit, just so you know we’re serious.” He hands Danny a hundred-dollar bill.

Danny’s eyes light up.

Danny takes it and inspects it closely, “This isn’t from the future too, is it?” he asks smiling then shaking his head in disbelief at what he just said. “I’m getting to be as crazy as you folks.” He laughs.

Sal laughs. “Nah…” she says looking around at the others with a smile. “I get the feeling that you’re your own kind of crazy, Danny boy,” she says, smiling at Danny.

He smiles at her with a chuckle.

“Danny! Let’s go! Trucks are waiting!” his partner yells from the Chris Craft.

“You better get going,” Hank says stepping forward.

Danny waves his shipmate over. Hank and Danny shake hands.

“Ok… Meet me at Tiny Underwood’s in a couple hours,” Danny says smiling.

“Tiny Underwood’s?” Kelly asks.

“It’s up by the harbor. You’ll find it,” he says climbing over the siderail and stepping into his Chris Craft.

“That Coast Guard is right about there, south by southwest,” Hank tells Danny, pointing towards shore. “Around three miles in,” he adds.

“They can’t catch this sweet gal,” Danny says, patting his Chris Craft. “Gotta go,” he says, then revs up the speedboat and disappears into the moonlight.

“Wow,” says The Kid.

Sal moves close to Hank and puts her arm around him.

“You okay, Hank?” she asks.

Hank runs his fingers through his hair, looking out to sea. “I suppose,” he says.

He looks at the crew and all the booze on board.

“We best get out of here,” he says, pointing to the cases of booze stacked on deck. “There’s Coast Guard out there somewhere…” he says turning himself in the direction Danny just took.

He moves to the helm, puts the Sally Ann in gear and heads to shore.

They get back to their secret little cove without incident and set anchor. For the first time since arriving in 1929, Hank steps off the Sally Ann. The crew, with Hank in tow, make their way to the side of The Montauk Highway where Chappy is dutifully waiting in the carriage, writing in his notebook.

“Good to see you again, Chappy,” Kelly says.

Hank with them, they climb into the carriage.

“Do you know of a place called Tiny Underwood’s?” Kelly asks him.

“I do… It’s a speakeasy up near the harbor. Only I don’t recommend taking the lady into that establishment,” he says with a warning. “Rather nefarious environs, if you know what I mean,” he says as he slaps the reigns, getting the horse moving.

“Sounds juicy,” Dave comments.

They make their way up West Lake Drive towards the harbor past Star Island. A short time later Chappy pulls the carriage left into the parking area of Tiny Underwood’s. A tinny piano can be heard accompanied by a wailing trumpet. Chappy calls out to Kelly as they exit the carriage. Kelly looks up at Chappy. "You must inquire about the Lobster Special," he says with a wink.

"I see," Kelly says.

They approach the entrance where a large doorman oversees entry into the small club.

He looks them over. "Is the lady attached to one of you fellas?" he asks.

"On my better days," Hank says stepping up and planting a kiss on Sal's sweet lips, which she doesn't pull away from.

"What of it?" he asks looking up at the large doorman.

Kelly steps up and slaps a twenty-dollar bill in the doorman's hand.

"We'd like the Lobster Special," he says with a wink.

The doorman pockets the bill and opens the door.

"Right this way, folks," he says.

They enter the small, lively club. A jazz combo plays "If I had My Way" by Merle Johnson and his Ceco Couriers. A few roughnecks sit at the bar with a couple of floozies while some well-dressed adventurers fill most of the tables. No sign of Danny yet, so they grab a large table, order some drinks and enjoy the music.

"This place doesn't look so tough," The Kid says looking around the room.

"You think he'll show?" Rollie asks.

“He’ll show,” Hank assures them. “But, until he does,” he says standing up, turning to Sal with a smile. “May I have this dance?” he asks with his hand out to Sal.

“Love to, captain,” she says placing her hand in his, allowing him to help her to her feet.

They make their way to the tiny dancefloor and slow dance to the bluesy jazz being played. It isn’t very long before Danny and a few of his boisterous fisherman cohorts enter. Hank excuses himself and walks over to greet them.

“Coast Guard never had a chance,” Danny says shaking hands with Hank. “Where can I get one of those radar machines?” he asks.

Nowhere for another twenty-five years or so,” Hank tells him with a smile. “Maybe we can hook mine up in your Chris Craft,” he smiles.

“Really?” Danny asks with a big smile.

“That’d give you a huge advantage over the Coast Guard,” Hank tells him. “They don’t even have this technology yet,” he assures Danny.

“That’s awful big of you, Hank,” Danny tells him. “Awful big…” he says, looking around the speakeasy.

“I can’t believe it’s really you!” Hank says emotionally placing his hands on his young grandfather’s shoulders and looking him in the eye. “All the stories you told me about this place and the rum-running days… Now to actually be here… Man, it just boggles the mind.” Hank shakes his head.

“It’s nothing less than surreal,” Danny agrees. “I want to believe it, but I have to confess, as much as I do feel a connection to you, it’s a lot to make sense of,” he says.

The two Sullivans stand there in the center of the speakeasy bewildered. A long moment passes amidst the jazz, clinking of glasses and boisterous crowd.

"So, what exactly is this all about?" asks Danny. "Your friend is pretty loose with a hundred-dollar bill," he adds.

"They're right over there," Hank says referring to the table with the crew seated around drinking. "C'mon, drinks are on me," Hank says, leading the way.

Hank and Danny Sullivan make their way over to the table.

"You all know Danny," Hank says pulling out a couple of chairs for them.

The crew greet Danny.

"Besides the fact that Hank is your grandson returned from a far-away time, I guess you want to know what we're up to and why we need your help," Kelly says with his classic trusting grin.

"It's fair to say you've piqued my interest," Danny says as he sips his drink.

Kelly looks around the table and begins. "As you know, we got caught up in a strange electrical storm of some kind and ended up here. It was July 4, 2019 when we boarded Hank's boat to retrieve a six-foot rocket filled with bank loot and valuable gems worth quite a lot of money," he continues. "Now we're trying to find the rocket which we believe passed through time ahead of us and could still be here, only we're not going to get very far without money," he says looking around at everyone at the table.

Danny sips his drink and looks at Kelly. "Let's say that everything you just told me is true," he says, raising his eyebrows with a doubtful expression in comic relief. "How do I fit into all this?" He looks over at Hank. "Other than maybe this fine fella here might be my grandson from the future all grown up," he says, smiling at Hank.

"Fair enough," Kelly says. "The thing is, as I said, we need enough money to keep up appearances, and to make investigations freely as well-heeled individuals so we can more easily further the effort to locate our rocket," he says, sipping his drink and looking around at everyone. "We have a plan to reverse the rigged roulette wheel in the casino at The Deep Sea Club, causing it to favor straight bets as opposed to the low odds bets it favors now," he tells Danny.

"You know how to rig a roulette wheel?" Danny asks impressed.

"I do..." says Dave with his mischievous grin.

"In order to do that, we need a distraction that will buy Dave here an hour alone with the wheel inside the casino," he says attempting to sound logical and methodical.

"A distraction, hunh..." Danny says. "That's where I come in," he says looking around at everyone.

"Smart man," Sal says lighting a cigarette in her fancy cigarette holder.

"And how exactly do you propose to take command of the casino with Capone's boys running security?" he asks.

Kelly smiles at Danny. "That's the fun part," he says smiling. "We set up a phony FBI raid of the club and casino," he says, matter of factly.

Danny laughs. "You know, when I first met you guys out at the rum line, I thought you were crazy... he says, lighting a cigarette. "Now I know you are," he finishes exhaling cigarette smoke.

"Maybe," Kelly says. "Maybe... But that doesn't mean we're not going to do it," he says, smiling at Sal.

"We need a few guys to play the FBI agents," The Kid tells him.

"We figured you and some of your renegade fisherman rum-runner pals would be game," Dave chimes in.

"Hmmmm..." Danny mutters. "A chance to outsmart Capone's security", he smiles, "Doesn't happen every day," he adds with a chuckle. "How do we do it and how much does it pay?" he asks, puffing on his smoke.

Kelly lays out the plan. The passport photos, the fake IDs, the cheap government-issued suits, the FBI-style hats, 38 revolvers, the works. Kelly tells him, looking over at Rollie, "We'll need two or three Ford sedans," he says.

"On it," Rollie says.

Danny glances over at Hank with a "Can-you-believe-these-guys" expression on his face.

Hank looks back at him. "I know," Hank says with a smile.

"We have The Kid, Rollie, Dave and me," Kelly says looking at Danny, "Can you get six men at two hundred and fifty dollars apiece?" he asks. "Paid in advance, of course?" he adds.

Danny plays the cool customer despite the fact that $250 in 1929 is close to $4,000 in 2019. He flicks the ash off of his cigarette and looks at Kelly.

“Plus, a bonus down the road if all goes well,” Kelly assures him.

“I won’t lie to you...” Danny smiles. “...for that kinda cash and the chance to make fools of Capone’s boys... I’ll have to beat ‘em off with a stick,” he assures Kelly with a giant smile.

Kelly’s giant grin emerges.

“Sedans?” The Kid asks disappointed.

“Yeah, Kid,” Dave tells him. “Sedans... The FBI didn’t drive hot rods to a speakeasy raid,” he says.

“I guess...” The Kid says a bit disappointed.

“Don’t worry, Kid, we’re gonna get you in a hotrod on that racetrack soon enough,” Kelly says.

“First things first,” Rollie tells The Kid.

“There’s a photographer in town who makes passport photos that we’ll need for the IDs,” Dave tells Danny. “What time can you and your crew meet us there this afternoon?” he asks.

“Oh, we ought to be back in around four o’clock,” Danny tells him.

“Then it’s all set!” Kelly says standing up and reaching out his hand.

He and Danny shake on it.

“See ya round four,” Danny says smiling.

Kelly tips the waitress and they exit Tiny Underwood's. The crew hop into Chappy's carriage and make their way to the Montauk Manor.

XIX

It's three a.m. the night of the FBI raid. They've agreed to meet on a deserted side street a block away from Tiny Underwood's, a less than three-minute drive to the casino. Dave has created convincing FBI IDs for everyone, they've been fitted for and are wearing cheap government-styled suits and are armed with 38 specials in G-Men-styled shoulder holsters. Rollie and The Kid managed to acquire three Ford sedans which are on the street idling and ready for action. There is a lot of chatter between the rum-runner fisherman gathered for the con. They're having a ball in anticipation of the raid, bragging and jostling each other about getting back at Capone's men. Kelly and the crew are happy to see them so relaxed and gung-ho. He, Dave, Rollie and The Kid feel confident that the rum-runners are more than capable enough to pull this off.

Kelly gathers them around, pulls out a wad of cash and as he pays each rum-runner fisherman the promised $250, he makes sure to stress that the pistols are only to be fired in an extreme case of self-defense. "As you probably know, the butt of a 38 in the back of the neck will knock anybody out," he assures them.

He looks around at the motley crew and smiles. "Okay, fellas, it's showtime," he says with a smile. "Hey, Danny, why don't you ride shotgun in my car," he says.

The ten bogus FBI agents pile into the cars and take off for Star Island. They get to the entrance where the armed guards are on patrol and screech to a stop.

"FBI!" Kelly says flashing his badge.

They burn rubber towards the Deep Sea Club casino while the guard races to the telephone inside the guard booth to warn that the FBI are on their way in. All mayhem breaks loose inside the clubs. Important guests such as then NYC Mayor Johnny Walker, are escorted out the back through the kitchen entrance.

The sedans screech to a stop in front of The Deep Sea Club. The FBI imposters leap from the sedans and bust into the casino, guns drawn. “FBI!” Kelly announces, flashing his badge. “Get them out of here!” he orders. Pointing his gun at crowds of gamblers who are stuffing as much cash and casino chips as they can into their pockets and purses.

“Okay, you,” Rollie says to a man who is obviously one of Capone’s security goons. “Give it up,” he says pointing his pistol at him.

Capone’s men don’t challenge the FBI and give up their weapons. The rum-runner fisherman FBI agents line the goons up along with all the other casino occupants against the exterior walls of the casino.

“Check the latrines,” Kelly shouts to a few of the fake FBI Agents.

They rifle through the men’s and ladies’ bathrooms and escort the few people hiding in them outside with the others. Once they’re certain no one remains inside the casino, Dave wastes no time getting to work on the roulette wheel, Rollie standing nearby.

“You got this?” Kelly asks Dave who is already busy removing a leg from the roulette wheel table.

Dave raises his eyebrows at Kelly, “Don’t I always?” he asks wise.

“One hour,” Kelly says as he checks his watch.

He runs outside to assist in rounding up the occupants of the Deep Sea Club speakeasy and to see if a payoff arrangement can be had with Carl Fischer who he imagines has to be somewhere nearby. Crowds of disgruntled patrons who have been rounded up at gunpoint, are lined up outside held at bay by the gun-yielding rum-runner fisherman FBI agents. Kelly enters the speakeasy to find Carl Fischer.

“What’s going on here?” A man asks loudly as one of the FBI Agents forcibly escorts him outside.

Kelly walks to him briskly, “FBI! I’m looking for Carl Fischer,” Kelly says flashing his badge.

“He’s out of town,” the man tells him. “Harry Johnson, club manager. I’m in charge until Mr. Fischer returns this evening,” he says.

“That’s okay, agent, I’ll handle this one,” Kelly tells a rum-runner FBI agent who has walked over to assist him. “Check the latrines,” he says.

Kelly guides Harry to the bar. “Let’s talk,” he says.

“You guys are worse than the cops,” Harry tells him.

“You have no idea,” Kelly says smiling.

“So, what is it exactly that you want?” Harry asks. I don’t see any Paddy Wagons out there,” Harry says, looking at Kelly suspiciously.

“What’s good for the goose is good for the gander,” Kelly tells him.

Manager Harry Johnson looks at him, unsure what he means by his innocuous remark. Kelly observes Harry closely, trying to learn something about him before he drops the bomb. Plus, he's stalling in order to give Dave plenty of time to work his magic on the roulette wheel.

"Let's just say I've decided to take a page from the Chief of Police's handbook," Kelly tells him with a wry smile.

"But you're the FBI," Harry says surprised at a request more befitting the local constabulary. "What's it gonna take?" he asks.

Kelly looks at his watch. He knows Dave needs a good forty-five minutes longer. He takes a few steps away from the bar, and strolls further into the club.

"Nice place you have here," he says. "Some high rollers frequent this haunt..." he says examining Harry for his reaction.

He steps closer to Harry, "I don't want to shut you down, Mr. Johnson," he says. "I do, however, believe a little respect must be paid its due to the hard-working law enforcement members of this fine community," he goes on.

"You guys aren't even of this community," Harry argues. "You're FBI for crying out loud," he complains, agitated.

"There is some curiosity as to how Mr. Fischer funded all of his elaborate projects," Kelly warns possessing knowledge the history he is now living.

Kelly knows that Carl Fischer lost a fortune in the Miami real estate bust of 1925 and the hurricane of 1926. Kelly's convinced that there's a fair chance there was a bit more at play than a few wealthy partners that allowed Carl to build Montauk. Perhaps a windfall of some kind helped him to pay 2.5 million dollars for the land, then finance construction of landmark buildings, most of which still exist in 2019. Kelly glances at his watch. Maybe he can learn something of value from Harry Johnson. An idea forms in his head. It's outlandish, but that never stopped Kelly in the past, and it's not about to stop him now.

"Let's see..." he says taking his time, "There's the Montauk Manor, The Montauk Yacht Club, The Montauk Inn, The Surf Club, The Tower, the inlet to Lake Montauk, and this place... The Deep Sea Club," he says taking in the speakeasy in which they're standing. "Very elegant," he says with a smile. "Not to mention the roads, plumbing and electrical lines throughout the entire town or his elaborate eight-thousand-square-foot private mansion," he says, playing for time. "Let me ask you something, Mr. Johnson," he says, leaning in closer. "How did Mr. Fischer finance all of these impressive projects?" he asks.

Harry looks at Kelly suspiciously. *Who is this strange man?* he asks himself. *And why all these questions?*

"Look, you want a payoff, fine," Harry says curtly. "The Police Chief is usually happy with a few grand," he says, looking Kelly in the eye.

Kelly looks at his watch. If all is going well with Dave, he should be finishing up in about fifteen minutes.

"Naturally, I'm a reasonable man, Mr. Johnson," Kelly tells him with a smile. "Three grand sounds about right," he says.

"Damn feds! The safe is back here," he says walking towards the back of the club.

Harry leads Kelly to his private office and opens the house safe. He pulls out two one thousand-dollar stacks of hundred dollar bills, gives Kelly a miserable glance, then grabs a third begrudgingly.

"This ought to keep you off of our backs for a while," he says handing Kelly the cash.

“This will do fine,” Kelly says stuffing the bills in his inside vest pocket. “We’re holding your people outside,” he says, looking at his watch. I’ll call my men off soon, and you can enjoy the rest of your evening in peace,” he tells him.

He holds his hand out for Harry to shake, which Harry does reluctantly.

Kelly exits to find that Danny and the boys have everything under control outside. He walks over to Danny.

“Having fun?” he asks speaking into his ear.

Danny keeps one eye on Capone’s goons. “Feels like Christmas morning,” he says smiling.

“We’ll be letting everyone go as soon as we’re finished inside,” Kelly tells him quietly.

Kelly enters the casino to find Dave and Rollie just finishing up. He struts over to the craps table, pockets three pair of dice and walks back to the roulette wheel. Dave tests his handiwork several times and it works perfectly. He looks at Kelly with his mischievous smile.

Let’s make some money,” he says.

Kelly gives Dave a big hug. “You’re a genius,” he tells him.

Kelly shows off the dice he pocketed. “Think you can do something with these?” he asks.

“Good idea,” Dave says. “Notice how many times they switched out the dice on The Kid the other night when he was having his lucky streak?” he asks.

“I most certainly did” Kelly says smiling.

He lifts the dice to his face and looks at them with affection, "Although the pair I palmed the other night with Sal are my favorites, I'm sure Dave will treat you all with the same love and affection," he tells the dice before stuffing them into his pocket, a huge grin on his face.

"I thought Hank speaking to his dead grandfather was strange," Rollie comments before checking the area for any loose tools or signs of them having been there.

"Carl's out of town, but I met his manager," Kelly lets them know.

"How'd we do?" asks Rollie.

"He was quite generous," Kelly says pulling out the three thousand-dollar stacks and holding them up for the guys to see.

"Not bad," says Dave. "Not bad at all... Especially for 1929," he says.

They exit the casino and make their way over to Danny and the other fisherman FBI agents who keep the angry crowd in check.

"Okay, let's wrap it up, fellas," Kelly tells them.

"Kelly stands in front of the large disgruntled crowd and in a loud voice tells them, "We are sorry to have disrupted your party, ladies and gentlemen. Please, carry on and enjoy the rest of your evening."

He and the boys get in the sedans and drive off. People are confused at first, but it isn't long before they are back in the speakeasy and casino roaring it up.

The sedans pull up to the dockage where Danny and the other rum-runners keep their speedboats stashed. They jump out of the cars and laugh it up, charged from the raid.

“Man, that goon nearly wet his pants!” Danny says to one of his pals.

Kelly walks over to thank them all and pay each of them a hundred-dollar bonus from the three grand he got off of Harry Johnson.

“You fellas can hold on to the suits, firearms and FBI badges,” he tells them. “Never know when we might need to go back in,” he says, smiling.

Danny walks over to Kelly. “Thanks again, Kelly,” he says offering a handshake. “It was a lot of fun,” he says.

Kelly smiles his big grin, loving the fact that Danny considers what they just pulled off to be ‘lots of fun.’

“You’re my kinda guy, Danny,” he says giving him a giant hug.

Danny looks at his watch, “We can still make Rum Row, fellas,” he says loudly to his fellow rum-runners.

“Yeah…” one of the rum-runner fishermen agrees. “McCoy’s probably wondering where we are!” he says laughing.

Kelly, Rollie and Dave stash the sedans in the reeds near the Sally Ann where Chappy is dutifully waiting in the carriage.

“Good evening, Chappy,” Kelly says stepping out of the brush.

Dave, Rollie and The Kid appear right behind him. The four of them climb into the carriage and take off for the Manor.

“Man, that was fun!” The Kid says.

“It was all right,” Rollie says.

“You think those goons are gonna recognize us when we return as gamblers tomorrow night?” The Kid asks.

Kelly smiles at The Kid. “It’s a funny thing... A man with a badge... Most people will rarely remember the face, only the badge,” he tells him.

“Yeah,” Dave says. “Cops and FBI agents become more like cartoons to the memory,” he says. “It’s as though they’re not real people. Just a badge,” he tells him.

“A source of fear,” Rollie adds looking at The Kid. “No passion so effectually robs the mind of all its powers of acting and reasoning as fear,” Rollie says.

“Interesting...” The Kid says thinking about it. “Makes sense,” he adds.

“Have an interesting evening, gentleman?” Chappy inquires.

“You writing about us, too?” The Kid asks Chappy.

“It hadn’t occurred to me, young man, however, now that you mention it,” he smiles. “I would suggest to you that there are far more intriguing subjects to write about. I must add however, that I am pleased to hear one of you quoting Edmund Burke,” he says looking at Rollie then slapping the horse with the reigns.

A fast-driving roadster passes them blowing its horn. The Kid watches it zoom past and race up the highway towards Montauk.

“That’s a car!” The Kid comments.

“Why don’t you see what you can learn about the races?” Kelly suggests.

“I’m on it,” says The Kid with a smile.

XX

Back in Nova Scotia at the same time of the same day, only in 2019, not knowing what has happened to his friends, and wary about contacting the authorities, lest he get them all arrested, Sparky has finally decided to give up waiting and grabs a flight back to Montauk. It's not long before he's back driving his taxi. He makes frequent trips to the commercial dock and to the Dock Restaurant to see if there has been any word about the Sally Ann. After speaking with the bartender at The Dock restaurant, and a few commercial fishermen, all he has learned is that the Sally Ann went out the night of that strange electrical storm and hasn't been heard from since. Now that they're gone, memories of his stimulating encounters with Kelly and the crew have become extremely vivid and he continues to write down everything he can recall. He feels in his heart that they're okay and somehow will return one day.

XXI

It's the next night and the crew is gathered in Kelly's suite at the Montauk Manor getting ready to hit the casino and take it for all it's worth. Dave has managed to load the dice and informs everyone that two pair have been loaded to favor hitting sevens for hard bets and the others to roll numbers found in what most seasoned gamblers, and croupiers alike, consider amateur bets known as The Field.

"Field bets? Why field bets? The Kid asks with a disgruntled face, "They don't pay anything."

"Betting the field will throw the croupier off and buy us more time to cash in on the pass bets when those dice are in play, Kid," Dave tells him.

"Oh... Good idea," The Kid admits. "That croupier must've switched out the dice a dozen times on me the other night. But, he was no match for Mario," he says laughing.

Dave presents two sets of dice to Kelly. "I fixed four pair, these will roll straight," he says handing Kelly two pair, "And these will favor the field," he says handing Kelly the other two pair of dice, "Be sure to keep them separate and know which ones you're rolling or you'll end up betting against yourself," Dave tells him.

The crew has rarely seen Kelly this excited about a scam. He checks to be sure he has each set of loaded dice in separate pockets then briefs everyone on how the loaded dice can be used to best effect. "You guys just follow my lead on the bets," Kelly tells them. "I'll palm the house dice, switch them out, roll Dave's dice, until all four pairs of the smart dice have been played out," Kelly tells them. "So bet big and when they switch out the dice, wait till I place a large pass or field bet, before you lay down," he says.

"When Kelly's done with the loaded dice, feel free to stick around for Mario's play," The Kid says, air-rolling dice.

"Don't get ahead of yourself, Kid," Sal tells him. "Luck, like love, is fleeting," she says.

"Words to live by, Kid," Dave assures him.

"Amen to that," Rollie says.

The crew walk outside and meet Chappy who is parked at The Montauk Manor in his carriage waiting for them. They make their way to the Deep Sea Club speakeasy to finalize the plan and to have a few drinks. Thinking it best to break up into two separate parties, Kelly and Dave enter the Casino followed soon afterwards by Sal, Rollie and The Kid. Kelly and Dave head straight for the craps table to get a pair of the loaded dice in play. Sal, Rollie and The Kid appear moments later pretending not to know Kelly or Dave. It isn't long before Kelly gets a roll. He switches out the first of four pairs and places a pass bet signaling Dave and the others how to place their bets. After three hits of sevens, the crew betting large and winning, the croupier pulls the dice off the table and introduces a new pair. Kelly palms them on the first pass and bets the field to signal the crew that he switched them out for a pair that pay in the field. They begin betting large amounts on low-paying field bets and winning. The crowd is getting excited and the croupier, as was hoped, is a bit miffed. Because low-paying field bets are paying out, it takes him a while to decide to switch out the dice. Kelly palms the new dice and switches them out for a pair loaded to roll sevens. The crew know to follow Kelly's lead and place large pass bets on Kelly's come out roll, as do other gamblers at the table following the action. They all win big. Cheers and shouting ensue. Kelly rolls the same dice again and most of the gamblers let it ride. Boom! All pass bets are paid out. The croupier switches out the dice. After all the loaded dice have been played out, Kelly and Dave move over to the roulette wheel. The Kid, Sal and Rollie stick around in case The Kid is still hot.

Kelly and Dave approach the roulette wheel where a high roller is already reaping the benefits of Dave's handiwork winning on straight bets he otherwise would very likely have been losing money on. They watch a roll spying on the croupier to see if he presses the secret button. He spins the wheel and rolls the ball.

"No more bets," he announces as he slyly presses the secret button.

Kelly and Dave smile as the high roller wins on a straight 23. Cheers from the crowd.

"Let it ride!" the high roller yells.

Kelly turns to Dave, "Look at that, the table is already primed," he says smiling.

Kelly and Dave manage to get past the boisterous crowd of gamblers feeding off of the excitement and find a spot at the table. Dave lays a large bet on a 35/36 split. Kelly lays an equally large bet on 35 straight. The croupier rolls the wheel and drops the ball.

"No more bets," the Croupier announces.

The croupier presses the hidden button again.

Various gamblers call out their numbers, "Come on, twenty-three!" the high roller yells.

The ball dances across the wheel, then stops finally.

"Thirty-five," the Croupier announces.

Kelly and Dave collect their winnings and place another bet. Hours later, there is a huge crowd surrounding Kelly and Dave cheering. Dave has a stunning, sophisticated woman on his arm.

At the craps table, The Kid's blonde is back and he's on fire again, winning big. Sal and Rollie have both amassed huge stacks of chips.

It's not yet three in the morning when the manager, Harry Johnson knocks on Carl Fischer's private office door in a near panic. Carl returned from a trip to Chicago already unhappy to learn about the FBI raid of the previous night and now the casino is taking a major hit.

"Show me," he yells standing up and marching towards the casino with manager Harry. Carl bursts inside of the casino and Harry runs over to the head goon in charge of security.

"We may be shutting it down early tonight, Max," he says.

Carl grabs the casino manager by the arm. "Where are we getting hit the hardest?" he asks, scanning the casino floor as a huge cheer erupts from the craps table.

Craps *and* roulette," Harry tells Carl.

Carl gets to the roulette wheel just as Kelly and Dave win another large bet paying thirty-five to one. They've won more bets than they've lost by far thanks to Dave's fix. As they organize their chips and lay down the next play, loud cheers and whistles blast out from the craps table where The Kid, still on fire, is causing all kinds of mayhem, winning roll after roll as Sal and Rollie cash in.

"Shut it down! Shut it down!" Carl tells the manager.

Harry makes a mad dash to the light control panel. He flashes the lights on and off signaling the casino is closing. Capone's goons make their way around the casino to ensure the message is clear, that the casino is closed for the night.

Kelly turns to Dave and smiles.

"They've decided to cut their losses." Dave chuckles.

"We shut them down," Kelly says.

"And in fine style," Dave says.

He turns to the lovely woman who has attached herself to him.

"C'mon, toots, let's grab a drink next door," he says.

"Sure, baby," she says, leaving a large lipstick mark on his cheek.

The crew join a large group of gamblers cashing in their chips. Carl Fischer is nearby with manager Harry Johnson who points out who the big winners were. Kelly recognizes Carl from old photographs of him he's seen.

"Keep it casual, but that's Carl Fischer..." Kelly tells them pointing with his chin. "It appears that Harry has zeroed us out as the big winners," he says.

"He knows who we are all right," Dave says, spying Carl, pretending to smooch with his lady.

"Check out Dave," The Kid says, smiling at Sal.

"Romeo IV in the making..." she says cracking wise.

"I think I'll go and introduce myself to Carl," Kelly says.

Kelly cashes in his chips and walks over to Carl Fischer.

"Mr. Fischer," he says hand outstretched.

Carl appears less than pleased to have to shake hands with one of the players who has nearly broken the casino.

"Yes..." is all he can utter, as he shakes Kelly's hand.

"John Kelly," Kelly tells him.

He looks around the casino as the gamblers finally make their way to the exit. Kelly's mind, as always, is searching for an angle. Then it comes to him.

"I understand you were once a celebrated racecar driver," Kelly says.

"What of it?" Carl asks, still disgruntled.

"Only that... You see, I was awful lucky this evening and I was wondering, if perchance, you were the gentleman organizing the auto-races here in town," he says with as much charm as he can muster.

Carl looks at him suspiciously but also thinking of a way he might perhaps turn this into a profitable exchange.

"I am," he says. "One of them... Why do you ask?" he adds.

"I have a driver I'm backing who would very much like to enter an event if you have one upcoming," Kelly says smiling.

"Who is your driver?" he asks. "I know most of the racecar drivers... Perhaps I know him," Carl states, very curious now.

“I doubt you’ve heard of him. He’s a young man from Scotland, just arrived,” Kelly tells him.

“What does he drive?” Carl wants to know.

“Actually, we’re only just now shopping for the automobile,” Kelly tells him with a grin. “Something very fast, I hope,” he says. “Since I’ll be betting on him.”

“Why don’t you drop by my office tomorrow and bring your driver along,” Carl tells him.

“It would be my pleasure,” Kelly says shaking his hand.

He exits the empty casino and walks next door to the speakeasy. As is usual, sweet jazz from the era fills the lively room. He spots the others at the bar and joins them. Dave is smooching with his date, as is The Kid. Sal and Rollie are seated together at the bar sipping cocktails, having a ball recalling the high points of their winning streak.

“That poor croupier couldn’t figure out what to do,” Rollie says. “No matter how many times he switched out the dice, we just kept winning.” He chuckles.

“And Kid luck over there played the lucky dummy to a ‘T’,” Sal says, looking up at Kelly who has just joined them.

“He’s a real natural,” Kelly says watching The Kid slow dance with his bombshell flapper date.

“He’s going to be happy to learn I just got us a meeting with Carl Fischer concerning a race,” he tells them.

“Nice move,” Rollie says smiling.

"He probably figures he can recoup some of his losses from this evening," Sal comments, sipping her champagne.

"He was practically biting at the bit," Kelly tells them.

"I bet," Rollie says patting his pocket, "We hit him pretty hard at the craps table.

"Dave and I took care of business at the roulette wheel as well," he says, a huge smile on his face, as he watches Dave with his young lady dancing to an upbeat tune.

"I was hoping Errol would be here tonight," Sal says looking around the club. "Probably back in LA hunting down some fresh high school girls," she quips, lighting a cigarette in her long, sleek cigarette holder.

"It's getting late... The Kid and I have a meeting with Carl Fischer tomorrow morning," Kelly says looking at his watch. "I'll go see if Chappy's standing by," he says.

Kelly exits the club and finds Chappy dutifully waiting. He spots Kelly. "Another late night, sir?" he asks.

"Good to see you, Chappy," Kelly tells him. "Let me round up the crew and we'll head down to the Manor," he says.

"Righto," Chappy says.

Kelly manages to tear Dave and The Kid away from their dates and the crew jumps in the carriage for their slow ride back to the Montauk Manor.

XXII

The next morning, Kelly and The Kid ride up in Chappy's carriage to meet with Carl Fischer.

"I'm thinking a Bugatti," The Kid says. "But it almost doesn't matter because whatever I end up driving, Rollie and Dave are going to give it an edge," The Kid says smiling.

"Dave mentioned that he can modify any present day supercharger," Kelly says.

"That's great for the quick blasts of speed I'll need to get out in front, but on that track, with hardly a straightaway in sight, it's all about handling. Suspension..." The Kid tells Kelly, happy to know more about something than his mentor.

"I see what you mean," Kelly says.

"Yeah, Dave and Rollie have an idea to outfit me with softer springs and modify the steerage to a rack and pinion design which no one else has even seen yet. That'll give superior grip and handling, which is what I'll need on that track," he says, air-driving.

Kelly loves that The Kid has already given it this much thought.

"You know, as much money as we won last night this could be the cash cow we need," Kelly says. "I plan to play into Carl Fischer's vanity as a champion racecar driver hooking him into making a fat wager on the race," Kelly tells The Kid.

Kelly and The Kid pull up to the speakeasy which isn't officially open yet. They step out of the carriage, walk to the entrance and introduce themselves, telling the doorman that Mr. Fischer is expecting them. The doorman has them wait while he checks it out.

A short time later he returns. "Mr. Fischer will see you now. Come in," he says, opening the door for them.

They enter the club where waiters are setting up tables, bartenders are organizing the bar and a Jazz Band is setting up. Harry Johnson walks out to greet them.

"Harry Johnson," he says his hand outstretched.

Kelly shakes his hand. Harry looks at Kelly like he sees a ghost. Luckily, he can't put it together. Kelly plays it cool as a cucumber.

"John Kelly," Kelly says accepting the handshake.

"Jackie Stewart," The Kid says in his Scottish accent, also shaking hands with Harry Johnson.

"Mr. Fischer is in his office," Harry tells them. Right this way, gentleman," he says leading them to Carl's office in the rear of the club.

Harry knocks on the door and enters. Carl Fischer is seated at his desk smoking a large cigar. A magnificent blue marlin hangs on the wall behind him.

"Come in, gentleman." He stands up in a cloud of cigar smoke.

He walks over to greet Kelly and The Kid.

“Mr. Fischer, good to see you again,” Kelly says shaking Carl’s hand. “Impressive,” Kelly says, pointing to the large marlin behind Carl’s desk.

Carl turns to look at it, “Took that baby out of the waters off Key West with Hemingway a few years back, he says smiling.

“This is my driver, Jackie Stewart,” Kelly says by way of introduction.

The Kid and Carl shake hands.

“I’ll be on the floor if you need me, Carl,” Harry tells him taking his leave.

“Thanks Harry. Bring us some whiskey, would you?” he asks.

“Sure thing, Carl.” Harry walks to the bar and prepares a tray with whiskey, ice and three glasses.

“It’s an honor to meet you, sir,” The Kid says. “You were a top driver in your day,” The Kid says in his brogue, shaking Carl’s hand.

“Very good of you to say. Have a seat, gentleman,” Carl says, inviting them to sit down.

Harry returns with the drinks. They sit in the lounge area of Carl’s office and make themselves comfortable.

“Can you tell us about the nature of your racetrack,” The Kid asks. “I’ve only heard bits and pieces,” he adds.

“Certainly,” Carl says as he pours the cocktails. “It’s a challenging little track loosely modelled after the Indianapolis Speedway with hills and plenty of twists and turns that loops around the golf course I'm building a little less than a mile from here," he tells them.

"Sounds challenging! Can't wait to see it!" The Kid says enthusiastically. He sneaks a wink at Kelly who finds The Kid very amusing.

"Mr. Kelly tells me that you're purchasing a new car. Have you chosen a model yet?" Carl sips his whiskey.

"I'm thinking the Bugatti 35," The Kid says, air-driving for a moment, winking at Kelly.

"How often do your races occur?" Kelly asks.

"We try to have three during the summer season," Carl says, puffing on his fat cigar. "The next one is less than a week away. If you have your wheels by then you'd be more than welcome to enter," he says turning to The Kid.

"We can do that, can't we?" The Kid asks Kelly.

"Absolutely," Kelly says with confidence.

Kelly crosses his legs, folding his hands on his lap in a non-aggressive position and looks at Carl.

"I imagine there is prize money involved..." Kelly says. Before Carl can comment he adds, "I will also imagine wagering occurs in conjunction with these races?"

"You imagine correctly, Mr. Kelly," Carl smiles, seeing this as an opportunity to recoup some of the money lost at the casino the previous night.

"In that case, we will be more than happy to enter your illustrious race," Kelly says sitting up.

"Harry handles all the details," Carl tells them.

He stands up, opens his office door and calls into the club for Harry. Kelly and The Kid stand up. Within moments Harry appears.

“Mr. Kelly is going to enter his driver in our next race. “Jackie Stewart is it?” he asks turning towards The Kid puffing his cigar.

“Yes, sir, Jackie Stewart,” The Kid says in his Scottish accent, smiling.

“I’m sure we’re happy to have you in the race, young sir, Harry says. “All pertinent details, starting time, regulations, entry fees, etc. will be available one day before the race here. Just ask for me,” he says, smiling and looking back and forth from Kelly to The Kid. He shakes The Kid’s hand.

He doesn’t know why, but he finds himself snarling at Kelly.

“See you then, gentleman,” Harry says running off to handle managing duties of the most glamorous speakeasy on Long Island in 1929.

Carl Fischer gives Kelly a look bordering on disdain, “I wonder, Mr. Kelly, what is it that you do?” he asks. “I know most all the finer people here, but you sir, remain a mystery,” he says as he sits down and pours himself a whiskey.

The Kid glances at Kelly with a slightly concerned expression. Kelly smiles, sits down, pours himself a drink, raises his glass to Carl, and looks him directly in the eye with a calm smile.

"It's no wonder," Kelly says. "I spend a considerable amount of time in Africa. Diamonds, mostly..." he says, sipping his whiskey.

The Kid sits down smiling and pours himself a drink. He's impressed how Kelly just turned a potentially difficult exchange into an opportunity to introduce the subject of diamonds into the conversation.

Kelly looks at Carl inquisitively. "Do you venture into exotic gems of value?" he asks as nonchalantly as he can.

"Gems? Who said anything about gems? he replies, maybe a bit agitated.

He takes a stiff drink, looks at Kelly, then his watch and says, "I really must be going."

He stands up briskly and walks to his desk. "I apologize, gentlemen, but I have some important matters to attend to," he says a bit short.

Kelly and The Kid look at each other with raised eyebrow. Kelly is more than intrigued.

He moves close to Carl, "Never invested in exotic gems then?" Kelly asks.

"Never!" he says, practically shouting, gulping down some whiskey.

The Kid stands back and watches, unsure as to exactly what is happening.

"I see... Pity really, they often prove to be good onvestments," Kelly says.

Kelly moves towards the door and opens it.

"Goodbye, Mr. Fischer," The Kid says in his Scottish. "It is a real honor to meet you."

"Yes, yes..." Carl remarks seated at his desk, acting strangely uncomfortable about something.

"See you on race day," Kelly says smiling and stepping out of the office with The Kid.

They walk through the club towards the exit.

"What was that all about?" The Kid asks.

"I'm not sure," Kelly says.

He stops walking suddenly and grabs The Kid by the arm.

"Did you see how nervous he became when I mentioned exotic gems?" Kelly asks.

"Yeah... that was weird," he says.

They stand there in the middle of the empty club. An idea pops into their heads at the exact same moment.

"Unless!" they both exclaim at the same exact time.

They move quickly towards the door and exit the club. Chappy is standing by. They leap into the carriage.

"This isn't a get-a-way, is it gentlemen?" Chappy says, enjoying that he can be a bit of a smart-ass with his generous clients.

"Ha! Not at all, Chappy. However, we do need to get to the Manor as quickly as is possible," Kelly informs him.

Chappy releases the brake, slaps the reigns and they get going to the Manor.

"It's entirely possible," Kelly says, looking at The Kid, his face electrified at the prospect of discovering where the rocket containing Demyan's exotic gems may have ended up.

"We should check with Dave," The Kid says.

"It is highly uncharacteristic of a man like Carl Fischer to act the way he did," Kelly said to The Kid. "It was as though we opened a wound," he says, thinking. "I mean, Carl is a wealthy daredevil. A man's man," Kelly tells The Kid. "A first rate promoter, and successful businessman, who made millions with the Prest-O-Lite. He makes a fortune inventing Miami Beach then after he losses a big hunk of his assets in the real estate bust of 1925 and the hurricane of '26 in that same Miami, which had to nearly put him under he comes to Montauk and starts all over again," Kelly says thinking aloud.

"He's got balls," The Kid says.

"Exactly, so why so nervous suddenly when we mention valuable gems?" Kelly proposes.

"Maybe because he found our rocket with Demyan's diamonds, and that's how he bought the whole town and built everything he built here," The Kid says.

They look at one another amazed at the possibility.

"We'll invite him fishing!" Kelly says.

"Fishing?" The Kid asks perplexed.

"Carl's a sportsman..." Kelly says. "See that Marlin hanging behind his desk? He was known... well, *is* known as Crazy Carl in some circles," he adds. "Air ballooning, speed boat pilot, airplane manufacturer. The man is a visionary!" Kelly insists. “He can imagine the future. That is a rare and valuable talent,” he tells The Kid.

Kelly and The Kid sit there quietly thinking for a moment.

“If he was the one to find the rocket, it’s possible that he hasn’t cashed in all the gems,” Kelly says. “We tell him we have a boat with new inventions that can help us catch big fish... Invite him aboard the Sally Ann, then approach him like we did Hank’s grandfather,” he tells The Kid thinking it through as he speaks.

“Yeah... and if he did find the rocket, he found the cash dated 2019 or whatever and since we know about it, he should believe we’re from the future and that it’s our rocket,” The Kid says thinking through Kelly’s plan.

They sit there thinking in silence a few moments as the carriage clatters along Flamingo Avenue towards the Montauk Manor.

“I’m still getting that race car!” The Kid exclaims.

“Absolutely, Kid... Absolutely,” Kelly says.

“What if we bust him by convincing him we’re from the future and all, but he isn’t willing to give up the gems?” The Kid asks.

“I’ll wager they’re in a personal safe in his office,” Kelly says looking at The Kid. “If he refuses to give them up, we’ll just have to steal them back,” he says, smiling.

Chappy pulls the carriage up to the Montauk Manor. Kelly and The Kid jump out.

“You better stick around, Chappy,” Kelly suggests. “I can send a waiter out for your lunch order if you like,” Kelly says with a smile.

"That would be most welcomed, Kelly, sir," Chappy says.

Kelly runs into the Manor excited to tell the others about his Carl Fischer theory and plans of inviting him deep sea fishing to find out if he's correct.

They walk to the glamorous dining room to find Sal, Dave and Rollie enjoying a lovely brunch. They can see Kelly is super excited about something.

"What's got you so charged up?" Sal asks sipping her coffee.

Kelly takes a seat, leans forward, elbows on the table and looks at each of them.

"The Kid and I may have discovered who came across our rocket," he tells them.

"Carl Fischer?" Sal asks, the realization dawning.

Kelly smiles at Sal. "Precisely," Kelly tells her.

"How do we confirm it?" Dave asks.

Kelly lays out the plan to invite Carl to go deep sea fishing.

"Sure..." Rollie says, "When he sees the instrumentation on the Sally Ann and some currency from 2019... That ought to do it."

"What if he's already cashed them all out or doesn't want to give them up?" Sal asks.

Kelly looks around the table slowly with a devious grin.

"Then we'll just have to steal them back," The Kid says. "Only, after the race next week," he adds, air-driving.

“On that note, your Bugatti will be here day after tomorrow,” Rollie tells The Kid. “Dave and I will take the train into the city and shop around for some goodies we’ll need to enhance performance,” he adds.

“Maybe we should all go,” suggests Sal.

“To see New York City in 1929,” Kelly says dreamily.

“The concierge tells me the train ride is only two hours long,” Sal tells them.

“That’s an entire hour less than in 2019,” remarks The Kid.

“That’s because there are far fewer stops,” says Dave.

“Maybe we can hire a private car on the train... But first, there’s no reason to let Dave’s masterwork on the roulette wheel go to waste,” Kelly says, looking around the table with his signature smile.

“Yeah...” Rollie says, looking around the table at everyone. “I haven’t had the chance to enjoy my work on the Roulette Wheel yet,” he adds.

“Roulette it is then.” Sal lights a cigarette in her long elegant cigarette holder. “After all, I will require some additional cash for shopping, dahling,” she adds, blowing a puff of smoke.

XXIII

That night the crew hits the casino again, winning big. Poor Carl has to shut it down early for the second night in a row. Once all the gamblers, especially Kelly and the crew have been escorted out, he orders Harry Johnson to have his 'boys' check the roulette wheel.

"Something's just not right," he insists.

The crew gathers outside the casino.

"Let's grab a drink at the club," Sal suggests.

"I'm buying," smiles The Kid patting his vest pocket full of winnings.

The crew saunters over to the speakeasy, grab a table and order drinks.

"It's time to see Hank," Kelly tells them. "See what he thinks about this fishing expedition," he adds.

"Let's grab him a hot meal," Sal says.

"Good idea," says Rollie.

The crew gets the chef to roast Hank a chicken and make a few sandwiches for Chappy. They get back in the carriage and ask Chappy to take them to the boat.

"Who wants to count?" Kelly asks.

"Give it to me," Dave says.

The crew pull out stacks and stacks of cash from their winnings at the roulette wheel and hand it over to Dave. He counts it up in an organized manner.

“There’s over twelve thousand dollars here,” Dave tells them. “Or about $200,000 in 2019,” he says looking up with his mischievous smile.

“Sweet,” The Kid says with a broad smile.

“Not bad,” Sal says.

“It’s more than enough to buy The Kid a car and make a few healthy wagers in his favor,” Kelly says.

“Your boy Carl didn’t look at all happy when he saw it was us who was cleaning him out at the wheel,” Sal tells Kelly.

“And that should give him just enough incentive to try and get his losses back at the races,” Kelly says.

Chappy pulls off to the side of the road he has now become familiar with. The crew get out and make their way to the Sally Ann with a roasted chicken for Hank. When they get there, Hank is standing on deck holding a shotgun. He sees it’s the crew, smiles and places the shotgun to his side.

“We should come up with a call, so I know it’s you guys,” he suggests.

“Good idea. I’d hate to get shot in the ass for no good reason,” Rollie exclaims smiling up at Hank.

Hank reaches down to help Sal aboard. Rollie hands her Hank’s meal.

“We got you a roasted chicken from The Deep Sea Club,” Sal says, handing him the tray of food with a sweet smile.

“That’s very thoughtful of you,” he tells her, carrying the tray into the helm.

The crew gets comfortable with some of the Jamaican Rum they purchased at Rum Row and tell Hank about their adventures in the casino and the developments with Carl regarding locating the rocket. Hank enjoys his meal as he listens.

“You gotta make it for race day!” The Kid tells him excitedly.

“I just might, Kid,” Hank tells him as he takes a bite from a chicken leg.

“I was thinking we could invite Carl to go fishing,” Kelly tells Hank. “He’s a real sportsman, so I think he’d go for it, and if he is the one who indeed found our rocket, the Sally Ann, with all her modern features would be the perfect place to convince him that we’re from a different time and the rocket belongs to us,” Kelly says.

“What if he doesn’t want to give back the loot?” Hank asks.

“Good question,” Kelly says. “I’m not sure yet,” he adds. “Stealing it back is always an option, He says winking at Hank. “As has been the case since we arrived here, we haven’t had the luxury of time to plan as carefully and in such detail as we usually would,” he says looking around at everyone. “The key is convincing Carl that we are from 2019,” Kelly says. “That will open up all kinds of possibilities,” he adds.

“Like we know world events that are about to happen,” Dave says. “Things he would like to know…”

“We could warn him of the impending stock market crash,” Sal says.

"Good call Sal. Carl is an extraordinary businessman of his time and loves a challenge. Once we convince him we are from the future and know about upcoming major shifts in world affairs, he will see it as a potential business opportunity," Kelly says, thinking aloud.

"Knowledge is power," adds Dave.

"...if you know it about the right person," Rollie says quoting Ethel Watts Mumford.

"And that we do..." adds Kelly smiling.

He looks at everyone with his signature mischievous thinking-cap grin that finds its way to his face when he is formulating the possibilities of a con.

"What do we know about Carl Fischer?" Kelly asks. "We know he loses practically everything in the end. At the time of his death, having been a multi-millionaire for years, his total net worth is fifty-two thousand dollars," Kelly tells everyone.

The crew is impressed with Kelly's knowledge of Carl Fischer. His wife Jane wrote a book about him..." Kelly tells them, as he pours himself a rum, takes a healthy swig and looks over at Dave. "Any further thoughts on how we can get back to 2019?" he asks.

Dave clasps his hands together in thought, "Right now I have a vague theory that there is a circular pattern to when the window opens," he says. He looks up at Sal, "Sort of like a woman having her period," he adds.

"The fourth of the month." Kelly muses.

"Maybe," Dave says. "That's my theory... But, there's no way to test it without risking being taken up into that vortex of space-time and ending up who knows where," he says with a serious expression.

"What's the worst thing that could happen?" The Kid asks, arms up with a shrug.

Dave looks at him knowingly, challenging The Kid with his eyebrows raised. "We could end up in Montauk 300 BC," Dave tells him.

"Interesting..." says Hank thinking about it. "What you're saying is that you're convinced whatever it is that exists out there is confined to this specific place on earth but could potentially land us at any point in time," Hank says, thinking it through.

"That's exactly what I'm saying," Dave tells him. "However, the conspiracy theory involves the US Military, so chances are favorable that it is a loop that involves only two eras in time," Dave says.

He's spreading his theory rather thin and he knows it.

"Yeah... Then and now..." Sal quips in her smart-ass tone.

"Wait!" Dave exclaims. "You might have something there," he says.

Kelly perks up and jumps to his feet. "We're a part of the equation!" he says excitedly.

"Precisely!" Dave says. "And that, my dear lady," he says to Sal, "...is likely the primary factor of the *then* part of your brilliant equation. The molecules that make up our bodies will remember where they come from, where they belong," he says. "It's biological energy and placement molecular memory," he blurts out, making it up as he goes along.

"I get it!" says Rollie. "Because we're from that time, we'll likely go back, if we get caught up in that storm again," he adds. "It's like muscle memory of an athlete, it's how a child learns to walk," he says. "Or get the spoon to his mouth. Through trial and error, repetition, creating physical memory..." he adds.

"Only on a molecular level," Dave says thinking aloud. "Which includes the Sally Ann..." he finishes.

They all stare at each other in confused amazement. There's a long silence.

"How likely?" asks Sal.

"How likely what?" Dave asks.

"How likely is it the primary factor in the *then* part of my brilliant equation?" she asks. "That we'll end up back in our time?" she asks.

"I don't know," Dave admits. "But there's only one way to find out," he says looking at Hank, then Kelly.

"OK," Kelly says, standing up and pacing the deck. "We all know there's only one way to test Dave's theory, and that is to do it. So first, we will get our gems back or since the possibility exists that we may never find them, put something else in place that will be there waiting for us, valued in the millions of dollars, when we return to 2019," he says smiling, as always, rolling with the punches.

"Yeah... and right now that involves getting Carl Fischer to bet big on my race," says The Kid, his hands on an imaginary racecar steering wheel.

Sal rolls her eyes watching The Kid. Kelly paces across the deck of the Sally Ann.

"The Kid may have something there. We can earn enough to purchase stocks for pennies on the dollar after the crash, and place them in a trust," Kelly says, speculating on how to take advantage of possessing advanced knowledge of the stock market crash.

"Black Tuesday," Dave comments.

"That's right," Kelly says. October 29, 1929, …it's only a few months away!" he says, thinking and pacing again. "Wall Street shut down in a panic for a little while after that, but when it reopened, stocks continued to drop," he says pacing the deck. "What stocks survived? Think, Kelly, think!" He says to himself.

"Union Carbide," Hank says.

Kelly turns his head to Hank, "You're a genius!" he says. "And a poet!" he adds. Everyone stares at him blankly, unsure what he means by poet. "Selling Prest-O-Lite headlamp business to Union Carbide is how Carl made his first millions! And it still exists today, only as a subsidiary of Dow Chemical," Kelly tells them.

"There is a certain poetic justice in that," Dave says. "A dark synchronicity," he adds.

"Coca-Cola!" The Kid exclaims.

"An oldie and a goodie," Dave comments.

"Kid, you're right." Kelly tells him. "Coca-Cola is another great one we could buy," he adds.

"If we were to ride the crash until November 3 of this year when the prices are essentially as low as they're going to drop, then buy as much as we can afford at the crashed market price, place it in a trust to be redeemed by so and so corporation, that's us, in 2019…" Kelly says.

"It will be worth many millions of dollars." Sal interjects.

"Exactly!" Kelly looks around at everyone.

"Then on November 4, we board the Sally Ann, where our illustrious captain will pilot us to the precise coordinates of the time loop. The tear in the space/time continuum, originally caused by the Montauk Project... And find out if it's going to get us back home," Dave tells everyone.

Hank and the crew sit quietly for a moment sipping their rum, a bit stunned from all that has happened in a few short weeks. A few weeks that feel like a lifetime... A lifetime being amplified by the notion of maybe getting back home.

Hank looks around at the crew.

"What exactly does this have to do with asking me to take Carl fishing?" Hank asks, sipping his rum with a wry smile on his face.

Kelly looks at Hank, smiling. "I guess we got a bit off track," Kelly admits.

"Just a bit," Hanks says. He walks closer to Kelly and looks him in the eyes. "If we can get back," he says, turning to look at Dave for a moment, "I'm all for it," he says.

"Okay," Kelly says, pacing the deck. "Tomorrow we go to the city. I'll find us a stock broker. Rollie, Dave and The Kid... You guys find whatever we need for the racecar," he says. He glances over at Sal.

"I'll be busy shopping, dahling," she says.

They all look at her questioningly.

"If we're going to step it up a notch, we have to look the part," she says in her defense.

"Sal's right," Kelly says.

He walks to the helm, pours himself a rum, takes a healthy swig, turns to the crew and smiles.

"Then we convince Carl into wagering substantial money on the race," Kelly stops and turns to The Kid, "This will only work if you win the race, Kid," he says.

"Nobody knows that track better than I do," he says confidently. "They're going to eat my dust!" he insists.

"Dust is right, too," Rollie tells him. "This won't be a Crown Vic in a modified video game," he tells The Kid. "This is a dirt track in the 1920s," he tells him.

"I can drive that entire course in my head right now," he says, closing his eyes.

"All the same, Kid, you better have Chappy take you around it a few times to refamiliarize yourself with it in three dimensions," Dave tells him. "The landmarks that are fixed in your head aren't there yet. It's a totally different racetrack now," he says.

The Kid nods his head in agreement, "Good point..." he says. "But!" he insists standing up, "It doesn't matter, cause I'm still gonna win that race," he tells them looking around at everyone.

"Then, after winning a big wager on the race, being the gentleman that you are, you invite Carl deep sea fishing," Rollie says to Kelly.

“I’ll catch us some big fish,” Hank tells them. “Fishing was... is a lot better in these days than in my time,” he adds. “I’m looking forward to getting out there,” he says gazing out to sea.

He looks around the Sally Ann, and then over at Kelly. “We’ll need deep sea rods and reels... some fighting chairs...” he says. “All I’ve got is longliner rigging. I’m a commercial fisherman... We’re going sports-fishing!” he says with a chuckle. “I’ll make a list,” Hank tells them.

“Got that, Sal?” Kelly asks.

“Sure doll, I’ll just add it to my list, hot shot,” she smiles.

Kelly looks at his watch. “Roulette, anyone?” he asks, smiling at the crew.

“You know I’m game,” Rollie says. “You game, Hank?”

Hank scratches his head, “I better stay with the boat,” he says.

“We’ll see you when we get back from the city tomorrow night,” Sal tells him with a hug.

The crew make their way through the reeds and back into Chappy’s carriage.

“Chappy, we’d like to pay a visit to the casino, please,” Kelly lets him know.

“Naturally, sir,” he says turning up the headlamps, releasing the brake and slapping the horse a few times with the reigns.

The carriage clatters along The Montauk Highway towards West Lake Drive.

“We’ll know fairly quickly if they’ve managed to reset their original rigging on the roulette wheel,” Dave tells them, handing out stacks of hundreds to everyone.

The crew pulls up to the casino and jump out.

“We’ll be back in a jif,” The Kid tells Chappy.

Kelly hands Chappy a hundred-dollar bill. “For your loyalty and discretion, Chappy,” he says.

“Happy to be appreciated, Kelly,” he says with a wink admiring the bill before stuffing it in his vest pocket. Kelly can’t help but smile.

“Chappy…” he says to himself entering the casino with a shake of the head.

He slaps a ten spot in the doorman’s hand and enters.

“Thank you, sir!” he hears from the happy doorman as the din of the noisy casino takes over.

Kelly joins the others at the cashier to purchase chips.

The crew gathers at the roulette wheel and sure enough Dave’s fix is still in. After a few hours of winning big, not wanting to bring undue attention to themselves forcing Carl to have to close it down a third time because of them, they decide it best to call it a night.

Chappy is waiting dutifully with the horse and buggy for them to return. The crew get into the buggy and Chappy takes off towards the Montauk Manor.

“Third time’s a charm,” Dave says, counting the loot won that evening.

"Apparently, whoever originally rigged that wheel isn't local." Rollie smiles while counting his cash.

The crew arrive at The Manor and make arrangements with the concierge for securing a train car to the city the next morning and turn in early.

Before dawn the next morning, Chappy is waiting dutifully outside the Manor in order to get them down the hill and across the street to the LIRR and catch the 5:39 a.m. to Pennsylvania Station. Sal brings him a cheese Danish.

"That's most kind of you, madam," he says, accepting the pastry.

They board the train in Montauk and arrive in NYC two hours later. For the crew, it's nothing less than surreal. They have entered a living museum of New York City in the roaring 20s. Kelly has often imagined what it would be like to live in another era and feels that he is living a long-held dream. Being in the city only amplifies those feelings. The crew hires a Yellow Cab for the day. Kelly meets with a few stock brokers while the crew make all of the purchases needed for the race car upgrades, deep sea fishing expedition, and new duds. It occurs to Kelly that it isn't quite dinner time yet.

"We should buy Chappy a limousine," he says.

"Yeah!" The Kid exclaims. "I mean, the horse and buggy's nice and all but if one more hot rod speeds by us on Flamingo Avenue, I'm gonna bust," he says.

"Not to mention refamiliarizing yourself with the track will play better in an automobile driving closer to the speed you'll be racing it in than in a horse-drawn carriage travelling five miles per hour," Dave adds.

That's right" exclaims Kelly.

The taxi driver assists them in finding a beautiful black 1927 Lincoln L series for a good price. After arranging to have what will become Chappy's Limousine loaded on a flat LIRR freight car with all of their purchases loaded into the massive trunk, they decide that they absolutely must visit the Cotton Club for a bite, a few cocktails and to see the great Duke Ellington.

They are shown a table near the bandstand and order a few bottles of champagne. Duke Ellington and his Cotton Club Orchestra is introduced.

Kelly is near tears.

They enjoy a lovely dinner, party through the night, then catch the late train to Montauk Point.

Chappy is waiting dutifully at the Montauk station. The Kid is the first to reach him.

"You know, Chappy, we really like you and all, but this old cart has got to go," The Kid says in a tone Chappy finds somewhat rude as the others catch up.

"Well! I must say, I..." Chappy stammers a moment looking at the crew staring at him.

"Time to put her out to pasture, Chappy," Kelly says stepping up behind The Kid. "Come with me," he says.

Chappy steps down from the carriage.

"The old gal is getting rather old," he says patting the horse's backside.

Chappy is not quite sure what's happening. Sal can see that he is somewhat confused about the odd goings-on.

"Worry not, Chappy," Sal tells him. "We have something exciting to show you."

They walk towards the station. Kelly checks his watch just as a loud period car horn is heard. Dave and Rollie pull up in the huge Lincoln.

"We've decided that if you're going to continue to be our chauffeur, you'll need a more suitable carriage," Kelly says waving his arm out and presenting the fine automobile.

"I'm not quite sure what to say, sir," Chappy blurts out, a bit flabbergasted.

"Why don't you just drive us up the hill to the Manor?" Kelly tells him. "Perhaps something will come to you along the way..."

Dave steps out of the driver's seat. "She's all yours, Chappy," he says, holding the driver's door open.

"I can't possibly afford such a fine automobile. And what about my carriage?" he asks completely taken aback.

"I have a feeling you'll figure it out, Chappy," Kelly tells him. "After you drop us off at the Manor, we won't need you again until five o'clock or so. I imagine that will be enough time to make arrangements," he says.

"Why yes, of course sir, but..." Chappy says, still flustered.

"But what?" asks The Kid.

"A car of this caliber costs more than I can possibly pay for, I'm afraid," Chappy explains.

"Don't be silly, hot pants, it's a gift," Sal tells him.

“Happy birthday, Chappy,” Kelly says, his hand outstretched.

Chappy shakes his hand. “I hardly know what to say,” he tells them.

“’Thank you’ will do just fine,” Dave tells him.

A large smile comes to Chappy’s face and he opens the door for Sal. She steps in with a giggle. Chappy ties off his horse and gets behind the wheel. He toots the horn a few times, giggling.

“You know how to drive this thing?” The Kid asks.

“If the engine is large enough, I believe I can get you up the hill, young sir,” Chappy says revving the engine with a big smile, getting used to the idea of having a Lincoln Limousine

The Kid laughs as Chappy puts the car in gear and races up the hill towards the Montauk Manor, smiling the entire time.

Back in 2019 Sparky keeps abreast of the ongoing FBI investigations. He’s seated in his taxi reading The East Hampton Star’s report on the bank robbery, happy to note that they are essentially clueless as to who may have pulled off such an elaborate theft. Because a joint effort of both the CIA and the FBI cannot prove that Demyan’s exotic gem collection was the motivation for the robbery or that it is connected to some type of espionage, and in part as retaliation for both the CIA and FBI questioning him as a potential suspect, Demyan is beside himself with grief accusing the FBI of not conducting a thorough enough investigation because he’s Russian. He has filed several lawsuits against both the Chase Bank and various law enforcement agencies, beginning with the FBI.

Sparky shakes his head with a smile, “You called that one, Kelly,” he says to himself before closing the newspaper and stuffing it between the seats.

XXIV

It's race day and The Kid couldn't be more excited. He rode the hard-packed, sandy track with Chappy a few times in the Lincoln then took a few test runs in the enhanced 1927 Bugatti 35B once it was ready. As shocked as he is that there are essentially no trees or homes along the track, The Kid feels confident he can win the race. As promised, Dave and Rollie have modified the suspension with softer springs for better handling and have mimicked a version of rack and pinion steering that will greatly improve maneuverability giving The Kid an edge over the competition. The Kid has chosen number 19 for 2019, signified by a plaque attached to the grill and painted on each side of the car. Crowds have gathered in force for the spectacle and are filling wooden bleachers that have been erected for the event. A loud brass band, several lemonade stands and, hot dog vendors create a festive, circus-like atmosphere along the sparse, sand-dune landscape less than half a mile from the ocean.

Dave checks the water in the radiator and wipes the hood clean with a rag. He looks at The Kid with a huge smile.

“It's all you, Kid,” he tells him, stuffing the rag in his back pocket. “This is the model with the large supercharger,” Dave says smiling. “Took Bugatti a while to accept that fuel induction wasn't cheating. But once he did, he did it right!” Dave tells him. “Plus, I gave it a few minor adjustments,” he says cracking his knuckles and looking around to be sure no one is listening.

“This baby puts out 138 horsepower,” Rollie adds. “Which for this day and age is pretty much as fast as it gets,” he adds.

“Big whoop!” says The Kid. “A VW in 2019 puts out more horsepower than that,” he says.

“True, only this car is a thousand pounds lighter,” Rollie tells him.

“Not to mention, while your competitors are out there sliding off the track, you’ll be able to hold the turns at a higher speed,” Dave tells him. “This Bugatti already had a slight advantage in that regard, even without our modifications, and now even more so,” he smiles proudly. “But, don’t get too crazy till you get a feel for what she can really do,” he adds.

Kelly and Sal are nearby speaking with Carl Fischer. Kelly and Carl shake hands. Kelly and Sal walk over to Dave, Rollie and The Kid.

“How ya feeling, Kid?” Kelly asks him.

“That’s Jackie to you friend,” The Kid says in his Scottish accent.

Dave gets close to Kelly and leans in, “How much did he go for?” he asks.

“He bit off the whole thing,” Sal tells him winking.

Dave looks over at The Kid and the Bugatti 35B. “I did everything I could do with what I had. He’s got an edge, but it’s still a competition… Anything can happen,” he says, looking at Kelly with a shrug.

Kelly walks over to The Kid, places his hand on his shoulder and looks him in the eyes.

“Love, honor and daring, Kid,” he tells him.

The Kid looks up at Kelly and smiles.

"I hope you bet on me using those same principles," he says with a wink.

"Remember Kid, just enough confidence, but not too much," Kelly reminds him from an early lesson long ago.

"You missed the race during the craziness at sea but ask Rollie about it sometime. I kicked ass!" he says smiling. "Had those cops playing bumper cars in my wake," he boasts. "You know... I ran that track on video more than a hundred times before the heist," he boasts. "Other than the houses and the trees, it hasn't changed all that much either. I can run this track blindfolded," he tells Kelly.

Kelly smiles, "I believe you could, Kid. I believe you could..." he says smiling. "Don't forget, it's three times around, so pace yourself and save the best for last," Kelly tells him.

"You know me," The Kid says with a wink and a smile.

"You tell him, Kid," Sal says, doing her part to pump The Kid up.

"The only real difference I felt on my practice runs this morning is the dirt track effect," he tells Kelly. "As soon as I set the parameters in my muscle memory reflex, I'll cream these guys," he says confidently.

Carl Fischer walks up. He looks over the Bugatti. "Nice wheels," he tells The Kid. "Best of luck out there," he says offering a handshake.

"That's mighty sporting of you, Mr. Fischer," The Kid says in his best Scottish accent, shaking Carl's hand.

"See you at the finish line," Carl tells him.

"I'll be the lad in the winner's circle," The Kid says with a wink and a broad smile.

"Deacon Litz may have something to say about that..." Carl laughs and walks off.

"Nice touch, Kid," Dave says.

"Who's Deacon Litz?" asks The Kid.

"Deacon Litz came in third at Altoona this year," Kelly tells him. "Carl's backing him. That's who we bet against," he lets him know.

"What number is his car?" The Kid asks.

"Number 35," Dave tells him speaking up.

"Screw him," says The Kid.

"That's the spirit, Kid," Dave says.

"Show him who's boss, Kid," Rollie says, patting him on the back.

"You look great, Kid. Leave 'em in the dust," Sal says.

The stands are full of spectators anxiously anticipating the start of the race, as the cars take their positions on the racetrack. The race is about to begin. The starter takes his place at the start line. He brings a large megaphone up to his mouth. "Drivers... Start your engines," he announces.

The roar of the 1920s race cars commands the entire area, coupled with the crowd yelling and cheering. Kelly, Sal, Dave and Rollie are on the sidelines cheering The Kid on. Suddenly Hank appears with Danny and some of the rum-running fishermen. The Kid sees them and gives a thumbs up with a broad smile.

"Fancy seeing you here," Sal says, cuddling up to Hank.

"Wouldn't miss it for the world," he says.

"Give 'em hell, Kid," Danny shouts over the roar of the engines, waving his fist in the air.

The Flagman steps forward. He waves the checkered starting flag in the air a few times, drivers are revving their engines. The Kid is licking his lips in anticipation, eyes locked on the flag. Down it goes and the drivers are off in a roar of dust and smoke.

The Kid finds himself three or four off the lead halfway up what will become Fairview Avenue. He hits the gas holding the first turn tight on the inside and gets himself into second place behind number 35, Deacon Litz.

"I knew it would be you," he says to himself, challenging Litz on the next turn heading south. Litz is no slouch and he's got a lot more experience on dirt than The Kid but that doesn't discourage The Kid. They're neck and neck at the first lap with three other racers hot on their tail. The number 12 car races past them on a straightaway at breakneck speed.

"What the?" The Kid exclaims.

The Kid won't be outdone and takes the lead on the next sharp turn. He races through the starting point to a green flag. Kelly, Sal, Dave, Rollie, Hank and Grandpa Danny are thrilled, jumping up and down as he speeds by in first position.

Nearby Carl Fischer is sweating it out as Deacon Litz zips by in second. The other race cars desperately vie for the lead on the last lap, giving it all they've got, and it gets crowded at the first turn of the last lap. The number 69 car flies off the track trying to pass The Kid, giving Litz a clear shot and he takes the lead on the downward leg south.

“Shit!” The Kid exclaims. There’s one more turn before the last straightaway. The Kid knows he must take the lead on that last turn to win the race. “Watch this, Litz!” he says as he hits the gas hard and takes the last turn at a daring speed leaving Litz in the dust and heads for home. He keeps it floored the whole way down the stretch. Litz has the bigger engine and is gaining on The Kid but there’s not enough track left, and The Kid wins the race.

Three other cars crashed out there and Litz takes second but The Kid… The Kid is in the winner’s circle just as he told Carl Fischer he would be. The engine is steaming from the punishment he gave it. Carl is not happy.

The announcer, Megaphone in hand steps onto the racetrack at the finish line and faces the bleachers, “Ladies and Gentlemen!” he says loudly addressing the impressive number who’ve turned out for the race. He checks a piece of paper with The Kids name on it, “Jackie Stewart of Scotland is the winner!” he shouts loudly referring to The Kid with a flourishing wave of his arm. The crowd loves it and cheers for The Kid while photographers flash away at The Kid posing with his Bugatti, waving and throwing kisses at spectators.

Kelly, Sal and the rest of them run over. Kelly lifts The Kid into the air. “You did it!” he says. Big hugs all around.

Carl Fischer walks over and congratulates The Kid. “Damn good driving, Mr. Stewart,” he tells him. “That risky move on the last turn really paid off,” he says shaking The Kid’s hand.

“I couldn’t agree with you more, but it’s mighty fine of you to say so,” The Kid says in his Scottish accent. “A true gentleman you are, sir, indeed.” He smiles.

Carl turns to Kelly. “Congratulations, John,” he says offering a handshake. “We’ll meet in my office in the morning to settle up, if it’s all the same to you,” he says.

“That’ll be fine, Carl,” he says, shaking his hand.

Deacon Litz walks over and congratulates The Kid. “Helluva race kid,” he says shaking The Kid’s hand. “You coming up to Syracuse this year?” he asks, inspecting the Bugatti.

“Ya know... I just can’t say,” The Kid answers in his Scottish brogue.

“Maybe Indianapolis next year than,” Litz says with a smile. “I’d like the chance to get back at you!” he says with a sporting smile.

“Sounds like a plan,” The Kid tells him in his best Jackie Stewart.

Deacon is intrigued by the unusual steerage and suspension. He bounces the car up and down. Dave watches him carefully.

“Smooth,” he says looking up at The Kid. “What’s this configuration?” he asks, referring to the custom home-made rack and pinion steering Dave and Rollie added.

“You like that?” Dave asks him.

“Never seen steering quite like this before,” he comments inspecting it closely.

“You’ll be seeing more of it in the future,” Dave tells him.

Deacon looks up at The Kid, “No wonder you were able to take that last turn so fast,” he says.

“I made that last turn from sheer skill,” The Kid insists, staying in character. “...and daring,” he adds, winking at Kelly.

Carl and Deacon stroll away.

The Kid turns to Dave and Rollie, “She handled like a dream, fellas. Thanks,” he says with a champion’s smile.

“You did us proud, Kid,” Dave tells him.

“Yeah, and you weren’t even being chased by the cops,” Rollie says, patting The Kid on the back.

“Nice work, Kid,” Sal tells him. “You ran that road like it was a video game,” she says, smiling.

“Smart-ass,” The Kid says and gives her a hug.

“Drinks are on me!” Kelly tells them walking up with Hank and Danny.

“Chappy’s around here somewhere,” Kelly tells them.

“Best not to leave this car out here overnight. We’ll follow you to the Manor,” Dave says, patting The Kid on the back.

They find Chappy, “Congratulations to you, young sir,” Chappy tells The Kid.

“Thanks, Chappy,” The Kid says. “Race you to the Manor,” he says smiling.

The crew meet The Kid at the Montauk Manor in Chappy’s new Limousine. He jumps in the Limo and takes the ride up to the Deep Sea Club, recalling the high points of the race and Carl Fischer’s reaction. Jazz fills the air as they pull up. The crew piles out of the Lincoln with Hank and Danny.

Danny enters the club, "Swanky," he says.

"C'mon, I'll buy you a drink," Hank tells him.

Danny stops and grabs Hank by the shoulder. He looks around the club, then at Hank, "Do I ever mention any of this to you when you're a young lad?" he asks.

"No..." he tells Danny, already having had to deal with the strangeness of their predicament.

"How can that be?" Danny asks.

"I don't really understand it, but it's because it hadn't happened yet, or something like that. As though there are two futures now because I got caught up in that storm and ended up here after I already knew you," he says not fully comprehending it.

"I want to ask you, but I already know I shouldn't, but how do I..." Danny stops, stares Hank in the eye, then thinks better of it and adds, "Eh... let's have a drink." Placing his arm around Hank's shoulder, they stroll to the table Kelly has procured for the group.

"Your finest champagne," Kelly tells the waiter. "Enough for the table," he adds slipping a twenty-dollar bill in the waiter's hand.
The waiter looks at the twenty and stuffs it in his pocket, "Right away, sir," he says as he rushes off.

They toast The Kid and drink all night. Several people who had attended the race come over to congratulate The Kid, who is still dressed in his racing attire. A few patrons ask to have photographers take their picture with him. Others send congratulatory bottles of champagne to the table.

Several flappers visit the table to congratulate The Kid, showering him with flirtations and kisses. He plays the Scottish race car driver, Jackie Stewart, loving every minute of it.

After celebrating for a few hours, they pile back into Chappy's Limo for the ride to the Montauk Manor.

"What a night!" exclaims The Kid, falling into the limousine, exhausted.

The next morning Kelly visits Carl at his office as agreed. Harry Johnson is there to greet him.

"Good morning, Mr. Kelly," Harry says meeting Kelly at the entrance of the speakeasy. "It's the strangest thing, but every time we meet, I can't help thinking I know you from somewhere," he says, shaking Kelly's hand.

"I just have one of those faces, I suppose," Kelly says smiling.

"I suppose," Harry says with a confused, maybe doubtful expression. He turns around, "Right this way. Mr. Fischer is expecting you," he says as he leads Kelly to Carl's office.

He knocks on the door, "Mr. Kelly, sir..." Harry announces loudly.

"Come in," Carl's voice is heard through the door.
Kelly enters the office and walks over to the large taxidermy Marlin hanging over Carl's desk.

"Fantastic," he says. "When did you hook this beast?" he asks Carl, shaking his hand.

"Oh... about three years ago, I guess it was." Carl tells him.

"Your reputation as a sportsman precedes you," Kelly says smiling. "After our transaction here today, I was hoping you would accept my invitation to go deep sea fishing," he says. "I have an associate with a large fishing vessel featuring experimental fish-finding equipment we're developing. Something I believe an inventor such as yourself would find interesting," he tells Carl.

"That was quite a race your driver ran yesterday," Carl says. "Please sit down," he tells Kelly, motioning to the chairs.

They sit down at the lounge area in Carl's office.

"I took a good look at your car. You seem to possess all manner of modern invention, Mr. Kelly," Carl says gazing at Kelly, eyebrows raised. "Deacon was impressed with the steerage and suspension of your Bugatti," he adds.

"Wait till you see the ship," Kelly says smiling.

Carl looks at his watch, "I have some early appointments so, best make good on my wager so I can get on with my day," he says. "I am a man of my word…" he adds, getting up and walking to his safe.

"I never doubted that for a moment, Carl," Kelly assures him.

"Still, I must admit surprise that a driver no one has ever heard of was able to beat Deacon Litz with such a high degree of style and bravado," Carl says turning the combination dial.

Carl opens his safe and pulls out ten bundles of hundred-dollar bills arranged in bundles sealed with paper strips a bank might use. "Your young Scotsman has an exciting future in racing ahead of him," Carl says. "Providing he doesn't kill himself first," he says, handing Kelly the stacks of cash.

Kelly examines the cash. He quickly assesses the amount and places it in his vest pocket. Kelly knows the ten thousand dollars would be worth over a hundred and fifty thousand in 2019.

"I hope you will accept my invitation. I would be honored to have a legendary sportsman such as yourself as my guest aboard the Sally Ann for a deep-sea fishing expedition," Kelly says smiling. "Captain Hank assures me we will catch large swordfish, tuna and marlin," he adds smiling. "And, as a sharp-minded industrialist, you'll find the cutting edge instrumentation we're developing fascinating to say the least," he adds.

"I'm always eager to see modern engineering. Yours is a very gracious invitation and I accept," Carl says smiling. "When are you thinking of hosting this extravagant fishing soiree?" Carl asks.

"Two days from now, this Thursday, weather permitting," Kelly says.

"That works fine for my schedule, John," Carl tells him.

"Your Yacht Club, dawn Thursday then," Kelly says.

Kelly offers his hand and the men shake on it.

"I realize you're a busy man, and will leave you to your work," Kelly says, turning towards the door. "Oh," Kelly says turning back to face Carl, "I should like to engage your fine chef to provide provisions for the trip," he says smiling.

"Of course," Carl says smiling. "Harry can arrange that for you," he says opening the door and calling for Harry.

They arrange to have food and drink delivered to the Sally Ann at dawn Thursday. Kelly makes his way to Chappy's Limousine and heads back to the Montauk Manor with his winnings.

XXV

It's dawn on Thursday. The Sally Ann is docked at the Yacht Club. Danny has been invited along as the only other experienced fisherman besides Hank. With Hank and Danny's help, Rollie, Dave and The Kid have used the past two days to outfit the Sally Ann as a sports fishing vessel. The long line rigging is stowed, a dining table has been built behind the helm and two deep-sea fighting chairs have been installed aft. Hank pulls up to the dock. Rollie and The Kid tie off. Hank walks out to the aft deck and takes in the new set-up of his longliner.

"Never thought I'd see the day," he says to Danny with a wry smile.

"She looks good, Hank," Dave tells him. "Hemingway would be happy to fish on this boat," he adds.

"Hemingway wouldn't be allowed to fish on this boat," Hank says, patting Dave on the back.

He walks to the helm and starts the big diesel engine.

A few porters arrive with trays of cold pheasant and the like along with plenty of cheer from The Deep Sea Club. Rollie and The Kid stow it in deck stowage they've customized expressly for that purpose, tip the porters, and let them know they're free to go as the crew will handle the service once out to sea. It isn't long before Kelly, Sal and Carl Fischer arrive. They climb aboard and Kelly makes introductions.

"And finally... our illustrious captain Hank Sullivan and his first mate Danny Sullivan. Hank, Danny, this is Carl Fischer," Kelly says with a smile.

“Welcome aboard,” Hank says shaking Carl’s hand.

Hank looks over at Rollie and The Kid. “Okay, shove off, fellas,” he yells.

Rollie and The Kid untie the moorings, Hank puts her in gear and off they go. The dawn sky becomes lighter as they idle through the inlet. Danny rigs a few lines for coastal fishing in order to catch some bait for the larger fish. Danny, Dave, Rollie and The Kid set lines and bait hooks as he tutors them on how to snag some strippers and blues. Carl and Kelly join them catching plenty of bait fish for the trip out. Once they’ve caught enough fish, Danny lets Hank know that they’re good to go. Hank revs up the motor and heads southeast into deeper waters where large tuna, shark and marlin can be found. At Kelly’s invitation, Carl makes his way to the helm to inspect the gadgets he’s been told about.

Hank is there with Sal, the boat making nearly fourteen knots.

“Fast boat,” Carl comments.

“She’ll do fourteen knots pretty steady,” Hank tells him. “We’ll be where the big fish are hiding in two hours or less.

“Since seeing the modifications made to the Bugatti, I’ve became curious about the new inventions you’ve told me about,” says Carl looking at the sonar fish finder, radar and GPS navigation system. “Fascinating looking gadgets... What is this one here?” he asks, pointing at the now unusable GPS navigation screen.

“That one isn’t operational yet,” Hank tells him. “One day...” he adds winking at Kelly. “This is a depth finder and will tell us how deep the sea is beneath us,” Hank tells him. So, we don’t run aground in uncharted waters...” he adds.

"What about this unusual looking apparatus?" Carl asks, referring to the fish finder.

"That one's a real beaut," Hank tells him. "This unit sends out sonar, ummm... sound waves under the water and then reads the sound waves bouncing back," he says turning it on.

The display shows underwater topography as they motor out to sea. Hank points to the ocean floor, telling Carl how deep it is.

"Now, whenever there are fish, the sound waves bounce those images back, letting us know where the fish are," he says. "It gives you depth, distance and heading, he says. "We'll use it to find fish once we get a bit further out," he adds, keeping the boat on course.

Carl stares at the amazing device as Hank shows him how it distinguishes between fish, seaweed, or an old sunken ship on the ocean floor.

"Fish are represented by little fish icons, weeds by little weeds and so on," Hank tells him.

"That's fantastic," Carl says amazed at the device.

"These are all very impressive devices..." Carl tells them with a big smile. "I should apologize, as to be frank, I doubted your claims, but see now that you were not exaggerating in the least, John. This is absolutely cutting-edge engineering," he says looking at Kelly with a smile revealing his amazement. "Downright futuristic," he says.

"You have no idea," Kelly says with a chuckle.

"When do you plan to take these gadgets to market?" Carl asks.

“We’re still in the testing phases, but soon, I assure you,” Kelly tells him with his broad grin.

Kelly looks at Sal as a signal. Sal places her hand on Carl’s arm.

“If you’d like, we have hot coffee, and a full breakfast set up on the aft deck,” Sal says, looking into Carl’s eyes.

“That sounds lovely,” Carl says, letting Sal lead the way.

They walk out to the aft deck and are met by Dave, Rollie and The Kid.

“Please have a seat, Mr. Fischer,” Sal says in an accommodating manner.

Carl looks at her, and like most men lucky enough to spend time with her, is deeply affected by her extreme beauty and allure.

“Please, call me Carl,” he says, smiling, pulling a chair out for her.

“Thank you, Carl,” she says, taking the seat.

Sal pours champagne as the rest of the crew join them at the table and enjoy breakfast while Hank and Danny take the Sally Ann southeast towards the shelf. By the time they’re through with breakfast, Hank lets them know they are out far enough to hunt for some big fish. Carl is anxious to see the fish finder at work and joins Hank at the helm. The fish finder reveals quite a few large fish not far off to the south. Hank suggests they bait their hooks and get ready to set some lines. Carl is adept at fishing and needs no assistance in getting his line in the water. Hank sets Kelly up and it isn’t long before he has a fish on his line. Kelly battles the fish for some time and finally pulls in a rather large big eye tuna.

“That’s a nice fish,” Carl comments just as his line gets a strike. He teases the line a while until there’s a solid bite. It’s bright enough now for everyone to see a huge marlin jump out of the water at the end of Carl’s line. Yelps and hollers from the crew. Carl is in his element fighting the huge Marlin. It’s clear to see that he loves deep-sea fishing and the thrill of the catch. Sal cheers him on till he gets the fish in.

“Oh… that’s a beauty,” says Danny admiring the catch.

“Nicely done, Carl,” Sal tells him with her alluring smile.

They fish a while longer, hooking a few more large fish. Carl and Kelly are having a ball reeling them in. Then, after an hour of losing bait without a solid catch, they decide to enjoy some lunch.

Sal makes sure the glasses are full. Hank lets the Sally Ann drift as they all enjoy the cold pheasant and other delicacies.

“I admire your courage developing Montauk the way you did, Carl, after that devastating hurricane in Miami,” Kelly says.

“That would have beaten most men,” Sal says, pouring Carl another glass of wine.

“You must have taken quite a hit,” Kelly says.

“I did,” Carl admits. “…but, and you will appreciate this, Jackie,” he says to The Kid, “if there is one thing I learned from racing,” he says sipping his champagne, “Cars don’t lose races, drivers do. No one will remember the second-place driver of a race…”

“There are some timid souls that will never know victory nor defeat,” Rollie says, quoting Teddy Roosevelt.

Carl looks over at Rollie and with a glint in his eye raises his glass, “To the great Theodore Roosevelt,” he toasts.

Everyone joins him in the toast.

“To Teddy,” The Kid says in his Scottish accent, emptying his glass.

Carl enjoys lunch with plenty of wine and things are progressing nicely. Kelly needs to prod some more and learn if his suspicions that it was Carl who found the rocket are accurate. It’s nearly two o’clock and he promised Carl he’d get him back to Montauk in time for a business dinner Carl has planned. The fish they caught are on ice in the hold and it’s time to dig into Carl’s psyche.

“I have great respect for a man who can pull himself up by the bootstraps after a devastation and turn it into a success,” Kelly says. “You are nothing less than a visionary,” he adds.

“To Carl Fischer,” Kelly says raising his glass.

“To Carl Fischer.” Everyone repeats in a toast. Glasses clink and the wine is finished.

“You are very kind,” Carl says graciously.

“Join me for an afternoon rum?” Kelly asks.

“You don’t have to ask me twice, toots,” Sal says, lighting a cigarette.

“Allow me,” Rollie says as he stands up.

He gets a few bottles of rum and some glasses. He pours drinks for everyone, serving Carl a rum first.

“Ladies first,” Carl insists passing the drink to Sal.

“Nice to have a gentleman in the crowd,” says Sal, lifting the glass in a mini toast to Carl before taking a sip.

“And what a fascinating gentleman you are too, deary,” she says as she gazes into Carl’s eyes. “To think that you somehow managed to realize such a finely executed vision of transforming the wilds of Montauk into an exclusive playground after nearly losing everything in the Miami hurricane,” she says, attempting to sound as innocent and genuine as possible. She looks up at him with doe’s eyes. “It truly is an astonishing feat,” she insists. “Adonis, move over,” she adds with a coy smile, polishing off her rum.

Hear, hear!” Dave comments, raising a glass.

“That’s very sweet of you to say, ...however, to be honest, I’m more interested in hearing about the amazing engineering of your fish finder,” he says while sipping his rum. “Who designed it? Perhaps I know him,” he says.

“That would be David,” Kelly says, pointing to Dave.

Carl looks over to Dave. “Very impressive work,” he says as Sal refreshes Carl’s cocktail.

“Thank you,” Dave says glancing over at Kelly for a moment. “Advancements in technology have always defined the future,” he says, sipping his rum. “Something I know you can appreciate as, my accomplishments pale in comparison to yours,” he says raising his glass to Carl.

"Perhaps I can steal you away from John and get you to work for my aeronautics company," Carl says, winking at Kelly.

Dave and Kelly lock eyes for a moment.

"Interesting that you should mention aeronautics," Kelly says smiling. "I understand that you've recently discussed aeronautic ambitions with Q.B. Noblitt..." Kelly adds, letting Carl know he's in the loop on Carl's ambitions. "Perhaps we might join forces to develop a fast-flying passenger airplane," Kelly suggests.

"I'm a big fan of Noblitt," Dave adds.

"As am I," Carl tells Dave.

"We recently tested a rather unique engine encased in a small missile which has gone missing in this vicinity," Kelly tells Carl, watching closely for his reaction.

Carl lifts his rum and takes a healthy swig. "Oh?" he says a bit nervously.

Kelly winks at Sal as Carl takes another healthy swig.

"What do you suspect happened to it?" Carl asks.

"We're not sure," Kelly says, observing Carl closely. "Either it sunk, or someone found it and is keeping it a secret," Kelly says, sipping his rum.

"Imagine an airplane the size of Vanderbilt's yacht that can carry people around the world. That's the future!" Dave says to Carl.

"That was the focus of our recent test," Kelly tells him. "Only the technology is so advanced, even we could barely understand it," he adds.

Sal pours Carl another rum, which he immediately takes a healthy swig from.

Carl finishes his drink and pours another generous one. Kelly looks around the table at the crew one by one. He is about to leap off that precipice into the unknown once again. Dave looks back at Kelly and just shrugs. Sal, the same. The Kid gives Kelly a don't-ask-me expression. Rollie is no help, either. Meanwhile, Carl has increased his consumption of rum steadily. Kelly wants to take the leap but knows it could backfire. He looks over at Danny and Hank in the helm. Danny took it pretty well, after all was said and done. Maybe, just maybe it'll be the same with Carl. Besides, he knows it has to be done. *If I'm wrong and Carl hasn't found the rocket, what will be lost?* he asks himself.

"Look around this ship, Carl," Kelly says peering into Carl's eyes. "You're intelligent enough to realize that the technology at the helm can't possibly exist yet," he says.

"What do you mean, can't exist yet?" Carl asks him, noticeably perturbed.

"Something occurred to me the other day when I asked you about precious jewels," Kelly says looking at Carl.

"What about them?" Carl asks appearing almost defensive.

Kelly pulls out a few 2017 one-hundred-dollar bills and holds them up for Carl to see.

"Ever see one of these?" he asks.

He places them on the table under the bottle of rum. Carl stares at them flapping in the breeze, held down by the bottle of rum. Carl, who has spent the past four years holding the secret about the rocket inside himself, is astonished to see the bills. What a great relief it would be to share what happened with someone. Anyone! His mind reels as he takes the one hundred dollar bills lifts them to his face and stares at them. He hadn't even told his wife. He knew even his closest associates would think him crazy or guilty of fraud. Showing anyone the rocket would likely have caused nothing but complications. Considering the contents... costly complications. Costly in smore ways than one. It was best to keep it a secret. But now, here are these people, who he barely knows, and they too have currency from the future. He is unsure what to do. He takes another swig of rum. Kelly, Sal, Dave, Rollie and The Kid sit there quietly staring at him. He looks up and focuses his eyes on the lot of them. He's carried this burden since 1925, alone. The desire to tell someone has become an overwhelming force he can no longer contain.

"It was July 4, 1925 during a fireworks exhibition land baron Arthur Benson held for some friends at the estate he'd built east of Ditch Plains," he says, handing the bills to Sal and taking a long sip of rum.

Dave's eyes light up. He can sense that a significant aspect of his theory is about to be proven. He looks at Kelly. They nod at each other.

"I saw something fantastic floating down to earth attached to a parachute," admits to them. "Everyone's focus was on the fireworks. I alone noticed it. I followed it to where it landed on the beach, more than a mile west of Arthur's estate right one the edge of town, and was astounded at what I found," he says taking another healthy swig of rum.

Trembling slightly, he looks around the table at everyone. He can't stop telling them about it now. The cat's out of the bag and he can finally let it off his chest. Whatever the final outcome, he's glad to be ridding himself of the gargantuan secret that has weighted his spirit down for years.

"Seeing it lying there on the beach steaming and hissing, expecting Buck Rogers to pop out of it," he laughs, "...left me somewhat dumbfounded at first. Naturally, once I opened it up and found its contents, I couldn't tell anyone about it," he says.

"Naturally..." Sal quips.

Danny walks out to the table, sits down and pours himself a drink.

Hank walks out on deck. "We'll be heading back now," he tells them. "Should only be..." he stops in mid-sentence sensing something significant occurring.

Danny looks up at Hank, "Have a drink," he says pouring Hank a rum.

Carl looks up at Hank, then around the table at everyone.

"Now you people," he says. "Exactly how... I mean..." he stammers, "Where did you come from?" Carl asks confused.

They all look at Carl, none of them sure what to say or where to begin.

"The real question is when are we from," Dave tells him, pouring himself a rum.

"Believe him, fella," Danny says with a wry expression. "Hank here is my grandson," he says looking at Hank fondly. "Come from a different time," he adds, taking a swig of rum.

By the reflex of logic alone, Carl is perplexed and doubtful, yet, having found the rocket with its futuristic contents just a few years earlier... not exactly disbelieving, or worse, in a state of shock.

Danny looks at Carl, “I’m from this time, too,” he says. “I know what you’re feeling... The ocean is a mysterious place Carl,” he adds looking out to sea. “Things happen out here that only God understands,” he says then polishes off his glass of rum.

Kelly looks around the table stopping at Carl with a kind, warm smile. “It’s taken us all a little time to get used to,” he says looking around at everyone.

That things have evolved to this point has everyone feeling emotionally distraught. Hank puts his arm around Danny’s shoulder. Sal pours herself another rum. The Kid looks up at Carl. He’s about to tell him something but then stops. He looks over at Kelly and just stares at him for a moment. Kelly shakes his head no in a barely perceptible slow motion, but The Kid gets the message and he will remain Jackie Stewart for the moment. Kelly doesn’t see the advantage of letting go too many secrets of their own just yet.

“It’s a lot to take in.” Kelly says, looking around the table at everyone, sensing the abyss over that precipice looming again. “We got caught up in a strange electrical storm of some kind on July Fourth in the year 2019, then ended up here on July Fourth of this year,” Kelly tells him.

Carl sits there silent. As fantastic as what he is being told sounds, the moment when he first discovered the rocket, a moment that remains etched in his brain, was just as fantastic. He envisions it as he considers that the questions fomenting inside of him these past years may finally be answered.

“We passed through a crack of some kind, in space-time out here somewhere,” Dave tells him with arms outstretched referring to the vast ocean that surrounds them. "Hank has the coordinates..." he says pointing his thumb at Hank. "We're not entirely positive, but it may be a side effect of a government experiment that occurred during World War II," Dave says, suddenly realizing there's no way Carl could know about WWII.

"World War II?" Carl asks, astonished.

Sal pours him a drink. "Don't sweat it, toots, we win," she tells him.

"The thing is, we arrived here after the rocket did, and have been looking for it ever since," Kelly tells him.

Carl is absolutely astonished, not sure what to think or feel. On the one hand, he's stunned by the idea of people traveling through time while on the other hand, he feels a great relief sharing his incredible story after years of loneliness holding it inside of himself. He sits there quietly questioning his sanity. Several long moments pass as the Sally Ann drifts with the current, the sun heading towards the horizon.

"Where's the rocket now?" Kelly asks.

"I buried it," Carl tells him taking another swig of rum. "Buried it in the sand near the ocean, where it landed. Then I bought the land and built my beachfront hotel, The Surf Club, alongside of it" he tells them. "In fact, it's fair to say that discovering the rocket, as you call it, is what inspired me to buy the land and build the Surf Club in the first place," he says looking around the table. "I couldn't risk anyone else learning about it," he says, looking around the table studying everyone's faces. "Owning the land that it's buried on and building the hotel there decreased the chance of it being discovered, he adds.

"And the gems?" Kelly asks.

"Most of them were sold and the money used to build Montauk," he says, looking at Kelly with slight shrug.

"What about the cash?" The Kid asks.

"I buried that separately in a metal box on the same property. I knew most anyone would think it was counterfeit and that I had perhaps lost my mind. I couldn't risk that... Then again, it is currency, albeit from the future, so I buried the box where it would remain accessible in the event it can one day be used. I can show you where it is," he tells them.

Kelly looks at his crew with a raise of the eyebrow.

"Sparky..." Sal says with a smile.

The crew stare at her a long moment.

"We better start heading back," Hank tells them, looking at the sky.

He finishes his rum, gets up from the table, shakes his head in amazement, heads to the helm and starts the huge diesel engine. Danny pours a fresh rum and joins Hank at the helm. Hank comes about and pilots the Sally Ann towards the Yacht Club. Everyone else remains seated at the table discussing the strange recent events. Carl begins to realize that he's on the hook for a lot of money. Then again, there was no way he could know who the strange object he'd found belonged to and no one ever came to claim or even inquire about it. Until now... He looks up at everyone with a curious expression on his face. He suspects they will likely expect some type of compensation.

"There's something you need to see," he says, looking around the table at everyone. "It's in my safe and then maybe you'll understand," he says. "There were a lot of personal effects in that rocket," he tells them.

"The safety deposit box contents," Dave says nodding his head and remembering loading them into the rocket.

"Right..." agrees Kelly.

"What about them?" Sal asks.

"There's one in particular you must see," Carl tells them. "A letter," he says. "A love letter..." he adds looking at them with a solemn expression.

Carl and the crew continue consuming large amounts of rum as the intensity of all that has occurred would otherwise be too overwhelming. The subjects of time travel as it relates to aeronautics and how the two may be connected one day in the future are talked about with much excitement as they allow the nature of what has happened to fuel their imaginations. More so, how looping through time might be used as a business venture. All of them having been affected, being brought together by the most unusual, even magical, circumstance, a unique camaraderie develops between them. By the time they arrive at the Yacht Club, Carl has agreed to return whatever gems remain. He invites them inside The Deep Sea Club to hand over the jewels and to show them the letter. Of the two, it is fair to say that the letter, a letter that Carl insists had a remarkable effect on him, has taken on a greater interest. Especially Kelly, who always fascinated with history, is very excited to read it. Hank and Danny will stash the Sally Ann and return to the club in Danny's Chris Craft, which is hidden in the cove near the future Crow's Nest, near the highway.

Carl leads Kelly, Sal, Dave, Rollie and The Kid into the speakeasy where the always wary Harry Johnson is there to greet them. Carl asks Harry to send in some refreshments and invites the crew into his private office.

"Please, make yourselves comfortable," he tells them, pointing to the lounge area in his office.

A waiter arrives with scotch and sodas and is told by Carl that he doesn't wish to be disturbed. The crew gather round the refreshments and anxiously wait for Carl to return from his safe with the love letter he so eloquently talked about. He walks over to Kelly and hands him the letter still in its original envelope.

"Would you read it aloud for everyone," he says.

Kelly takes the old letter, looks at it a moment, then around the room at everyone. Carl pours himself a scotch and sits down in one of the overstuffed chairs. Kelly stands up and walks over to Carl.

"I think you should read it," he says handing the letter back to Carl.

"Yeah, Carl, why don't you read it to us?" Sal asks.

"If you insist," Carl says, accepting the letter back from Kelly.

Carl holds the letter in his hands like a new-born baby. He takes a long drink of scotch, pulls a pair of eyeglasses from his vest pocket, puts them on and opens the letter. He looks around the room at everyone, his face registering deep emotion. He holds the letter in front of his face, gets it in focus and begins reading:

My Dearest Aileen,

I was happy beyond description to receive your very sweet letter. Barely a day has passed that I have not thought of you. In fact, not one day has passed... I would not have survived the near fatal injuries sustained in the Blitz were it not for you. Strange that I should survive the beach landing at Normandy unscathed only to come near death in London only a year later. I know in my heart that it was your beautiful smile that kept me alive through the most harrowing nights fighting for my life in that hospital. That you made the great sacrifice to serve as a nurse in the war-torn city of London, not having any duty whatsoever to do so, being Irish... With Ireland maintaining neutrality throughout the war, tells me much about your wonderful character and loving heart. I have often wondered if you were not a nurse at all, but an angel sent by God to protect and console me.

Now that the war is over, and having written to every hospital in Ireland, at long last, I have found you. My heart is consumed with the deepest feelings of love for you. I have never stopped thinking about our wonderful conversations and your reading Yeats to me late into the night, as I lay there on the mend.

Today, I have a thriving fishing boat in the beautiful seaside village of Montauk Point in New York, the closest point to Ireland in the USA! We can have a wonderful life together here. Montauk is a magical place with what many consider the premier fishing port of the entire world. Primarily, thanks to a gentleman named Carl Fischer, who, in the 1920s, using dynamite, blew apart the sandbar that separated Lake Montauk from the Block Island Sound, creating Montauk Harbor. Carl came here and transformed what was then a sleepy fishing village into the summer paradise it is today! He built The Montauk Manor, a giant castle-like resort high on a hill... The Montauk Yacht Club, and several other still popular hotels and hot spots that, to this day, attract vacationers and sports fishermen alike. And we're only a few hours away from New York City by train!

Aileen, it is my hope that you will accept my invitation to come here and see this wonderful place for yourself. And of course, me... I love you, Aileen and ask, from across the sea, for your hand in marriage. I offer these lines from the great Irish poet William Butler Yeats which you read to me one evening and which now echo in my mind and fuel my heart...

"I have spread my dreams under your feet.
Tread softly because you tread on my dreams."

Yours with deep affection and the greatest of love,

Gordon Ryan

Carl is near to tears, as is everyone. He folds the letter and places it back in the envelope with great care. He wipes his tears and looks up at the crew.

"I found this letter in the rocket before I began my first construction here," he tells them. "It felt to be providence... A sign from above..." he says, before realizing the irony of what he just said. "From above..." he repeats smiling.

The crew and he laugh about it.

"I am often forced to wonder would I have made all these wonderful constructions without having first discovered this prophetic letter," he tells them.

"Yet it was written decades after you did all those things," Dave says.

Once again, the perplexing nature concerning the consequences of traveling through the dimension of space-time consumes their thoughts, inspiring an endless stream of what-ifs. The lot of them sit there in silence, thoughts racing through their minds as they consider all manner of possibility and of what is to come. Several moments pass.

“It’s like what came first, the chicken or the egg,” The Kid says, breaking the spell.

“The Ouroboros,” says Rollie.

“The what?” The Kid asks.

“King Tuts snake eating its tail,” says Rollie.

The word is from the Greek and means tail devourer or one is all,” Kelly tells him.

“Hence the phrase, ‘It’s all Greek to me’,” Sal quips getting a few laughs.

“Or what Jesus said, that he is the Alpha and Omega,” adds Dave.

Hank and Danny arrive and join them in the lounge area of Carl’s office.

“This is getting to be ‘It’s-a-Mad-Mad-Mad-Mad-Mad-Mad-World’,” Sal says, smiling.

Hank laughs. “Let’s hope not,” he says.

Of course, Carl and Danny have no reference for Sal’s Mad world comment. Kelly looks around the room at everyone. He stands up and starts pacing the floor trying to work things out in his head as he has done many times during this caper.

“We gave the fish to Harry Johnson, like you asked, Carl,” Hank announces.

Carl is happy to hear something tangible to deal with.

“He didn’t look happy about it, either,” Danny says, laughing.

“Thanks, fellas. Scotch?” Carl asks.

“I could use one,” Danny says.

“Please, help yourselves,” he tells them.

Danny pours drinks for Hank and himself and they get comfortable on the sofa as Kelly continues to pace the floor.

“Okay… Let’s break it down,” Kelly says, continuing to pace the floor. “There’s a lot going on here, …things we need to consider,” he says, turning to Carl. “Can I see the gems that remain?” he asks.

Carl looks up at him, “It’s only fair,” he says, standing up. “Come with me.”

Kelly follows him to the safe. Carl unlocks it, places the letter inside with great care and takes out a small black velvet cloth tied together with a string and hands it to Kelly.

“This is what remains of the gems I found,” Carl tells him. “I buried the futuristic metal case they were in along with the rocket,” he says.

Kelly unravels the cloth revealing what looks like about twenty carats worth of diamonds and a large ruby. He turns to the crew.

“Not bad,” he says.

Dave walks over, “We never had a chance to check if any of these have laser engraved serial numbers,” he says, taking one in his hand and looking at it in the light. “I’ll need a microscope of some kind,” he adds.

The Kid walks over, “What if they are lasered?” he asks.

“If they’re lasered, they may be worth more here in 1929 than they would be in 2019,” he says. “We’ll have to do some math to figure it out... Black market in 2019 verses open market today,” he says looking around at the crew. “Either way there’s not a lot left from our original haul,” he says, looking at Carl accusingly.

“Ease up, Dave,” Sal says joining them at Carl’s desk near the safe. “Carl said he’d make good, and he will,” she says.

She looks up into Carl’s face with an innocent girl-like expression, “You will make good, won’t you Carl?” she asks.

“There was no way I could know anyone would ever lay claim to them,” Carl says in his defense.

“Carl’s right,” Kelly tells everyone. “The question is, what do we do now? How do we use the value of Demyan’s Diamonds to take advantage of being in 1929?” he asks everyone.

“The man stole our loot, plain and simple,” insists Rollie, walking over and entering the conversation.

“Hold on there, hotshot. That’s not the whole story and you know it” Sal argues.

“Sal’s right,” Kelly says giving Carl a kind smile. “Then again, you took what was not yours, Carl. You didn’t wait to see who the rocket might have belonged to,” he adds. “Maybe you will consider making us partners in one of your properties. We did help to finance them after all...” Kelly tells him.

Hank and Danny listen from the sofa not sure where this will all lead as Carl grapples with Kelly’s bold suggestion. Kelly’s mind is working quickly to find a solution, as is Carl’s. They both know everything has changed. The crew has finally located the rocket, but not all the loot remains. One man has benefitted from finding it and deep down everyone in the crew knows they would have done the same. Now what?

“Okay look,” Kelly says. “What time is your dinner tonight?” he asks Carl looking at his watch.

“I nearly forgot,” Carl says looking at his own watch. “I must get ready. My dinner is in an hour,” he says.

“Let’s stick around and grab a bite here at the club,” Kelly suggests to Hank, Danny and the crew, taking charge. He looks at Carl, “Can you let Harry know we’ll need a large table for dinner?” he asks.

“Now you’re talkin’,” The Kid says.

“There’s a news flash...” Sal says, lighting a cigarette.

“Certainly,” Carl says. “I’ll have him find you at the bar when your table is ready,” Carl tells them.

Kelly walks over to Carl. They shake hands.

“We’ll work something out that will satisfy all concerned,” Carl assures everyone.

“I know,” Kelly responds.

“Now if you don’t mind, I want to dress for dinner,” he tells them.

He walks to his office door, grabs the doorknob, stops a moment and turns to everyone and smiles.

"I truly am sorry to have taken your gems. Naturally, what they were doing in that infernal rocket in the first place is mysterious, to say the least," he says to Kelly, eyebrows raised. He opens the door to the vestibule leading to the speakeasy, "Enjoy your meal," he tells them as they exit his office.

Kelly is the last to leave. He stops at the door and looks into Carl's eyes, "You realize that until this is fully resolved, it will be a thorn in both our sides," he tells Carl as a warning.

"I know," Carl tells him.

"I'll never keep that bunch under wraps till morning," Kelly tells him. "I suggest we meet after our prospective dinners and resolve everything this evening," he tells Carl in a no-nonsense manner rarely seen in Kelly.

Carl knows when he's licked. Short of engaging Capone's men to knock them off and ending up with Capone on his back, he knows he has to make a deal, so he agrees to the meeting. Kelly walks out towards the bar. Finally, Carl is alone. He walks to his desk, sits down in his chair and weeps. It soon evolves into a full out wailing that causes his entire body to convulse in deep sobs. Four years of inner turmoil and unexplained mystery that might have destroyed many a good man, Carl kept it all inside, never telling a soul. He sits at his desk and sobs for fifteen minutes straight. He pulls himself up from his desk, freshens himself up in his private bathroom, dresses in a fresh suit and tie, combs his hair, looks in the mirror and winks at himself.

"Things could be worse," he tells himself. "Remember that," he says before turning off the lights and entering the club.

Kelly strolls through the speakeasy as the crew enjoys drinks at the bar. The place is already lively with patrons enjoying an elegant dinner and floor show. He stops and looks around the loud and lively speakeasy. A large part of him has not fully grasped the intensity of all that has happened since July Fourth with any worthy degree of perspective. As is usual for Kelly and the crew, it has been full steam ahead, but now... this moment! They have located the rocket and here he is, standing in the middle of the glamorous Deep Sea Club speakeasy in 1929. He cannot help but to be astonished. He stands there taking it in as his mind races a mile a minute. He looks over at the bar. There's the crew, his crew, having cocktails in a speakeasy in the roaring twenties. A wry smile comes to his face.

"Your table is ready, Mr. Kelly," the voice of Harry Johnson interrupts his thoughts.

Kelly turns around, sees Harry, looks him in the eyes, steps forward and gives him a giant bear hug. Harry is unsure what to make of it.

"A simple gratuity will do, sir," Harry tells him, feeling uncomfortable by Kelly's emotional gesture.

Kelly reaches into his pocket and hands Harry a fifty-dollar bill.

"You are a beautiful man, Harry. Don't change a thing." He smiles uncontrollably.

Harry is even more miffed by the comment than he was when Kelly gave him the bear hug.

“Thank you for saying so, sir. Right this way,” he says turning.

Kelly tells him he’ll fetch the others and meet him in a moment. He saunters over to the bar where Sal, Dave, Rollie and The Kid are enjoying cocktails discussing Carl and the rocket.

“Our table is ready,” Kelly says, smiling at them.

He puts his arm out for Sal and they follow Harry to a large table not far from the band. Harry pulls out a chair for Sal and they all take seats at the table which is set for dinner with a menu at each setting.

“Four bottles of your finest champagne, please Harry,” Kelly tells him.

“Right away, Mr. Kelly,” Harry says, dashing away towards the bar.

Dave peers out at a table on the other side of the room, “There he is,” he says pointing to the table with his chin.

The gang look over at the table to see Carl joining a group of wealthy-looking men who appear to be engaged in a business discussion of some type.

“Carl has agreed to meet with us after dinner this evening,” Kelly tells everyone.

“Good,” Sal comments while lighting a cigarette. “The last thing we need is Carl skipping town on us,” she says, blowing a puff of cigarette smoke.

A waiter appears with the champagne, and a tray of champagne glasses. He pops the cork and serves up the champagne amidst the sweet twenty’s music wafting through the club. Kelly raises his glass. “To the strangest town we’ve ever visited,” he says.

“Twice,” Sal quips.

“Hear, hear!” says Dave among laughter as he downs his champagne.

“Wait till Shin finds out how far his rocket flew,” Rollie says with a chuckle. The crew cracks up laughing.

“To Montauk,” says The Kid, downing his drink.

“To the end that never ends.” Sal toasts, feeling philosophical.

“Can we order some chow?” asks The Kid, grabbing his menu and opening it.

“Sure, Kid, whatever you like,” Kelly says, feeling elated.

“I’m thinking lobster bisque, then prime rib,” The Kid says looking over the menu.

“What? No caviar?” Sal asks.

The Kid looks over at Rollie, then across at Kelly. “You think we’ll ever get back?” he asks.

“I don’t know, Kid. But if we don’t, Carl’s convinced you have a heck of a future as a race-car driver,” Kelly says smiling.

“You’ll have to change your name, of course…” Dave quips.

The Kid’s not exactly jumping for joy. Considering the circumstances, the crew has adjusted incredibly well since arriving in 1929. Kelly knew to keep them all busy, but at times like this, the slower moments that affords them the opportunity to reflect on the reality of what has happened to them, thoughts that would otherwise not have the luxury to unfold, creep into their heads. The Kid, perhaps, has been affected more than the others. Kelly can see it in his face.

“Look… the plan is to put some things in motion now that will pay off in 2019. A payday big enough that will allow you to buy Lamborghinis in every color they make, Kid. But,” he looks at Dave, “There's no guarantee we'll find a way to get back,” he adds.

“Yes, and so far, the only method I've devised of finding out is to follow Hank's coordinates back to the precise point in the ocean where it happened on the Fourth of July,” Dave says, looking at The Kid. “However, we can't even try until we're ready to go back because if my theory is correct, that there's a recurring loop that exists out there, once we're in it, we're in it. There's no way to control it,” he says. “It's a do-or-die one-shot deal,” he adds finishing his glass of champagne and pouring another.

“Which is why the next order of business is to put something in motion that will be there waiting for us when we return. Purchasing a large parcel of real estate, or stocks…” Kelly says, thinking.

“Automobiles, stamps, art, wine…” Sal adds.

“Touché,” Kelly says smiling. “Bond certificates…” he adds.

“Pretty much all the things we have made careers of stealing and or forging…” Rollie adds with a smile.

“Yes! Then place it all in a trust we can claim when we return to 2019,” Kelly says.

“If we do this right, it'll make Demyan's Diamonds look like chicken feed,” Sal says.

"Exactly," Kelly agrees with his mischievous smile. "My friends, we have an opportunity to pull off the greatest caper ever executed in the history of the con," Kelly tells them. "The Time Machine Scam," he names it with a big gesture.

"This will go down in history as the greatest con ever perpetrated," Dave says.

"Waiter!" shouts Kelly, grabbing the attention of a waiter.

The waiter walks over, "Yes sir?" he asks.

"We're ready to order now, but first, bring us a bottle of your finest scotch whisky," he says. "Macallan, if you have one," says Kelly.

"Right away, sir," the waiter answers and dashes to the bar.

The waiter returns with the scotch and glasses for everyone.

Kelly pours the whisky as they order an extravagant meal.

"Keep an eye on Carl," Kelly says, looking at Rollie.

"Never let him out of my sight…" he tells Kelly.

The crew enjoys an elaborate meal in the lively speakeasy. The subject of Carl Fischer, the gems and how to proceed dominates the conversation. They decide they want to see the rocket and the remaining contents of the safety deposit boxes.

"You know he found more than that sappy love letter in there," The Kid insists, sipping his scotch.

"Hardly sappy, Kid," Sal tells him. "That was an expression of true and desperate love," she says.

"She's right, Kid," Rollie tells him. "That letter speaks of an unrequited love, spanning years and an ocean, that you can only hope and have the privilege to suffer through one day," he tells The Kid.

Sal smiles and looks over at Rollie, "I always suspected there was something more than larceny and famous quotes in that head of yours," she says.

"A romantic..." Dave comments.

"Speaking of which, look who's back?" Kelly tells Sal, pointing with his chin to Errol Flynn.

Sal looks over, sees Errol Flynn and smiles.

"I'll be damned... That's Errol Flynn," Dave says somewhat astonished by the sight of seeing the American icon. "This may be the best vacation I've ever been on," he says laughing.

The crew laughs uproariously.

"In like Flynn," The Kid laughs.

"How's Carl doing?" Kelly asks Rollie, who has the best view of his table.

"Looks like a business meeting of some kind," Rollie says.

"Among his exploits, Carl was a bootlegger, don't forget," Kelly tells the crew. "Could be anything, really... Does he look happy?" Kelly asks Rollie.

"Yeah, there's no sign of duress of any kind. They're just partying," he says.

"The well-heeled enjoying a night out, devising new and exciting ways to increase their fortunes," Kelly defines the exchange. "This is what Carl lived for," he says, turning around to catch a glimpse of his would-be nemesis.

"I believe the proper vernacular is 'lives' for," Dave says smiling with a raise of the eyebrow.

"Is Chappy out there waiting for us?" Sal asks suddenly.

"I suppose he is," Kelly says.

"Maybe we should order him a meal," suggests Sal.

"I'll go check. I could stand to stretch my legs," Kelly says standing up and walking towards the exit.

Sure enough, Chappy is out there much like Sparky would have been, scribbling notes in his notebook. Kelly offers to have a hot meal delivered to him, which he gratefully accepts. Kelly heads back into the speakeasy and arranges for a waiter to deliver a full course dinner to Chappy, complete with a fine bottle of French wine.

Kelly returns to the table. "He was writing in his notebook," he says.

"Just like Sparky," Sal says thinking about their pal who was left behind.

"I wonder what Sparky's doing right now?" she asks looking posh as she lights a cigarette exhaling a large puff of smoke.

Everyone turns to Sal through her cloud of smoke with strange expressions. She too suddenly realizes the absurdity of wondering what Sparky's doing at that moment, as they are in 1929 while Sparky remains in

2019 which technically won't happen for another ninety years. Dave looks up at her excitedly, maybe putting something together in his head.

"What's today's date?" He asks.

"August 11," Rollie answers. "Why?"

"Somewhere out there in the ocean is that interruption in the space-time continuum... And at the end of that loop, somewhere, it's August 11, 2019," he says. "Right now. Not in this time, yet still at this very moment..." he adds letting his mind imagine it.

Dave looks around the table with a fantastical expression as the jazz, clinking of glasses, loud shouts and laughter from partiers fill the air at the speakeasy.

"The same number of days has passed for Sparky as it has for us," Dave tells everyone.

"So?" The Kid asks.

"So... I wonder what Sparky's doing right now, too," Kelly says smiling at Sal.

The crew sits there dumbfounded as the 1920s roars around them scored by the Deep Blue Sea house band's rendition of "Ain't Misbehavin'."

"Does that mean we can get back?" The Kid asks.

"Anything's possible, Kid. Anything's possible..." Dave says with a smile as he pours himself a tall whiskey.

Kelly looks at his watch. "How's Carl doing?" he asks Rollie.

“The man can drink some booze,” Rollie says, gazing out towards Carl’s table.

“He nearly drank himself to death,” Kelly tells them. “It gets worse after the stock market crash,” he says sadly.

“Couldn’t we warn him?” Sal asks.

“Maybe… if we can gain his trust to the degree it would take to convince him,” Kelly says.

“He trusted us enough to tell us about the rocket and return the gems he didn’t cash in,” says The Kid.

“True, but that was primarily because after years of holding the secret of the rocket inside himself, he was bursting at the seams,” Sal answers.

“Yeah. Did you see the look on his face when he let it out?” asks The Kid.

“Like a kid on Christmas morning,” Kelly says sipping his scotch. “How can we not tell him?”

It occurs to Kelly that by warning Carl of the impending stock market crash it essentially makes him a part of the crew. A partner…

“Carl always said that he didn’t think in terms of money… He just liked to see the dirt fly,” Kelly tells them.

“Sounds about right,” The Kid says, smiling.

“If we tell him and he believes it to be true, we are essentially making him a part of the crew,” says Dave looking around at the others for reactions.

“Exactly…” says Kelly. “What would be so wrong with that?”

“The man’s a legend,” The Kid says.

“Touché,” agrees Dave.

“They’re getting up and shaking hands,” Rollie tells everyone from his bird’s eye position at the table.

“Why don’t you bump into him on your way to the powder room, Sal?” Kelly asks.

“You read my mind,” she says, standing up.

She turns towards Errol Flynn throwing him a coy wave then struts over towards Carl shaking her hips a bit more than usual.

“Why Carl, dahling!” she says, practically walking right into him.

She leans up and kisses him on the cheek. Carl doesn’t resist.

“Are you going to introduce us to your charming friend?” one of the men asks Carl, taking in the gorgeous Sal.

“The lovely Sally Ann,” Carl says, winking at Sal. “May I introduce some of my business associates? John Collins and the board of the Montauk Beach Development Corporation,” he says with a lavish wave of his arm signifying the other men standing around the table mesmerized by the gorgeous Sal.

“Pleasure to meet you gents,” Sal says. “Carl?” she asks alluringly taking Carl’s arm and kissing him on the cheek again. “Promise you’ll dance with me,” Sal insists.

“How can I refuse an elegant lady a turn on the dancefloor?” he says smiling. “Gentlemen…” he says turning to his partners before scurrying off towards the dance floor with Sal.

Kelly and the gang watch the whole thing. Kelly smiles broadly, charmed by Sal's fantastic ability to turn grown men into little boys.

Sal and Carl cut the rug for a few dances, when she leads him to their table. The crew greet him warmly as he takes a seat. Kelly pours him a scotch. Carl lifts his glass and turns in his chair, slowly making eye contact with everyone there ending with Sal.

"It warms the heart to know that, whatever year you're from, we're still dancing," he says taking a healthy swig of the scotch.

"I'll drink to that," Kelly says raising his glass.

"Rather..." Says Dave lifting his glass.

The crew lift their glasses and drink merrily, more and more becoming a part of the roaring 20s.

It isn't long before the subject of the rocket's contents and where Carl buried the cash come up. It has become apparent to Carl that Kelly and company went to extravagant lengths, even with his limited knowledge of the world as it exists in 2019, in order to fill that rocket with valuable items, and blast it out over the sea in order to retrieve it in stealth. As much as prior to the Volstead Act, Carl's endeavors remained within the bounds of the law and ethical standards, that he now finds himself bootlegging, running a speakeasy, rigging roulette wheels, befriending notorious gangster Al Capone and the like, he cannot help but to feel a certain kinship with the crew. A feeling amplified by the fact that they are the only living creatures in the world who know his dirty little secret of discovering the rocket and capitalizing on the value of its contents.

“As fascinating as it is to consider how a rocket filled with precious jewels, a large amount of cash from nearly a century in the future and a plethora of personal effects, found its way here, how and why those items found their way into the rocket in the first place feels to me, to be an equally significant part of the story,” Carl suggests finishing off his scotch and pouring another.

Kelly looks around the table at the others with raised eyebrows, then at Carl with his signature grin. He knows that Carl has just opened the door to an extremely delicate if inevitable conversation.

“Time travel makes for strange bedfellows,” Kelly says, pouring himself a scotch and raising it to Carl.

“Indeed,” Dave says.

“Be that as it may, bedfellows we are,” Carl says winking at Sal.

“Hold your horses, hot pants,” she says with a smart-ass grin.

Carl gets a kick out of Sal’s sassy response.

“Fair enough,” he says smiling.

Carl scans the table slowly, looking at each of his new friends from the future. He takes a long sip of whiskey. “You seem to have a firm grasp on history,” he says and then laughs suddenly, “On what for you is history anyway…” he adds with a comical shake of the head.

“You don’t know the least of it,” Kelly says with a chuckle.

Ideas and concepts are racing through Carl's head faster than he can fathom. Carl Fischer may be a celebrated daredevil who has made a remarkable career of trusting his instincts and throwing caution to the wind, but suddenly, in this moment... in the face of these stunning turn of events... has he met his match? He looks at everyone with a befuddled expression on his face, fills his glass and takes a healthy swig, flabbergasted.

"Tell me I haven't gone mad," he says.

"There are some crucial things you need to know," Sal says looking up at Carl with the most sympathetic expression.

"History is about to take a major turn," Kelly tells him. "And the only people who know about it for certain are seated at this table," he says.

The lot of them sit there silent for a moment as the jazz rolls on and the twenties roar around them.

"Let's retire to my office," Carl suggests. "It's too loud out here," he says.

"Let's," Kelly and Sal say simultaneously, then laugh about it.

Carl and the crew get up from the table and walk towards Carl's office at the back of the club, stopping often as many a patron greets Carl enthusiastically, cracking wise or just making festive hellos. Finally, they reach the sanctuary of Carl's private office. They stand there quietly staring at one another.

"Now what?" The Kid asks, looking up at his mentor.

Kelly begins pacing the floor. Carl pours himself a drink and takes a seat in an easy chair. Sal joins him, as does

Dave and Rollie. Kelly turns to Dave with an excited expression, then turns to Carl.

"Want to come back with us?" Kelly asks him.

Carl is expressionless. He looks at the gang, then at Kelly. "To 2019?" he asks.

"Do you think he could come with us?" Kelly asks Dave.

Dave looks at Carl, then at Kelly, then at the others. He takes a healthy swig of whiskey.

"I don't know," he says. "I don't know if any of us can get back," he adds, looking around the room at everyone.

It's quiet again. Did Kelly really just ask Carl if he wanted to go back with them?

What if I could go? Carl thinks to himself. *Why would I? What would I gain? What would I lose?'*

Kelly is pacing the floor. Everyone grapples with the question... *What would I do if I were Carl*? Most of them know by now that historically, it doesn't end well for Carl. He loses everything when the real estate boom of Montauk busts. Then the crash of '29 finishes him off in the following years. By 1932, every property in Montauk went into receivership. After being a multi-millionaire, Carl ended up living in a cottage in Miami surviving on a $500 a month salary paid to him by his old partners to do promotional work. Then in 1938, completely out of character, he builds his last project, a blue-collar paradise. Key Largo's Caribbean Club, a fishing club for men of modest means. Called "the poor man's retreat," it's later featured in the film *Key Largo* with Bogart and Bacall. In 1939, Carl dies in a Miami hospital of a stomach hemorrhage caused by his massive consumption of alcohol. Should they forewarn him so that he might avoid his fate. Could he? Would he? Can he? Some events may simply be irreversible. Plus, do they want such a legendary figure from another era to be a part of their tight-knit crew. What about Sparky?

What if none of us can get back, Kelly thinks to himself as he paces the floor. *We could still survive... But some of the worst years in American history are upon us, who would want to stay?* he wonders. *The depression is about to set in, then World War II, then...We likely wouldn't see what comes next. Maybe, The Kid... He's young enough. But why not try to get back. And why not take the great Carl Fischer along for the ride?* He stops thinking and pacing the floor and faces Carl.

Much like Kelly and the crew, Carl is no stranger to that moment of standing at the precipice of the unknown. Of staring into the abyss unsure what awaits him when he lands were he to leap in. A place he has found himself many times before as daredevil, titan of industry, builder and entrepreneur. Of all his many daring exploits, setting race-car speed records, air ballooning, risking large sums of money transforming mangrove swamps into high-priced paradises and the like, this just may be the most daring and unusual leap he has ever considered. Kelly and the crew struggle to keep up with Carl's voracious appetite for booze as the speakeasy swings into the wee hours. Carl realizes that Kelly and his friends likely know things that he would like to know. There is a very unique opportunity here. One that has likely never happened before and may never again occur in the history of all mankind. He grabs a hold of his balls and leaps into the abyss.

"I have never backed away from a challenge, however unlikely the outcome, in all my days, and I don't intend to start now," Carl says, raising his glass.

"Talk about watching dirt fly!" Kelly exclaims.

“To watching the dirt fly!” Dave chimes in, raising his glass to Carl.

“It is not in the stars to hold our destiny, but in ourselves,” Rollie says, raising his glass, quoting Shakespeare.

They all toast.

Carl leaps to his feet and not unlike Kelly would, begins pacing the floor. The crew can’t help but notice the similarity.

“We have a unique opportunity here,” he tells them. He focuses on Kelly, “I have capital and contacts in this era and you,” he scans each of them again slowly, one by one, ending with Kelly, “You possess knowledge of future events that all the money in the world couldn’t buy,” he says, forever the visionary entrepreneur.

“Not that it hasn’t been attempted…” Kelly adds with a chuckle.

“We have a plan,” Kelly tells him. “And you’d be welcomed to be a part of it,” he says boldly.

Kelly looks around the room seeking approval from his crew for his bold statement. They all make favorable expressions.

“It’s sort of a short long-term investment,” Kelly says, then begins laughing so hard he can’t speak.

They all join in the laughter letting go of a huge amount of tension that has built up in them. Even Carl gets the joke and laughs along with them.

“A short long-term investment.” Carl continues laughing.

They all collapse to the sofas and easy chairs.

“This calls for champagne,” Carl says, reaching for the phone.

“I knew I liked you,” Sal says with a smile.

Carl calls Harry Johnson and orders champagne for everyone.

After they enjoy the champagne with lively enthusiastic toasts, it is agreed they will meet at the Surf Club the following day where Carl will show them the location of the safety deposit box contents and the cash from the Chase bank. Sal is excited to take a swim in the Olympic-sized salt water swimming pool Carl had built there.

The crew finds Chappy waiting dutifully in his new limousine and pile in for the ride to the Montauk Manor.

“What a night,” The Kid exclaims as Chappy pulls away.

“What a world,” says Dave.

XXVI

The following day they meet at the Surf Club as agreed and Carl shows them where he stashed the cash and safety deposit box contents for safekeeping. They dig up the steel case Carl had hidden the cash in and count it. There is a little more than $250,000. It's decided that they will return the safety deposit box items to the Chase Bank anonymously, although they're not sure whether they should load the items onto the Sally Ann or leave them where they are, then dig them up when they get back, if they get back.

Now that Carl is essentially a partner, if not actually a part of the crew, their escapades at the Deep Blue Sea Casino are over. They must assess their current investment potential which presently consists of an unnamed amount from Carl in exchange for the gems he used to build Montauk, the cash remaining from the safe they robbed on Vanderbilt's yacht, winnings from the casino, the race winnings and the as-yet-to-be-determined monetary value of the gems Carl returned. They have a few months until Black Tuesday and if need be, they decide they can always use Dave's loaded dice at a casino in the city or up island to increase their purchasing power at the stock market after it crashes.

The concierge at the Montauk Manor acquires a microscope for Dave and he learns that the gems are indeed laser etched with serial numbers. It is decided they will sell them and use the cash to buy Union Carbide and Coca-Cola stocks at hugely deflated prices after the crash and hold them in a trust that they can access when they return to 2019. Kelly remembers that after the stock market crash, diamond prices slump because no one can afford them, so they must sell these quickly while they still have great value.

They head to the Sally Ann and work on a solid plan of action in order to move things forward. Chappy remains parked in the nearby dunes. It's been a few days since Hank has heard from anyone and he is happy to see them.

"Hi, Hank," Sal says accepting Hank's hand to help her aboard.

"Hello, pretty lady," he says.

The crew along with Carl climb aboard the Sally Ann. They can't help but notice Hank's surprise at seeing Carl with them.

Sal gently takes a hold of Hank's arm. "Carl's coming with us," she tells him.

"To 2019?" Hank asks, somewhat astonished.

Kelly explains the new arrangement to Hank. Carl assures him that he doesn't expect a free ride and that Hank will be compensated handsomely if he gets Carl to 2019 safely.

"The time travel fee..." Kelly smiles.

They may not realize it, but the Sally Ann represents a tangible element of home for the crew and there is a comfort level that being on board provides.

"Got anything to drink on this boat?" Carl asks.

"I could stand a rum," says a smiling Sal. She finds the rum and pours a few drinks. Kelly, Hank and the rest of the crew join them. Dave scribbles some figures on a piece of paper as he sips rum.

"What are we looking at?" Kelly asks.

“These aren’t exact figures but they’re in the ballpark and even with inflation, full stock price recovery and uncollected dividends, we won’t be buying Dick Cavett’s Stanford White any time soon,” he says. “We need to increase our stock-buying power drastically in order to make this work,” he adds.

“I won’t know what I can give you until I talk to the bank and my partners, but I’m sorry to say it won’t be close to the current day value of the gems I used. The Montauk constructions are meant to be long-term investments.

The crew are a bit gloomy wondering how this plan is going to pay off if they can’t buy enough stocks. It’s quiet as they sit around sipping rum.

“Wait!” exclaims Kelly having an inspiration. We’re thieves, are we not?” he asks, jumping to his feet and looking around at the crew. “We’re looking at this all wrong! Do you realize how easy it would be to rob say... Tiffany and Company now in 1929,” he asks with a mischievous smile.

“Absolutely,” says The Kid.

Of course!” exclaims Sal.

“Joy is of the will which labors, which overcomes obstacles, which knows triumph,” Rollie states, quoting William Butler Yeats.

“And we know for certain they won’t be laser etched with serial numbers,” says Dave smiling.

Carl looks at his newfound friends, admiring their spirit. “I do believe you may all be crazier than I am,” he says, laughing.

And he’s not exaggerating. Carl is the one taking the bigger gamble, as he is considering liquidating all that he owns and betting it on reaping the benefits ninety years in the future. A place he has serious doubts even exists creating on-again, off-again bouts of uncertainty deep within him. There are moments when he questions his sanity but once Black Tuesday, October 29, 1929 happens, just as the crew told him it would, he decides, however radical and strange things have become, that he is making the right decision to continue with the plan. He creates his trust as The Apollo Holding Company.

Now they must choose a bank to hold the trusts registered with the State of New York, a bank, that will still exist in 2019. Kelly informs everyone that The Manhattan Company, started way back in 1799 is now, in 1029, Manhattan Bank and in 2019, will be, ironically, the JP Morgan Chase & Company, or simply Chase Bank.

It's Sunday, November 4th and all the arrangements have been made. With the settlement amount from Carl for the gems he had taken, the crew has managed to purchase nearly $500,000 worth of Union Carbide and Coca-Cola stock certificates and place them in a limited liability corporation they have named Sparky Enterprises Limited. Dave figures it should be worth close to one hundred million in 2019. Hank has gotten them back to the exact coordinates from when they first arrived to 1929 a few months earlier. They wait until dawn, but nothing happens.

The crew is gravely disappointed. They're truly worried that they'll never be able to get back. A gloom permeates the mood as Hank pilots the Sally Ann back to Montauk.

A few days pass but they refuse to give up, vowing to try again on December fourth. In the interim they pull off a few successful heists in New York City in order to invest more into stocks for the trust as prices continue to plummet. Sal has the brilliant idea to begin purchasing stock certificates they can physically take back to 2019 with them.

"Who knew what dear grandmother was keeping in that old trunk in the attic," Sal says innocently, then laughs.

On the fourth of December, then again on the fourth of January, February, March, April, May and June they go out to the coordinates that first swooped them into 1929 to no effect. Winter and Spring have come and gone, but the crew has not given up hope.

They walk into the Deep Sea Club to grab some dinner. Afterwards they stroll over to the casino for a little fun, maybe pick a few pockets... They enter the casino and are surprised to find Carl at the craps table, drunk out of his skull and losing terribly.

Kelly approaches him, Hey Carl. What's goin' on?" he asks.

Carl doesn't respond. The croupier gives Kelly a worried look and shrugs his shoulders. Kelly shakes Carl's shoulder trying to get him to respond.

"Carl!" he shouts over the din of the noisy casino.

Carl rears back and punches Kelly square in the jaw, "Why the hell is everybody calling me Carl?!" he yells out in a drunken stupor. "Get away from me!" he shouts angrily.

Rollie runs over and easily pins Carl on the ground. Sal and The Kid help Kelly to his feet. "He's got a punch," Kelly says, rubbing his jaw.

Casino security rush over to take control of the situation. Behind them is Carl. The real Carl. Kelly, the crew, security and the croupier look from one Carl to the other, not sure what to make of it.

“Wait a minute,” Sal exclaims. “He really isn’t Carl.”

“He’s a dead ringer,” Dave exclaims.

The two Carls, stare at one another.

“What’s going on here?” Carl asks.

“And just who might you be?” the other Carl asks.

The two men stare at one another. Carl is dumfounded.

He pulls himself together and insists, “I’m Carl Fischer. I own this casino!”

Kelly and the crew and now half the people in the casino watch the odd scene unfold.

The croupier runs over, “We all thought it was you, sir. He’s lost everything. Been drinking heavily all night,” the croupier exclaims.

“What’s your name, fella,” Kelly asks the man rubbing his jaw.

“What’s it to you?” the man asks belligerently.

Rollie steps up to the man and very calmly looks him in the eye, “My friend asked you a question,” he says with an authority few would challenge.

The man wavers on his feet a moment but he knows he’s beat. “Hoffer,” he says. “James Hoffer. What’s it to ya?”

Carl grabs his security man by the sleeve, “Bring him to my office,” he tells him. “You guys come, too,” he tells Kelly.

Kelly and the entire crew walk next door to the rear entrance of The Deep Sea Club and enter Carl's private office. Carl and the look-a-like, Jimmy, stand there staring at one another.

"The resemblance is uncanny," says Dave looking from one to the other.

"Sit him down," Carl tells his security man. "You can go," he tells him.

"If you say so," the security man says.

"Don't worry pal, we got this…" Rollie assures him.

The security man leaves the room and heads back to the casino.

Carl walks over to Kelly. "I just had an interesting idea," he says.

"Ladies and gentlemen… allow me to introduce Mr. Carl Fischer," Carl says presenting the drunken Jimmy Hoffer who is presently sprawled out on Carl's sofa.

"Brilliant!" says Kelly. "You leave town with us and no one ever knows," he says impressed at how quickly Carl dreamt up such a wonderfully devious plan. "Welcome to the crew," Kelly says with his hand outstretched.

He and Carl shake hands. Sal, Dave, Rollie and The Kid are impressed.

Carl picks up the phone at his desk and calls Harry Johnson.

"Harry, can you bring a pot of coffee to my office?" he asks.

Carl walks over to the sofa where the drunk James is sitting and takes a seat. He puts his arm around his shoulder as a sympathetic gesture.

“Where are you from, fella?” he asks.

“Coney Island,” says James.

A waiter arrives with the coffee. Carl pours a cup for James.

“Here, this will help sober you up,” Carl tells him.

James accepts the coffee.

“I lost it all,” he says, taking the cup and sipping from it.

He looks up at Carl, “You know... I’m a big admirer of yours, Mr. Fischer, being a builder myself.” He takes another sip of coffee and straightens himself out on the sofa. “Not on your level of course...” he adds.

“Interesting,” Carl says looking over at Kelly who is listening closely. He looks over at the crew who just stand there watching the exchange between Carl and his doppelganger in utter amazement.

“Maybe we should give these gentlemen some privacy,” Kelly tells them.

“You’ll stay, won’t you?” Carl asks Kelly.

“Sure, Carl,” he says taking a seat in one of the overstuffed chairs. “I’ll meet you guys next door in a little while,” Kelly tells his crew.

“You got it, chief,” Dave tells him.

The crew leave the room.

“I have a proposition for you that could relieve you of your financial burden,” Carl tells James.

Kelly is smiling, watching Carl operate.

“Yeah?” James asks. “What do you have in mind?” he asks.

Carl explains that he must leave on a journey to a far-off locale but needs to maintain a presence in Montauk. That hiring James to play him would be the perfect solution.

“You would assume my identity. For all intents and purposes, you will be Carl Fischer with no one the wiser,” Carl tells him.

“The things money can buy,” exclaims James, shaking his head. “God knows I’m desperate enough,” he adds.

James is in dire financial duress and came to the casino that night with every penny he had in a desperate act, hoping that lady luck was on his side and that he might win enough to crawl out of the mess he’s in. With no family ties of his own to prevent it, he feels he has no choice but to accept the strange proposition. To avoid having a lawyer know anything about his transfer of identity, Kelly and Dave assist Carl in shifting his identity to James Hoffer and James’ to Carl Fischer.

The crew have amassed quite a few precious diamonds at post stock market crash deflated prices, keeping them for what they know will be an astounding value in 2019. They have continued to purchase stocks as the prices unceasingly plummet in the months following Black Tuesday. Each has also acquired special items to take back. Sal has two trunks filled with period designer clothing, Dave, a collection of timepieces, Rollie has a genuine Samurai sword from the twelfth century and The Kid has stashed the Bugatti 35B in the garage of Carl’s house on Foxboro Road, hoping to get it back one day. “Even if I have to steal it,” he says. Just for fun, as he put it, Kelly has purchased a case of 1911 Chateau Lafite Rothschild Pauillac wine. They even got a gift for Sparky, a 1926 Rolex Oyster Perpetual. Appropriately, the first waterproof watch.

XXVII

It’s the afternoon of July 4,1930. Chappy stops the car in the dunes near to where the Sally Ann is stashed. The crew accompanied by Carl Fischer, now legally James Hoffer, step out of the car.

“If we’re not back by dawn,” Kelly says emotionally, looking around at the crew standing around the limo. He looks back at Chappy. “Enjoy the new ride,” he says, patting the Lincoln affectionately. He reaches into his pocket and pulls out ten hundred-dollar bills, “This is for you. Take some time off and write that book!" he says. He gives Chappy a hug.

Chappy is beside himself as he accepts the stunning amount of cash; nearly $15,000 in 2020. He holds it in his hand, completely dumbfounded.

"You're a good man Chappy," Says Carl offering a handshake.

"See ya around, Chappy," Dave says with a warm smile.

Chappy shakes Dave's hand, "Perhaps..." he mutters, then turns to the beautiful Sal.

"Which reminds me. I have a gift for you." He tells Sal.

Chappy reaches into the Lincoln, grabs two novels and hands them to a somewhat perplexed Sal. She accepts them and looks at the strange titles. *'Travels and adventures of Little Baron Trump and his wonderful dog Bulger' and 'Baron Trump's Marvelous Underground Journey.' By Ingersoll Lockwood.*

Sal looks at them amazed at the strange titles. She peers up into Chappy's eyes and smiles warmly. He winks with a knowing expression. "Love, honor and daring..." he says. Sal kisses Chappy on the cheek tenderly, bringing a sweet smile to his face. "Love, honor and daring," she repeats warmly.

"See ya, pal," The Kid says, patting Chappy on the back.

"Take care of yourself, buddy," Rollie tells him with a grin and a handshake.

They walk off knowing that if Dave's right and they travel back to 2019, they'll miss their friend. They arrive at the

Sally Ann to find Danny Sullivan on deck with Hank. They help the crew board the Sally Ann.

"It's gonna be awful strange seeing you as a small child, if I remember all this," Danny says, giving Hank a big hug.

"I know," Hank says with a tear in his eye.

"Good luck out there," Danny tells him.

"Thanks, ...Grandpa," Hank says, barely holding it together.

Danny jumps aboard his Chris Craft and takes off, waving goodbye.

The crew gathers around the helm with Hank as he starts the huge engine and navigates his way back to the precise location in the sea where it all began. In part because the rocket appeared four years before they did and, using an algorithm he devised on his tablet, Dave has theorized and is now convinced that the interruption in the space-time continuum is on a yearly not monthly loop, as he first suspected. Carl is with them and, like the crew, is hoping Dave's theory of an annular loop for the interruption in the space-time continuum is correct. A few hours later they arrive at the location it all started.

Kelly checks his watch. It's nine p.m.

"Taking into account that congress abolished daylight savings time after World War I until 1942 when FDR brought it back, calling it 'War Time', if anything's gonna happen, it should start in the next half an hour," he tells everyone.

Hank is busy keeping the Sally Ann from drifting off the coordinates against the current, Carl is scratching his head unsure what to expect and the rest of the crew is just plain nervous.

"Whatever happens, I want you to know, it's been fun," Hank tells everyone.

"A true adventure," says Rollie.

Carl pours himself a rum and raises his glass, "To making dirt fly!" he says.

The sky begins to darken as though a squall has come upon them suddenly. The sea begins to rage as thunderbolts light up the sky.

"This is it!" exclaims The Kid.

The wind increases as electrical flashes from lightning far above, light up the sky. The crew hold on tight as once again the Sally Ann gets knocked around like a cork in a washing machine. The sky is a spectrum of exploding colors and dropping closer every second. The sound is deafening. They can barely hear one another now as the sea crashes over the bow while massive thunderbolts light up the sky around the Sally Ann.

"I'll be damned!" Carl exclaims. "Is this what it was like last time?" he asks at the top of his lungs as the heaving of the boat knocks them all about.

"Exactly like this!" Kelly shouts.

"It's like Déjà vu," Rollie exclaims.

Once again, the boat twirls around and around as the sky and sea appear to have merged into one. Powerful electrical flashes come within reach of the Sally Ann.

"This again," exclaims Hank. "Better hold on, little lady," he tells Sal.

They fly wildly through the electrical whirlwind as loud explosions made of electricity engulf them. There are moments when it feels as though the Sally Ann is being torn apart. Everyone holds on tightly, protecting themselves from being tossed around too badly. Then in a flash, it's dead quiet. Once again, just as it occurred a year ago, the Sally Ann seems to be floating in a netherworld of sorts. Then boom! The ship crashes into the sea surrounded by a dense electrical fog. Once again it feels as though the sea crashed into the boat since they felt as though they were floating not falling. The Sally Ann continues to bounce around as a scattering of crackling electrical charges continue to light up the dense black fog they once again find themselves in.

Carl is astonished. "That was one some kinda ride!" he says smiling.

"Get a load of Evel Knieval," Sal says cracking wise.

The sky continues to crackle and flash thunderbolts, but the sea is no longer raging wildly, and a general calm permeates the crew.

"I don't wish to alarm anyone, but before we begin celebrating, until we can confirm, you should all know..." Dave says looking at them with a dire expression, "We could be anywhere."

"What do you mean, anywhere?" Carl asks staring at Dave angrily. "I thought you had this down to a science?" he adds, yelling at Dave.

Everyone turns to Carl in disbelief as thunderbolts continue to light up the dense black fog. He stares back at them with an angry expression for a long moment, then let's go of a giant laugh. Kelly, the crew and Hank crack up laughing. After they've all had a few laughs, Hank tries the GPS and knocks on the Radar display a few times. The electronics are unresponsive as the sky continues to light up and crackle with thunderous crashing.

"Let's get out of this fog," shouts Hank. He attempts to start the engine. Nothing.

"We'll have to wait it out like last time," Kelly comments.

At the same time, Sparky is dropping a few tourists off at the lighthouse in his taxi. It's a gorgeous day without a cloud in the sky. He tells his fare that if they look out at the horizon from the top of the lighthouse they will see the curvature of the earth.

"It's the most subtle and poetic curve," he tells them illustrating it with his arm outstretched gazing out at the ocean. He is shocked to see lightning flashes and dark clouds isolated to a small area a few miles out to sea.

Being a fan of astronomy, Sparky always carries a set of binoculars with him. He yanks them out of his knapsack as his passengers exit the taxi. He places them up to his eyes and focuses on the darkened cluster about five or six miles out in the ocean.

"Would ya look at that," he says to himself.

He grabs his cellphone and calls the Coast Guard station on Star Island.

"Hello? Hello?" he asks excitedly, looking through the binoculars. "Yes, do you have any reports of an isolated storm east of the point?"

He listens a moment as he peers out to the spot in the ocean.

"Wait! The lightning has stopped," he says, placing the phone down and staring out at what now is just an area of dense black fog.

Back on the Sally Ann, the fog begins to dissipate. Hank tries starting the engine again. It cranks several times and finally starts. He turns on the GPS and sure enough they're in Montauk.

"There's the Inlet!" he says excitedly pointing to the GPS display.

"Fascinating," says Carl seeing the modern equipment working for the first time.

Hank begins navigating the Sally Ann back home. They've been gone an entire year.

Sparky keeps his eyes on the fog which appears to be thinning by the moment. He sees a boat come out of the fog but can't tell what kind it is because it's still too far away for the magnification of his binoculars. He follows it as it moves closer.

"I'll be damned," he says when he recognizes it as a commercial fishing boat.

He continues to track the vessel as it comes closer. He considers the possibility that it could be the Sally Ann and begins to laugh out loud. He puts the taxi in gear and races to the harbor. Ten minutes later he pulls up to the commercial dock, puts the taxi in park and runs out to the end of the slip where the Sally Ann once tied on. Nothing there. He decides to drive up the street to the inlet near Gosman's restaurant. He jumps out of the taxi and looks out to see with his binoculars. There are a number of boats in the water, so he examines each one. Finally, he sees her. The Sally Ann motoring towards the inlet! He laughs uncontrollably, happy to see her. He runs out to the end of the jetty jumping up and down trying to get their attention.

“Look! It’s Sparky!” Sal exclaims and waves. “Sparky!” she yells at the top of her lungs.

Sparky yells back. “Ahoy!”

The crew runs to the starboard of the Sally Ann yelling and screaming loudly, happy to see their friend. Hank blows the loud horn.

All Sparky can do is laugh in ecstatic near disbelief.

He jumps in the taxi and drives back to the commercial dock. Hank backs her in. Rollie and The Kid tie her off as Sparky jumps aboard.

“You’re late!” Sparky says with a huge smile.

Big hugs all around.

“Where have you guys been?” he asks Sal.

Sal rolls her eyes, “Where haven’t we been?” she says laughing.

“Why are you dressed like that?” he asks.

Kelly looks at Sparky with a big smile, “Have we got a story for you,” he says.

“Yeah, you have a book to write now,” Rollie tells him with a pat on the back.

Hank kills the engine and walks out on deck.

“Welcome home, Captain,” Sparky says, smiling.

Sparky notices Carl. "Hitchhiker?" he asks, pointing to Carl.

"Sort of… Sparky, meet James Hoffer, James this is Sparky," Kelly says.

Sparky and Carl shake hands.

"What kind of name is Sparky?" Carl asks.

"A very special one," Sal says, smiling at Sparky and giving him a warm hug. "It's so great to see you again, Sparks," she says. She steps back and adds, "Wait till you hear what happened to us," she says.

"Carl, if you'll excuse us a moment, I have to confer with my associates privately," Kelly says.

Kelly, Sparky, and the crew gather at the bow.

"What's the skinny with the investigation?" Kelly asks. "We've been out of touch…" he adds.

"The FBI left town months ago," he tells them. "You didn't leave them much to go on," he adds.

"Thank you, ladies and gentlemen," Dave says taking a bow.

"What about Demyan?" Sal asks.

"He accused the FBI of bungling the case by not giving it the same attention they would have were Demyan not Russian. Especially once the CIA got involved. Stuff like that," Sparky tells them. "He's suing everybody," he adds as laughter gurgles up in him from finally seeing the crew again.

"CIA?" Rollie asks.

Kelly smiles, “Doesn’t matter. Sounds clean enough,” he says. “Sorry about Nova Scotia,” he adds.

“Yeah…” says The Kid. “I forgot about that… How long did you stick around?” he asks.

“I was there for a week waiting for you guys. What happened?” he asks. “And just now I was dropping off at the lighthouse… I looked out to sea and spotted that weird black, electrical storm. That was you, wasn’t it?” he asks.

Hank joins them, “Rollie’s right, Sparky. You have a doozy of a story to write in that book of yours,” he says.

“What’s the plan?” Hank asks Kelly.

“Yes, how do we proceed?” Carl asks, appearing behind Hank.

“We’re going to need a shovel and a flashlight,” he tells Sparky.

A shovel?” Sparky asks.

“Yup… Oh, and we need a hotel but not until we reinstate our credit cards…” Kelly announces. “And claim our trust,” Kelly says turning to the crew with a wink and a smile.

“Does the Yacht Club still exist?” Carl asks.

“Yes, but as of last year, it’s called Gurney’s Star Island,” Sal tells him.

“It remained the Montauk Yacht Club and respected your legacy for close to a hundred years, until this recent change,” Kelly tells him.

"Yeah, and none of us likes that they changed the name," The Kid adds.

"They could have called it Gurney's Montauk Yacht Club or The Montauk Yacht Club at Gurney's or by Gurney's. Or any number of respectable names but I guess they had to put their own stink on it," Sparky tells him. Then looking at Carl, strangely, turns to Kelly and asks, "Wait, his legacy?"

"Until this Gurney's fiasco, the Montauk Yacht Club had a brochure that told the history of the man who built it, Carl Fischer," Kelly tells him.

"Yeah… it's as though they're trying to erase ninety years of history," argues The Kid.

"And as we know, that can't be done," Dave says, laughing.

"Like that!" exclaims Sparky. "What exactly do you mean by that?" he asks peering at Dave.

"We have a lot to tell you about, Sparks, but first we need to load in," Sal tells him. "We brought you a gift," she says, handing Sparky the Rolex.

He opens the box and is amazed. "I love vintage timepieces," he says. "Is this a fake? It's brand new," he says looking up at the crew with a strange expression on his face.

"We'll explain everything tonight at dinner, but now can we back the taxi up this dock?" Kelly asks, turning to Hank.

"Sure, it'll hold a truck…" Hank tells him.

"All right," Sparky says and puts the watch on.

He steps off the Sally Ann and looks up at the crew, "You never cease to amaze..." he says before jogging down to get the taxi.

He backs the taxi up the dock to the Sally Ann. Rollie, The Kid, Dave and the rest of them load Sal's trunks, assorted suitcases, Kelly's case of wine and the rest of it, including a case of Jamaican Rum.

"I need a drink," Hank says as he steps off the boat.

"My kind of Captain," Carl says with a smile. "Is there a drinking establishment nearby?" he asks.

"C'mon," Hank says stepping off the Sally Ann. He looks at Kelly. "I'm keeping him as collateral," he tells Kelly.

"Don't worry, Hank, I'm a man of my word, and as agreed there will be special compensation for time travel," he assures Hank with a wink.

"Time what?" exclaims Sparky.

"No need to worry, my good captain, as agreed, there will be special compensation for getting me here safely," Carl assures him.

Hank looks towards the Dock Restaurant. "I'm going to have a lot of explaining to do," he says. "If anyone asks, we've been fishing in Southern waters all year, off Mexico," he says.

"Fine... Now, about that drink?" Carl asks.

"Follow me," Hank tells him.

"Remember, you're James Hoffer now," Kelly tells him.

"Righto," Carl says.

They agree to meet back on the Sally Ann later that night. Hank and Carl stroll down towards the Dock Restaurant. Rollie and The Kid make an idiot check to be sure nothing they want was left behind on the Sally Ann. The Kid pops his head up from below deck, "Good to go," he says jumping up on the deck.

They pile into the taxi and drive down the dock to the street.

"We need to hit that hardware store in town," Kelly tells Sparky.

"Man, I missed you guys," he says. "I always knew that someday you'd find your way back," he says, turning onto West Lake Drive and heading to town. "But you have to tell me something," he says excitedly. "There's no way I can wait till tonight. For instance, what's the shovel and flashlight for?

"We're going to have a few hours to kill before dark, and we'll tell you all about it," Kelly says.

They drive to town.

The Kid looks up at the Tower. "Surreal..." is all he can say.

The others are experiencing similar feelings being back in a very different Montauk, yet, still Montauk...

Sparky pulls up to Becker's Hardware in town.

"We should get a pick-ax, too," suggests Rollie.

"Good idea," says Kelly. "Can you change a hundred?" he says handing Sparky a 1928 hundred-dollar bill.

Fascinating…" Sparky says taking the bill from Kelly. "Kind of goes with the watch…" he adds holding it next to the mint vintage Rolex Oyster on his wrist, his eyebrows raised high.

He looks into Kelly's eyes. "Are you serious?" he says, his face not wanting to believe what his mind is already putting together.

Kelly smiles, looks back at Sal, Dave, Rollie and The Kid a moment.

He looks back at Sparky, "Let's get the tools, then we'll tell you the whole story over dinner," he says.

Sparky makes change. Rollie and Dave take the cash and go inside Becker's to get a shovel, pick-ax and few flashlights.

"Where to?" Sparky asks with a smile.

"The Manor?" Kelly asks, turning to the crew.

"Wow…" The Kid says.

"Where else?" Sal asks. "But, is that a liquor store?" she asks pointing up the block from the taxi.

"Yeah, that's White's Liquors," Sparky tells her.

"Let's get a few bottles of something bubbly," she suggests.

"C'mon. I'll buy," says Sparky.

He and Sal get out of the taxi and walk up the street to White's Liquors. They enter and the owner Tom is there.

"Nice music," Sal says referring to the Jazz Tom always has playing in the store.

“Sparky…” Tom says with a welcoming smile. “Moving up in the world…” he says, referring to the gorgeous Sal.

Sal winks at Sparky. “I’d say I’m the one moving up,” she says, taking Sparky by the arm then kissing him on the cheek.

“What are we looking for today?” Tom asks.

“Something bubbly,” Sal says. “Love your music by the way,” she adds.

“Thank you, a good friend of mine makes CDs for me,” Tom says winking at Sparky, the person who burns Tom the CDs.

Sal chooses a few bottles of chilled champagne. Tom places them in insulated sleeves so they’ll stay chilled. Sparky and Sal make their way back to the taxi and Sparky drives the crew up to the Montauk Manor. They’re a bit blown away at being there again.

“Seems like just yesterday…” Dave comments peering at the Montauk Manor, a mysterious look on his face.

It’s so spooky, they can’t even laugh. During dinner Sparky gets the whole story. It’s difficult to believe but it’s as good an explanation as any concerning where they’ve been an entire year and why they’ve returned dressed the way they are loaded with hundred year old currency.

“You’re buying, Sparks,” Sal tells him. “Unless you guys have enough modern cash to cover this feast,” Sal says turning to the guys.

“None of our credit cards will work. Until the bank opens in the morning, all we have is period money,” Dave informs him.

"Until we dig up the steel chest..." Kelly says.

"They're actually quite valuable," Dave tells Sparky handing him a few of the hundred-dollar bills.

"I know..." Sparky says smiling. "Unreal!" he says. "How much do you think you're going to make?" Sparky asks.

"Dave figures well over a hundred million dollars," Sal tells him.

"You know that if this works it will be the greatest con in history," Sparky says, smiling.

"Legendary!" The Kid says.

"But who'd believe it?" Dave asks.

"People will want to believe it," Kelly says as he sips his wine.

"What about Carl?" Sparky asks. "And who's James Hoffer?" he asks.

"That's one of the more incredible parts of the story," Kelly tells him.

"Carl had a doppelganger," Rollie says. "A blue-collar type of guy who, like Carl, was also a builder. A guy from Coney Island," he adds.

"Coney Island or not, it was spooky," The Kid says.

"They could have been identical twins," Sal tells Sparky.

"You know, when you think about it, it's as though it had to happen this way," Kelly says.

The crew gaze at one another again, the amazing and mysterious events of the past year nearly overwhelming them. Sparky is not sure what to think.

"As history tells it, the last thing Carl built was The Caribbean Club in Key Largo," Kelly tells Sparky. "All his life he built first class resorts for the well-heeled… the best people… the rich and famous, and then, totally out of character, he builds a resort that was called a 'poor man's paradise.' Think about that… And there's no record that I know of that tells us of him having a change of heart, an epiphany of some kind that motivated him to suddenly build a resort for men of moderate means," Kelly continues.

"It is however the type of resort James Hoffer would have built," Dave says.

They all look at one another, considering the probabilities and being amazed by them.

"This time-travel business can get awfully complicated," Sal says. "Wait till Carl sees the Manor!" she adds lifting the tone.

"Yeah…" The Kid agrees.

"Carl Fischer was a visionary!" Sparky exclaims. "He goes to Miami, finds mangrove swamps then, sort of like, when Bugsy Siegal envisions Las Vegas in the Nevada desert, Carl envisions a luxurious winter playground of hotels, yacht clubs, fine restaurants and builds it. Then after he loses nearly everything in the real estate bust near the end of 1925 and the hurricane of 1926, he comes to Montauk where he finds some fisherman, sheep meadows, a few Stanford White mansions, and creates a summer playground for the same crowd. Dave's right, from everything you've told me, The Caribbean Club is exactly the kind of place James Hoffer, builder from Coney Island would construct. As though it were a dream of his, and Carl helped him to achieve it," Sparky says completely fascinated by the astounding likelihood.

He looks around at everyone, amazed at this turn of events. "It's something he would never have had a chance to build were it not for Carl switching identities with him... And would Carl have ever switched identities with James Hoffer if you guys hadn't shown up and offered to bring Carl here?" Sparky asks as conjecture.

"Like I said..." Sal insists, drinking her wine. "This time-travel intrigue is tricky stuff."

"Speaking of time... it's time to get back to the Dock Restaurant to grab Carl and Hank," Kelly says, tapping his watch.

"Don't forget there are fireworks tonight," Sparky says.

"Yes, there are... And once again they'll be the perfect distraction for our treasure hunt," Dave says with his devious smile.

"You know, it's not unusual for people to dig fire pits on the beach," Sparky tells everyone, "We should pick up some firewood so if anyone sees us digging, it will appear as though we're just digging a firepit," he says.

"Sparks!" Sal says affectionately.

Kelly looks over at Sparky with a big smile. "Best wheelman ever!" he says.

"There's a guy on Flamingo Avenue, on the say to the Dock Restaurant, who usually has bundles of firewood for sale on the side of the road. He leaves a coffee can out for the five bucks," he tells everyone.

“Nice,” Rollie says.

They pile into the taxi and drive up Flamingo Avenue. Sparky pulls over at the wood rack at Flamingo and Duryea Ave. They load in a few bundles and Kelly stuffs one of the vintage hundred-dollar bills in the honor system coffee can.

“This’ll be a nice surprise for whoever this guy is,” Kelly says.

When they get to the Dock Restaurant, Carl and Hank are drinking at the bar. There’s a festive atmosphere with the locals at the Dock happy and excited to see Hank again.

Kelly gets them into the taxi and Sparky drives everyone to the Surf Club. The town is already buzzing with excitement in anticipation of the Grucci fireworks. Carl stares out of the window at 2020 in utter amazement. Finally, they reach the Surf Club.

“That’s not the Surf Club I built,” he tells them.

“I’m afraid your original hacienda style stucco cabanas were washed away by the sea in a series of hurricanes sometime back in the 1950s,” Kelly tells him.

“Carl frowns, then with a sudden smile says, “They kept the name, at least!”

They unload the shovel, pick-ax and firewood at the dead end street on the ocean. Sparky stashes the taxi and meets them on the beach behind the Surf Club. Dave pulls out a map he’d drawn the night Carl had shown them where he buried everything. Carl notices it and laughs.

“You won’t need that,” Carl tells Dave as he begins walking to the spot. “If they followed the original footprints of the club I built, your cash should be…” he looks up at the Surf

Club a moment, takes a few steps to the east and says, "right here..."

Sure enough, he has led them directly to where the cash is buried. Rollie and The Kid dig it up and open it. Sparky is amazed. As is Hank.

"You guys are something else," Hank says, shaking his head with a smile.

"That's a lot of money," Sparky says.

"We're going to need your help in getting us a few rooms tonight," Kelly tells him.

"Yeah, you can't get a room without a credit card these days no matter how much cash you have..." Dave says. "Not like in 1929," he adds with a chuckle.

"Hey Sparky, drive us to the city tomorrow?" Kelly asks.

"Sure," he says. "But if you want rooms tonight, I better call around. It is the Fourth of July in Montauk..." he says as he dials a number on his cell.

Kelly counts out fifty thousand dollars and hands it to Hank.

"This is just an installment," Kelly tells him. "We'll contact you after we claim our trust and get our cells turned back on in the city tomorrow," he tells him.

"You guys are all right," Hank says, accepting the cash.

"As promised, I'll have something substantial for you tomorrow as well," Carl assures Hank.

Kelly counts out twenty thousand and hands it to Sparky, "For expenses, Sparks," he says.

With his cell phone to his ear, Sparky takes the cash with his free hand, “Sounds good, five rooms are preferred but whatever you can work out,” Sparky says speaking into the cell.

“Let’s stay for the fireworks,” Sal suggests. I brought champagne,” she says, holding up the bottles she and Sparky bought from White’s Liquors earlier.

“Why not?” says Kelly.

They build a fire and sit around it, passing the champagne.

“Five minutes to blast off,” Dave says looking at his watch.

“A little different than last year’s fireworks,” The Kid says. He lifts a bottle of champagne, guzzles some down and passes it along.

“Just a little,” says Rollie, accepting the bottle from The Kid.

They enjoy the fireworks, then make their way to Sparky’s taxi.

“I’m sorry that after ninety years and maybe a dozen different owners the present owners of the Montauk Yacht Club have changed the name to Gurney’s Star Island,” Sparky tells Carl.

“So, I’ve heard… I just may have to buy it back,” Carl says with a smile.

Sparky drives everyone up to what until recently was rightly named The Montauk Yacht Club and gets everyone checked in. They agree to meet around eight the next morning to make the trip into the city.

Carl and the crew have no problem claiming their fortunes. They make their way back to Montauk where Carl hosts a celebration at The Montauk Manor. At one point he breaks down in tears. The crew and Carl each give Hank a million dollars.

Kelly and the crew invite Sparky on a trip to Europe. Sparky has always wanted to go to Istanbul, so they hit the casinos in Istanbul, before heading off to Monaco where the crew plan the caper they had in the works before Montauk and for which Kelly and the crew originally used Montauk as a warm up for. Having always loved aviation, Carl is fascinated by the jet plane. He decides to join them in Monaco for the caper, just to watch the dirt fly. They have a ball pulling off what The Kid calls the second greatest robbery ever. Carl returns to Montauk unsure what he'll do next but decides it's time to slow things down for a while. At least until the Indianapolis 500...

Sparky finished his book and even though he has millions in the bank, loves driving his taxi. "Sometimes, I'm not exactly sure why, but I find the taxi the perfect place to write. Besides, you never know when you might meet another interesting crew," he says, a big smile on his face.

Winter has set in and the streets of Montauk are bare. The tourists have all gone. Most of the hotels and restaurants are closed. A lone figure wearing a long dark overcoat and Fedora strolls along the sidewalk past the Chase Bank. He stops and looks up at the Montauk Tower. "You're still standing tall," he says to himself with a wry smile.

The End

Montauk Time

New York-born French-Italian writer Peter Bové is a naturally prolific creator from whom work spills out with incredible frequency and range. A poet and fine artist from an early age, he is also a musician and composer, a novelist, a screenwriter, filmmaker, actor and performer, as well as philosopher, astronomer and carpenter. He began his career studying fine art at The New School in New York City where he delved into myriad art forms, eventually exploring performance art, theater and film. This voyage of discovery led to a long and successful career in entertainment and commercial media, however never diminishing his passion for drawing and painting or the written word. Over the years, he has continued to produce written and fine art pieces, which he is now working to bring into the public eye. Mr. Bové has always been motivated and inspired by love and faith in opposition to the misery and corrupted ideals of the world we live in. This underlying theme is reflected throughout all of his compositions and the resolution of this conflict continues to be the beacon that guides his artistic journey. Mr. Bové currently lives in Dallas, Texas, on a hill, where he can get a good view of the stars and bring them down to earth with paper, canvas, paint and the mighty pen.

Made in the USA
Middletown, DE
25 July 2020